WOLF IN A FALCON'S NEST

Joanna let up slowly. Bailly's whole body slumped when she let go. He instantly grabbed his throat with one hand. Joanna drew her pistol while she grasped the back of Bailly's chair and swung him around.

"I told you I do not have time for games, scum. You will tell me what you know. Put your hands behind your head and get up." She prodded him at the waist with her pistol, nudging him around to the front of the desk. He would not try anything now.

"First I will tell you what I know," she said, coming to close range and tapping the weapon against his chest. "And then you will tell me the rest. . . ."

BATTLETECH®

I Am Jade Falcon

Robert Thurston

A ROC BOOK

ROC
Published by the Penguin Group
Penguin Books USA Inc., 375 Hudson Street,
New York, New York 10014, U.S.A.
Penguin Books Ltd, 27 Wrights Lane,
London W8 5TZ, England
Penguin Books Australia Ltd, Ringwood,
Victoria, Australia
Penguin Books Canada Ltd, 10 Alcorn Avenue,
Toronto, Ontario, Canada M4V 3B2
Penguin Books (N.Z.) Ltd, 182-190 Wairau Road,
Auckland 10, New Zealand

Penguin Books Ltd, Registered Offices:
Harmondsworth, Middlesex, England

First published by Roc, an imprint of Dutton Signet,
a division of Penguin Books USA Inc.

First Printing, March, 1995
10 9 8 7 6 5 4 3 2 1

Series Editor: Donna Ippolito
Cover: Peter Peebles
Mechanical Drawings: Steve Venters and Dwayne Loose

Printed in the United States of America

To my sister and brother,
Dona and Alan Thurston

Thanks to Eugene McCrohan for all the BattleTech conversations he endured with me and the many insights he provided into the BattleTech world.

Map of the Inner Sphere Coreward Sector

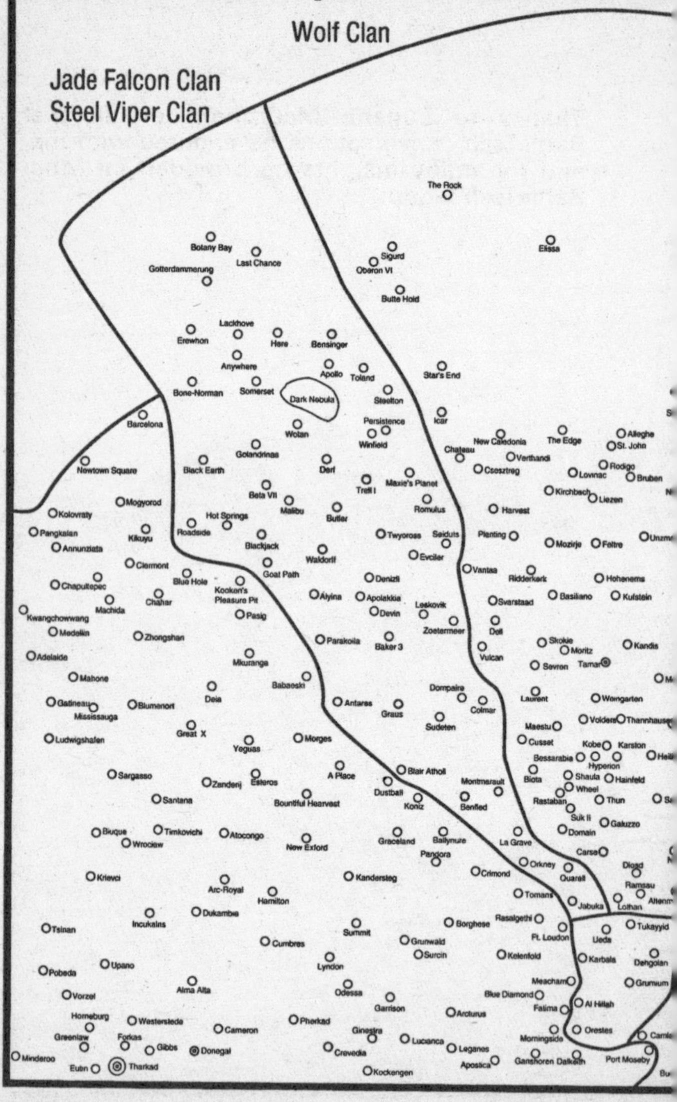

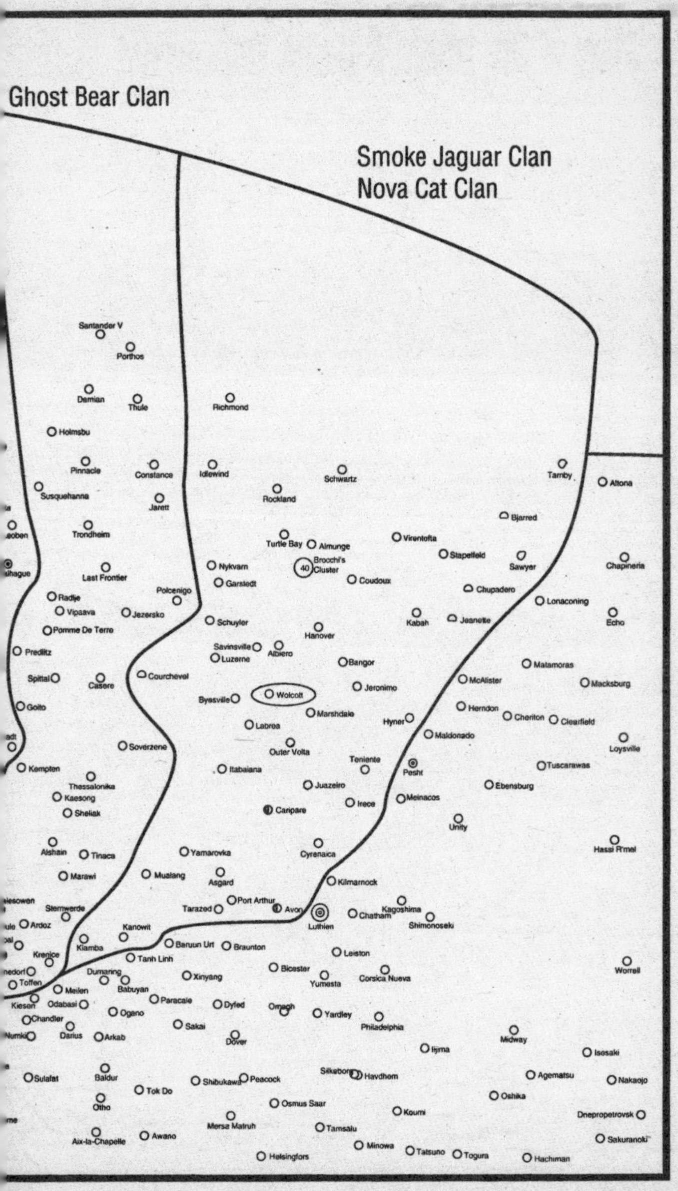

Ghost Bear Clan
Smoke Jaguar Clan
Nova Cat Clan
Santander V
Porthos
Damian
Thule
Richmond
Holmsbu
Pinnacle
Constance
Idlewind
Schwartz
Tamby
Altona
Susquehanna
Jarett
Rockland
Bjarred
Trondheim
Turtle Bay
Almunge
Virentofta
Brocchi's
40
Cluster
Stapelfeld
Sawyer
Chapineria
Last Frontier
Nykvarn
Garstedt
Coudoux
Chupadero
Lonaconing
Radje
Polcenigo
Vipaava
Jezersko
Kabah
Jeanette
Echo
Pomme De Terre
Schuyler
Hanover
Prediltz
Savinsville
Albiero
Luzerne
Bangor
Matamoras
Spittal
Casere
Courchevel
McAlister
Macksburg
Wolcott
Jeronimo
Byesville
Goito
Marshdale
Herndon
Cherlton
Clearfield
Hyner
Labrea
Maldonado
Soverzene
Outer Volta
Loysville
Teniente
Kempten
Itabaiana
Pesht
Tuscarawas
Thessalonika
Juazeiro
Ebensburg
Kaesong
Irece
Meinacos
Sheliak
Caripare
Unity
Alshain
Tinaca
Cyrenaica
Hassi R'mel
Yamarovka
Marawi
Mualang
Asgard
Kilmarnock
Sternwerde
Port Arthur
Tarazed
Avon
Kagoshima
Ardoz
Kanowit
Luthien
Chatham
Shimonoseki
Kiamba
Baruun Urt
Braunton
Krenice
Tanh Linh
Leiston
Worrell
Dumaring
Bicester
Toffen
Meilen
Babuyan
Xinyang
Yumesta
Corsica Nueva
Kiesen
Odabasi
Paracale
Dyfed
Omagh
Yardley
Chandler
Ogano
Philadelphia
Darius
Arkab
Sakai
Dover
Midway
Iijima
Isesaki
Sulafat
Baldur
Silkeborg
Havdhem
Agematsu
Shibukawa
Peacock
Nakaojo
Tok Do
Oshika
Otho
Osmus Saar
Koumi
Dnepropetrovsk
Mersa Matruh
Aix-la-Chapelle
Awano
Tamsalu
Sakuranoki
Minowa
Tatsuno
Togura
Hachiman
Helsingfors

Prologue

For years Joanna had rarely been aware of her dreams, sometimes even wondering if she dreamed at all. But that had all changed now. Almost from the day the Clans made their truce with the Inner Sphere, not only did she dream, but her dreams seemed to haunt her waking hours, sometimes for days afterward.

In a dream that recurred, with only occasional variations, Joanna was slogging through the dense underbrush of a forest, her legs feeling like they were made of 'Mech endosteel, plus many extra layers of ferro-fibrous armor . . .

As she pushed through the thorny growth, she recalled training in just such a forest. Years ago. Too many years ago.

Separated from her sibko, she'd been pursued by the falconer in charge, a strong, burly man named Barnak who loved to give pain. That day she had tried to push her high-booted legs through underbrush just like this.

When she reached the edge of the forest, Barnak jumped her. With the grace that burly men can sometimes achieve, he swooped down from a heavy branch, then seized her by the throat and pushed her fiercely against the trunk of the tree in whose branches he'd been hiding.

Growling and cursing in that falconer way, he called her the worst warrior cadet he had ever had the miserable duty to train. She would fail, he announced with some pleasure. She would fail even before she qualified to climb inside the cockpit of a 'Mech. She would fail in a simple test or she would crumple emotionally, breaking down the way only the weakest Jade Falcon cadets ever did, the ones who wound up in the most humiliating Clan castes after they flushed out of warrior training.

"You have not a chance of winning your Trial of Position, you nasty, foul creature. You will not even get that far, you are so nasty. You are so nasty you suck the dirt and bugs among these leaves and birdlime."

As he spoke Barnak kept ramming her body against the hard, rough tree trunk, which scratched her back and left it bleeding with cuts. Her friend—she had a friend then, an actual *friend.* What was his name? What had happened to him? Joanna could not picture him now, but he had applied herbal salve to her wounds later that night.

"Give up now, nasty," Barnak whispered hoarsely. "You will fail, nasty! As sure as feathers molt from birds, you will fail."

Enraged, she managed to break his hold on her and push him two steps away. He stumbled, but even though Joanna was sure it was a fake to draw her assault, she jumped at him, screaming. Raining ineffective blows against his face and torso, she hated herself for not being able to hurt him with her fists, for not being able to wipe away his calm smile, for not breaking his damned arrogance. Suddenly she leaped up and bit him on the face, savoring the taste of his blood on her tongue.

Barnak shrieked in pain, which she had little time to enjoy, since he then proceeded to give her one of the worst beatings of her life.

Afterward, lying among the brush, with the hundreds of little cuts on her back throbbing with pain and the thousands of little pains from his beating, Joanna peered up at Barnak through swollen eyes and smiled with her own best arrogance. She was delighted to see blood streaming down from the laceration just below his cheekbone.

At the end of training, when she had been the only one of her sibko to succeed in the final trial, Joanna had confronted Barnak with the kind of defiance she had learned from him.

"You wished to speak with me, nestling?"

"Admit you were wrong, Falconer Barnak."

"Wrong about what?"

"Saying I would not succeed."

"Yes, I *did* tell you that."

"So, admit you were wrong. Or fight with me in the Circle of Equals."

He laughed. "No, I will not fight you now. What I did in the forest, I did for you."

"*For* me? How could it be for me?"

"You hated everyone. Your hate caused you too many mistakes. So I focused it on me. You hardly noticed the others after that day. You trained fiercely, and with a ferocious anger, a rage even. A rage directed at me and at life, but not your sibkin. Everything you did in your training from then on, you did well."

"You *are* an arrogant bastard!"

"I hope so. And I hope I never see you again."

And, except for some final ceremonies, she had not.

Yet, Joanna realized now, she had never really gotten Barnak out of her system. When her own time came to serve as a falconer in charge of training sibkos of young cadets, she had treated her charges with the same brutality she had learned from Barnak, insulting them, prodding them, humiliating them, driving them. And producing some of the finest warriors ever to test out as Jade Falcons.

In her dream, she still feared Barnak. Branches might hide him, yet she knew he could dive gracefully again. She also knew she was a fool to worry about that ancient falconer, who was no doubt long gone or by now relegated to lower-caste status. There seemed to be worse creatures all around—cold, staring eyes in the forest darkness.

She entered a clearing. Suddenly her legs were lighter. She could run, which she did. She could fly, which she did. She soared over the high grasses of a strangely hued meadow. Each step took her higher, made her feel lighter.

Ahead of her, a few kilometers distant, she saw an array of MechWarriors and BattleMechs engaged in heavy combat. A *Mad Dog* was breaking apart, its pieces drifting above the scene for an impossibly long time before falling. An Elemental rode the shoulder of a *Summoner,* pounding at its armor with an ax.

Suddenly she wanted to be a part of this battle, so she sailed toward it. Speeding across the meadow, she was like a kestrel swooping across a plain.

She understood that what she was about to join was a bloodname melee. She had seen enough of those. In her last bloodname try, Joanna had been forced to start with a melee, for no Jade Falcon warrior wanted to sponsor someone as old as she. She had won the melee and gone all the way to the final round before losing. The defeat had only deepened her rage. She deserved a bloodname. At any age.

Even though she was not in a 'Mech and had no weapons, Joanna plunged into this new melee fearlessly, her arms flailing wildly, her legs kicking out. Still able to fly, she sailed up and down the mighty BattleMechs, disabling them, turning their own firepower against them, setting off fireworks displays decorated with flying armor. Once she merely kicked at a BattleMech chest and the 'Mech fell. It crashed against another 'Mech, which toppled another, until a whole line of the awesome machines lay in a high, twisted pile. She climbed the pile.

Standing atop the last 'Mech to fall, its hot metal burning the soles of her feet even through her boots, Joanna surveyed the devastation she had caused.

The giant, bulky bodies of the Elementals were broken into sections, and MechWarriors hung out of their cockpits in twisted, lifeless positions. Smoke, bits of armor, and tiny pieces of fire were carried on the breeze above the debris.

She felt exhilarated. The bloodname was hers. She raised her arms in victory.

"You have not won yet," said a voice from somewhere in the smoke of battle.

"Aidan? Is it you?"

He strode out of the smoke, step firm, manner confident, his smile annoyingly cheerful.

"And so we meet again, Joanna."

"Why are you here?"

"You must fight me to win the melee."

"Fight you, but why?"

"We are the sole surviving MechWarriors."

"What are you doing here?"

"I am here to compete for the bloodname."

"You already have your bloodname."

"Now I want yours, the one you are trying to earn."

"That is not fair. I deserve my chance."

"Nothing is fair. That is the way of the Clan, *quiaff*, Joanna?"

It was difficult to argue with the truth.

"But you are dead, Aidan. You died in the fighting on Tukayyid."

"That is correct. And you must fight me now."

"I will not."

"Then you have failed. Again. You lose, nasty."

"You never called me nasty. That was Barnak."

For a moment Aidan looked like Barnak, then he was Aidan again.

"I will fight you then," she said.

An assault rifle drifted upward from below and she grabbed it. Leaping off the high pile of 'Mechs, she floated to the ground and strode toward Aidan. As she approached him, his features began to change. His skin grayed and became metallic. His eyes lost their amiability and became hard, metallic. The shape of his face became angular, and metallic. He began to grow upward and outward. Soon he stood over her, a BattleMech, fully weaponed. He had become the *Timber Wolf* in which he had died. All his weaponry was now aimed at her.

"That is not fair. I have only this rifle."

"This is a melee, Joanna. Nothing is fair."

"I know—that is the way of the Clans. Am I not the one who first drilled it into you?"

She raised her rifle and began shooting at him, wildly. From deep inside the *Timber Wolf* that was Aidan, she heard him say, "I am sorry, Joanna." Then, he fired his weapons at her in a barrage, each direct hit forcing her backward. Then he raised one of his 'Mech's enormous feet. It became a dark cloud blotting out the sky above her, until Joanna could see no more, only the huge foot coming down straight at her, to crush her like a bug, to—

And then she woke up.

Sweat covered her body. For a moment, she could not tell the difference between sleeping and waking. A giant BattleMech resembling Aidan seemed a dark fog shape in the surrounding mist.

She was outside her quarters, sleeping on the ground without covering, her head resting on an equipment pack. How had she gotten here? Had she lost hours or merely drunk too much and fallen asleep the way drunks did, abruptly and gracelessly?

Excess of drinking was not common among Clan warriors. Because their lives were so controlled, they rarely used stimulants. They had been taught, after all, that being a warrior was stimulant enough. Nevertheless, over the years

Joanna had developed a taste for strong wine and a peculiar Clan drink known as a fusionnaire. In spite of the ache in her head, she could have used one of those high-powered concoctions right now.

As she struggled to her feet, her legs as stiff as if they really had slogged through dense underbrush, she thought of the new MechWarriors, the ones who had finally been sent as replacements for the brave warriors lost on Tukayyid. They were not like her, but then who was? More important, they were not like any MechWarriors she had ever known. They were a new breed, restless with the truce, vicious in contrived raids, close-ranked in their behavior.

They looked like Clan warriors right enough, yet in a strange way that Joanna could not quite define they were different.

I hate them, she thought.

Aidan seemed to invade her mind. She heard his voice saying, "But you hate everyone, Joanna."

And she very nearly said aloud, "Almost everyone, yes."

1

Western Training Zone
Pattersen, Sudeten
Jade Falcon Occupation Zone
1 July 3057

"What do you mean, they don't want to serve with us?" Joanna demanded.

As she spoke the question, her eyes widened, increasing the fierceness of her ever-angry look. The eyes had almost no color in them, were just the lightest shade of gray in certain lights, a gray that made artillery comparisons appropriate.

"I mean, they do not want to serve with us," Star Commander Horse said laconically. "Also, Star Captain Joanna, I did not use the contraction." His half-smile, used increasingly these days as bad times verified his amused and bemused view of all things, irritated Joanna.

"That is correct. *I* am the one who used a contraction. I needed to. Sometimes you need to."

"You know me. I wouldn't argue that."

"You—oh, I see. Horse, your need for sarcasm outweighs anything sensible."

"Sorry, Captain."

The back of Horse's right hand ran along the line of his chin, as if searching for his recently shaved-off whiskers. In the weeks since he had executed the beard, Joanna had told him at least a hundred times that he looked years older. Though most warriors would have hated hearing that because remarks about aging were considered insults within the Clans, Horse only laughed.

With them was MechWarrior Diana, also a member of Joanna's Star. The three veteran Clan Jade Falcon warriors were lounging on a hillside, enjoying a rare pleasant day on the unpleasant world of Sudeten. Most days on this planet were wintry with strong winds, but today the breeze was mild and the temperature cool without requiring cold-weather outfits. The three warriors were dressed in wrinkled battle fatigues, with all indications of rank removed. Rank was not emphasized in the truce zones.

Joanna and Horse sat on the hillside's short spiky grass, leaning back on their elbows. Diana sat propped against a tree. The tree bark was hard and sharp, but she barely noticed its roughness.

About a half-kilometer from the foot of the hill lay the remains of a Battlemech factory and supply depot that had been turned into a salvage yard. Both the building and the depot had been severely damaged, rendered useless by warfare. The factory walls still stood, scorched and scarred by a devastating attack. Most of the roof was still there, too, though pitted with jagged holes. But even from this distance they could see that the factory was a shell. The windows were broken, with debris poking through the shattered panes.

The scene was like a boneyard whose graves had all been opened and the corpses scattered everywhere. These corpses were, of course, metal ones. Pieces of BattleMechs were mixed together just like bones piled on a battlefield, not a single torso with a limb still intact. Metal arms and legs intertwined and entangled unnaturally. Heads were mixed in among the piles or lay on the ground, upside down, or on their sides, or straight up as if the rest of them might still be buried, an archaeological fragment of a mighty king's statue. Horse had recently read an ancient poem about a monument to an ancient king, also a giant head in a desolate area, and had suggested the comparison to the others, who hadn't a clue to what he might be talking about. Within the mounds of the 'Mech graveyard were also the crushed remains of many vehicles.

The breeze rattled the 'Mech pieces. On some days, when the wind was fierce, the lighter fragments would bounce and skid across the ground, often banging against the 'Mech limbs or the walls of the factory.

Joanna thought the ruins seemed to scream at them that their lives were like such debris, scattered about a desolate landscape. Once they had been warriors wholly devoted to war, to the Clan invasion and its many battles. Jade Falcon warriors, each one skilled and brave. Now, with the uneasy fifteen-year-truce between the Clans and the Inner Sphere, they were idle, mere garrison troops with a few duties on insignificant planets. Like most other Clan warriors, they were a bit edgy, hungry for tasks worthy of their fierce military training.

Staring back at Horse, Joanna took a deep breath to calm herself. "Again, do they say why they do not, *do not,* wish to serve with us?" Her repetition was meant to emphasize her elimination of the contraction.

"They have more reasons than you have bad habits, Captain."

Joanna could not talk. Anything *anybody* said these days made her angry. As a delaying tactic, she ran her hand through her long hair. It felt bristly and disheveled, a battered victim of Sudeten's frequent winds. Touching it made her think of the thick streaks of gray that now alternated with her darker tresses. Before the invasion and the truce, she had been unconcerned about her gray hair. Now she wished that, like a village fishwife, she could eliminate the gray with some dark dye. Though Joanna believed a warrior should never use cosmetic subterfuge, there were moments when she would have preferred it to a blatant display of gray hair. Ah, well, she thought, I guess I am long over the hill, as much as a warrior can get.

"Horse," Diana said, leaning away from her tree, "I swear, you become more of a 'Mechhead every day. Talk straight to us. I want to know about the canister babies, too, especially if they are handing us cheap insults."

Horse's glance at Diana was filled with affection. It was not the affection of a lover, for he and Diana had never coupled, despite the many opportunities. It was the affection of a family friend, which was, after all, what he was. Diana was freeborn, as was he, a shame they'd both had to confront all their lives. They usually won any battle that reached honor duel stage, yet they knew that—in spite of their skill and courage—they would never really be accepted, even by fair-minded trueborns. Trues always believed that their genetic origins as beings created from carefully chosen genetic materials in Clan laboratories made them superior to frees conceived and born in the old ways, so there was always a holding-back among trues, even in their friendly associations with frees. A trueborn saying went: Trues do things, frees are things.

When Horse looked at Diana, he saw his trueborn friend, the Jade Falcon hero Aidan Pryde. The close resemblance was not surprising to a freeborn like Horse. There was, after all, some consistency to freeborn genetics. While trues from the same sibko tended to look like each other in a generic way, a free's physical attributes came from his or her parents. Horse had never known Diana's mother, Peri, but he had known Aidan better than anyone else in the Jade Falcon ranks. In certain lights Diana resembled her father strongly. Of course, since Peri had come from the same sibko as Aidan, Diana must look like her, too.

What had been strong features in Aidan were equally strong in Diana, but hers were more artfully sculptured. She was, Horse thought, a beauty. Like drawings and paintings of blue-eyed damsels, the kind he had seen illustrated in some of the books Aidan had collected. Books were not exactly popular among warriors, or the common folk for that matter, but Horse had grown to like them. He had learned from Aidan the virtues of nonessential reading and now loved the collection as much as Aidan had. Like Aidan, he kept the small library hidden away, but often disappeared to peruse one of the volumes.

"These replacements are a new breed, Diana. It as if they have been pushed out of the nest too soon, before they are ready to become falcons."

"You do them a kindness, Horse, to call them falcons at all. But I agree. I have never seen any warriors like them."

Joanna growled. It was the sound of a caged animal. "They are jackasses," she said. "Freebirths."

Diana caught her breath. She never got used to the casual and vile use of the term *freebirth* for her kind. But she knew Joanna respected her as a warrior, and the term was not intended to insult her.

"Star Captain Joanna," she said, "these jackasses have proven themselves qualified to be warriors. They passed their Trials of Position. They are warriors. *Trueborn* warriors."

Diana's irony was lost on Joanna. "I know a freebirth

when I see one. Whatever sibkos spawned those imbeciles must have had some defective genetic strains somewhere."

Horse laughed. "You demean Clan science. The new warriors come from so many different sibkos. Do you mean to say the whole program is being sabotaged by defective DNA?"

"You mean that as sarcasm, *quiaff*?"

"*Aff.* I like the idea of defective DNA ruining some strains."

"I could report you for merely saying that, Horse."

"You could, but you will not."

"Do not depend on it. I am a trueborn Jade Falcon warrior and proud of it. Praise the Clan."

"Praise the Clan," Horse responded, then added with a gleam in his eyes. "And praise Aidan Pryde."

Horse's ridicule of the oaths irritated her, but the sarcasm in his voice was so subtle he could never be accused of it. "Praise Aidan Pryde, that is what the new ones keep saying, the imbeciles. They treat Aidan as some kind of god."

"I say it is one of the few good things they do."

"Nothing they do is good. Aidan would have hated being fawned over."

Joanna vividly remembered the ceremony where Aidan's genetic materials had been accepted for inclusion in the Clan Jade Falcon gene pool. It had been a stirring celebration, made more so because it redeemed Aidan's years as an outcast. Had he died before the Clan invasion of the Inner Sphere and his subsequent heroism on Tukayyid, he would now be mere dust on some insignificant planet, his genetic materials decomposed with the rest of him. Of course, the basic genetic materials still existed, in Diana, but few people knew she was Aidan's natural daughter. Perhaps Diana would have children and then—ah, the mind could explode with theories like that.

Odd the way things work out, she thought. Time and opportunity guide a warrior's fate. While Aidan was one of the few people she admired, Joanna was aware that his worth would never have been known had fate not placed him in the battle for Tukayyid. And even before Tukayyid, fate seemed to have also played a part in the winning of his bloodname. Aidan had not even been nominated. He'd had to qualify through a melee, a free-for-all among unnominated candidates. After that victory, he had gone on to prove himself with the bravery and the skill to be expected of a well-trained Jade Falcon warrior. *Of course he was well-trained. I was his falconer.*

Unlike her trainee, Joanna had failed to win a bloodname in several vigorous and hard-fought attempts. In each try she had been one of the last to fall. *Fate, no reason to fight it. Hate it, yes, but why do I dwell on it so much? I'll die without a bloodname, and that is that.*

2

Western Training Zone
Pattersen, Sudeten
Jade Falcon Occupation Zone
1 July 3057

Diana saw that Joanna was contemplating her existence. Her metallic eyes got a little distant and her mouth formed a hard, bitter line whenever she was thinking about her life, her fate.

Unsettled by the look in Joanna's eyes, Diana turned her attention to the ruined factory and the depot beside it. One of the unattached heads was a *Timber Wolf*'s, the same type of BattleMech in which her father had met his death. Her memory of his death was confused, especially since she had been going in and out of consciousness, injured and trapped in her own 'Mech. She had heard Joanna tell Aidan that Diana was his freeborn daughter, but not his reaction. That her father had protected her while the Elemental Star Commander, Selima, rescued her, made Diana believe that Aidan might have been affected by Joanna's revelation. His defense of her and the valiant fight he put up to help other groups of warriors escape in the DropShip *Raptor,* together with all his heroic acts on Tukayyid, had earned him fame as a hero and his deserved place in the gene pool.

Diana's thoughts of her father were interrupted by the appearance of five warriors at the base of the hill. So deep in thought, she had not noticed their arrival till now.

One of them said something that made the others laugh uproariously as he pointed up at the three veterans on the hilltop. The laughter was accompanied by some hearty backslapping and arm-punching. Maybe Joanna was right about these new warriors being fools and jackasses. Come to replace the brave Jade Falcons who had died during the invasion, they did not seem worthy of that honor. They were a bit too arrogant, conceited. They had accomplished nothing, yet they preened as if their genetic materials had already been selected for the gene pool.

The quintet started walking up the hill, their strides long and almost in sync. To Diana, they looked like an army of vanity, marching in exaggerated step. Each wore recreational fatigues, which were basically martial arts uniforms in battle colors. The cloth was starched and clean, the fit tight. Diagonally across their chests, each also wore a wide band whose color combinations indicated their original sibkos, the bands as carefully arranged as the rest of their outfits.

The practice of displaying sibko colors on dress uniforms was unheard of. Any warrior would prefer signs of his or her achievements to symbols of origin. At shoulder level on the band each wore a Jade Falcon patch that showed a mighty falcon in flight. The whole display seemed ridiculous to Diana.

"What do these fools want?" Joanna muttered.

"Nothing we have to worry about, *quiaff*?" Horse said, his voice characteristically laconic.

"Shove your *quiaff*. We should kick their worthless backsides all the way back to their homeworlds."

"Calm, Joanna, calm."

"You never address me by my rank anymore, you insolent freebirth."

Horse guffawed. "My abject apologies, Star Captain Joanna."

"Oh, stuff it, Horse. Apply for a transfer. I will grant it even before the disk is in my hands."

"Unlikely, Captain, unlikely."

"I hate you, Horse."

"Just like you do everyone else."

She grunted. "What is the name of the fool in front?"

"Cholas," Diana said. "They say he is a skilled fighter."

"And the others?"

"The big one is Ronan." Big might have been a kind

word, for the man was muscle on the verge of fat. He had odd, secret eyes, made even more strange by the masklike tattoo of his neural implant. "Castilla is the tall one." Rather slim except for broad hips that were probably to her advantage in close combat, Castilla might have been beautiful but for the hard, thin line of her mouth. "The dark one is Haline." A rather large woman, Haline was nearly as muscular as Ronan but much shorter. "Oh, and that other one is Fredrich." He was neither tall nor short; neither big nor small; neither handsome nor ugly. Diana found him thoroughly ordinary.

Watching Cholas lead the way up the hill, she had to admit he was an impressive figure, so tall and well-muscled, with a certain grace to his movements. They had coupled one night soon after his arrival, but he had behaved with such detachment and with such a distant look in his eyes that Diana wondered if he was bored. They had not coupled again, and she did not regret that.

"Star Captain Joanna," Cholas called as he came near, "we have been seeking you."

The colors of his sibko band were particularly garish, orange thrust against yellow streaked with red. Snakes in fury.

Joanna growled her response. "For what purpose, MechWarrior?"

"It seems you will be needed back at base shortly. A new arrival has entered DropShip skies and will be here presently. You should be eager to meet him."

Joanna glanced back at Horse and Diana, her look showing scorn for the intruders. "I should be eager to meet him? I should be eager for anything? And why is that, MechWarrior Cholas?"

"He holds special interest for us all. He is one of the wonders of Jade Falcon warriordom."

Horse roared. "Jade Falcon *warriordom*?"

Cholas walked to Horse. "You laugh. Why?"

"Nothing, friend. Just the phrase. I find it . . . eloquent."

Cholas did not seem to comprehend the sarcasm. "I am glad you do, freebirth."

Cholas turned away, missing the quick change to anger in Horse's face. He returned his attention to Joanna. "The new arrival is our new Cluster commander, and I must tell you he is an officer of esteem. His defeat of his three opponents in the Trial of Position was so impressive that he entered the ranks as a Star Captain. Then he immediately sought his bloodname and—"

"Bloodname?" Joanna asked. "Immediately? How in hell could he go after a bloodname before being tested in actual combat?"

"I did not mean immediately, actually."

"Then why did you say it, *eyas*?"

The word *eyas*, the name for a newly born falcon, was a grave insult to anyone who had won his Trial of Position to become a warrior. Cholas started to reply, but Castilla came forward to say coolly, "It was not, of course, immediate in actual time. But in relative time, it has seemed so. The star colonel did—"

"Star Colonel? This fledgling is a star colonel, too."

"Of course," Castilla said coolly. "To be our Cluster commander, he would have to be, *quiaff*?"

"Oh, *aff*. I am not used to such a rise in the ranks."

"It is the new dream," Cholas interjected. "You warriors who preceded us in the Inner Sphere invasion have paved the way, and we give you honor, but now—when this blasted truce ends—it will be our war, and we will smash our way straight through to Terra, you will see."

"I will not hold my breath. Do you realize you will no longer even be young when the truce ends?"

"Only if the truce is not broken. But we doubt that."

"I am cheered by your certainty. You were about to say, Castilla?"

"I was going to tell you that the star colonel was blooded before winning his bloodname."

"In our invasion? I heard of no young hotshot star colonel who—"

"No, not as part of the invasion, though I am sure you would have heard of him if he had been. He won his fame wiping out bandits in the homeworlds. He bid particularly low, then won the day practically singlehanded, slaughtering many and—"

"Excuse me, but are you praising this hero for a skirmish? A *skirmish*? Is that how a warrior becomes eligible to compete for a bloodname these days? A bit of combat seen while exterminating vermin or with some discontented laborers and techs—"

"Star Captain Joanna," Castilla interrupted, struggling to keep control of her voice, "the rebels were hardly ill-equipped villagers. They had stolen sophisticated weaponry and even had their own BattleMechs."

" 'Mechs, I suppose, that they could operate with the skill of trained warriors?"

Castilla was a bit disconcerted. "Well, I guess the filthy freebirths had not much training, but their leader was a freeborn of extraordinary skills, a worthy opponent who had undergone training with—"

"I am unconvinced. I will meet with this . . . this hero in my own good time, Cluster commander or not. Dismissed."

Cholas stepped angrily toward Joanna, but Castilla held him back with an exquisitely shaped, multi-ringed hand.

"We have not finished telling you about him yet. His name is Star Colonel—"

"I have heard enough about this new brand of hero. I do not wish to hear his name." "—Star Colonel Ravill Pryde." Castilla supplied the name with satisfaction in her voice. Her diagonal mouth seemed more than ever like a slash, a scar.

For a moment all three veteran warriors were speechless.

"Pryde," Joanna finally said weakly. "His bloodname is Pryde."

"Yes," Cholas said loudly, his arrogance restored. "Ravill Pryde. He is of the same bloodright as Star Colonel Aidan Pryde, hero of Tukayyid." He examined the disbelieving stares of the three veterans before announcing further, "I would think that you all, as survivors of that battle, would want to meet someone of that noteworthy genetic heritage."

"Praise Aidan Pryde," Ronan said in a voice that seemed too high for his bulk. The others joined in the invocation.

Joanna shuddered. Shuddering was a new reaction for her, but how could she avoid it when she had to listen to the foolish words of these new warriors? Even though she had admired Aidan's bravery, she hated the way these imbeciles invoked his name.

"You served with Star Colonel Aidan Pryde, Star Commander Joanna, *quiaff*?"

"*Aff.* Of course I did!"

"And you scorn our praise of him."

"No. Well, yes, I do."

Ronan pushed Haline aside and stepped forward.

"Be careful what you say, *quiaff?*" he said menacingly, and Haline nodded agreement. Castilla's mouth was twisted angrily, and the ever-silent Fredrich glared. Only Cholas appeared calm.

"Careful?" Joanna said. She walked to Ronan. Although she was tall, Ronan hovered over her. "Why should I be careful? Because I knew him and you five did not, I am a better judge than you of what was or was not praiseworthy in him. He was a hero, I agree. *I was there with him on Tukayyid and when he made his last stand, and you were not!*"

"That gives you no cause to mock him or us," Castilla said.

The remark drew a smile from Cholas. Horse glared at him, thinking that this was the one you would not trust. One of the major Jade Falcon virtues was a belief in directness and a hatred of deception. When either value was in jeopardy in battle, Horse believed, the battle could be lost.

"I mock only you," Joanna said, her voice low. The backs of all five warriors stiffened. Joanna looked at each one, in turn. "Aidan Pryde was a human being. He was also the hero you claim, but he was not—*not* a legend, not some superhuman clown of myth." Ronan and Castilla bristled at the word *clown*. "Look, my dear *eyasses,* there was a battle and—like all battles—there was much confusion. At the end of it, we were retreating. Retreating. Most of us would have died if Aidan Pryde had not sacrificed his life to help others escape."

And while I escaped, Diana thought.

"It was a heroic action, yes," Joanna continued, "but should we not view it as the act of a Jade Falcon warrior doing his duty—instead of a god visiting us briefly from some far-off place? How much—"

"His genetic materials were used in the Jade Falcon eugenics program sooner than any warrior's in history," Cholas said calmly.

Joanna whirled on him. "And—?"

"And I believe that proves that others of Clan Jade Falcon regard Aidan Pryde in the same way we do. Praise Aidan Pryde."

"Praise Aidan Pryde," the others echoed.

For a long moment Joanna stared at Cholas. Then she said quietly, "This discussion is over. You must give me respect. Dismissed." None of the young warriors moved. "I said, dismissed."

Cholas raised his hand to his comrades. "This is enough. We will go." He turned and began to walk away, then threw back some last words over his shoulder. "We will respect the rank. We have to, Star Captain. Even when it is a rank that has often been lost." Joanna glanced at Horse, anger in her eyes. He gestured for her to remain calm. "But respect for the person? I do not think so. Not when a Star Captain chooses to spend her time with freebirths!"

Before he had gone two steps more, Joanna had leaped at his back. The rough push she gave him knocked them both to the ground. When Cholas tried to get up, Joanna seized his shoulders and pinned him to the ground. He screamed in pain. Screaming was not a typical Jade Falcon response to an attack, and it surprised Joanna.

Cholas' allies, momentarily stunned, began to edge toward the scuffling pair. Diana and Horse ran forward and pushed themselves between the two fighters and Cholas' comrades.

Cholas, his calm regained, muttered to Joanna, "What is the matter, Captain? Do you deny that your friends are filthy freebirths? Or do you deny that they are your friends?"

She tightened her hold, making Cholas grimace. "You, my dear *eyas,* are the real freebirth here."

"Do not insult us by comparing us with *them*!" Ronan shouted. "This is not honorable. We have the glory of being—"

"Oh, stuff it," Horse said. Ronan rushed at him, but Horse quickly incapacitated him with a sharp punch to the stomach. Ronan went down in a heap, choking. Haline grabbed his arm and struggled to help him up, but for the moment the big man could not move.

"Let us not start a team tussle here," Joanna said and stood up. "You may go."

"No," Cholas said softly as he stood up. "No, we will not go."

"Oh?" Joanna asked.

"I have the honor of challenging you to a duel in the Circle of Equals."

Joanna's eyebrows raised in ridicule. "That is what you want?"

Horse lined up on one side of her. From her belt Diana removed the studded gloves that Joanna had once given her and slowly put them on. She strolled casually to Joanna's other side. Cholas' four allies took up similar positions on either side of him.

"I do."

"*We* do," Castilla said, joining arms with Cholas.

"Yes," said Haline, and the others nodded assent. All five had soon linked arms.

Joanna stared at them for a while, then said, "That is very pretty, your ritualistic display of allegiance. I have always respected the importance of ritual, but only when it is in the service of something worthy."

"Let us start," Cholas said, breaking the link with the other and taking a step toward Joanna.

"That means you wish to bid first?"

"It is your right, I believe."

"Never mind formalities. You begin."

"There is little to bid. I wish to fight with you in a Circle of Equals. You may choose weapons. I will even cede you place."

"We are so generous and polite, the two of us. But why make this a private matter? Since you have insulted us, I will—"

"Wait. My challenge comes from your insult to me."

"Whatever. I will bid that my . . . my freeborn friends here, the honorable *Star Commander* Horse and *MechWarrior* Diana, will join me in fighting the three best warriors among you. Do you accept, Horse? Diana?"

"You need not ask," Diana said. Horse merely nodded assent.

"Very well, then. We three against the three best of—no, that would not be fair to you. We three against *all five* of you and, since no formal Circle has been established on Sudeten, we will make the circle here on this hillside. What say you?" Cholas' voice dropped and his words were drenched in hate. "It is not an acceptable bid. It is not even a fair bid. You insult us."

"Oh? How?"

"You ask that all five of us, all trueborns, dishonor our weapons against a threesome that contains two freebirth scum. We will not have that. This batchall must be canceled, it must—"

"All right, Cholas. You will have your way."

Cholas, satisfied, stared contemptuously at Horse and Diana. His stare was quickly imitated by his four allies.

"I bid away my two freeborn friends," Joanna said placidly.

"No!" Diana shouted. "That is not fair. It is playing into their hands. In the Circle of Equals, we are equal, too. We must fight."

"No, Diana. Once you are bid away, you must accept it. That is the way of the Clans."

"I know, but—"

"Silence, MechWarrior Diana." Joanna turned back toward Cholas. "I bid them away then. I will take on all five of you myself."

Cholas opened his mouth to protest, but Joanna would not allow it.

"You cannot argue until my bid is finished. I fight all five of you *eyasses*. The Circle will be drawn, and only the six of us will enter. We will bring no weapons into the Circle. But it will not be merely hand to hand. I draw the Circle around the supply yard below. We will fight there. Anything inside the Circle may be used. That is my bid. What say you?"

"I say, I will fight you alone," Cholas said.

"Unacceptable. That does not beat my final bid. I win. We go with the last legitimate bid. You can bid away your comrades only if you can come up with a bid that ranks lower than mine. And that bid is an admission of cowardice."

"But—"

"The bidding is over. You must all fight with honor in this honor duel. What say you?"

Cholas was crestfallen. "Bargained well and done."

"Bargained well and done. Well, then—Horse?"

"Yes, Star Captain Joanna?"

"Such an honor duel requires the services of a RiteMaster, *quiaff*?"

Horse's eyebrows raised slightly, but Cholas asked the question first. "I know nothing of this term, RiteMaster."

Joanna laughed scornfully. "You *are* fresh from the canister. Do you still play with toy 'Mechs? A RiteMaster is required whenever an honor duel ratio of four to one is exceeded. It is considered that the wide odds must be compensated for, and the RiteMaster therefore provides the rules of combat for all the warriors within the Circle. He or she establishes the limits of the battle, when each warrior may step into the Circle, and where each of the warriors must be placed when entering the Circle. Horse is an experienced RiteMaster and he will—"

"We protest!" Castilla shouted. "No such role existed in our training, no such—"

"You are out of training, or so I am told. You must play by the rules of *real* warriors now."

"Even if we accept your ruling, MechWarrior Horse cannot be RiteMaster!" Cholas cried, a slight whine in his voice. "He is a freebirth and we cannot follow the orders of such scum."

"Diana could also serve in the role."

"This is some kind of ploy, is it not? A freeborn may not serve as RiteMaster, of that I am sure. Only a trueborn can be RiteMaster!"

"But all of you trueborns are already engaged in the honor duel. It would not be fair for a participant to be RiteMaster."

"How can we trust a . . . a freebirth, like this foul filth?"

Joanna held the enraged Horse back. "This freebirth, as you persist in calling him, is a Jade Falcon warrior, battle-tested and valiant."

"But—"

"Are you trying to back out, MechWarrior Cholas? Cancel the bid? You may, of course, with my blessing, and it will be a delightful story to tell back at base. Well, *eyas*?"

Cholas glanced at the others. They all nodded. "All right," he said. "We accept Horse as the RiteMaster."

"Very good then. Let us get down to the site."

The five young warriors descended the hillside at a swift, determined pace. The three veterans followed, slower but with just as much determination.

"I never saw a RiteMaster governing the Circle of Equals," Horse remarked. "And I am an *experienced* RiteMaster? I never even heard of RiteMasters before."

"Neither have I," Joanna responded. "I may be daring, but I am no fool. I will not go up against five warriors who are both young and fresh from training without some kind of edge. The RiteMaster just may be that edge."

"Whatever you say. I will do anything to see these arrogant bastards get their comeuppance."

Joanna smiled. In Horse's freeborn world being called a bastard was just as insulting as the word freebirth. Trueborns did not like the implications of being called bastard.

"I never knew you to be do devious, Joanna."

"Good bidding is never just what is said. It is what is concealed beneath the words."

"Just what bidding ritual is your source for that?"

"My ritual."

"Sometimes, Joanna, I nearly sense you joking."

"I sense you as a freebirth, Horse. No joke there."

"But you're fighting them for calling me just that."

"Are you sure?"

"With you, I am never sure."

"Make it tough on them, RiteMaster. But they must survive. We are too far away from the homeworlds to lose even such pitiful replacements as these."

Diana followed behind the two as they quickly fleshed out the role of the RiteMaster. She did not care for the deception. Joanna, especially, was not usually devious. Jade Falcon warriors did not usually endorse such tactics. Forceful, direct action was the honorable warrior's way. Still, she thought, with such arrogant idiots as these, traditions could be ignored. She would have liked to get her own hands around their necks.

Thinking of hands reminded her of the studded gloves. It seemed appropriate that she should slip these gloves, a gift to her from Joanna, into Joanna's belt before she entered the Circle. Which she did.

3

Salvage Yard Number 3
Pattersen, Sudeten
Jade Falcon Occupation Zone
1 July 3057

Joanna crouched on a tipped-over forklift, standing on its flat snout and peering out from between its two long elevating prongs. She had heard a noise a few meters away, from beyond the twisted torso of some Inner Sphere BattleMech she could not identify. The machines were too broken up to provide clues to the origins of the various parts. This 'Mech's right arm, ending in a fist, reached slightly backward, as if beckoning ground troops onward.

A human head, shaped almost like a 'Mech's, peeked momentarily out from a tangled network of burned-out wires. Ronan, she thought, because of its shape and size. *Of course, the biggest one would be sent in first. Cholas, the conceited peacock, will be the last to enter the Circle, probably with hopes of finishing me off after the others wear me out. He is officer material, all right.*

While walking to the factory area, she and Horse had planned the honor duel carefully. Horse, assuming his newfound role of RiteMaster with ease, had decreed that the five warriors must step into the circle at ten-minute intervals and that they must stay apart. "Honor duels are based on the concept of one-on-one combat," he had improvised joyfully, "and so group fighting techniques must be avoided." Diana, standing well behind Horse, had suppressed several smiles as he invented rule after rule.

Horse had ordered each of the warriors to different points of the Circle. They had obeyed him reluctantly, obviously irked at having to accept a freeborn's dictates. Whenever one of them looked disgruntled, Horse gave him or her a stare that would have overheated metal.

Joanna had been allowed a five-minute head start into the circle. Behind her, as she entered the salvage yard, she heard Horse reminding her opponents that Star Commander Marthe Pryde, Gamma Galaxy's commander, had recently prohibited honor duels being fought to the death. The ranks of the Jade Falcons had been too depleted during the invasion of the Inner Sphere for the leadership to risk losing warriors to infighting. The fierce and violent Falcon warriors chafed at the order, but knew it was for the good of the Clan.

It was going to be hard for Joanna to pull her punches. After settling herself onto the forklift, she had speculated on the new Falcon Guard commander. She dreaded having to meet him, especially since he came from Aidan's bloodline. She wondered how Marthe Pryde, so cool, so distant, so self-contained, would react to the new glorymonger bearing her bloodname. Would she resent the man's overbearing reputation, that of a warrior who was achieving legendary status without ever having seen true combat? One thing was certain: Joanna could never accept a star colonel who should still be sucking nutrients out of his canister feeding tubes.

Ronan, the imbecile, clattered around on the other side of the 'Mech debris, obviously trying to draw Joanna to him. Well, that was as good a ploy as any. Joanna would carry the fight to anyone, especially a proven fool.

Descending from the forklift, she edged forward, stepping carefully around bits and pieces of 'Mechs and other instruments of war. As she approached the fallen BattleMech, she noted that the damaged surface of its gesturing arm offered many possible handholds.

Up close, the acrid smell of thick oil sludge and the burn odors of wiring were enough to overcome the staunchest of warriors. But Joanna had fought in so many battlefields and strolled through so many of these 'Mech graveyards that she noticed the smell only in passing.

Climbing slowly without even trying to see if Ronan had spotted her, stopping at each handhold provided by the many pitonlike shards on the arm's surface, she made her way to the top of the arm and was able to nestle into the vee between the thumb and fingers. Glancing up, she saw distant, heavy storm clouds heading toward the area. On Sudeten storms came suddenly and seemed to emerge out of nowhere.

Looking down, she scanned the area for a sign of Ronan, who was still wearing that bright-colored band. The fool could not have been more obvious if he had covered himself in luminescent paint. Glancing at her wrist-chronometer, Joanna saw she had about four minutes to dispose of Ronan before the next opponent would enter the Circle, so she could not dawdle with her arm casually wrapped around a BattleMech thumb. Better to dispose of this Ronan swiftly. A little surprise, and a bit of dirty fighting—yes.

Even though the time was short, she waited her chance. Within minutes Ronan came her way, strolling audaciously across the debris below Joanna. Grasping the upper surface of the 'Mech thumb, she worked herself outward until her body hung loosely from it. As the thumb creaked softly from her weight, Ronan stopped and looked up, obviously astonished to see Joanna hanging there some six meters overhead.

At that instant Joanna dropped straight down and caught him dead center in the face with her heavy cleated boots. Ronan yelled in pain as Joanna's weight pushed him backward among the scattered fragments of 'Mechs and metal. Quickly rolling off Ronan, Joanna worked her way around like a sea crab, finishing with her legs beside the younger warrior's head. Ronan crawled sideways, away from her. She sat up and, like a child not quite ready to walk, wiggled on her backside after him.

Squinting through bloody eyes, Ronan raised his head to find her, giving Joanna her chance to trap his thick neck between her legs. Squeezing her powerful thighs together, she held Ronan's head tightly squashed between them. His arms flailed but they could not reach Joanna to do any damage. All he could do was struggle in her grasp, trying to get air down his constricted throat. As Joanna increased the pressure, Ronan finally gave a weak grunt and his eyes closed. She immediately released some of the pressure, just enough to keep him alive. Then, when he was obviously unconscious, she released her legs from his neck and stared at the still-breathing Ronan. It would have been so easy to strangle him, but rules were rules.

A glance at her chronometer revealed that the second opponent had entered the Circle about two minutes ago. Dispatching Ronan had taken too much time.

Sensing movement in the distance, Joanna looked to her right, toward the factory. Certain that somebody had moved near a window, she got to her feet and raced toward the building. In front of her an open door, hung half off its hinges, beckoned her in. But going through there might make her an easy target for ambush. Two windows to the left of the door, she saw a flash of movement. A trick of the light, maybe, or her next foe heading toward the door in order to jump her.

She chose the second window to the right of the door as the one to dive through. Unfortunately, that one's glass was unbroken.

Accelerating her pace, Joanna rushed at the window. Ducking her head as she lunged through it, she caught most of the impact with the back of her head and her shoulders. Shards of glass spraying around her, she somersaulted, sprang to her feet, and quickly looked toward the half-open door. Beside it, just turning away from her ambusher's nest, was Haline.

So, the giant male fails and they send in the chunky female. These fools are not strategists, that is clear.

Haline went into a crouch as Joanna rushed her. In her hand Haline held a long piece of metal. Some bit of garbage she'd plucked from a trash bin, no doubt. No need for tactics with this one. Joanna ran straight at the crouching Haline, who held the improvised weapon steady. She appeared quite ready to inflict a mortal wound, rules or no rules. Joanna could just hear her. "I did not mean to kill, but in the heat of battle and with Joanna coming at me . . ."

Timing the move for the last possible instant, Joanna doubled over and rushed forward. Sailing in under the weapon, she rammed Haline in her considerable stomach, shoving her hard against the wall. Although Haline was able to bring the weapon down onto Joanna's back, Joanna's maneuver neutralized the force of the blow, especially one landing on a hardened, battle-scarred back like hers.

She pushed harder at Haline, knocking the wind out of her. Then she slapped the steel pipe away and began hitting the bulky warrior over and over. It was no contest. In half a minute, Joanna had knocked Haline unconscious, her face streaked with blood as she slid to the floor.

With this clash over quickly, Joanna had gained precious time, about four minutes. It was unlikely that Ronan or Haline would be any problem for a while, which gave her a chance to think.

A glance around the interior of the factory showed her that this floor contained one large room, with several smaller ones in a row at the other end. There could be other rooms beyond them.

It was easy to see how Haline had found a weapon so quickly, with all the pieces of metal lying around, some in bins, some of it merely scattered over the floor. Benches and tables, machines and conveyor belts, work clothes and tools, were similarly littered about.

The first-floor ceiling had collapsed at one end, adding wood and metal to the debris piles there. What ceiling remained sagged over the middle of the room. It could fall at any moment—a spot of bad weather, a rumble in the ground, a passing BattleMech pounding with its heavy feet.

A doorway in the far wall led to some stairs. Thinking it might be useful to scan the terrain from a second-story window, Joanna decided to go up to the next floor. Might not be safe, but what was life without risk?

The stairs were rickety, like the stairways leading to mystery in dreams. Joanna took them two and three at a time, always ready to grab the railing on the left side of the stairwell, a railing that had come partially off its moorings. Despite a resounding crack given by one protesting step, she reached the top of the stairway safely. She still had at least two minutes before her next opponent entered the Circle. If she guessed right, it would be the silent Fredrich. Then Cholas would send in the wicked-looking Castilla.

Pitted with holes, the floor spread out in front of her like a wooden version of the outer landscape, with plenty of hillocks and ruts. Here and there pieces of office furniture remained. A couple of cubicle walls still stood. Fragments of wood and metal were littered over the floor, and charred bits of paper were all that was left of some forgotten bureaucratic ritual. The Inner Sphere, she had heard, was quite addicted to paperwork. For the Clans the only records that mattered were the codexes of trueborns, each warrior's personal record, including everything from unique aspects of his DNA to all the important deeds of his career to the names of the warriors from whom he or she descended.

Joanna started toward the nearest window, nearly tripping when a piece of floor sagged beneath her. Cracking and creaking sounds accompanied her entire trip to the window.

Looking out she saw the hill where the original challenge had been made. Diana sat at its base, shifting around nervously, staring futilely into the Circle. Horse stood nearer the Circle, but farther away to the right. Another step or two more and Joanna would have not have been able to see him. His hand raised, Horse was staring at his chronometer. Joanna thought she had some time left, but realized she did not when Horse lowered his hand. The next opponent, whoever it was, entered on the other side of a pile of 'Mech parts. If she could get to the roof she might be able to see him, but Joanna saw no stairway to the roof. The only way to get there was through one of the holes in the ceiling.

Well, so she was caught between a floor that might collapse any moment and a roof that was not in much better shape. It seemed like the story of her whole existence.

Making her way to an overturned desk propped against the wall, Joanna ignored the ominous noises, the floor's instability, and the gaping hole just in front of the desk. From there, she examined a window set high in the wall. It was just below a narrow hole in the roof that extended all the way to the top of the wall. Her plan, so clear when she had instantly conceived it on the other side of the room, now seemed doubtful. But she did not want to tiptoe back across the floor, and she did not want to jump out the window, and she did not want to drop through a hole in the floor, and there was a warrior stalking her below, so she decided to call on her acrobatic skills, which were probably rusty.

Joanna tested the desk and the floor around it gingerly. The floor seemed to give way when she prodded it with the toe of her boot, but she had no time to worry about that. Using a light fixture for balance, she managed to climb to the top of the desk.

Switching her hand to another light fixture located to the left of the desk and higher, she used it to guide her left foot toward the ledge of the window. The window glass was gone, but the frame was intact. With one foot on the sill, Joanna put both hands on the light fixture and shifted her body toward the sill. The movement made her kick the desk away before she'd planned to, and the floor beneath the desk shifted with a loud crack. Gradually, slowly, the desk slid toward the hole in the floor, teetered at its edge for a moment, then fell through. A large chunk of the floor went down with it.

It seemed like a long time before the desk hit the next floor down. When it did, its loud impact set off a series of echoes, a chain of noise that no opponent outside could miss. Twisting her neck painfully, Joanna managed to get her head around the side of the window while one hand stayed on the light fixture and the other slid sideways to gain an unsteady grip on the near side of the window. She had to look around her upper arm to see out the window. What she saw there was Fredrich standing on the ground and looking up at her with an enigmatic smile. Had he a weapon he could have easily picked her off. He watched a moment longer, then began to walk casually toward the factory entrance.

So here I am, Joanna thought, one hand clinging to a light fixture, another on a window frame that feels like it is separating from the wall. The floor beneath me has collapsed, and the desk I climbed up on has fallen through a hole, so I can't go back. One leg on a sill, the other hanging free. Now what?

"Well," she said aloud, "the roof is still an option."

Working her free leg onto the sill, she was left in a particularly uncomfortable position—tilted sideways, her hands clutching the light fixture and the window frame. But Joanna had no time to contemplate her next move, since the fixture began to separate from the wall.

She moved her right hand to the window frame while swinging the left outward so that, at the finish of her maneuver, one hand clung to the outside of the frame, and the other to the inside. This at least allowed her to shift her body and achieve a precarious balance.

She heard Fredrich walking on the floor below.

The hole in the roof was only a few centimeters from the top ledge of the window. A portion of roof beam was exposed. Releasing her hands from their positions, relying on her own fine sense of balance, Joanna let herself fall backward while reaching up and grabbing the ledge. Her feet nearly slid off the sill, but she managed to keep them there.

Using the side of the frame for leverage with her feet, she managed to pull and climb upward until her chin was above the upper ledge. Swinging her body outward, she let go of the ledge with her left hand and grabbed the lower ridge of the exposed roof beam. Perhaps miraculously, the beam held.

Now she had one hand on the beam and the other still on the window, with her legs dangling awkwardly. In an athletic maneuver that would have been impressive even for a young warrior, and might be regarded as phenomenal for an old one, she planted her feet against the wall beside the window while simultaneously shifting her window-ledge hand to join her other hand at the roof beam, but on the higher ridge.

The adroit movement made her look down. Fredrich stood below, ever silent, looking up at her curiously. She was surprised he did not laugh out loud. She must have been some sight, spread out like a dropcloth between the window and the hole in the roof.

Pulling herself up as well as she could and rapidly shifting her lower hand to the upper ridge, she bent her knees and kicked away from the wall. While her hands held on tightly, the power of the kick sent her legs across and upward. Twisting herself upward at the same time, she forced one leg against the jagged edge of the hole and managed, by squirming her body, to get her other leg above and onto the surface of the roof.

She wondered if Fredrich was being entertained by her ungainly gymnastic exhibition, especially now that her hands were on the beam and her crossed legs at different parts of the hole's border. And now what?

Working her hands along the roof beam, hand over hand, hand under hand, she bent her legs until she got the upper hand further onto the roof. When she felt ready, she disentangled the other leg and swung it onto the roof also. Now her body was twisted, angled, and a bit unsteady. *Now, for my next trick . . .*

With both legs on the roof, she pushed herself backward along the beam, each move getting more and more of her body onto the roof. Finally, with a push upward and a roll to her left, she was completely on the roof.

For a moment, she lay on her back, looking up at the densely clouded sky, and took a deep breath. Every muscle in her body seemed exhausted. Not a good sign when there was still a lot of fight ahead. Maybe she no longer had the reserves. Maybe the Clans were right in their belief that older warriors should be weeded out.

Maybe she was, after all, too old.

Maybe she was.

With surprising agility Joanna leaped to her feet.

I do not think so, she thought.

4

Salvage Yard Number 3
Pattersen, Sudeten
Jade Falcon Occupation Zone
1 July 3057

Ignoring her pain, Joanna struggled to slow down her breathing. Her heartbeat was also too rapid. Looking down through the hole, she searched for Fredrich. He was gone. No surprise there.

She walked to the north side of the roof and saw no movement in the supply depot area. On the east, overlooking the building entrance, Horse studied his chronometer, then motioned another young warrior into the Circle. Beyond, thick black clouds were heading this way.

At the west edge Joanna saw nothing but desolation below, and the south view was pretty barren, too.

Fredrich must be still in the building somewhere. But where, and how could she find him?

As if in answer, a low rumble preceded the opening of trap doors near the middle of the roof. What appeared to be a small building rose up through the opening. A sliding noise came from the other side of this structure.

As she walked toward it, Fredrich strolled around its corner to face her. He was smiling, probably a rare event in his life. Gesturing toward the structure, the usually silent warrior spoke in a calm, almost melodious voice. "The elevator still works, so I took it." Letting out a scream that would have scattered birds in flight, Joanna rushed at Fredrich. He went into a crouch, then somersaulted into her attack, his feet straightening in mid-roll and catching her in the chest. The kick knocked the wind out of her.

As she stumbled backward, Joanna realized that in the old days such a simple maneuver could never have taken her by surprise. Regaining her balance as Fredrich sprang to his feet, she beckoned at him, taunting, "Come on, Freddie boy, let us just mix it up. Nothing fancy, nothing acrobatic."

She hoped to make Fredrich fight her on her own terms, but suddenly began to regret the tactic. He countered every punch she threw, none of hers landing with any force. In the meantime, he scored a couple of punishing blows on her body.

As Joanna staggered backward, Fredrich pursued her, leaping, and kicking her so hard at shoulder level that she was momentarily dazed. Everything seemed to fly around her, including a half-dozen menacing Fredrichs.

By shaking her head Joanna brought everything back into focus. Fredrich had taken a few steps back to assess the situation, then started toward her again. Fortunately, her next step backward was a slow one, or she would've stepped right off the roof. She quickly reversed the step, saving herself from a two-story plunge.

Fredrich countered sideways. Not even a young warrior like him would be fool enough to rush her at a roof edge.

Now the two of them stood face to face along the rim of the roof.

"Either one of us goes off-balance even an iota and the other gets to push the rest of the way. Come on Fredrich. Play."

Joanna knew that if Fredrich got in just one of his strong punches, she might indeed be the one to sail off the roof, so she had to attack. She abruptly rushed him, conscious of each step as she ran along the roof edge.

With hands clasped together, she knocked him sideways, away from the edge. It was a blow so illogical in their precarious circumstance that it worked. As Fredrich stumbled and fell flat on his face, Joanna leaped on him and rained blows, most of them ineffective, on his back. When she finally managed one good one by his ear, his body suddenly went limp.

Joanna rose from her apparently unconscious victim—but

too soon. Fredrich, with a sudden athletic spin, his body partly raised in the air, kicked at Joanna's knees. She went down onto her backside, dazed by the intense pain from the kick. Scrabbling to a crawling position, Fredrich propelled himself at her, pushing Joanna back onto the roof's rough surface.

He was strong, this silent young falcon. Joanna felt her limbs weaken as he pressed them down. With all the strength she could muster, like a contestant in an arm-wrestling match that was going bad, she pushed back. Slowly, in gradual stages, she discovered that she, old falcon that she was, was just that little bit stronger than her adversary. The veins in both their necks stood out like ragged branches as each strained against the other. Gradually, with renewed confidence, Joanna shoved Fredrich off her body. Grunting from the effort, she rolled in the other direction and went into a crouch, ready for Fredrich's next assault.

Finally there was an emotion on Fredrich's face. Rage. He obviously did not intend to lose a contest of strength to an aged Jade Falcon warrior. Maintaining his silence, he jumped at her, arms flailing. She fought back but her blows did not seem to affect him. She realized why. He was in what some called "the Jade Falcon fury," that state when everything irrational in a warrior rose to the surface and it did not matter how stupidly he or she was fighting because it worked.

He shoved at Joanna. She resisted weakly and, with one massive heave, he sent her right to the edge of the roof. She was able to balance for a second with her arms waving. Then he hit her again—merely touched her really—and she felt herself slipping off the edge of the roof. Reaching out with both hands, she grabbed for the edge as she went. Grating pain in both arms nearly made her lose her already precarious hold.

The building's rough-textured wall offered good traction for her boots, and she began to climb back onto the roof. One arm already on the surface, she stared up into Fredrich's unemotional eyes. With excruciating pain traveling from fingertip to shoulder joint, she reached up with her other arm and grabbed at his arm, the one whose hand was in a fist meant to finish her off. She yanked at his arm and jerked him toward her with such force that his own momentum completed the job, and he cleared the edge of the roof. He nearly pulled her all the way off with him, but Joanna held on.

For a moment, she held onto his arm, her own crooked arm and her feet firmly planted on the side wall, keeping her safe. She stared at him hanging below her. Although his eyes were calm, there seemed to be tears in them. No, they were not tears. The moisture came from a scattering of raindrops that had begun to fall.

"You think I can pull us both back onto the roof?" she said. "I doubt it."

Joanna let go. His fall was relatively short. When he hit the ground, there was the distinct sound of at least one bone breaking.

Back on the roof, Joanna lay flat on her back for a brief time, too tired to move. She wanted to quit now. But there were still two more imbeciles to face, so she stood up wearily. One thing she would have to thank Fredrich for. He had discovered the elevator.

As the elevator doors opened on the ground floor, she was tensed and ready to fight anyone waiting there. But no one did. No surprise. If she was right, Castilla was outside somewhere, and—of the five young warriors—that one seemed the smartest. And a smart one would not want to encounter Joanna in this debris-ridden trap of a building. Joanna was, after all, an old Jade Falcon, and old falcons were fierce in a cage.

Castilla sat on a bent propeller blade beside a pile of other remnants from a smashed VTOL. Large drops of light rain made an erratic pinging melody as they fell on the many pieces of metal scattered all over the junkyard.

"I saw some of what happened on the roof. I would not have been as dumb as Fredrich so close to the edge, nor would I be moaning as much as he is now."

His moans were low, just audible. With similar injuries, Joanna might have moaned, too, but she was sure the proud and cruel Castilla would not.

"Would you like to rest a bit, old woman?"

"Why should I?"

"For one thing, you look like the rag end of a 'Mech exhaust. For another, I would not take much pride in defeating you while you are worn out."

"What makes you think I am worn out."

"If you are not, then you are superhuman."

"I am a Jade Falcon warrior."

"So am I."

"Not really. Not yet."

"A clever answer, Captain Joanna, but we do have a philosophical disagreement, the two of us."

"Philosophical disagreement? Is that how warriors talk these days? What kind of new breed are the scientists putting out?"

What Castilla's angled mouth did now might have been a smile. A harder rain was falling, and water streamed down both women's faces and off their hair.

"Well, we have idle time and plenty of opportunity for discussion. I meant, put into the *vocabulary* of a veteran warrior, that we are *all* warriors from the time we win our Trials of Position. It does not matter whether we are still unblooded or whether we have been through many battles. It does not—" Joanna's derisive grunt made her stop. "Do you disagree?"

"I do not even care! All I see is that, in addition to your other traits, you *eyasses* are boring, too. Philosophy! Are you sure you have not been hanging around freebirth villages?"

A flash of anger sparked in Castilla's eyes. "I know nothing about freebirths. You are the freebirth expert."

Joanna moved threateningly forward. "You lecture to me? You still have canister fluid in the cracks of your skin."

"I may be inexperienced, but I will get the experience. You, however, my dear Star Captain, will always be a freebirth-lover!"

Castilla stood up. Joanna was ready to engage her, but another voice interrupted them. "Well spoken, MechWarrior Castilla."

Cholas emerged from the shadows beneath a ruined, slightly bent and twisted 'Mech knee. His hair and face were dry, untouched as yet by the heavy rain. Cholas, like Ronan, still wore his grotesque decorative band. His was made of a shiny material and had too much red in it.

"You have done well, Star Captain Joanna. Three victories. Castilla and I had not expected that our turn in the Circle would even come. Thank you, Castilla, for delaying our freebirth-loving opponent so I could join."

"I could have finished her off alone," Castilla said in a sinister voice.

"Do not be so sure of that," Joanna said. "Your strategy,

if it deserves that name, is stupid. I will ignore the fact that you presently violate honor duel rules, for obviously you new-breeds cannot be bothered by the tradition. No matter. You have, with your precious delaying tactic, given me time to get my wind back. I will gladly take on the two of you at once, and get all this over with."

What am I thinking? I can barely stand up—and here I am issuing foolish challenges. If this pain in my back gets any worse, I'll have to hobble out of here.

Touching the painful spot on her lower spine, Joanna's hand happened to brush against the gloves Diana had placed in her belt. Realizing immediately what they were, she gave them a casual tuck to make them even more secure.

"We do not wish to violate any cherished tradition," Cholas remarked, as he walked alongside Castilla. "We will face you one at a time. *Quiaff,* Castilla?"

"Anything to get this over with," Castilla said, as she took Cholas' chivalrously offered arm. "We two can couple all the earlier then."

Joanna's laugh was more derisive than usual. "Couple? You think about that in the midst of a fight?"

"It is . . . exciting after combat. Cholas and I . . ."

"You pair *are* a new breed, all right. What kind of warrior considers field tent lust while still in a fight?"

Castilla's face matched Joanna's in scorn. "I pity you, old one. You are missing so much."

The idiocy of their words filled Joanna with anger. She burst into a quick run, ignoring the pelting rain against her face. Cholas and Castilla assumed battle postures. Either one could have knocked Joanna backward—if she had gone straight at one of them. Instead, she ran between them, stopping only to elbow Cholas aside while she landed a mean kick on Castilla's hip. Both young warriors were sent reeling and sliding on the wet ground.

Joanna sought position. Better to show these *eyasses* the value of a strategic retreat, she thought, as she ran under the 'Mech knee from which Cholas had originally emerged.

She came out into an open area. Ahead of her was a 'Mech head resting a bit crookedly on the ground, and she realized it was exactly what she needed, a confined position that would give her a strategic advantage. She ran toward it, her pace increasing as she heard scuffling feet slipping and sliding behind her. She chose not to look back. After all, the younger warriors might be running faster than she was—no point in knowing that.

The hatchway leading into the 'Mech head's cockpit was open and facing the ground. From ground level the opening was just above her head. If her arms, weary from hanging off roofs and windows, did not fail her, she could make it.

Without breaking stride, Joanna jumped up, grabbed the hatchway's lower rim, and pulled herself up and in. The sounds of pursuit suddenly stopped. The only noises were the loud beating of the rain against the 'Mech's outer surfaces. It sounded like the rain was now mixed with hail.

Twisting around to peer out of the hatchway, Joanna saw Castilla and Cholas standing below, arms akimbo and feet spread apart. Their clothes soaked through and their hair in wet tangles, they were obviously enraged.

"Going to ground?" Cholas shouted.

"In an *honor* duel?" Castilla yelled.

"Just as honorable as your ganging-up strategy."

"Now you are just being testy," Cholas said. His diction was so precise and his manner so foolish that he did not sound like a Jade Falcon warrior at all. This brat better rise up the ranks quickly, Joanna thought, or he will be assassinated by members of his own Star.

"You will have to fight me one at a time now," Joanna said softly. "See? There is strategy and strategy. But why am I giving you simple basic training? They tell me you passed your Trials."

Her insult clearly rankled them. Castilla lunged forward, but Cholas put his hand on her arm and drew her back. They began whispering together. Joanna could hear none of their words.

Damn! Now they are conferring! I wish I had a weapon. Then I could just shoot the both of them and be done with this.

Joanna could see that the cockpit interior had been scavenged for all usable parts. Clan techs and warriors must have performed the scavenging for they were even more thorough than the Spheroids. That should have given her Clan pride a boost, but right now it was irritating because if left her with only useless junk for weapons. It was a small cockpit. She could stand up in it if hunched over, but she could also touch the two opposite walls appreciably stretching her arms.

Cholas and Castilla had completed their deliberations, and

Castilla was approaching the 'Mech head. With the back of her hand, Joanna agitatedly wiped the rain and sweat off of her face, then glanced down at the cockpit floor. Nothing much there but nuts, bolts, wire. If only she had kill privileges in this honor duel, the wire would have been a godsend.

The cracked shell of a console lay on one side of the compartment. It was obvious from all its black streaks that the scanner originally housed in the shell had been burned. Reaching for it, Joanna wrenched it from its weak moorings. A few short wires dangled beneath its jagged border.

She felt the 'Mech's head lurch as Castilla hit its side running, then Castilla's hands immediately appeared on the bottom rim of the hatchway. With as much force as she could accomplish in the cockpit's close confines, Joanna brought the console shell down, jagged end first, onto Castilla's hands. Castilla yelped with pain, but she wiggled one hand—blood flowing from several cuts—from beneath the console. Grabbing the console with it, she pushed upward with such power that the upper end of the shell smashed into Joanna's face. Joanna gave out her own sudden yelp, the pain momentarily making her dizzy. Blinking, she pushed at the shell, trying to slam it back onto Castilla's hands, but the younger woman intruded her hand inside the shell. Using a backhand thrust, she flung the shell out of Joanna's hand and out of the hatchway, It clanged against the side of the hatch on the way down. With a grunt loud enough to reverberate off the cockpit's walls, Castilla pulled herself upward and in. Keeping her head down, she rammed it against Joanna's already throbbing nose.

Joanna pushed at Castilla's shoulders, but the young warrior's strength was impressive. While resisting Joanna, she slowly set her legs on the bottom rim of the hatchway and achieved an edge in leverage. The leverage was only marginally useful because the cockpit was too compact for successful infighting. Castilla shoved at Joanna and slammed her back against the wall. Joanna responded with a shove that immediately bounced Castilla's back against the opposite wall.

In the closeness of the cockpit the odor of their wet uniforms was overpowering. Water squeezed out of the cloth each time one grabbed the other's clothing.

Castilla worked her elbow up and tried to drive it into

Joanna's throat. She did cut off Joanna's air supply for a second, but the threat of death only drove Joanna to gather that extra little bit of strength. With excruciating effort, she was able to counter Castilla's maneuver by twisting her head sideways, then shoving Castilla away.

Their legs interlocked as lovers in passion, but their passionless attempts were futile. They fell awkwardly to the floor, still holding onto each other. Neither could render effective harm to the other. All they could do was squirm around and then wind up in distorted positions.

"Castilla."

"My name is ugly in your mouth."

"Your mouth is ugly."

The wrathful Castilla could do no more than squirm more and mutter, "Your breath is foul."

"Enough," Joanna said. "We can trade insults later. But why fight in here any longer? This is not fighting, it is erosion. Our strength wastes away. We need to get out of here."

The cockpit's heat was stifling, adding to all the other odors, Joanna was perspiring profusely, the sweat and the smells making breathing nearly impossible.

"Bargained well and done," Castilla said. "Since I am closer to the exit, I will go to it. Then, you."

"As you wish."

Castilla twisted and squirmed toward the hatchway, leaving Joanna sitting on the floor to watch. As Castilla stood and leaned her head through the hatchway, turning her body for the climb down, Joanna raised both her legs and kicked at Castilla's hip. The unanticipated move sent the younger woman straight through the opening. Joanna smiled as she listened to Castilla's relatively subdued scream as she fell. Scrambling quickly to her feet, she looked out to see the other warrior lying in an enormous puddle at the base of the 'Mech's head, blood streaming down one side of her face. The way she held her left arm, it was surely injured.

Castilla twisted her mouth into its most grotesque position yet as she screamed, "That was not fair!"

"I do not recall agreeing on fair."

"Freebirth!"

Joanna jumped straight down and deliberately landed on Castilla's uninjured arm with both heavy-booted feet. Puddle water splashed high.

"*That,* my dear young *eyas,* was not fair." She kicked at

the young warrior's ribs as hard as she could. "That was not fair either." She strode away, satisfied that Castilla was incapacitated. "But what I did—all of it—was well within the way of the Clans, MechWarrior Castilla."

Cholas was nowhere in sight as the rain and hail now seemed to be coming down in a flood. A flicker of movement to her right, where some battered servomotors were piled high, was either a trick of the weather—or Cholas. Joanna moved toward where the flicker had been.

"It is up to you now, Cholas," Castilla shouted. "Do not fail us!"

Joanna's response was laughter, loud and derisive.

She slogged on, across wet ground that was rapidly turning into muck.

5

Salvage Yard Number 3
Pattersen, Sudeten
Jade Falcon Occupation Zone
1 July 3057

Cholas stepped out casually from his hiding place behind the pile of servomotors. The laser pistol in his hand was pointed somewhat to the left of Joanna. He probably intends to whip it around fancily and kill me with his finesse, she thought.

In spite of the increasing torrent, Cholas seemed relatively dry except for strips of wetness on his clothing.

"Where did you get that?" Joanna asked, coolly gesturing toward the weapon.

"Oh, this? I found it."

"Impossible."

"Why is that, Star Captain Joanna?"

"All this junk has been picked clean by Clan techs."

"An honorable profession, scavenging. Impairs wastage."

"You may not use that weapon. We bid away our personal weapons, you know that."

"Yes, and I left mine behind with Horse. I do not know how this one came to be where I found it."

How convenient, thought Joanna. Aloud, she said, "However that pistol came to be here, you may not use it."

"I believe we agreed we could use whatever we discovered here. Well, I found *this*. I regret to use it, but I do not choose humiliation. You have humiliated us thus far, and I do not like that. This will be spoken of back at camp and we will be the laughingstock of—"

"You should have considered that before issuing the challenge."

"And what kind of Clan warriors would we be if we had shied away from a fight?"

"About the same kind you already are."

"You use words the same way you fight, Star Captain."

"A Jade Falcon warrior hurt by words? Tell me, Cholas, are you an actual Clan warrior or is this some kind of dramatic performance?"

Cholas sent a beam toward Joanna's feet. It left a short trail of smoke as it gutted the ground in a narrow line traveling toward the toe of her boot. The line immediately began to fill with rain.

Joanna sighed. This pistol was not powered down.

But she was not bothered by the danger, the one thing this fool had not figured on. He did not suspect how little she cared whether she lived or died.

"Do you plan to kill me then, Cholas?"

"It is not allowed by the bid."

"You do not seem one would hesitate to violate a bid."

"I am Clan!"

"Oh, yes, I forgot."

As Joanna began to walk toward him, her boots sloshed through a deep puddle.

"So shoot, Cholas. You know how to shoot, *quiaff*? Push back on the little piece below the barrel. We experienced warriors call it a trigger. But you will learn."

"Do not mock me! I have earned the right to be called warrior. I won my Trial—and, I might add, won it convincingly."

"I do not doubt that. I won my Trial, too, and I thought highly of myself afterward. But Trials are not skirmishes, and skirmishes are not battles, and battles are not wars. You will learn all that—if you do not shoot yourself in the foot first."

Cholas aimed the pistol. Joanna stared at his hand. In spite of her age, she had better eyesight than most. The other warriors joked that she could see a drop of sweat seep out of a pore. An exaggeration, perhaps, but her vision was good enough to see, in spite of the downpour, the skin of Cholas' trigger finger as it slightly bulged out when he began to squeeze the trigger, enough so that she could dodge to the side just in time to avoid the laser's azure beam.

She broke into a run to her left and dived behind a lone 'Mech leg propped up nearby. The leg, bent at the knee, formed an impressive triangular tower. Water streamed off it onto her head.

The area had become misty. Although she could no longer see Cholas, Joanna could hear him cursing. A rare thing, a warrior's curse, but not unknown when a tactic failed.

"That was quick, Commander Joanna!" Cholas called out.

He was trying to get her to respond so that he could learn her location. She remained silent. Studying the leg, she saw that several sheets of metal were missing at a spot just below the knee joint. The leg was hollow inside.

On the other side of the leg she found, at ground level, a small triangular maintenance panel that would allow her access to the limb's interior. She crawled into it and was soon kneeling uncomfortably inside the hollow thigh. *At least it is dry in here. Score another point for Clan technology.*

It was an easy crawl upward to the knee joint. When she came to the edge of the opening, Joanna looked down. Below, she could see her footprints. The rain made them look like foot-shaped puddles.

Above the sounds of the storm, she heard the splash of Cholas' steps as he approached the 'Mech leg. He walked slowly and made no attempt to disguise the noise. Though still not able to see him, she sensed him making his way along the lower part of the leg, slowly and cautiously. When his left foot came into view, Joanna raised up slightly, ready to jump.

"Cholas!" It was Castilla. She came forward, dragging one foot behind the other.

"Stay back, Castilla."

"But the two of us can—"

"Let me do this alone. I do not need your help, Castilla."

"We always—"

"Be quiet. I can do this alone."

"I love you, Cholas."

"Quiet. Not here."

Joanna nearly tumbled from her position. Had she heard right? An expression of romantic love between Clan warriors? That was village stuff, words for lower castes to relieve their disappointments about not being trueborn, not being warriors.

Cholas came further into sight, holding his pistol high. He now stood where Joanna had waited only moments before. Castilla came closer, limping.

There was no time to plan. Joanna knew only that she could not stay where she was. She quickly secured a grip on two handholds, drew her legs up, and swung through the knee-hole. As her legs arced outward, she released her grip and dropped down onto Cholas. Just before her feet made contact, one connecting with his head and the other with his shoulder, Castilla shouted a warning. But too late.

The fall forward propelled Cholas' face straight into Joanna's muddy footprints. Joanna lurched sideways and sprang to her feet as Cholas twisted around, his face spotted with mud. His gun hand was still free and he aimed at Joanna. She leaped at him, grabbed the arm holding the weapon and slammed it into the muck. The gun tumbled away, handle over barrel. Joanna intended to jump for it, but the still-agile Cholas slipped out of her grasp, rolled away, and rose to his knees. Using his arms to drive him forward, he butted Joanna in her chest. The blow was not strong, but it sent Joanna stumbling back. As she got up again, she suddenly realized how winded she was.

For a moment the two combatants, Cholas on his knees, Joanna wobbly on her feet, stared at each other. Cholas' decorative band had ripped and was soiled in several places. *Too bad, Cholas. Hope you have a spare for parades.*

Castilla limped into view. An odd smile distorting her odd mouth, she reached down and retrieved the pistol.

Joanna's shoulders slumped. "You, too? Is there no one in your group who can fight without props?"

"I do not know what you mean. We have been taught that the important goal is to prevail. We will prevail."

Cholas stood up. "Do not shoot her, Castilla. I want to finish her off myself."

Castilla casually shoved the pistol into her belt. "We will both finish her."

Joanna smiled. "It is no problem for you to violate *zellbrigen*?"

"To win, yes," Castilla said.

"Emphatically," Cholas said and came at Joanna, arms raised, fists clenched.

As she went into defensive posture, Joanna felt as if all the energy had drained out of her. Cholas' first blows showed he was not as weary as she. Still, she found the power for a sharp jab that sent him reeling backward.

Castilla limped past Cholas. Joanna blocked her first loose swing, but then Castilla got in a backhanded strike that sent Joanna stumbling back.

Wiping blood from her mouth with the back of her hand, Joanna realized the odds were simply against her. These two, even injured, were still too strong at this point in the contest.

But she gained a moment as the two attackers stood there, apparently relishing the prospect of victory. Seeing their overconfidence Joanna faked some staggering. She let her arms fall limply to her sides and added to the drama by making her eyes look dazed. She wanted the pair to stand still for the few seconds she needed to reach for the studded gloves Diana had stuffed into the back of her belt. It had been a long time since Joanna had used gloves in a fight.

Continuing to stagger, she performed a particularly dramatic whirl and wobbled her legs so that they looked about to collapse—a move designed to keep the gloves out of sight. She looked down at them briefly. The metal studs were arranged into a Jade Falcon star. Each stud was pointed and hard.

She pulled the gloves on and turned around to see her two attackers moving in for the kill. Letting her arms hang limply so they would not notice the gloves, Joanna peered at Castilla and Cholas through drooping eyelids. The more she got into the sham, the more effects she was able to create. Seen through swinging strands of her wet hair, her eyes no doubt effectively feigned exhaustion.

The downpour was getting heavier.

"This reminds me of our Trial, Castilla." There was something resembling affection in Cholas' voice. "When we worked so well together to—"

"You two qualified together," Joanna said, her voice pretending weakness. Well, some of the weakness was pretense, at least.

"Yes. Castilla saved me when she—"

"Spare me the folk tale." Joanna's voice was stronger as she eased out of her fake slouch. "I knew you could not qualify completely on your own, Cholas."

Startling them both, Joanna gave her battle scream and

rushed straight for them. Cholas flinched as she came at him, but then she veered to her right instead to confront her weaker foe first.

She pushed Castilla back against the side of the 'Mech foot before hitting her. The first blow of the studded gloves ripped across Castilla's face and left a long, bleeding cut. The second collapsed Castilla's stomach and left her bent over, choking. A strong leg sweep, punishing Castilla's injured leg, sent the young warrior sliding down to the muddy ground.

Cholas jumped on Joanna's back and tried to encircle her neck with his arm. The tactic might have worked, but the clothes of both warriors were slippery from the rain. Besides, Joanna was now strengthened by a rage that let her flip Cholas off and throw him against the 'Mech leg, which tottered from the impact. As Cholas pushed away from it, it began to sway back and forth above them.

Joanna moved in on Cholas, each blow she delivered making effective contact with his face or body. Each blow also either drew blood or was so painful that his face was soon contorted in agony. The last blows sent him crashing against the 'Mech leg, his head bouncing off it with a loud clang. The leg rocked back and forth more, creaking and making that odd screech so common to BattleMechs.

His eyes dazed, Cholas ran under the leg and fell to the ground on its other side. His shoulder slammed into a puddle so hard that the impact splashed out most of the water there. Joanna started after him, but then a heavy downpour of water falling on her head made her look up. She realized that the tottering leg had reached the point of no return and was about to fall.

Castilla, on her knees beside the 'Mech foot, was still groggy. She seemed unaware of the movement of the leg, whose foot was about to fall directly on her.

Running over to Castilla, Joanna reached down and grabbed her legs, then quickly dragged her body away. The 'Mech foot came crashing down, just centimeters from Castilla's head.

Dropping Castilla's legs, Joanna pitched backward, exhausted. She could see the star pattern on her gloves. Some of the metal stars had drops of blood on them still, but the rain was quickly washing them clean.

She could fight no longer. If either of these *eyasses* had anything left in them, they could beat her now. She was like that fallen 'Mech leg. She would topple over at the slightest touch.

Pulling off the gloves, she stared down at Castilla, whose eyes were open. The younger MechWarrior winced several times at the rain hitting her face, but refused to turn her head away from it.

"You should have left me there. I do not want to be indebted to you."

"No debt, Castilla. *Quiaff?*"

"But—"

"Quiaff?"

"Aff."

"That was too weak, insincere. *Quiaff*?"

"AFF!"

Snapping her gloves militarily against her thigh, Joanna walked over to the prone Cholas. He was conscious. Seeing her, he tried to rise to a battle stance, but he could barely move.

"Do not bother, Cholas. This honor duel is over. I win, *quiaff?*"

"Well . . ."

These fools are hard to convince.

"QUIAFF?"

"Aff."

Joanna moved a couple of steps away. The rain was letting up. Like her, the storm had no more fight in it.

"Those gloves, they are not a fair weapon," Cholas muttered.

"Who said they were a weapon?"

"But you—"

"Quit your whining, Cholas. I wore the gloves, you had the pistol. Cancels out, *quiaff*? Anyway, what warrior's manual lists gloves as weapons?"

"On your hands, they—"

"You are ridiculous. These gloves are proper warrior issue for a cold-weather planet."

"But the studs—"

"The studs are garish warrior decoration, like your foolish sibko bands. Just fashion, Cholas, just fashion."

Joanna slapped the gloves fiercely against her thigh, then walked with surprising energy out of the improvised Circle of Equals.

6

Falcon Guard Headquarters
Pattersen, Sudeten
Jade Falcon Occupation Zone
1 July 3057

There was something wrong with Star Colonel Ravill Pryde's face, Joanna thought. It did not look like the face of a real person, but reminded her of a hastily sketched drawing.

The cheekbones. It must be the damn cheekbones. They are too high in the face, too pointed. Pointed like sheer cliffs. Jutting out too far. Touch them, you could cut yourself. They make his eyes too narrow, turn them into caves behind the cliffs. Slitted, plunging the eyelids downward, but not quite hiding the eyes, which stare out like laser rays, ambushers hiding in the caves. They are mean eyes. I should like mean eyes—they are tough eyes, warrior eyes. But these scare me. They are like the eyes of some demon. And that high forehead makes them seem all the smaller, all the narrower. His hair, cut so close, is just enough to keep him from being bald. His mouth is too friendly. Too much smile, too many teeth. White teeth. Yet the effect of the smile is to take attention away from the eyes' secrets.

What really surprised her was the man's body. Not only was he shorter than most warriors, he was abysmally thin. The standard, short-sleeved uniform of the warrior displayed bony arms whose veins stood out. The swooping Jade Falcon on his unit insignia looked larger than it should, although it had to be the same size worn by the other Falcon Guard warriors in the room.

Abnormally thick tufts of chest hair stuck out from the open neck of his shirt. If there was anything Joanna especially hated on a male warrior, it was heavy chest hair. It was ugly and sometimes smelled bad. Ravill Pryde's boots were so shiny, their light seemed like the source rather than the reflection.

As he addressed the warriors assembled in the sparsely furnished wardroom, he moved among them gracefully. A lot about Ravill Pryde was graceful. His walk, his gestures, the way he tilted his head and leaned slightly forward when listening to another. He did *most* of the talking, though, and the warriors, newcomers and veterans alike, seemed rapt by his words.

Joanna, leaning against a wardroom table, shifted uncomfortably and wondered if anyone else in the room could see through Ravill Pryde's act, or was she the only one? If so, did that made her mistaken? Had she become so enmired in her misanthropy that no one new could impress her?

Or maybe was she the only one who saw clearly.

To her, Ravill Pryde was a pompous, fraudulent little weasel. And to Joanna, weasels had no place among the fierce, proud blood of Clan Jade Falcon. The universe suddenly seemed smaller.

Ravill Pryde stopped in front of the young warriors, four of the five Joanna had fought and eight others. Two of them were in her own Star. Although prone to a good deal of secret snickering, they had been performing their assigned duties adequately. And what was adequate for Joanna was arduous compared to what the other Star officers asked.

At the forefront of the group were Cholas and Castilla, the effects of the honor duel still glaringly evident on them. Ronan and Haline stayed in the background, hiding their bruises. Fredrich was in the garrison infirmary with two broken legs.

In addition to the cuts Joanna had inflicted, both Castilla and Cholas' faces were severely bruised. Castilla's left eye was swollen shut. Both young warriors struggled to stand upright, but the posture was obviously painful for them.

Ravill Pryde put a hand on the shoulder of each one. "I

see we have a pair of real warriors here, their courage showing in their wounds."

Cholas and Castilla both smiled, the distortion of Castilla's smile revealing her pain.

"I have been briefed on the honor duel. You should have won, *quiaff*?"

"Aff," replied Cholas, glaring past Ravill Pryde at Joanna.

"Well, a lesson or two learned in an honor duel can be valiancy later, even when you lose. Just continue to conduct yourself with proper Jade Falcon daring and courage. Now that I am here, I expect to see your skills, and the skills of all Falcon Guards, rise to higher levels, *quiaff*?"

Aff," Castilla and Cholas said together. Others among the young warriors nodded agreement.

Joanna, grunting scornfully, looked away. Her grunt was a bit too loud, and it caught the attention of Ravill Pryde. He looked over his shoulder at her.

"You have a comment, Star Captain Joanna?"

"None at all."

"You were merely clearing your throat?"

"Aff."

Detecting something in her voice, Ravill Pryde scowled briefly, then turned his attention back to the young warriors.

"Well, I am the newcomer in this room. Like all Jade Falcon warriors, it is my duty to prove myself to you, not yours to prove yourselves to me."

What does he mean by that? Nobody has to prove anything to anybody else in a wardroom!

Joanna leaned toward Horse and whispered, "Is this *stravag* full of hot air or what?"

Horse shrugged. "He seems full of something."

Cholas spoke up, as if on a staged cue. "We are all anxious to hear about your Trial of Position, Star Colonel Pryde."

Ravill Pryde was conspicuously pleased by the question. Before speaking again, he surveyed the entire room except for seeming to skip conspicuously over Joanna.

"How much time have we? Do you really want to hear?"

All of the young warriors nodded eagerly. The veterans displayed, as befitting oldtimers, less emotion, but most indicated interest. Joanna glanced theatrically at her chronometer, the exaggerated gesture greatly amusing Diana and Horse.

Ravill Pryde missed the gesture, but did perceive the others' reactions. He walked over to Horse and Diana. "I enjoy jokes. How about letting me in on this one?"

"No joke," Diana improvised quickly. "We are . . . just a cheerful and happy pair of warriors." Her subsequent smile would have charmed anyone. Almost anyone. Ravill Pryde frowned.

"You are both freeborn. To do as well as you have—especially you, Commander Horse, as a warrior and as Aidan Pryde's chief ally—you must be quite brave. I am glad to serve with you. Let me remind you, though, that you *are* freeborn and must abide by the rules and customs of caste. I do not intend to allow any trueborn to be insulted in any way by any freeborn, *quiaff?*"

Joanna wanted to leap at Ravill Pryde's back, but instead she said calmly, "Who died and made you Khan, Star Colonel?"

He spun around to face her. There was anger in his eyes, but he kept his voice in control. "I am no Khan, but I am a trueborn warrior and therefore—"

"And I am also trueborn, but that does not mean I may insult Jade Falcon warriors at will."

"Insult whom? Them? How did I insult them? I merely pointed out they were freeborn and—"

Some red had come into his face, but the blades of his cheekbones were drained and white, almost as though freshly sharpened.

"This is not some safe little homeworld," Joanna said, "where *rules* and *customs* are laid out simply. We are warriors here, and we have fought together in the invasion, in war, and we know rules and customs do not always apply. You will learn that, Ravill Pryde. For now, take it from me, we have proven ourselves."

The young warriors began to shout out protests, and Cholas stepped forward. "Star Colonel Pryde has proven himself in his Trial, entering service as a Clan warrior with the rank of full Star Captain."

Joanna pointedly ignored Cholas. "I give you full credit for your achievement, Ravill Pryde. But that does not mean—"

"And he has a bloodname," Castilla shouted. "Match that, Star Captain Joanna."

Joanna was ready to battle the injured Castilla all over

again, but Horse held her back. At this moment he was perhaps the only one in the wardroom strong enough to do so.

"I choose not to press this issue," Ravill Pryde said. "There will be time for us to—to resolve this matter later. For now, I apologize if I have offended any warrior in the room, even a freeborn one. It is not my intent to open wounds. Yet, anyway."

Ravill Pryde stared into Joanna's eyes for a moment. Neither gave way. He returned his attention to his audience, and Horse gestured Joanna to a chair, where she reluctantly settled.

"You wished to hear about my Trial," Ravill Pryde said, and again the young warriors called and shouted enthusiastically. Even the veterans edged in closer so as not to miss a word.

Ravill Pryde put one of his legs on a chair. After carefully straightening out the crease of his trousers, he began.

"I do not think anyone had any doubts that I would succeed in my Trial of Position."

It's clear you had no doubts, Joanna thought.

"But I also knew it would be a waste for me to qualify only at the MechWarrior rank. Do not take that as a criticism of your own achievements, my fellow warriors. It was just that, well, I felt a sense of destiny, something perhaps unusual for a cadet. Most of my sibkin, I observed, concentrated only on winning the Trial. I looked beyond. In that respect, I suspect—if you will realize that my comparison is made in all humility—I was like the revered Aidan Pryde."

"Praise Aidan Pryde," chanted several of the young warriors. Some of the veterans, however, exchanged puzzled glances.

Who does he think he is? He has not fought a major battle, and he compares himself with Aidan? And he used the name just to invoke that ritual response, the stravag!

"My comparison of myself to the revered Aidan Pryde is not casual, my dear companions. I think . . . I think that, in a way, I was taken over by his young spirit during the Trial itself. You look puzzled. How can that be? You have done some mental calculations and realized I could not possibly have styled myself after him, since he had not yet performed so heroically on Tukayyid, and his name was still unknown back in the homeworlds, and it was long before his genetic legacy was accepted for the gene pool. How, you ask rightly, could the spirit of a warrior still alive have inspired me so? "But recall that I said the *young* Aidan Pryde. In fact, I had never so much as heard the hero's name when I came to my Trial. Nevertheless, he was the protagonist of a long-standing Crash Camp legend. Only later, after Aidan Pryde's valiantness was known, did we discover that he was the daring young man of the legend. In his first Trial of Position Aidan Pryde risked a daring maneuver, jumping his 'Mech over his three opponents and trying to defeat them all. He nearly succeeded but was defeated by the treachery of his Trial-mate, who entered the melee caused by his own unique strategy and shot him down to win her own Trial. I understand the Trial-mate achieved two kills and became a Star Commander."

That is correct. And it was a legitimate maneuver on Marthe Pryde's part. I always thought Aidan deserved it, and maybe became a better warrior because of it. He suffered, yes, had to pose as a freeborn for many years—but that is probably part of this stravag's damn "legend." I hope Marthe Pryde finds out he calls her treacherous.

"The Aidan Pryde strategy was, of course, one of many falconer stories. The falconers recounted it as a warning not to overreach, even though some of us took it differently. Well, not surprisingly, me being a *Jade Falcon* warrior, after all, the story inspired me. I knew, knew inside, that I had to attempt a similar strategy."

"But you risked failing altogether, like Aidan Pryde did," MechWarrior Ronan said. For a moment, Ravill Pryde scowled. Obviously he did not like being interrupted.

"Yes, I did that. I risked all. Risk is a characteristic I share with the revered Aidan Pryde."

"Praise Aidan Pryde."

Joanna felt nauseous. And she could not help but think Aidan would have hated such blind hero worship.

"By the day of my Trial I knew what to do. It was necessary to correct the legendary strategy, to make it work."

The more he described the Trial, the more expressive Ravill Pryde's thin arms became. He seemed to wave one arm or the other to emphasize each important detail. To Joanna he looked like a semaphore with sticks.

He spent some time setting up his version of the Trial, telling his spellbound audience of the bleak and rugged terrain, the attacks of some freeborn trainees brought in just to make the Trial harder (he defeated every one he faced, of course), the climb up into the cockpit of his *Timber Wolf.* His Trial opponents soon appeared, in a tight line, just beyond a deep but narrow canyon.

"Well, that canyon threw off my strategy a bit. It was narrow but just a bit too wide to step across, and I wished that my 'Mech could have been configured with jump jets, so I could switch to Aidan Pryde's original strategy. My Trialmate's foes were also on the other side of the canyon, but there was a bridge where she was. While she could easily cross it, it would have been a waste of time for me and would have forced me into a confrontation with her Trial opponents. No, I had to play the hand given me.

"Recall that I had given away some firepower in order to add the second Streak SRM. But that was all right. I intended to win, using only my PPCs and the SRMs. Immediately, as my first opponent 'Mech, an ominous *Gargoyle,* came forward, I saw the way. The Aidan Pryde strategy would work, I was certain, at least in the way I intended to adapt it."

Ravill Pryde took his foot off the chair and stood before them, his hands held in front of him. His stance resembled the battle-ready position of a pilot, and his small stature made the stance seem faintly ridiculous—to Joanna, at least.

"I knew it was imperative that I dispose of the first foe quickly. I went forward slowly, deliberately lumbered so that, to my enemies I would look uncertain, as if severely disoriented by their unexpected appearance on the other side of the canyon. Near the edge of the canyon, I fired off the first of my PPC barrages. My timing was good and I sliced off a good bit of armor from the *Gargoyle*'s right torso. It staggered him a bit. He was standing so close to the canyon edge that a rain of armor pieces plunged down into its depths. I hammered at him with my PPC while his SRMs did a fair bit of damage on me. I will not bore you with the details, since the *Gargoyle* turned out to be such an easy mark. Its next burst was way off target, and I knew that something had to be wrong with the pilot. A stray shot, perhaps, had pierced the cockpit and maybe wounded him.

"I knew what I had to do. If I continued knocking armor off the torso, I could get to something vital, the fusion engine or the gyro, but that would waste a lot more ammunition. I backed away four or five steps from the canyon, then bent my torso, a feint that allowed me to aim my PPCs directly at the *Gargoyle*'s lower legs. I let off a punishing fusillade, forcing the legs backward and the upper body forward. More firing on the lower legs and I sent the *Gargoyle* toppling. As I had figured, it fell forward across the canyon, its head, face down, and its shoulders on my side of the canyon, the lower part of its legs on the other. And you know what I did then?"

Ravill Pryde surveyed the blank looks of his audience, then announced smugly, "For a moment while the *Gargoyle* was stretched insecurely across the nine-meter gash, it formed the makeshift bridge I had planned for it to be. Since my *Timber Wolf* had fine running capability, I ran it across the back of the *Gargoyle* and, in three or four steps, was on the other side. I did not slow my stride but immediately ran straight at the other two 'Mechs, a *Warhawk* and a *Summoner.* My weight had been too much for the fallen *Gargoyle,* and I heard it fall into the canyon behind me."

There were several sharp intakes of breath as Ravill Pryde described his derring-do with a cavalier enthusiasm.

"That strategy," Castilla said, her voice awed, "it was like Aidan Pryde using 'Mechs as stepping stones in the middle of the Prezno River on Tukayyid so that our forces could get across and capture the bridges."

Ravill Pryde smiled. "I suppose so. Of course that had not happened yet. I doubt that Aidan Pryde knew anything of my achievement, but perhaps he did. Anyway, here is the kicker. I ran straight at the *Summoner,* so that its pilot would think he or she was to be my next foe. I was feeling really fine by this time. I was already a qualified MechWarrior, was I not, so that anything I did now would not take away my essential victory. But I wanted more than anything to excel in my Trial, to make it a Trial that would be remembered. I kept my PPC firing, and the *Summoner* landed several hammering blows on me. My armor was getting paper-thin. I kept coming. At short range the *Summoner* was devastating. In a moment it would have finished me off.

"But see, up to this point I had not used my Streak SRMs. When I got close enough to the *Summoner,* I suddenly veered to the right, upped my speed, and started running into the space between the two 'Mechs. I knew my heat levels were raising rapidly, but I was also certain my *Timber Wolf* could take whatever the other 'Mechs had to offer and be done with it before heat reached the danger point.

"The *Summoner*'s pilot saw I was creating a melee and started firing his large pulse laser at me. My armor was chipping away so fast, and in such big chunks, that in spots there was none left. I was extremely vulnerable, but that did not matter. As soon as I had stepped just a bit past the line, so that the melee was created, I used my *Timber Wolf*'s superb adaptability to come to an abrupt stop and step back across the line so that I ended up directly between the *Summoner* and the *Warhawk*. Without waiting for my *Timber Wolf*'s feet to settle, I twisted to the right, launching my Streak SRMs, and even before they impacted, I twisted left and engaged the *Warhawk* with my PPC. The *Warhawk* exploded. Again I twisted and brought my crosshairs down on the *Summoner*, finishing him off. I was pretty much done, too. My heat was high and only stubbornness kept me from ejecting. But I had won. It took me a moment before I began to relish the fact that I had earned a Star Captaincy."

The young warriors, obviously inflamed by the tale, looked at Ravill Pryde as if they wished to be him.

"And so I am not exaggerating when I say that I may credit my success to Aidan Pryde, whose name I did not even know until much later, but whose later heroism became even more legendary than his daring cadet exploits."

Several young warriors seconded the reverence by mumbling ritualistic and awed praise.

"Star Colonel Ravill Pryde?"

"Yes, Star Captain Joanna?"

"When you turned the Trial into a melee so that you could fire on the other 'Mechs . . ."

"Yes."

"What happened to the other trainee, your Trial-mate?"

Ravill Pryde's face became grim. "She lost, I am afraid."

"And did her loss have anything to do with your invocation of the melee?"

Ravill Pryde seemed uncomfortable. "It was unfortunate, but she was defeated by her trio of foes once the melee was initiated. But mine was a fair tactic, and my Trial-mate praised me for it."

"I do not doubt that. Where is she now?"

"I am not really sure."

"You have no idea?"

"She is a tech somewhere."

"Is she content, do you think?"

"How would I know that?"

"Oh, just a question—though the answer, it seems to me, is obvious. I mean, what cadet who had nearly become a Jade Falcon warrior and lost only because of circumstances would be satisfied ending up as a tech? Sorry to interrupt."

"You express half-formed opinions rather freely, Captain Joanna, especially for—well, I will get into that later. I will treat your remark as the normal initiation, the normal Trial of Greeting, as it were, for a newcomer to your garrison. That is what it is, *quiaff*?"

"Oh, *aff*. Definitely *aff*."

Joanna was not sure why she had even spoken. The fate of a cadet during a Trial of Position was of no concern to her. Everyone in a Trial took the chance that something would interfere with a probable success. That was what a Trial was about. It was like war in that respect. Stray shots finish off heroes, terrain controlled some battles. Still, she felt that she had provided a troubling footnote to Ravill Pryde's egotistic tale.

"Tell us about the winning of your bloodname, Star Colonel," Haline asked, her eyes wide. "It is incredible to win one so soon after a Trial of Position."

Ravill Pryde seemed pleased by her question, but he said, "I think one story at a time is sufficient. I will save that one for another idle night, although I hope we do not have too many of those."

The other warriors, including the veterans, gave a small cheer at those words. Jade Falcon warriors did not relax well. To them, the truce with the Inner Sphere was like a serious illness eating away at what was, for them, a vital organ: the need for war. It was, after all, what they were bred for.

Ravill Pryde made an expansive gesture that seemed to include the whole roomful of warriors. "I thank you, my fellow Jade Falcons, for making me feel so at ease in your midst. I know it is not always easy to welcome a commanding officer, especially after all that many of you have been through together. I am honored."

Unused to such politeness, the veteran warriors exchanged confused glances. The young ones, though, reveled in the new officer's manner and words. Joanna thought that their admiration, so openly displayed on their faces, was revolting.

"I would like to get down to work now. I know it is evening and we are off-duty. But the way of the Clan cannot abide wastefulness and I believe in using all my time for the good of the Clan. I will be setting up my barracks office now. Star Commander Horse, I would see you in my office in a half hour, prompt, *quiaff*?"

"*Aff.*"

"And Star Captain Joanna, please see me in one hour, *quiaff*?"

"For what?"

"We will discuss that then, *quiaff? Quiaff*?"

"All right, *aff.*"

The new warriors frowned at Joanna, making it clear that they unanimously despised her. That did not particularly bother her. She had always drawn the hatred of others. Still, she had not confronted such open hostility since her days as a falconer at Crash Camp on Ironhold, when even cadets from sibkos not under her supervision hated her thoroughly. Well, no matter. When it came to hatred, she had always given back more than she got.

Ravill Pryde marched briskly out of the room. Joanna asked Horse and Diana to meet her outside on the parade grounds.

The planet Sudeten, with its erratic weather patterns, was favoring its inhabitants with a warm but windy evening. The previous night it had been raining, rain with some sleet in it, battering the barracks walls so hard it had kept Joanna awake.

Wind velocity picked up within seconds of the three warriors coming together. Joanna felt it pounding at her back, giving added emphasis to her spirited words.

"What do you two think of this . . . this Ravill Pryde?" she asked the only two friends she had. It *did* nettle her that they were both freeborn. She had never adjusted to freeborns the way Aidan Pryde had, but he was an anomaly among Jade Falcon warriors.

"Ravill Pryde is unusual."

"Why do you say that, Diana?"

"Well, it is rare to see any Jade Falcon warrior boast, but there is something different in the way he does it. It is not just telling tales of his prowess, it is more like he is trying to create a mythic image of himself long before he has done enough to have his genetic legacy accepted into the gene pool."

Horse looked amused.

"What do you say, Horse?"

"I am not sure. He does seem to be promoting himself as a hero, yes, but there is something I admire in him, a touch of Aidan Pryde per—"

"Oh, come on, Horse," Joanna exclaimed angrily. "Aidan was your comrade. How can you even begin to compare him to—"

"Let us say then that Ravill Pryde has some potential. I will wait and see."

"And the two of us are wrong to judge him so harshly on short notice?"

"In a way, Joanna, in a way. Don't forget that he did win his Trial and bloodname rather convincingly and that he is a star colonel, however young and inexperienced in war itself. These are accomplishments."

"Can you not see? He has no rage in him. A Clan warrior should have rage. At least under the surface, ready to erupt. Ravill Pryde does not show even an iota."

Horse smiled. "How can you tell what form rage will take?"

"I can tell. Believe me, I can tell."

Joanna felt frustrated. She wanted Horse to agree with her, and here he was waffling on the matter. That was not like Horse. This Ravill Pryde was affecting them all.

"Go away, both of you. I need to think."

Diana and Horse were used to Joanna in such a mood. There was no point in arguing with her. They simply left her alone.

She began to walk. *It is wrong for Ravill Pryde to earn a bloodname so young, especially when a bloodname has been denied me. And his youth guarantees he will hold the bloodname for years. Even if I am too old now, I would sacrifice anything to win a bloodname, even if it only came on the last day of my life.*

Thoughts of age created a sick knot in her stomach. Joanna was not used to being affected by pain, even from the wounds of war. Now her stomach often hurt, and she got headaches.

She nearly tripped on a fallen branch that had been wrenched off a nearby tree by the progressively fierce wind. The wind burned her skin and made it difficult to stand straight. She picked up the branch, which was twice as long as her arm. Like all the branches on this planet, all the trees, it was quite heavy. If it had been leaf-bearing, it would have been too unwieldy to lift. Its bark was rippled with sharp points, which cut into the skin of her hands.

Holding the branch up, a task achieved with some exertion, Joanna felt the powerful force of the wind bending it and pulling her forward. She ran a few steps, adjusted her control of the branch to the wind, and stopped.

How old is the tree this comes from? Could I saw that tree open and count its rings? Would it be older than me? Would this branch be older than me? She strode to a nearby tree and began to slam the branch against its trunk.

I cannot be this old. I cannot be plagued with stomach aches, headaches. I was never meant to be this old. I should be many years dead. In battle I have always fought well. I have always risked all. I should have died a thousand deaths. How has it come to this? Am I like this branch, broken away from the tree, but still intact? Will I live out this life in some lower caste or in some Galaxy of ancient warriors, or die in bed with my body wrinkled and emaciated? That cannot happen. It cannot happen. I will not let it. It cannot happen. I will not let it. *It cannot happen. Cannot!*

Over and over Joanna slammed the branch against the tree trunk. The contact of wood on wood was loud and echoing. Eventually she realized that the stinging pains in her back were not signs of age, but a sudden hailstorm of small but plentiful pellets. Throwing the branch as hard as she could, she let the fierce wind take it high and away.

"That, my dear Horse, is rage," she whispered.

She felt better.

7

Falcon Guard Compound
Pattersen, Sudeten
Jade Falcon Occupation Zone
1 July 3057

Joanna encountered Horse a few steps from the door to Ravill Pryde's quarters.

"So that fraud is taking over the Falcon Guards," she said abruptly. "In the place of Aidan Pryde?"

"That is correct."

"But he is not battle-tested."

"He has commanded many engagements—for genetic legacies, for—"

"All back in the homeworlds, *quiaff*?"

"Aff."

"That is not battle experience. It is play."

Horse, unusually serious, took a deep breath. "It is the way of the Clans, Joanna. You know that. Rank is all."

"But the command should go to a proven veteran, like Star Captain Alejandro."

"His promotion is recent, more recent than Ravill Pryde's earned rank. Alejandro is not yet bloodnamed. Ravill Pryde is. In fact, Joanna, look around at our units. How many bloodnames do you count?"

When Aidan Pryde had been given command of the Falcon Guards, the troops he'd been given with which to reconstruct the unit were warriors either too old or whose codexes carried some taint. The result was that the new Falcon Guards possessed few bloodnames.

"True enough, Horse. But there will be no joy in following Ravill Pryde into battle."

"When did you ever feel joy, Joanna? Your bitterness is, in some ways, the same as mine, but I hide it and you don't. Of course you will follow Ravill Pryde into battle. You're a Jade Falcon officer, a BattleMech pilot—one of the best I've ever seen—and you are Clan. You'll do what you must."

He let the words stand and awaited a response. How ironic that these sentiments should come from Horse. There had, after all, been a time when Joanna had hated Horse. Yet in the years that had served together, observing his prowess and his loyalty to Aidan Pryde, seeing him protect Diana, she had ceased hating him somewhere along the line. She felt no affection for him, but she did not hate.

She did not hate Diana either. Even in their first real encounter, when Joanna had taught Diana some lessons in a Circle of Equals, she had admired the young woman's spirit and skills and began noticing a resemblance to Aidan. Diana was so complete a Jade Falcon warrior that it was hard to view her as a mere freeborn.

There must be something wrong with my life, if all I can claim after all this time—instead of glory, instead of a bloodname, instead of an honorable death—is the friendship of two stravag freebirths.

"Joanna?"

"You are right, Horse. I will do what I must, you know that. But, if you use one more contraction, I will tear out your heart, you freebirth scum."

He smiled. "That is better. Sounds more like you."

"What would you know, *stravag*?"

He laughed. "Why not keep your appointment with our new leader?"

Joanna started to walk past Horse, then stopped and looked over her shoulder at him.

"What did he want to see you about?"

Horse hesitated, which was very unlike him. "I wanted to wait to tell you," he said slowly. "He wants me to resume my old role in the command Cluster."

"Transfer you from my Star?"

"Yes."

"The bastard."

Horse flinched. Bastard, with its freeborn connotations, was an especially forceful curse word within the Jade Falcons.

"You must transfer?"

"Yes."

"It is stealing, Horse. He does not want you in my unit. There is already resentment from—"

"No, it is not stealing. Why would a trueborn officer want to steal a freeborn from another trueborn officer? It is because of Aidan Pryde. I was Aidan's closest friend. The idea of having me in his unit seems to give Ravill Pryde some kind of, well, comfort. Of course I'd rather remain in your Star, but in a way I am flattered."

Joanna wanted to smash something. "You almost like Ravill Pryde, do you now, Horse?"

"No, but I respect him—"

"Leave me," Joanna growled.

Horse walked away without a backward look.

"The bastard," she muttered, and even she was not certain whether she meant Horse or Ravill Pryde.

Ravill Pryde let his bombshells fall quickly and forcefully.

"I am to remind you that your rank is based on your codex. After the normal review, it has been determined that your place is as a star commander. You revert immediately to that rank and will wear the proper insignia."

"Star Colonel Ravill Pryde, I request what is my right—a Trial of Position to win back my rank."

Ravill Pryde sat at his desk, one like no other officer had here on Sudeten. He must have dragged it with him all the way here to this inhospitable planet. Made from dark, polished wood, the big, heavy piece was filigreed all the way around its upper edge in falcon insignia.

Ravill Pryde got up and came around the desk. He was so much shorter that Joanna could not help feeling a definite sense of physical superiority.

"Negative, Star Commander Joanna. I deny you any appeal."

"With all due respect, I believe that such a judgment exceeds your authority."

"It does not. In the five years since the Truce of Tukkayid, the Falcon Guards have grown weak and perhaps a bit stale. I have been charged with returning the unit to its former levels of ferocity and efficiency. The performance of the Falcon Guards has deteriorated, perhaps because of the unusually high number of freeborn warriors, and it is my duty to—"

"You speak against freeborns, yet you appoint one to serve in your Cluster."

"I see you have spoken with Star Commander Horse."

"We have served together a long while."

Ravill Pryde leaned against the desk and stared at Joanna. She looked away, for the first time noticing the pictures hanging on the walls. Clan warriors rarely decorated their quarters, but when they did it was usually with images of war or falcons or sometimes some scene from village life. These prints had obviously been liberated from Inner Sphere worlds during the invasion. She wondered how Ravill Pryde had obtained them—and why.

"Star Commander Joanna, you look stiff and uncomfortable standing there. Would you like to sit down?"

There was something unctuous in the way he spoke, in the grandiose way he gestured toward a heavily stuffed armchair, another piece of furniture no doubt transported to the wilds of Sudeten by this man. The cloth of the upholstery was intricately designed in an abstract pattern, with many interlocking bars and curved lines. "I prefer to stand, Star Colonel."

"As you wish." His pause seemed intentionally dramatic. "Star Commander Joanna, you have served the Falcon Guards—and, for that matter, Clan Jade Falcon—well, and for many years."

The last remark nettled Joanna. There was generally an insult in any remark that alluded to a warrior's age.

"Does that mean that the disgrace on Twycross is no longer a part of my codex?"

Joanna often wondered if she would ever escape the humiliation of Twycross. Even though she had been a member of the Falcon Guards for only twenty-four hours, the shame of the defeat attached to her as one of the few survivors. On that infamous day, an Inner Sphere warrior had, by exploding hidden mines, set off an avalanche in a pass called the Great Gash. The explosion had buried and virtually destroyed the Falcon Guards, whose disgrace had reverberated throughout the Clans. Joanna herself had been reduced from the rank of Star Captain to Star Commander. And even that she had only maintained by defeating two BattleMechs in the Trial of Refusal she'd demanded to win back some rank. Otherwise she would have been left a mere MechWarrior.

"Twycross remains in your codex, as you no doubt realize. I will take your comment as unfortunate sarcasm, but I suggest that you rein in your anger during this meeting."

"Are we Clan warriors, the two of us?"

"Why do you ask that?"

"I am unused to polite conversations."

"Star Commander Joanna, I had hoped that this meeting might be amicable. Obviously that is not your way."

"Or the way of the Clans."

The small, slight man seemed ruffled as he leaned away from the desk and walked directly over to her. But, Joanna noted with a perverse satisfaction, he was not angry. As before, she could see no rage in him.

"I will be brief, Star Commander Joanna. You are to be reassigned."

Looking up at her, he let the words sink in. Taken completely by surprise, Joanna could barely breathe.

"Reassigned? I do not want to join any other Jade Falcon unit."

"You are not to be reassigned to a combat zone. Your days as a warrior are over. I know that will be hard to accept, but the Khan wishes to sift out warriors past their prime. Warriors like you, Joanna."

"But . . . I mean, what are you saying?"

"I am saying that you will, in a month's time, be relieved of your Star command, and be sent back to the homeworlds—to Ironhold, to be exact."

"I have already served as a training officer. I do not wish to—"

"You will not be a falconer."

"What curse *are* you putting on me then?"

"You are a Clan officer, Star Commander Joanna. You accept whatever duty the Clan has for you, *quiaff*?"

"*Aff*, but I have always been a warrior, and I must end my days as a warrior!"

"I understand very well such sentiments. Your misfortune is that you have survived—and with skill and bravery, I might add."

"I volunteer to be reassigned to a unit of old warriors and fight my last battle alongside them."

"A solahma unit? I imagine that option was considered, but the wisdom of the Khan has superseded that simple solution. Your skills have been recognized. Seeing that your codex is a distinguished one, he has decided that you would serve best as the commander of a sibko incubation and nurturing facility, that you—"

"A canister nursemaid? You are saying that I have the skills to be a canister nursemaid, to watch over vats and nurseries, to—"

"Joanna, the assignment is an honor. You will not be performing simple tech duties. You will command the entire facility. You will be the warrior caste's eyes and ears in that place, our liaison, our representative, our falcon. This assignment is, in fact, a great honor!"

"It is imprisonment! A life sentence! It is punishment, is it not, for Twycross—a delayed punishment, but a punishment nevertheless!"

"How you can say that? The order comes from the Khan himself. He has chosen you."

"Would *you* want such an assignment, Ravill Pryde?"

"I am bloodnamed. It is not an assignment for a warrior with a bloodname. It is one for a warrior not bloodnamed but who has distinguished him or herself in battle. It is a reward, not a punishment. And there is more. The position carries with it a great posthumous reward—to have your ashes mixed with the nutrient solutions for a new sibko."

That stopped Joanna. Short of winning a bloodname, the desire to have her ashes used to nourish a Jade Falcon sibko had become her greatest ambition. Yet—was it worth the shame of being a canister nanny?

"Well, Joanna? You understand better now?"

"Do I have any right of appeal?"

"None. It is for the good of the Clan. In time you will see and accept that."

"Never."

Ravill Pryde sighed. To Joanna, his sigh seemed especially unwarriorlike. It was the sigh of a bureaucrat, not a warrior.

"I am surprised that you feel this way," he said. "With your permission, I would speak personally for a moment, *quiaff*?"

"*Aff*. What worse can you tell me now?"

"I have been fully informed about the honor duel fought

yesterday, Star Commander Joanna. You performed admirably, but you were a fool for fighting it. The Circle of Equals is a place to resolve great offenses, not to quibble over such trivialities a—"

"Trivialities? They insulted me and my friends."

"Those friends are freeborn, therefore trivial."

"You are willing enough to steal one of them for your Command Cluster."

"True. But that is based on merit. I would not fight an honor duel over Star Commander Horse." He straightened. Standing as tall as he could, in his crisp uniform, with military bearing, Ravill Pryde looked like a leader, in spite of his height. "You have been in the field too long, Joanna. Too much combat and the nerves get stretched taut, as I think happened to you. Everything becomes like war, a matter of life and death. In this case you did not react sensibly. You endangered yourself and inflicted damage on others, and that is waste and the Clan abhors waste. When a warrior becomes so old that his judgment falters, reassignment is definitely in order. I congratulate you on the honor the Khan has bestowed upon you. Let us hear no more about it. Dismissed."

He wheeled around in military fashion, returning to the elegant chair behind his elegant desk and sat down. Dwarfed by the chair's high back, Ravill Pryde again looked too small for a warrior.

Joanna did not move.

"Dismissed, Star Commander."

"Ravill Pryde—"

"I would remind you to address me by my rank."

"Star Colonel Ravill Pryde, are you not aware that many older warriors continue to serve the warrior caste here in the Inner Sphere?"

"Name one."

"Kael Pershaw."

"He is an advisor to the Khan."

"Natasha Kerensky of Clan Wolf."

"You dare compare yourself to a bloodnamed warrior? Though she is aged, Natasha Kerensky is not you, Joanna. She *earned* her position with the Wolves, and unlike you, she has never stopped advancing up through the ranks. And she has risen high, even to the position of a Khan of the

Wolves. But when she is too old to be a Khan, she will die or be removed to serve her Clan in another way.

"You are arrogant and audacious even to suggest such a comparison. The decision has been made. Dismissed."

"Ravill Pryde, I would fight you in a Circle of Equals. I formally make that challenge."

"Neg, you may not challenge me. Not on this issue. I have merely communicated orders from above to you. They are, after all, not *my* orders. You do not duel with the messenger, Star Commander."

"I would duel with you because your manner is arrogant and supercilious."

"We do not fight an honor duel over my addressing you properly as your superior officer."

"I would duel with you because you are the lowest kind of freebirth, Ravill Pryde."

He smiled. It was a tight smile, without humor in it. "Not bad, Joanna, not bad. But such insults are simply another triviality, not worth fighting an honor duel over. You must do better.

"I would—"

"Dismissed! Now!"

Turning sharply, she marched toward the door.

"Star Commander Joanna!"

He keeps reminding me of the demotion, the stravag. I will think of a challenge that falls within his damn rules. I will!

"I remind you that my combat skills were proven in my original Trial and my bloodname contests. I am not an ordinary new warrior like Cholas, Castilla, and the rest. With your considerable skills you managed to defeat all five of them. But you would not defeat me. So, persist in this challenge, and I will slaughter you. It is as simple as that. It will be Twycross all over again for you. That is a promise. Accept your reassignment with grace, and we will have an amicable month together. I can learn from you, and I would rather learn from you than fight you."

Joanna said nothing. She merely turned on her heel and left Ravill Pryde's quarters. Something inside the room fell when she slammed the door shut. She hoped it was one of those *stravag* Inner Sphere prints.

Outside, she came upon the branch she had used against the tree trunk. Probably carried by the wind, it seemed to have been searching her out. She picked it up and snapped it in two against her leg with a loud, echoing crack. Joanna hoped, but did not care much, that the cracking sound belonged to the branch and not her leg.

8

Watch Command
Jade Falcon Command Center, Wotan
Jade Falcon Occupation Zone
7 July 3057

Kael Pershaw peered at the data sheet his aide had just handed him. In the dimness of the command center, its numbers were difficult to read, especially for one with only one good eye. And that eye was not exactly twenty-twenty anymore, either.

Not wanting any of his subordinates to observe his vision difficulties, he casually sat down at a console and set the sheet down on a computer keyboard. The glow of the monitor screen helped to bring the document's letters and numbers into focus.

The information on the sheet had been obtained through the interception of some Wolf Clan messages. As head of the Jade Falcon branch of the Clan Watch, the intelligence arm of the Clans, Pershaw was immediately sent any intercepted dispatch that seemed more than routine.

"What do you think, Kael Pershaw?" his aide, Star Commander Deval Huddock, said. Huddock always spoke most deferentially to his superior, but carefully avoided use of any rank. Though Kael Pershaw still wore the insignia of a Star Colonel, his warrior days were over and everyone knew it.

"Give me another minute, Huddock," Pershaw, never known for courtesy to his subordinates, growled.

He picked up the paper to examine it closer. By doing so, he lost the advantage of the light and had to slam it back down. The move depressed some keys and a jumble of misinformation appeared onscreen. After he lifted the paper slightly, one key still remained depressed. That produced several lines of dancing <'s until he released the key and erased them.

"So, Huddock," he said finally, "the only meaning I can take from this is that Clan Wolf has somehow been infiltrating spies into Jade Falcon units."

"That is my interpretation also, sir. The key word seems to be burgess."

"And why is that?"

Pershaw had great respect for Huddock's judgement. It was the reason he had given him such authority in spite of a rather mediocre service record. Although Huddock had succeeded in winning a bloodname, he had suffered from a condition that prevented him from properly using his neurohelmet to pilot a BattleMech—a condition techs sometimes called brainslip. Fortunately for Huddock, he had caught Pershaw's attention, and Pershaw had arranged for the warrior to join the staff of the Jade Falcon Watch. Pershaw never regretted his decision.

Huddock's looks were as average as his military exploits. His face was round, and his eyes generally had a deeply focused appearance.

"Burgess was a famous Terran spy about ten centuries ago, sir."

"He must have been *very* good for his name to endure so long."

"I am not sure about that. Names of traitors have a tendency to survive without any memories of their deeds. At any rate, I know Burgess was English."

"I understand they were devious, Englishmen."

"I do not know, sir."

Pershaw continued to study the report. "How will we be able to tell which units might have been infiltrated?"

"It is hard, but not impossible. Because of the truce, there are two kinds of troop movements now. Most units are fixed in position and travel only when their commanders wish to issue a challenge to other Clan units or conduct raids. Infiltrators could join units in two ways. First, if young enough, an agent could pose as a new freeborn warrior fresh from training."

Kael Pershaw nodded thoughtfully, though the expression on his ruined face was unreadable. "Very good, Huddock. It would not be difficult to modify the codex of a young warrior to match that of another person because a newly minted codex is nowhere near as extensive as a veteran's."

"Exactly. Once the forgery is complete, the spy merely hops the next JumpShip to one of the worlds in our occupation zone and connects easily with a unit."

Pershaw could not suppress his outrage. "If any freebirth scum has killed off a newly qualified Jade Falcon warrior to take his place, I will personally see to it that he or she has his skin peeled off alive."

"The spies are not exactly freeborn, sir."

The remark, so characteristic of Huddock's habitual literalness, made Pershaw smile and calmed him down. "I meant freebirth in the obscene usage, not the actual one, Huddock."

"Oh, I see."

"What is the other possible means of infiltration?"

"Well, uh, we have been replacing many older warriors and—"

"Warriors as old as myself?"

Huddock, who also did not perceive irony, seemed embarrassed. "I do not think age can be counted in years, Star Colonel Pershaw. It should be judged through effectiveness. Old Clan warriors are those whose combat ability is in question and whose reassignments are of a nonutilitarian nature."

Pershaw laughed. "You are a diplomat, Huddock. Perhaps we should make an ambassador out of you."

"I would treat the assignment as an honor, sir."

"Huddock, if you continue to serve me well, perhaps I should think about transferring you to the diplomatic service, *quiaff*?"

Huddock, as usual, did not catch the sarcasm. "I wish to serve the Watch as long as I am needed, sir."

"Diplomatic, if not wise perhaps. The Watch has yet to earn much respect among Jade Falcon warriors, most of whom rate anything less than battle prowess as beneath their attention."

Huddock found it particularly diplomatic at this moment not to respond to Pershaw's bitter commentary. After a pause, he picked up the thread of their earlier talk. "Many of our old warriors are being transferred to solahma units. Since we currently have little call to send such units out for sacrifice missions, they are being used mainly for minor guard duties and occasionally for raids that would be, well, slightly dishonorable for regular Jade Falcon warriors. Transfers of personnel in and out of these units is not a matter of stringent scrutiny. No one much cares about the codexes of solahma warriors. They will all die soon anyway."

"Yes, I can see that. For some of us, even those at command level, the old, used-up warriors rate only just slightly above freeborn warriors in our estimation. I can see commanding officers expediting transfers just to get rid of them."

"Some older freeborn warriors have also been assigned to solahmas."

"Logical, logical. And I can see where you are going with this, Huddock. It is relatively simple to insert a spy into such a unit, especially since the troops and officers are below-standard and morale is generally so low that few bonds are formed among individuals. I wonder, though, what could be gained by using solahmas for intelligence work?"

"Well, like any intelligence work, the task is essentially one of gathering information. Place any good observant agent anywhere, and something he or she sees or reads or hears can prove to be useful. And we know the Wolves rely much more on agents and informants than we do."

"Up to now."

"Sir?"

"I think we will place an agent of our own into one of these old-timer units, Huddock. After all, when in Rome . . ."

"Rome, sir?"

"You surprise me, Huddock. You know about England ten centuries ago and know nothing about Rome?"

"If it is in a file anywhere, I can learn, sir."

"Do not bother, Huddock. I have other, more important things for you to do. And thank you. Your insights have been useful. I will assume charge of the project from here."

After Huddock left, Pershaw sat back and considered his dilemma. The Jade Falcon branch of the Clan Watch did not have an active spy organization. Almost all of his activities were devoted to the accumulation and interpretation of information. This was because the Clans, and the Falcons especially, viewed covert missions as conduct unbecoming a warrior. Gathering information was another matter altogether—information was ammunition. He would have his staff begin to examine the documents on new arrivals to Jade Falcon units. There might be discrepancies. Whatever happened, the rooting out of such infiltrators would follow accepted procedures.

But the old-warrior units, that was another matter. Honor was not in question there. He should find operatives of his own. It would be radical for the Watch to send out covert agents, but it might work.

And almost immediately Kael Pershaw thought of one old warrior who would be perfect for such a mission. Nobody, Wolf Clan or otherwise, would ever suspect such a bad-tempered, bitter, and generally disagreeable warrior of being a spy.

9

Falcon Guard Compound
Pattersen, Sudeten
Jade Falcon Occupation Zone
7 July 3057

In Clan mythology there were few gods, just a general belief that some higher intelligence might be governing the chaos. As more and more planets were added to the known worlds, the possibility of a higher power began to seem ever more unlikely. Or perhaps likely—since the vastness of the universe could explain why the gods had to keep very busy and could not attend to everything.

Warriors, in particular, did not hold much store in the idea of a god or gods who cared very much for people. Something approaching religion was practiced in villages, particularly by the craftsman classes. Professional castes, like scientists, also tended to give lip service to philosophies resembling some old Terran religions, but it did not go much deeper than that.

Warriors had no use for gods. If anything, they were their own gods. All Clan warriors were willing to die for their Clan but, like Joanna, they did not wish their deaths to be meaningless. Bravery was meaning, sacrifice was meaning, waste was not. Any Clan warrior whose death was wasted took disgrace with him into eternity. Of course, it was an eternity that few believed in. There were no devils or demons in Clan mythology. Any living being could be a devil or demon, and most Jade Falcon warriors would have been proud to be viewed as such.

After a few days of serving under Star Colonel Ravill Pryde, the newly demoted Star Commander Joanna was willing to consider him the worst kind of devil. When she expressed that idea to Horse, he replied laconically, "There was just such a devil in old Terran literature. He lived in the pit of hell, chewing on traitors."

"How do you know so much about Terran literature?"

Horse, realizing he had slipped up, merely said, "You pick up a lot of garbage when you are a freeborn."

"I do not doubt it."

Horse had long ago discovered that he could weasel out of any conversational difficulty simply by blaming it on his freeborn heritage.

On his first day of command, Ravill Pryde had called a meeting of all officers, during which he announced that the unit was becoming inefficient. "Warriors who are not constantly facing combat grow stale and dull," he said, acknowledging that it was harder to maintain battle readiness in a period of truce. "Like the falcon, we must constantly sharpen our claws."

"Sitting idle, we lose our edge," he went on. "We become argumentative." Saying this, he made a point of staring at Joanna, who of course glared right back at him, resisting the obvious comeback—who said argumentativeness was bad in a warrior? "These raids that the other Clans, and even other Jade Falcon units, are engaging in are mere exercises in wastefulness. There is little point in depleting our own forces in minor skirmishes when we must be prepared to resume the invasion of the Inner Sphere should the truce be nullified—and believe me, my warriors, that it will. The Inner Sphere is governed by guileful leaders. The truce is just a smokescreen for them."

The new warriors relished Ravill Pryde's interpretations of politics and history. It fit their own conceptions well. In their minds Jade Falcons were honorable and all other peoples were not—including all other Clans and, especially, the people of the Inner Sphere. Nobody could be trusted in the bizarre labyrinth of Inner Sphere politics, with its shifting allegiances and changing borders. If someone wished to imply that the Inner Sphere contained nothing but bandits, traitors, and worst of all, freebirths, it would be believed wholeheartedly. As for the other Clans, the simple truth was that none were as noble or as fierce as Clan Jade Falcon.

Joanna had to shut her eyes to keep from seeing the smug faces of the young warriors when they cheered on Ravill Pryde. She wondered if they went on and on like this about the Clans in Inner Sphere encampments. Perhaps they cursed the evil Clans, perhaps they condemned the Clans for barbarism in combat and politics, perhaps they found the Clan style of living unsuited to whatever tastes they considered sophisticated.

It turned out that Ravill Pryde's program for sharpening the claws of the Falcon Guards was just as malevolent as his personality. He made everyone, officers as well as MechWarriors, MechWarriors as well as techs, arise before dawn to practice group calisthenics. He claimed the calisthenics made a warrior more alert in the cockpit and a tech more effective in field repair. It was difficult to argue with him since he performed the exercises at the highest levels, outlasting everyone else.

Though Joanna had been notorious for such tactics as a falconer, a week of the calisthenics left her feeling neither healthier nor more alert than before. If anything, she felt worse. There were aches and pains in places she would not have considered possible.

Enduring muscle pains, she pushed up yet again from the ground. She believed that exercise had its place. She had always exercised, but with her own regimens and in her own time. In her view, group exercise might be fine for instilling obedience in warrior cadets, but it was virtually worthless for training alertness in a cockpit. A warrior's normal routines kept him fit—and alert. A warrior's *exercise* should be up to the warrior only. That was Joanna's physical fitness credo, anyway. So, her face to the ground and her arms straining to perform still another pushup, her exercise was carried on more by the force of her cursing than by actual strength.

"You may stop now, Commander Joanna," Ravill Pryde announced. Even though he had performed the entire exercise routine with the warriors, he seemed annoyingly refreshed. "There is no need to go beyond the set limits." He smiled amicably, and it seemed as if his eyes actually twinkled. Joanna could not abide the idea of a Jade Falcon warrior whose eyes actually *twinkled*. "Especially for you,

Commander. You will not require all that much physical fitness when you assume charge of your nursery."

Many of the other warriors, who were now standing around her, laughed quietly. Ravill Pryde seemed pleased by their approval of his little joke.

"At ease, warriors." There was a general shuffle as the exercisers relaxed. "You have done well. In only one week, you have improved considerably."

Joanna, who had not quite caught her breath, struggled not to show it. Her eyes caught the gaze of Castilla, whose contempt for Joanna always seemed present in her eyes.

Ravill Pryde spread his arms. "I have to tell you, my fellow warriors, I am feeling very happy today. This world seems perfect." In the distance behind him, the usual storm clouds were forming. The air was bitter cold. The landscape was barren. Some perfect world, Joanna thought. "I think we, Jade Falcons and thus the best the Clans have to offer, can do anything."

Many warriors cheered, veterans as well as new warriors. Every morning Ravill Pryde made an inspiring speech, and every morning they cheered.

"Warriors," he went on with more pleasure than seemed necessary to Joanna, "I think that soon we will take the opportunity to show our individual prowess. I plan a series of games in which we will exercise the skills, power, and spirit we have gained here. It will be—well, the one word that fits is glorious. It will be glorious."

Spare me, Joanna thought, not knowing that was just what Ravill Pryde intended to do.

Ravill Pryde demanded that each officer prepare reports and other documents before the midday meal. Joanna, marked for departure, could have avoided this duty, but her deep feelings of vengeance made her work harder at the task. Diana, adept with figures and words, received Joanna's grudging acceptance of her help.

"I understand that, in the Inner Sphere, they thank assistants for their help," Diana said one morning as she assembled printouts of the morning report, which was Ravill Pryde's newest administrative wrinkle.

"In the Inner Sphere they coddle their domestic animals, too. A Jade Falcon warrior demands no gratitude for doing his or her duty."

Diana, though amused, responded in mock anger. "Duty? I volunteered for these tasks so that you—" She realized suddenly that she had overstepped.

"So that I what?"

"Never mind."

"You are getting bad habits, Diana. Respond!"

"Well, I meant to say, so that you might not waste your time on such work."

Joanna smiled ruefully. "You meant so that I might not tire myself. Another lie. If you are going to be so deceptive, why do you not defect to Clan Wolf or—better yet—to this new breed of warriors? Some of the others already have, after all."

"You misunderstand, Joanna." Diana was generally allowed to address Joanna without mention of rank, unless other officers were around. "They are not joining up with the newcomers. They are just responding to their enthusiasm."

"Are you already on their side? Like Horse, that freebirth bastard."

Diana bristled at the double epithet but, ever the diplomat in her dealings with Joanna, said calmly, "I am not on their side. You know that. I believe Ravill Pryde and his prydelings to be the most arrogant, most officious—"

"Officious? A definite Inner Sphere word. And you call them prydelings?"

"Well, I—"

"No, I like it. I like it."

"And Horse is no traitor. He is merely doing his duty."

"The bastard."

"No, Joanna, no. Be fair. Horse has proven himself as a warrior. Among freeborns and most trues, he is already something of a legend. As a key member of the Command Cluster, he has been awarded an honor that is proper for his achievements, despite his birth. I wish he were still in our Star, too, but—"

"But nothing. You are infected with Inner Sphere logic, Diana. All that book-reading, I suppose."

"You know about the books?"

"Yes, I know about Aidan Pryde's little library. Big library, really. And I am aware of how you and Horse carry on with all that reading. And see what good it has done you. You, with your distorted ideas; Horse as Ravill Pryde's pet warrior. Book-reading! I am glad I have never read any book other than the proper manuals required by the Clan."

"Joanna—"

"Dismissed, MechWarrior Diana. I have had enough of you for one day."

Diana wheeled about and headed for the door of Joanna's quarters, which was in its usual state of disarray. If anything, the room had gotten ever messier since Ravill Pryde's arrival.

"Diana?"

"Yes," Diana replied stiffly.

"You will come again to help with the reports tomorrow morning?"

"I will come."

"All right, then. Thank you for your help," Joanna growled.

Diana seemed pleased as she left. Joanna threw up her arms in disgust. *This damn Inner Sphere virus is everywhere. Perhaps it would be better if, as the Wardens encourage, we pulled back entirely from the Inner Sphere.* The Wardens, a political faction of the Clans, had opposed the other faction, more thrillingly called the Crusaders, on the subject of the Inner Sphere invasion from the beginning. Joanna shuddered at thinking like a Warden even for a moment. Nothing disgusted her more than the unwarriorlike politics of the Wardens.

10

Falcon Guard Compound
Pattersen, Sudeten
Jade Falcon Occupation Zone
7 July 3057

The normally calm MechWarrior Diana had become more and more agitated since Ravill Pryde's assumption of command. The newcomers, this new breed of warriors, were too annoying, even for her. Their insults about her free birth had become too frequent, and were crueler than any she had heard before. They seemed to seek out any opportunity to voice clever slurs. She particularly disliked the way the new levels of vituperation accompanied Ravill Pryde's ebullient slogans about happiness and satisfaction. If one listened to the new commander, everything was fine and dandy within the Falcon Guard ranks. Every day on this ugly planet, with its dangerous, foul weather, was a perfect day. Every goal achieved was a victory equal to success in combat. He smiled too much; his voice was ever-cheerful. When he strutted among his warriors, he was like a haughty barnyard animal lording it joyfully over the other farm creatures.

Though it was not like her, Diana hated him. She could usually brush off the natal insults, having adjusted early in life to her Clan status. It was the way of the Clans and she accepted it. Knowing that she was the daughter of Aidan Pryde had also helped her ignore the slurs of the truebirths. Indeed, her whole life was devoted to being the kind of fine warrior of whom her father would have been proud. But this new breed did get to her. Each time they smugly offered an insult about her birth, she wanted to rip off the mouth that uttered the words.

Walking away from Joanna's quarters, her thoughts concentrated on a wish that Ravill Pryde's cheerful, "perfect day" attitudes could be punched out of him so the unit could go back to its normal surly and combative ways, she did not notice the approach of Cholas.

"MechWarrior Diana."

He smiled, but the friendliness was not sincere. Standing a few steps behind him stood Castilla, unsmiling, her mouth twisted into a crooked line that seemed impossible to maintain.

"Yes, MechWarrior Cholas?"

"We have not coupled since my first days here."

For Diana the memory of that event now seemed grotesque. She had, of course, not known Cholas then.

"That is true, Cholas."

"Let us couple tonight. I wish it."

"No."

"No? What kind of Jade Falcon warrior are you, to refuse so quickly and with such force?"

"And you two, what kind are you?" Diana asked belligerently. Castilla walked nearer, her fists clenched. "You two cling together like you have been more than sibkin, like you have a special attachment, as if you were lovers."

The word *lover* was a tricky one in Clan lexicology. In some cases it could be construed as simply descriptive. In the villages of the labor caste, love was a common disease, and villagers often thought they were in it. Perhaps the idea brightened their drab days.

For warriors the word was usually insulting. Any romantic use of the word *love* was alien, nonexistent. Calling two warriors, especially sibkin, lovers was a deep insult, suggesting that their affection, which was rare among warriors anyway, was somehow unnatural, that their coupling was something more than mere sexual exercise, that the warriors were essentially behaving like freeborns. Jade Falcon warriors could not *love* each other. It was, in fact, a deeply disgusting thought.

"Take that back, Diana," Cholas bellowed. "It was unfair."

Diana started to walk away. "Then couple with yourself, Cholas."

He ran after her, grabbed her shoulder, and turned her toward him roughly. "Do not speak such filth to me. I do not have to—"

"Just couple with yourself. It will be more satisfying than being with me."

"I do not . . . do not do such things. They are forbidden."

"But not unknown. Here." She took the studded gloves from her belt and offered them to him. "Use these. To enhance your pleasure."

"YOU FREEBIRTH BASTARD!"

Backhanded, he slapped her across the face. The blow was quick. Caught by surprise, Diana reeled backward, Cholas pursuing, keeping up a steady flow of insults and getting in one more backhanded slap. When finally able to respond, Diana positioned her leg between his and kicked upward. Her legs were strong and the pain Cholas felt had to be excruciating. He doubled over, gasping.

Castilla ran up and, using Cholas' back, leapfrogged over him. The moment her feet touched ground, she thrust herself forward and head-butted Diana in the chest, knocking her off her feet. Leaping on top of her, Castilla began pummeling Diana's face. She was strong and used her leverage to advantage. Diana got woozy and would have passed out, but Cholas seized Castilla's shoulders, and threw her off her victim. "I will finish this," he said and kicked at Diana's side. This time, though, Diana had a moment to prepare, and she rolled away. The toe of his boot merely grazed her.

When she sprang to her feet, crouched and ready, she found herself under attack from both Cholas and Castilla. She was confident she could handle them both, but she quickly discovered that they worked precisely as a team. One hit her on one side and, a half-second later, the other landed a blow elsewhere. Diana suddenly realized the value of a strategic retreat. Rolling with the punches as best she could, she slipped backward.

She was about to give it up, fall, and feign unconsciousness when she heard the voice of Ravill Pryde ordering the combatants to stop. He pushed both Castilla and Cholas aside with surprising force for such a thin and small man.

"Ah," he said, "MechWarrior Diana. This is unconscionable, a freebirth provoking trueborns to wasteful fighting. Come to my quarters."

"They attacked me."

"That changes nothing. Perhaps I will reprimand them for being overzealous. MechWarriors Cholas and Castilla, you are dismissed. MechWarrior Diana, follow me."

Within five minutes they reached Ravill Pryde's office in the headquarters building, where Diana was struck by his neatness. Not a paper was out of place. As he eased himself into an ornate chair behind his ornate desk, he commanded Diana to sit on a hard bench placed against the wall across from the desk. She noticed that he looked more normal-sized seated at the desk. He must have had the chair built up so as not to look like a child sitting there. But she still thought he totally lacked the appearance of a warrior. His soft looks and somewhat graceful demeanor had little of the Jade Falcon aura about them.

He briefly glanced at some papers set in the desk's center, then disposed of them in several trays and upright slots on the right side of the desk. Wiping away a spot from the surface of the desk with the cuff of his well-creased sleeve, he turned his attention to Diana. "I have studied your codex, MechWarrior Diana, as I have all the warriors in my command. I have also examined the files and computer records left behind by the former unit commander."

He peered coolly at her as if he expected her to ask what he had found. *Fat chance,* she thought.

"You are, MechWarrior Diana, a most interesting warrior, especially for a freeborn. Most superior officers have little desire to know about most freeborns. Freeborn warriors do not, after all, have much opportunity to rise in the ranks, no chance to compete for a bloodname, and little prestige within a unit. Their codexes usually go unread and often the contents are not kept up to date."

Again he looked for a response from her, and again she supplied none. He took a single sheet from one of the upright file slots and examined it for a moment. It occurred to Diana that he was subtly structuring the entire speech, with planned pauses and expressions, inflections, and gestures.

"I see that your mother was a scientist known as Peri Watson. To all intents and appearances, then, this was the surname of your father."

For once Diana could not hold back a response. "My father?"

"Well, yes, this Watson is listed as your father. That is correct, is it not?"

"Not in a—" Diana stopped suddenly, wondering why she had the feeling that he was trying to trick her. "Yes, he is my father."

Ravill Pryde smiled in that annoyingly cheerful way so characteristic of him. "No, he is not. Assigning a surname is merely a village custom, common when a warrior sires a child."

Even though Diana was freeborn and knew the caste system well, she was nevertheless rendered uncomfortable by direct references to conception and birth, particularly when they were not used to insult.

Ravill Pryde put the paper onto the surface of the desk, his hand lying flat on top of it and rearranging it so that each border of it was parallel with a side of the desk.

"I admit I am trying to provoke you, MechWarrior Diana, and I can see that is the wrong tactic with you. What I mean to say is that I know this Watson is not your father. I have studied you for a while, since before I was assigned here."

"Me? But why?"

"Because I was so fascinated with the career of the great hero Aidan Pryde, I launched a study of him. Originally I intended to compile information that I could use to write a history of his achievements."

This Ravill Pryde was full of surprises, she thought. In addition to his exploits as a Jade Falcon warrior, he was also a Loremaster? Scholars were so rare in the Clan that Diana—who, after all, had some respect for books—could not help but feel a bit of awe for Ravill Pryde. She still despised him, but now it was a slightly different him she despised.

"I came across documents, dry records listing who was on duty and not on duty, that contained an indication that Aidan, then an astech, was away from Ironhold for a long while. Searching further, I found some travel documents involving no less than our quarrelsome Star Commander Joanna, so I sent transmissions to places she had visited."

"Wait," Diana interrupted, her interest in the man's words leading her to drop her aloofness, "why was it necessary to track Joanna's trips?"

Perhaps pleased by her interest, Ravill Pryde spoke with even more enthusiasm, his smile of pleasure making him look like a child with a new toy.

"You see, I had already established that Joanna was one of Aidan's falconers, and I saw that she had also been involved with the freeborn unit where he did his second stint of training. The possible connection between them during the missing time period tantalized me."

"What happened then?"

"I received a transmission from one place, a planet named Tokasha. It seemed that the files of one law enforcement administrator at a spaceport contained a notation of Joanna's arrival there with a tech named Nomad. I already knew that Nomad had been Aidan's tech back on Ironhold. The return trip listed a third person, an astech with a different name from Aidan. Of course, I knew immediately that it had to be him. You get a sense for such things when you are engaged in research. Such pursuit can be every bit as exciting as chasing another 'Mech across a battlefield."

Diana resisted commentary on that absurd idea. How could anything so mundane be as exciting as combat—for a warrior, at least? This Ravill Pryde was an oddity and a half.

"I was able to take a brief leave and so I went to Tokasha, where I traced Joanna's movements to a science station that was doing genetics research. The files yielded very little, but there was a man at the station who at first I could not abide because he was quite old. My experience with extreme age had been rare and, initially, merely looking at a person so old made me nauseous. All the wrinkles, the stringy white hair, the palsy, the brown spots on the back of the hand—all such characteristics were loathsome to me. I think we come out of the canister with feelings of repulsion toward age, *quiaff*?"

"I would not know, Star Colonel. As you well know, I came out of no canister."

For a moment he seemed ruffled. "You are quite right in correcting me. I would certainly suffer shame if I made such an error in public, attributing true birth to a freeborn. I apologize."

"You need not apologize to a freeborn."

"Perhaps for you I should make an exception. I will explain. This old man, who heard my questions to the station leader, came to me that night in my quarters. He told me his name was Watson. Your *alleged* father."

"Alleged, sir? Your records verify it, do they not?"

"Those records verified a lie. This man, this Watson, would die soon. You could smell death on him. I told him I was tracking the travels of a former warrior named Aidan. He saw through my story. 'The hero of Tukayyid?' he asked." Ravill Pryde picked up the paper from the desk and handed it to Diana. "This is what Watson told me. Read it."

She took it, guessing what it must contain. It was a detailed account of how Aidan came to Tokasha, found Peri—who had once been a member of his sibko—and hid away in the station. Joanna and Nomad located him there and took him away. Nine months later, Diana was born. Watson testified that Diana was the daughter of Peri and Aidan. Records did not indicate the details of birth, since by someone's official dictate Aidan had become a nonperson. He would not really emerge again until many years later when he revealed his true identity after he devised a plan to defeat the Wolves at Glory Station. Watson had allowed himself to be named the father purely to satisfy the demands of recordkeeping.

Diana had known Watson, but never as a father. She had spent her earliest years at the Tokasha science station, and he had been around. A man of immense girth with a slurred, sarcastic way of speaking.

"So you see, Diana, although you are a freeborn, you are at the same time something more than a freeborn."

"I do not understand," she said, placing the paper back on his desk, at a deliberately skewed angle. Ravill Pryde did not reply until after he had rearranged it to its former geometric symmetry.

"You exist in a state between free birth and true birth. Yes, you were conceived and birthed in the disgusting freeborn manner, but at the same time, look who your blood parents were. For a freeborn, your genetic heritage is astounding. I have never come across anything like it. First, your parents were both canister-born. Usually freeborns have only one trueborn parent. Two is a definite rarity. Second, not only were both Aidan and Peri trueborn, but they came from the *same* sibko. This establishes a fine genetic heritage. Technically, your genes have almost the same purity as that of a trueborn. That, in my view, raises you somewhat from freeborn status."

"Will you make me a trueborn, then?"

"Diana, you know I cannot do that. What satisfaction you may take from this must be purely personal, the knowledge that you are genetically advanced among freeborns. Of course, you still rank below trueborns."

"Which puts me in some kind of limbo?"

"How do you know the concept of limbo?"

Diana shrugged. "Am I dismissed now?"

Diana enjoyed Ravill Pryde's look of exasperation.

"No, you are not dismissed. I do not understand you, MechWarrior Diana. I tell you something that should please you, and you scoff."

"You told me nothing I did not already know, except that Watson posed as my father for bureaucratic purposes. Having others perceive that detestable man as my father is not, well, pleasing to me."

"Do you not even derive some satisfaction that your commanding officer regards you as more than a mere freeborn?"

"For all I care, you can call me freebirth till Sudeten's sun goes nova and I will not be, as you say, satisfied. All you are really saying is that I am halfway between acceptable and not acceptable. But halfway is essentially the same as *not* acceptable, since there is really no such thing as half-respect from others. May I go now? Sir?"

"Sit down. I will speak no more about your origins. When you are ready, we may discuss the matter again. I also see in your codex that you have scored high in the literacy aspects of your training, and I know from camp rumor that you do most of Star Commander Joanna's reports and recordkeeping for her. You are wasted on such low-level administration."

Ravill Pryde did seem to have an obsession about waste, Diana noted.

"As a MechWarrior you do not really have the rank for your new post, but neither does anyone else in the command. I have decided to appoint you coregn. Of course, as freeborn you cannot have a full coregn appointment. I will specify that it be only for administrative duties. You will represent me in some situations, but you will have no command duties. And I will excuse you from any duties of coupling with me, as some coregns are required to do. I do not think, frankly, I would derive any satisfaction from the experience."

"Because I am freeborn, *quiaff*?"

"Aff."

"I see. I have never heard of a freeborn as coregn."

"That may be so. It probably is. But we are in a combat zone, and compromises must be made. If some qualified trueborn is assigned here, I may change your assignment. Until then, you are coregn. You may not, as you know, refuse me on this. Now you are dismissed."

After she had left, Diana was not sure what had happened. She had come to Ravill Pryde's quarters expecting to be disciplined for the fight with Cholas and Castilla, and had come out as a warrior in genetic limbo—and coregn, to boot.

It was difficult enough to have to take it all in. It was harder now to envision telling Horse.

Even worse, telling Joanna.

11

Falcon Guard Compound
Pattersen, Sudeten
Jade Falcon Occupation Zone
13 July 3057

Joanna's dreams, like her life, became more chaotic. In her current recurring dream, Aidan still turned into a BattleMech, a different type in different dreams, but now he seized her in his 'Mech fingers and lifted her off the ground. Bringing her up to his 'Mech head, he held her close to the cockpit. Peering in, she saw Ravill Pryde at the controls. The sight always shocked her awake.

She was scheduled to return to the Clan homeworlds in just over two weeks. Whenever she thought about it, her anger seemed to take control of her body, to make her heart beat faster, to force throbbing tension into her limbs, to make her feel she wanted to smash the nearest object worth smashing. She hated being made a nanny, even a ranking nanny.

The stravag has even ruined my last days. First he takes Horse into the Command Cluster and then he makes Diana coregn. He is promoting freeborns all the while encouraging hatred of them in the ranks.

She asked Horse what the new commander was up to. The conversation took place in her quarters one morning, just an hour after she had awakened from a vivid dream.

"Up to?"

"All this extra training, the assignments of you and Diana, the emphasis on correct procedure, the reports and all the rules."

"What do you object to?"

"What is not there to object to? The man is unClanlike."

"You want my, well, interpretation?"

Interpretation was not a word Joanna cared for. It was too much like decoding what was not decodable.

"Go on, Horse."

"Ravill Pryde is obsessed with Aidan."

"Obsessed?"

"Think about it. He performs a legendary cadet trick during his Trial of Position, then he finds out that the cadet who started the legend was Aidan Pryde, the hero of Tukayyid. He is excessively proud of bearing the same bloodname as Aidan, whom he hero-worships. He arrives on Sudeten to find he will command the remnants of Aidan's unit. Then he takes me into the Command Cluster. Why is that?"

"You proved yourself a hero, too. You may not know it, but some legend has gathered around you."

"Mere campfire tales. My assignment to the Command Cluster is irrelevant to my experience. It's mainly because I was Aidan's friend and fought side by side with him that Ravill Pryde wants me at his side, too."

"I was on Tukayyid, too. I fought side by side with Aidan. Look how contemptuously Ravill Pryde treats me."

"I'm not sure why, Joanna. Perhaps it's because you're being rotated out, and so aren't of any use to him. Or maybe you conflict with his general cheeriness. You're darkness, he's sunshine."

"Does he let you use so many contractions around him?"

"Not a one."

"And you obey him in this?"

"For the most part."

Joanna grunted and looked away. She thought of her dreams and Ravill Pryde inside the cockpit of Aidan's 'Mech. Ravill Pryde mimicking Aidan. Perhaps Horse was right, and she was seeing it, too, in those dreams.

"What about Diana? Making her coregn?"

"Diana told me that Ravill Pryde knows her background. Do you see the implications?"

"Keep it simple."

"Diana is Aidan's daughter. Ravill Pryde is obsessed with

Aidan. He gives her a position close to him. It's as if he has substituted himself for Aidan, her father."

"You could be right. I saw him look at her yesterday. There was something in the look that he could not hide. And it makes me sick to my stomach. A Jade Falcon warrior, who grew up in a sibko, thinking of himself as a *parent*? It is, it is, well, disgusting."

"Only to a trueborn. We freeborns understand the miracle of birth."

"Now you are taunting me with foul words. Go away, Horse."

"Joanna—"

"GET OUT!"

With fierce effort Joanna got control of herself. Her stomach settled.

It seemed to her that Ravill Pryde was some kind of monster. Yet, she realized that, for others, he was a forceful leader. True, he was a taskmaster, but one who was welcomed by all the warriors. He was renewing the spirit of men and women who had been somewhat soured by the frustrations of the truce. He himself was a superior warrior who had earned his rank in a spectacular fashion. Even Horse seemed to tolerate him.

She must fight him. But how? He had found ways to slip out of every challenge. He obviously considered it wasteful to go up against a warrior soon to leave. He did not want to fight her, but it had to happen. Somehow Joanna would make it happen.

As it turned out, it was Diana, and not Joanna, who made it so.

12

Falcon Guard Compound
Pattersen, Sudeten
Jade Falcon Occupation Zone
20 July 3057

Diana came very close to taking the entire high pile of hardcopy left her by Ravill Pryde and transforming it into trash. She considered ripping the papers to shreds, then feeding them to someone she hated. Cholas or Castilla, maybe. Maybe both. Ravill Pryde had said he wanted someone efficient enough to perform the coregn job; what he really wanted was a bondsman.

She muttered frequently under her breath as she did the figuring, noting, arranging, computering, file searches, keyboard entries, and general tasks of extreme boredom. The work was bad enough, but the publicly cheerful Ravill Pryde was not much help. The good humor he displayed outside the office was absent inside, where he was intense, sometimes fidgety, and irritable. As soon as someone else came into the room, he would instantly resume his sunny demeanor. She wondered whether he had appointed her coregn just to have someone with whom he could reveal his true colors. Since she was freeborn, no trueborn would believe her if she claimed that Ravill Pryde had a nasty side to his character.

Even complaining to Horse did little good. When she mentioned her problems with Ravill Pryde, Horse merely said he was glad to hear the Star Colonel had a dark side and that he had seen hints of it himself. And forget talking to Joanna. It only cheered her up to hear about Ravill Pryde's character flaws.

Much of the work Diana did seemed remarkably unimportant, and there was definitely too much of it. Any idiot could see that, and she was just the idiot to keep doing it.

Yesterday she had discovered something else about Ravill Pryde. A temper that might have startled anyone taken in by his cheerful act. It had surprised Diana, anyway.

While examining some daily reports she had printed out at his request, he suddenly gave out an exasperated sigh.

"Diana, this is wrong!"

She looked up from a report whose statistics she was checking.

"What is wrong, sir?"

"Look, this column is off by one, and that put the total off by five."

Diana examined the numbers he pointed to.

"That is true. I made a mistake."

"Is that all you can say? You made a mistake?"

"It is a fact. What else should I say, sir?"

"You should apologize for it."

"I fail to see why."

He sputtered a bit. "You—you fail—fail to—"

"I did my job, *quiaff*? But I made an error, a simple mathematical error, easy to rectify."

"What if it had gone up to Galaxy level with the error intact?"

"Then perhaps they would have found it and corrected it. Or not."

"That is an incorrect attitude. Our figures *must* be right."

"Why? Especially if they are not found?"

"If they are discovered, it will reflect on our unit."

"And so? Why should warriors care about numbers?"

Ravill Pryde took a few moments to compose himself. He came around the desk to the work table at which she sat.

"Do you not agree, Diana, that a miscalculation in battle could result in further error that might lead to a severe loss in materiel or personnel?"

"Of course. But such miscalculations *are* made in the field, and corrected—by the seat of the pants, as they say—and not in an office weeks and months beforehand. And you have little time to retrieve essential data while you are faced with attack on three sides."

"What good is this talk about combat in these circumstances? You are coregn now. You must rise above warrior concerns."

"I would rather not. I will always be a warrior. I did not ask to be coregn."

"No one ever asks to be coregn. It is a conferred honor."

"Unconfer it if you wish. But I will not apologize."

"Freebirth!"

"That is true. What of it?"

Abruptly, he slapped her. Her skin stung from the force of the unexpected blow. She stood up.

"Do you wish to settle this in a Circle of Equals?" she said calmly.

"I have abolished honor duels. And perhaps you forget, an honor duel cannot be invoked over conflict in the performance of duty."

"You hit me."

"As is my command right. Warriors must accept all types of punishment, you know that. Plus, it is the custom that *freeborn* warriors are to avoid honor duels at all times, except among their caste. Sit down and do your job, freebirth."

From that moment on, Diana vowed revenge.

Ravill Pryde had already left for an inspection of a barracks when she finished entering a list of current ammunition loads into the computer. Closing the file, she began to study the onscreen menu of directories. There were several that she had not yet worked on, and she decided to check them out. Opening one after the other, she discovered the same kind of dull information that was at the heart of recordkeeping everywhere.

"How many battles are really won with data?" she muttered aloud. "Bang, you dirty *stravag,* I have your number—rounded off to three decimals."

Buried in a directory labeled Victory she found, placed in a folder within a folder within a folder, still another folder marked Personal. Personal? she thought. I would like to see what Ravill Pryde considers so personal that he hides it so deeply within files.

When she attempted to open the Personal file, the screen displayed a request for a password. For the first time since she had become coregn, Diana felt some excitement. Password? What kind of word would an arrogant dimwit like Ravill Pryde use for a password? The possibilities were, perhaps, wide, but the challenge would make her days more intriguing.

For the next few hours Diana tried such likely words as Falcon, Ironhold, Pryde, Ravill, Duty and many others. When she heard the colonel returning, she quickly aborted her attempts and, her fingers flying over the keyboard, sped back through his intricate pathway of folders to the data file she had originally been working on.

"Still compiling the ammo data?" Ravill Pryde asked pleasantly.

"There was a glitch."

"I am glad to see you taking more care with the data."

"My duty, sir."

During the next two work sessions, Diana went to the Personal folder whenever Ravill Pryde was gone. All attempts at working out the password failed, but Diana did not mind because the task made the time rush by. Any regular work she had to do, she did quickly in order to return to the pursuit of her quest.

On the third day she was ready to give up. Fingers resting on the keys, she searched her mind for a new word to try. The proper password could be merely a set of meaningless letters, she realized, but she doubted it. If he was anything, Ravill Pryde was methodical. He would use a word, one that he could remember easily. The key to the password could be in the man's personality, his psychology, his military beliefs.

For a moment she could not think of a single word. Then she recalled Ravill Pryde's reverence for her father, so she quickly typed in the name Aidan. The computer made a strange noise but, after a split second, returned its official rejection of the password. She tried Aidan Pryde. That did not work either.

She stared at the name in the rejection message for a long while. As she often did, she thought how her mother had cleverly concealed her father's identity by giving Diana a name that was an anagram of Aidan. In the dialog box for the password—for no reason she could imagine except to see the rearrangement of the familiar letters—she typed in Diana, then waited for the computer to tell her No.

Instead, the screen flickered, the computer made some different sounds, a new dialog box approved "Diana" as the password, and scrolled out a long menu of files.

For a long time Diana stared at the screen without reading anything on it. The password was *her* name. Why? She shuddered at the thought.

What kind of sick kestrel is he? He knows my background, so he uses my name as an essential password, he appoints me coregn against all methods of procedure even though he is a stickler for proper procedure, he bashes me in the head for making a clerical mistake, he hovers over me like a . . . like a father over a freeborn daughter!

Growing up in a village whose population was completely caste-bound, Diana had seen many fathers in spite of not knowing her own. That had given her a concept of parentage that trueborn warriors could not approach in their minds. But it made no sense to her that Ravill Pryde could even think of regarding her in that way—like a daughter!

Yet the man was so enmeshed in his hero worship of Aidan Pryde, and he had placed such emphasis on her being Aidan's offspring that she wondered if it were possible that Ravill Pryde was deranged enough to see himself as some kind of surrogate for her real father. No, she thought, that was absurd. How could it be? He came from a sibko. He would be disgusted by the concept of father—or would he? Why did it disturb her so, her name as his password? The man was just being clever. After all, who would have imagined he would use *Diana* as his secret password? No one. Except Diana herself.

To distract her mind from these troubling thoughts, she scrolled through the menu. The names of the files suggested little. They were mostly dates and locations. From what she knew about Ravill Pryde's codex, she was able to deduce that these files contained information relating to his tours of duty.

She opened one and found a bland, diarylike listing of day-to-day activities, records of duty and jobs performed. This was very like Ravill Pryde, to make lists of even his minor accomplishments and to keep the lists in a computer folder marked Personal. Very like Ravill Pryde, but not particularly like a warrior. It all reminded her of the neat ways in which he arranged the papers on his desk.

Scrolling down the menu, she noticed one marked Kerensky, a famous bloodname held exclusively by the warriors of Wolf Clan. A most honored bloodname also, for it was the revered General Aleksandr Kerensky who had led a fleet of ships into exile from the Inner Sphere some three hundred years ago, taking with him almost the whole of the Star League army. The descendants of those exiles would evolve under his son Nicholas into the Clans in their new home worlds far from the Inner Sphere. A curious choice of file name, she thought, so she opened the file.

The information on its initial pages so stunned Diana that for a moment she could not catch her breath. Then she carefully read the first part of what was a very long document.

And began to perceive her opportunity for revenge.

How could she accomplish it? she wondered. If she confronted Ravill Pryde with the information, he would find ways to keep her from using it. Most likely, he would not stop at reprimand. He would see to it that she was transferred out of the unit, or possibly even arrange for her death, maybe kill her himself.

No, it would be useless to confront him. But Joanna could.

Ravill Pryde was likely to return soon, so she printed out the document's first four pages only. That was enough to make the case. That night she took them to Joanna.

13

Southern Pole
Sudeten
Jade Falcon Occupation Zone
24 July 3057

Cooling vests worked fine when the heat was building up, but they were no better than just another layer of clothing when cold seeped into the cockpit. Inside her gloves, Joanna's fingers felt stiff and frozen.

Even the *Mad Dog* was affected by the blizzard it walked through. It did not respond quickly to Joanna's touch, but—like her—it was fighting the battle of keeping its joints and other movable parts from freezing up. It needed to engage Ravill Pryde in his *Timber Wolf*, get some heat rising from its pulse lasers and LRMs.

Forty-eight hours after Ravill Pryde accepted the challenge, he and Joanna had marched their 'Mechs into a DropShip for a quick suborbital flight to the southern pole's ice floes. Ravill Pryde did not mention why he had chosen this frozen wasteland as the site for the Trial of Refusal. Nor had he offered an explanation of why it had taken so long to reply. But Joanna had learned from Diana that the Star Colonel had spent hours pouring over Inner Sphere geological surveys and recent meteorological reports after accepting her challenge. Why was this delay necessary? Why not settle the matter immediately on the training fields of Sudeten? Obviously he was looking for some advantage here in this mind-numbing cold. Some type of trick or deceit he could use. But what that was Joanna could not fathom.

How could this man be so against freeborns, when he himself used so much freebirth-style deception and trickery? Or was she doing freeborns an injustice by thinking that? Such deception was, after all, closer to a Wolf trick than anything a freeborn might think up.

All her years of bitterness, all the hate that had built up in Joanna was not focused on Ravill Pryde. She would be happy to defeat and kill him. And despite the ban on duels, he had not been at all reluctant for this honor duel to be to the death.

Outside Joanna's 'Mech, the planet Sudeten was unleashing all the weather punishments if could. The blizzard, together with its high winds, lashed at the *Mad Dog*. By comparison, the day she had spent fighting the five new warriors had been positively balmy. The *Mad Dog*'s metal groaned, whined, and threatened her as revenge for the job it was being asked to perform. Like a recalcitrant cavalry horse facing bad weather, it seemed to want to return to its stable to fight another day.

Sensor information could not be relied on in these conditions. Caught between the minus sixty-degree frozen hell on the outside and the sunlike heat of the fusion plant buried in the belly of the 'Mech, the electronics of the sensor arrays started to fail. Twisted and warped, critical connections between subcomponents would break, only to be restored again with the next jarring footstep. As Joanna moved her 'Mech forward, Ravill Pryde's *Timber Wolf* would appear on the secondary screen one second and then be lost in the next. But enough information got to Joanna that she could guess where he was. He was now moving away from her.

Ravill Pryde had told the warriors of his command that the idea for the coming games had first come to him two years ago when he was in charge of an outpost near the Periphery, an assignment that had required the pursuit and ensnaring of bandits, but little else. Until the unit was sent into the Inner Sphere to bolster the Falcon forces there, the assignment had been too easy and too calm. As a palliative to boredom, he had devised the plan for the games—contests of physical strength, skill, and endurance fashioned on the principles of Trials of Bloodright. Warriors, after all, could be strengthened by healthy struggle and competition.

The games had been a great success then, as—he promised—they would be now. More than anything else, they would afford the present warriors the chance to achieve glory in a time when the glory of combat was being denied them.

Even though Joanna found the idea of the games foolish, she immediately requested the opportunity to participate.

"These events are for the warriors who remain here," Ravill Pryde responded. "You are leaving soon. There is no point to your participation."

"I am still a warrior."

"That may be so. But nothing would be proven by your competing in the games. I deny your request."

Joanna had not been surprised by his response, so she had an answer ready. "What about the melee? You cannot deny me that."

Seeing he had been outmaneuvered, Ravill Pryde sighed. "No, I cannot deny you that."

Joanna was afraid her *Mad Dog* would freeze in place, so she kept it moving. Ravill Pryde had to be somewhere in front of her, even though his blip on the scanner screen seemed to jump around unnaturally. There were no jump jets on either the *Timber Wolf* or the *Mad Dog*.

Despite his erratic image, Ravill did seem to be moving his 'Mech in the same general direction—toward a relatively flat and newly frozen plain of ice.

"I think it is a fine day for competition," Ravill Pryde had announced at the start of the games. "What do you say, warriors?"

The new warriors, of course, cheered approval, while the veterans joined in the general elation with a milder enthusiasm. The day he had praised was indeed one of Sudeten's better efforts. It was clear, more cool than cold, and free of any type of precipitation. For Sudeten, a rare day.

Ravill Pryde spread his arms, forcing most of his audience to look at the level game field. It had been worked on by Elementals—who would not participate in the games because of their unfair edge in most of the physical events—to make most of it smooth and dry.

Made more spectacular by the view behind it, the field ended at the shore of a wide lake, called by some Sudeten Lake because they had no idea what the planet's citizens had named it. On the other side of the lake rose high, jagged cliffs. For exercise, some warriors had crossed Sudeten Lake to climb them. In spite of the intense survival training that all warriors underwent, only a few had actually reached the top. The rest said that handholds were rare and the surfaces would not accept a piton even if you asked politely. Because the lake had not caught up with the latest weather change, what seemed like a thousand ice floes bobbed across its surface. When the weather changed, as it did that night, the ice floes would join quickly, creating a ragged, icy surface upon the lake itself.

Joanna ripped through the melee, showing even the experienced competitors a fierceness and bravado that went beyond Jade Falcon standards for fierceness and bravado. No weapons had been allowed in the melee, and the games overall involved few weapons. Joanna used every hand-to-hand combat technique and martial arts skill in her repertoire. The new warriors seemed astonished by her proficiency, while the old ones, who were familiar with Joanna's considerable abilities, were merely resigned. When she turned toward the command dais to claim victory, even Ravill Pryde seemed impressed.

The game competitors stood in a line for the start of the next stage. Joanna took a position at the end, with the other competing warriors spread in a straight line to her right. Ravill Pryde had ruled that the normal bloodname number, thirty-two, was too many for the games, so sixteen competitors would be sufficient.

With an unusually clear sky making his movements and gestures more vivid, the Falcon Guards commander performed an intricate ritual of his own devising, interrupted often by the chanting of the ritual word *"Seyla"* from the assembled warriors, the loudest cries coming from the warriors in competition. Joanna felt as if her eardrums would burst, and she refused to join in. She stood silent, conserving her energy for the games.

Horse was resplendent in ceremonial robes, even though, as a freeborn, he was not entitled to wear a cloak decorated with falcon feathers, as the trueborns did. Ravill Pryde had excluded the warriors in his Star from the games, saying he wished to represent the Star alone. Since Diana, as coregn, was also attached to the Command Cluster, she would not compete either. Joanna was glad. Having Horse and Diana in the competition would have been an impediment to her plan. In the structured competition of the games, she could more easily work up fury against opponents she hated. As it happened, she did hate almost everyone else in the entire unit, whether she knew them or not.

Following the last echoing chant of *"Seyla,"* Ravill Pryde jumped down from the dais. He did not look once at Joanna as he took his place in the center of the line of competitors. Diana, in her role as coregn, drew the match-ups from a set of special coinlike pieces of metal that had been placed in an ordinary bowl. The "coins" were intended to duplicate those used in bloodname match selections. Each was inscribed with the name of a contestant, except for Joanna's which was simply inscribed "melee winner."

Joanna drew Star Captain Evlan, from Trinary Echo Nova, as her first round opponent. She liked the draw. Evlan, although she kept to herself, was a good officer and would definitely test Joanna's mettle. She was only four or five years younger than Joanna and was on the verge of being an old-timer herself. A short, compact woman with long, dark hair and a wide mouth, she was inclined to fight in a conventional way, whether in a 'Mech or hand-to-hand.

From another bowl, Diana drew the events in which the first-round contestants would compete. Joanna and Evlan would be first. Diana announced that their event was a noncombatant one, a simple run to the shore of Sudeten Lake and back.

A run? Joanna thought. Simple? The one event in which Evlan—and, for that matter, most of the others—had a clear advantage over her. This sounded like some kind of *savashri* strategy from Ravill Pryde, yet there seemed no way he could manipulate the match-ups, not with Diana drawing. It must be fate.

Ravill Pryde came forward. "Let me remind you both that there is no route to follow for your race. Any route will do. Further, there are no strict rules to the contest. As in all Jade Falcon competitions—whether combat, honor duel, or game—the emphasis is on winning. Any way you can find to win, it is—"

Joanna did not wait for Ravill Pryde to finish his sentence. Instead she elbowed Star Captain Evlan in the stomach, brought her fists down on the back of her neck when she doubled over, and kicked her to the ground. Before Evlan felt the dirt in her mouth, Joanna had broken into a run toward the shore of Sudeten Lake.

In her cockpit now, staring at the ice that was forming over her viewport, forming faster than the heaters that bordered it could melt it, Joanna smiled as she recalled that race. As she reached the lakeshore and was dipping in the toe of her boot as a defiant sign that she had completed that lap, she could hear the steps of Evlan in pursuit. Joanna pivoted and ran toward her opponent, whose speed was impressive, especially considering how hard Joanna had hit her. As the two, running in opposite directions, were about to pass, Evlan sending a fierce glance Joanna's way, Joanna suddenly veered toward Evlan and brought up her forearm. With as much power as she could muster on the run, and with her body slightly tilted, she slammed her forearm into Elvan's neck. The Echo Trinary leader flipped backward, landing on her back, choking.

Even with that edge, Joanna had to put on speed to nose out Evlan at the finish line.

She sat on the other side of the line, out of breath but feeling positively defiant. "Good strategy, Joanna, you filthy *stravag,*" Evlan whispered to her while passing by. Joanna smiled.

A few moments later Ravill Pryde easily pinned his opponent from Trinary Bravo Eye, the strong and determined warrior Bish. Perhaps emulating Joanna, Ravill Pryde kneed Bish in the back to make his frontside pin more effective. Joanna's next opponent had been the grizzled, and not easily deceived, MechWarrior Boz from Trinary Charlie Eye. The event drawn was with combat knives, with each participant wearing protective padding and headgear. Boz, a veteran, was an expert with the thirty-centimeter-long, serrated blades. Joanna regretted that she had too often disdained combat knives as inferior and decadent weapons. The Medusa whip or her glove-encased hands were her preferred hand-to-hand weapon. But she was not really daunted by Boz's skills. She felt inspired, and inspired people did not worry about trivial details like an opponent's superior expertise.

Boz waded in, thrust and parried with quickness and certainty. After a few clanging exchanges and Boz's first score on her shoulder, Joanna said to herself that she was not patient enough to work her way through such a polite match. Diving in under Boz's next knife thrust, she flung away her own knife and grabbed him around the legs, sending him stumbling backward and off his feet. Whacking his knife arm against the ground, she made him release it.

Standing up quickly, she watched him scrabble toward the weapon. She walked beside him for a couple of steps, then brought her boot down on his wrist. Boz yelled in pain, but even before he could grab at the wrist, Joanna brought her boot down again. She listened with satisfaction to the sound of the bone cracking in his wrist. Then she told him to pick up the knife and fight her, to finish off the match.

He got up, holding onto his wrist and looked at her in disgust. She picked up her combat knife, then his. Offering him the knife, she smiled. He took the weapon in his other hand and tried to wield it. His moves were almost comical at first, then he lunged forward and tapped Joanna on her face mask with the tip of the blade. Two hits, in Boz's favor.

Growling, Joanna knocked Boz's knife away and scored her first point. Two others came with similar maneuvers. After her third hit, Boz angrily flung away his knife and managed a desultory nod of congratulation as he walked slowly away, holding onto his injured wrist.

Ravill Pryde was furious at Joanna's tactics. "As you said," she remarked as she walked by him, "anything goes."

Ravill Pryde and his next opponent drew a swim in Sudeten Lake, fifty meters out and fifty back. He was matched with MechWarrior Castilla of Trinary Alpha Beak Two. With Castilla as the opponent, Joanna found herself cheering the Falcon Guards commander on. It gave her great pleasure to see Ravill Pryde climb onto an ice floe fifty yards out and dive over Castilla's head to swim back to shore with smooth, even strokes. Both swimmers came out of the cold lake with their skins tinged blue but exhilarated by the close contest. Castilla had swum with impressive strength toward the end, but her prowess had urged Ravill Pryde on to victory.

* * *

How would you like to go swimming now, Ravill Pryde? Joanna thought as she maneuvered her *Mad Dog* through the intense blizzard. This section of ice had not been frozen for long. *All I have to do is blast through three meters of ice, and you can see how well your skill and tricks serve you in a 'Mech sinking to the bottom of this arctic ocean.*

The blip flickering in and out on her scanner screen had to be his *Timber Wolf.* She was zeroing in on him, ready to launch a long-range missile from her 'Mech's left torso. It would be exploratory, a definite risk, but it might goose the Falcon Guard commander into some kind of action. Or did he intend to merely hide in this blizzard and perhaps declare the match a draw when the day ended? The weather might just hide his cowardice effectively for the others.

For a moment she again got a sudden image of the strange look Ravill Pryde had given her after she defeated Boz. The round of eight had by then dwindled to four surviving competitors. He had drawn the formidable Star Commander Rhayna from Trinary Bravo Beak, while Joanna had to face the equally tough Star Commander Zabet, the leader of Boz's Star. Ravill Pryde and Rhayna had to climb opposite sides of a standing 'Mech, using freestyle mountain-climbing techniques. As he later explained, he had scaled several peaks on one of his assignments, and so was undoubtly too experienced for Rhayna. He reached the 'Mech's head well ahead of her, then terminated his descent with a most graceful jump from the 'Mech's hip.

Joanna fought Zabet in a whip duel. As a former falconer, Joanna had vast experience with whips, and she managed to entangle Zabet's arm in her thong and pull him to the ground even before he could land a strike on her. She pulled the thong roughly away and lashed it at his face, drawing blood very near Zabet's left eye. Another flick and Joanna created another line of blood, this time beside his right eye.

She could have continued toying with Zabet, but Ravill Pryde intervened, saying Zabet would not be allowed to continue. Zabet protested, but the Falcon Guard commander could not be swayed. Zabet's glare at Joanna as he capitulated and withdrew was filled with enmity. *Well, I have never won many friends around here, anyway. But I could apologize to him, to all my opponents, for my unorthodox tactics. I could apologize. I could. No.*

Joanna walked straight up to Ravill Pryde and said, "We

are the finalists in your little competitions, Star Colonel, *quiaff*?"

"*Aff*. You have done well for an old warrior, Star Commander Joanna."

"So then, why not allow me to remain here on duty instead of shipping me off to the nursery?"

He frowned. "Neg. The will of the Khan and the Falcon Clan cannot be so easily disregarded. Your assignment is the best use of your skills."

"Best use? But I have here shown my prowess as a warrior. How does that—"

"The fact that you have reached the finals of these games does not mean that you should remain a warrior. Perhaps it displays your skills and that only confirms how great will be your use to the Clan in supervising a genetics station."

Joanna had expected to be turned down, but had wanted to give Ravill Pryde his fair chance.

He turned to the dais to hear the nature of the final event from Diana. Joanna nudged his shoulder.

"A private word with you, Star Colonel."

"Now? When the last event is—"

"What I have to say concerns the last event."

He waved away spectators as he led her over to one side of the dais.

Searching for the illustrious Star Colonel now, realizing that she had again lost the blip that she had been sure was his location, Joanna savored that conversation with him.

"You lead us under false pretenses, Star Colonel Ravill Pryde, quiaff?"

"I do not know what you mean, Joanna."

"I mean this. I have seen your personal file. It is strange, I must say that. You see, I have read with great interest the parts about your genetic legacy."

He seemed alarmed. "Joanna—"

"No, let me speak my piece. I read that your sibko was created as part of a secret project, a series of genetic experiments that, as its outcome, mixed DNA from the Pryde line, a Jade Falcon line, with DNA from another line. Apparently such experimentation has been going on for some time and—"

"Joanna, I would suggest to you that you terminate this

conversation immediately. What you are delving into is a clandestine operation that is highly secret. There are—"

"I am sure I am not supposed to know about it. It is so miserable, so revolting, that—"

"No, wait. I mean it is dangerous for you to know. The trouble it would cause you is immeasurable. If you think you are being sent to a wasteful assignment now, you would be sent to the remotest place possible, the absolute end of the universe, if you pursue the matter beyond this conversation."

"I do not even care to do that. It is between you and me, as far as I am concerned. But Jade Falcons are honorable, and would not resort to extreme measures if I spoke out."

"Yes, if you deal with warriors and leaders of warriors, with Khans and ilKhans, but this project, as you call it, is the domain of the scientist caste."

"I know that. I know they are involved, but—"

"No, I am saying that none of the Clan's warrior castes knows about this. Not the Khans or the Loremasters or any of the bloodnamed. Nobody knows that I know my origins. It *must* be kept secret. The scientist caste is more powerful than you think. It is composed of freeborns, and the way of honor that guides the warrior caste is unknown to them. You see—"

"I do not see, and it does not matter. I am only concerned with you, Ravill Pryde, and the lie that you live. If what I read had not concerned *you*, I would ordinarily have found the information thrilling and even a source of pride that our scientists were so devoted to breeding us as the best warriors possible. I am for genetic progress, who would not be? But the shock, as you must realize, came when I identified the sources of the genetic mixture."

"Forget you ever heard about this, Joanna. There is no reason to go on. We must finish the games and then I will try to discuss this with you."

"No, I will speak now. I am not patient, even you know that. When I perceived that the mixture was not of one Jade Falcon line with another Jade Falcon line but a 'mating,' if you will accept such an ugly word, of a Jade Falcon line with that of another Clan, I was angered. How could you improve our lines in any way with genetic materials from any other Clan? We are the best bred of all warriors. But I was sickened when I saw that, for your sibko, the Jade Falcon materials were combined with those from Clan *Wolf.* That is an experiment so ugly that I cannot believe that our scientist caste even considered it. It is diluting our genes, not enhancing them. It is—"

"Joanna, it goes beyond just our scientist caste. I am not sure how. I have not found out. But the plans come from elsewhere, and not from the Jade Falcon leadership either. We must end this conversation. It is too potentially dangerous. I vow to you that—"

"I will not hear your vows. I am only using this information to get what I want, a revocation of the nursery assignment."

"But—"

"I do not wish to go to Ironhold."

"You wish to blackmail me into allowing you to stay here?"

"Neg, although that is tempting. No, I wish only what I deserve. A chance. A chance to prove I should remain with the Falcon Guards. I wish, for our games event, to fight you in our 'Mechs. An honor duel, if you wish to call it that. If I defeat you, you must revoke my travel orders. If you win, I will go quietly, and keep this information about you to myself. No, no, we will not even do it that way. Let us make this all simpler and ensure that the winner is properly rewarded. Let us make this a fight to the death. You leave orders for the revocation of my new assignment, and I—I will be dead, so I will no longer be a problem for you."

"A problem. No. A dilemma perhaps, but not a problem."

"Whatever. What do you say?"

Ravill Pryde paused and looked over his shoulder, where the assembled warriors watched the two of them with apparent curiosity and fascination. He turned back to Joanna, saying, "Bargained well and done. We will announce this honor duel as the new final event of the games."

"Agreed."

He started to walk away.

"Ravill Pryde!" she called out, deliberately leaving off his rank.

He turned. She walked up to him and whispered, "I despise every Wolf trait in your genetic legacy." Joanna then turned and walked away. She had made the final insult for psychological reasons. After all, with a man who had qualified as Star Captain in his cadet Trial of Position, a bit of psychology could be useful.

There was a lull in the storm. For a moment Joanna saw Ravill Pryde's *Timber Wolf* just a few hundred meters from her *Mad Dog*. In the swirling snow it was a mere outline walking away from her. Maybe he was not aware of her presence nearby. Maybe his scanners were off, too, and he did not know where she was. Maybe it was a good time for an ambush. Reacting quickly, she triggered a salvo of SRMs and found out how aware of her presence he was. The *Timber Wolf*'s antimissile system transformed her SRMs into fireworks—brief and colorful fireworks but ineffective. The snow became heavier again. Her last sight of the *Timber Wolf* showed that it continued out onto the field of ice. She had no choice but to pursue him, piloting blind since her detection systems had now chosen to display for her images that very much resembled the snow outside.

14

Southern Pole
Sudeten
Jade Falcon Occupation Zone
24 July 3057

The next few minutes were dreamlike. The *Mad Dog*'s footing seemed wildly insecure, as if the 'Mech were too light and likely to fall. Joanna kept telling herself that its weight would keep it upright. Yet, as the 'Mech progressed through the storm, systems disoriented by weather, Joanna felt disoriented, too. She had been in battles with poor visibility many times, but had always been able to see at least some shapes or reflections in front of her. Her guidance and scanning systems had usually shown minimal function. But this—this was like swimming in foam. Oddly, the effort required for the *Mad Dog* to move through the storm seemed to demand extra heat from its operating systems. In addition to the sounds of the storm, Joanna kept hearing a strange sizzle where the frigid snow struck the hot 'Mech surface.

Why do I need this fight? What drives me on, keeps me at it? Maybe this storm is some kind of sign, telling me to accept the humiliating assignment and go tell soothing stories to sibko brats fresh out of their canisters. Maybe Jade Falcon command, in its wisdom, is making the right decision for me. I'm supposed to believe that, I know. I am not supposed to defy what is ordained for me by them. My kind of defiance is Clanlike enough in battle, but outside of combat it becomes—what?—antisocial behavior? To be antisocial among Jade Falcon warriors is something of a distinguishing mark. Still, most warriors would accept these orders without complaint, no matter how angry they might feel about them. Only I would go to elaborate lengths to battle the commanding officer for the right to change orders. I know that, and in a strange way I am proud of it. If Aidan were here, he'd tell me, you're at it again, Joanna.

Yet, in no way do I feel disloyal. I don't know why. All I know is that all my life, all my warrior life, I've dreaded surviving to an age where all I could hope for was some degrading assignment like this one. I used to think that the worst that could happen was that I would become cannon fodder in some solahma detail, joining some little gang of ancient warriors no longer useful to their units who gratefully do their duty by going forward to certain death just to buy time for the real warriors. Damn it, I am one of the real warriors, still one of the real warriors. To go down in flames, be a casualty of a battle that means something—that is the kind of fate I always hoped for. To die with weapons firing, like Aidan Pryde. Freebirth, all those battles I've been in—and always won, or at least survived.

I could grow very old. There could be years of nursery duty. Years! I cannot even think in terms of years. It is disgusting, living to be old. How can the older warriors, Kael Pershaw, Natasha Kerensky, and the rest consider growing old? They have duty, yes, but what good is duty when your bones hurt and being in a 'Mech is just a memory? Pershaw's a wreck, but he goes on. Why?

It might be better for me to lose this little fracas with Ravill Pryde. Everyone knows he is a ristar, three in one blow, bloodname a gift, Cluster command before he has even seen real combat. It would even be a heroic and honorable death, to lose in an honor duel with a hero-to-be. Might become an important part of his epic sections in The Remembrance. *I can see him dragging my body back to his little prydelings. It all fits. Except I cannot die that way either. Something keeps me going. Something keeps me fighting. I am Jade Falcon. That may be it. I am Jade Falcon.*

The last idea pleased her. Just being Jade Falcon was sufficient. It had made a hero out of Aidan Pryde—who, after all, was no ordinary warrior either. In his way he was just as defiant as she was.

But he managed to die, damn him!

Well, there was no point in such unClanlike meditations. Best just to find Ravill Pryde and his *Timber Wolf* and reduce them both to junkyard scrap.

But where in blazes was he?

Another jarring footstep and her sensors came back online. Looking at the secondary screen Joanna saw a massive pressure ridge of ice and snow before her. A few more steps brought the ice cliff into view, thrusting high into the sky.

"Impressive, is it not, Star Commander Joanna?" Ravill Pryde said, breaking communications silence for the first time since the fight had begun.

She felt quite vulnerable, knowing that he could attack her from behind. Immediately she began to rotate the *Mad Dog,* not an easy task on the ice. The 'Mech was too heavy to fall, but that did not stop it from slipping and sliding a bit as she laboriously turned it one hundred and eighty degrees. She had her lasers ready to fire, but the *Timber Wolf* was not where it should have been. According to her scanners, she should be facing him, but from her viewport all she could see in front of her was chaotically swirling snow.

"Storm's got my systems haywire, too, Joanna. But I know where you are. Let me take a good look."

To her left, the *Timber Wolf* emerged from the curtain of snow. Seen from the front, the 'Mech looked much less fierce that its namesake. With its missile racks seeming to make the shoulders slump, its low head, and its arms bent so tentatively, the 'Mech looked humble.

Joanna decided to bide her time for a good shot, having wasted the first volley. A quick systems check revealed that the 'Mech's internal heat buildup was unusually high, perhaps the result of using too much power to force its way through the storm. Looking out through the viewport, she saw some condensation, some mist, around the *Mad Dog* as its heat met the cold of the air. There was no similar mist around the *Timber Wolf,* so Ravill Pryde apparently was not encountering similar heat complications.

"Save your fire for now, Joanna. I wish to talk."

"Talk. You are a strange Jade Falcon, Ravill Pryde."

"I am that, perhaps. From your point of view, anyway. But that is not what I want to discuss. I am willing to call this duel a draw. No one can see us. I do not wish to destroy you. You are too valuable to the Clan. I would be satisfied to let the others believe we fought to a draw. It would also give you great honor."

"No warrior ever plans a draw."

"Maybe. But I am willing, in order to avoid a battle that is essentially wasteful. If I kill you, the Clan loses an essential warrior. If you kill me, the Falcon Guards are suddenly leaderless. Who can say when an adequate replacement might be dispatched here?"

"Who said you were adequate?"

"Do not waste our time with badinage, Joanna."

"I do not even know the word."

"What about the draw?"

"What about my transfer to the canister nursery?"

"I cannot change that."

"Then I will not accept a draw. Warriors bid before battle, not during. You are some different kind of warrior, Ravill Pryde."

"True, perhaps. I offer the draw one more time."

"Bargained poorly and not done at all, Star Colonel."

The sound that now came over the line was strange. Was it possible the Falcon Guard commander was chuckling?

"Let the battle resume then. I will allow you to fire first. First, that is, if we do not count that foolish missile burst of a few minutes ago."

"You wish me to initiate the battle? I do not like that."

"Maybe, maybe not. But the storm is getting worse and we should not dawdle. Fire when ready, Joanna."

His supercilious tone made Joanna angry enough to do just that. With a curse she triggered a fierce barrage of laser fire at the *Timber Wolf,* but Ravill Pryde had moved his 'Mech sideways into the heavy snowfall and disappeared. Before he vanished, Joanna saw big chunks of his 'Mech's ferro-fibrous armor dislodge. Her lasers had done significant damage, she was sure.

But why didn't the stravag return fire? He did nothing. Just walked away like a coward.

Joanna had little time to ponder his actions, for the *Timber Wolf* had now reappeared in a different spot. She noted quickly that it was not the location shown on her screen. Ignoring the once again failed sensor and targeting system, she fired her lasers at the *Timber Wolf* by instinct. Her shots sent much more armor flying off and disappearing into the snow. Ravill Pryde still did not return fire.

She decided to try missiles again. Some of them, probably thrown off course by the worsening storm, went over the *Timber Wolf*'s head. At least one missile hit, though, and it looked like the *Timber Wolf* was in trouble. Before she could be sure, it again faded out of sight, the weather its shield.

The stravag has not fired once since the battle commenced. How could he have prevailed in a Trial, won a bloodname, with tactics like this?

"Star Commander Joanna." Ravill Pryde's voice was near a whisper. It came soothingly over the commline. Another attempt to disorient her?

She could not see the *Timber Wolf* anywhere, but her screen showed it to be only a few meters away, practically on top of her. Perhaps the phenomena were not caused by malfunctioning equipment. Perhaps Ravill Pryde could render his 'Mech invisible.

"Will you gab so much in a real battle, Star Colonel?"

"I do not often get someone worth talking to. But this time I am only trying to help."

"Help your enemy? What kind of warrior are you?"

"Not your kind, apparently. But no matter. I am reviewing my battle ROM recording of our last encounter and—"

"You review your opponent's tactics in the midst of a battle?"

"Well, yes. It is useful. For instance, I can see from reviewing the battle ROM that your *Mad Dog* is overheating. Dangerously overheating, looks like."

Joanna glanced at her heat monitor, which did, as she knew, show a dangerous heat rise, but how could she be sure that such information was not related to the malfunctioning of all the other equipment? She looked out the viewport, trying to locate the *Timber Wolf* and finish it off. All she could see was the madly spinning snow. Apparently there was no mistake about her 'Mech's heat levels, however. The ice that had begun to form on the viewport had melted away.

"I am not overheating, Ravill Pryde. We have not fought enough for that."

"You may not be overheating, but your 'Mech surely is. And we have fought enough. In these conditions more demands are put on any 'Mech. Just the effort of moving through this—"

"Stow it! This is too much chatter. You are merely using some new kind of psychological method. You are as cunning as Cholas and the rest of the prydelings."

"Prydelings? You call them that? I am not sure whether it is an insult or a compliment."

"Come back into my sights and we can end this!"

"Oh, I am sure we will. But I would suggest that you do something abut your heat levels. You see, the heat output of your leg-mounted heat sinks is melting the ice below you. Your 'Mech is slowly sinking through one of the thinnest sections of ice. You only have two meters under you, and your 'Mech has already gone though half a meter of that. And, by the way, here is a little added problem."

The *Timber Wolf* charged out of the storm toward her, firing.

But the *Mad Dog* did not rock with impact.

"You missed, scum!" she shouted gleefully as she sent another laser burst at the *Timber Wolf*. More of its armor sheared away as it again went out of sight.

"I missed you, yes, Joanna. But then I was not, in fact, aiming at you. I was using my Thunder LRMs and firing them toward your 'Mech's feet. you are, at this moment, surrounded by a minefield."

Joanna stared at her scanner screen which, indeed, did show that the area in front of her and to each side was littered with Thunder LRM mines. Each warhead was volatile. Trying to move through them at this moment, while vulnerable to an attack from Ravill Pryde, would be well-nigh impossible. She could do it, but—

The *Mad Dog* rocked suddenly and felt as if it were about to fall. One leg had slipped lower. Ravill Pryde had spoken the truth. The ice beneath her *was* melting. Her heat was too high, and would definitely cause the *Mad Dog* to fall through the ice.

"Shut down, Joanna. I will cease my attack. You may either concede defeat in this honor duel, or we will resume when you are ready."

"I want no gifts from you."

"Nevertheless, I refuse to finish you off under these conditions. Shut down all your systems."

"Finish me off? Come where I can see you and let me finish *you* off first."

"I am not as damaged as you may think. Face it, Joanna,

the fight is over—for the time, at least. Shut down." The *Mad Dog* shifted again and Joanna's stomach lurched with it as the 'Mech seemed to sink lower in the ice. Working frantically, she powered down every system she could think of. She took the leg-mounted heat sinks off line, and made no unnecessary moves. The lurching stopped.

Why is he declaring this truce? He could merely step forward now, while the minefield prevents me from moving this machine, and annihilate me. What is he up to? Why do I know he is up to something beyond what he says?

As she waited for the heat levels to sink low enough to start up the 'Mech again, Joanna studied the minefield. It did not really surround her, as Ravill Pryde had said. Mines had been placed only on three sides. But with the high cliff in back of her, she could not back up a step and go around one side of the minefield. So the mine placement, while not exactly an encirclement, was one in effect.

The stravag deliberately guided me here. It was his plan all along! Why? Why does he not just fire at will and reduce me to debris? That would at least end all my problems. A warrior's death—not graceful or admirable, but at least a warrior's death!

The only way out was through the minefield. She could set off a couple of mines without being sufficiently damaged, but it would give Ravill Pryde, if he resumed the fight at that moment, an excellent opportunity to take effective potshots at her. Still, based on potential strategies, it seemed the best one. Perhaps it could be managed if she could angle her *Mad Dog* to her right.

That is what she would do, Joanna decided, as she studied the steadily falling heat levels. Having calculated the point at which she could safely start up again, she watched the measurements sink to that level. As soon as she could get the 'Mech moving again, which would come before her weapons were ready, she would make a quick dart through the minefield, using the kind of feint and move tactics that Ravill Pryde himself was employing, and make this conflict even once more.

Probably detecting that Joanna had re-started her 'Mech, Ravill Pryde again spoke. "I am about to teach you a lesson, Star Commander Joanna. It is in the nature of tactics and strategy, something the Jade Falcons could use more of. We should perhaps study the Wolves in that respect."

Only someone with Wolf genes could say that to a Jade Falcon warrior, Joanna thought.

"Try to move your 'Mech."

Just what I was about to do, freebirth. But something was wrong. The *Mad Dog* was not responding.

"The air temperature is such that once your heat sinks were taken off line, the water immediately froze again. Right now your 'Mech's legs are encased in ice. You will not be able to take a step for some time. A trap, *quiaff,* and a good one, *quiaff*?"

Now in his voice was the arrogance that had been missing earlier. Joanna refused to answer as she continued to work her controls, trying to make the 'Mech operational. Systems were coming on one by one, their lights flashing readiness on her console, but to no avail.

The *Timber Wolf* stepped forward and fired its large laser at the *Mad Dog*. Ravill Pryde kept his shots away from the torso of Joanna's 'Mech while crippling her left-shoulder missile rack. Launching a missile of his own, he directed it to a heavy branch jutting out of the cliff, which fell on the other missile rack and knocked it loose. It merely hung there, now useless. As a fillip to the assault, he concentrated fire on the *Mad Dog*'s left arm and amputated it from the body. Suddenly, when Joanna's weapons systems did become operational, all she could use was the right-arm laser. She fired it immediately, but her shots went wide.

"That is enough, Star Commander Joanna. I do not wish to toy with you."

"End it then."

"No. You want that too much."

"This fight was to the death. You agreed."

"I did that. But remember, this is actually the final event of the games. I have won. That is sufficient. I do not wish to kill you and I will not. I prefer humiliation over death, and we will revel in your shame as we send you off to your new assignment. I have won, Joanna. Accept that, and leave it at that."

Joanna could not recall ever feeling so frustrated. What madness drove this *stravag* on?

"Of course, if you *wish* to die, you may. You have one weapon left. Use it to explode the mines. If they do not destroy you, maybe they will be enough to break up the ice and open a hole that will take your *Mad Dog* straight to the bottom of this lake. Look around you. This ice floe that we fight on is floating over an ocean of frigid water. The sea bed is more than four hundred meters down. At one hundred meters the seals of your 'Mech will fail and the engine compartment will flood. At three hundred meters your cockpit will be crushed by the weight of the water around it. By the time you hit the bottom, you and your 'Mech will be crushed flat.

"But what I suggest is this. Put your survival suit on and climb down from your 'Mech. I will give you a ride back to the DropShip in my *Timber Wolf*. Or perhaps you could ride on my 'Mech's shoulder like a pet monkey. Either way you will get back to the warmth and safety of the DropShip."

"I could still tell them about your Wolf genes, about our traitorous scientist caste. That might take the spirit out of your victory, Ravill Pryde."

"I doubt that. As you have said, you are Jade Falcon, you are honorable. You agreed not to speak if we had this little fracas, and you will keep your word. Few would believe you, anyway. They would just see an embittered, humiliated warrior. Even if the spy, your freeborn associate, backed you up—well, she is merely freebirth scum and her words would carry even less weight than yours. Do what you wish. I can counter it. At any rate, this storm is not over and will probably get worse. Leave your 'Mech. I will send a party out to retrieve it soon enough. We cannot waste a good BattleMech, after all. By the way, it is nice and warm in my cockpit."

"I refuse to ride with you."

"But how will you return?"

"I will walk. I need the air."

"You will freeze to death."

"I will not ride with you!"

"So be it, then. If you make it back to shore, I will be there with your travel orders in my hand. Farewell, Joanna."

The *Thunder Wolf* again performed its disappearing act into the storm.

How could the filthy stravag do this? I deserve to die with honor. Nobody deserves this humiliation. He wanted to humiliate me from the beginning. That was his battle plan. I could kill him. I will kill him. But no, whatever I do, this humiliation will remain. It is not as bad as Twycross, even though on Twycross I was only part of a unit defeated igno-

miniously. But here, here on Sudeten Lake, the same attaches to no one but me. The stravag! The bastard! He knows that wherever I go, people will hear about this. At the canister nursery the sibkin might one day taunt me with it. Ravill Pryde is the lowest form of Clan warrior. There must be more Clan Wolf in him than his genetic blueprint shows.

She stared out the viewport at the raging winds and heavily falling snow. She sighed. Ravill Pryde was right. She could not survive out there. She would die. Joanna sighed again.

No, she would not be that lucky.

15

Falcon Guard Compound
Pattersen, Sudeten
Jade Falcon Occupation Zone
1 August 3057

"Not packing yet?" Diana asked from the doorway of Joanna's quarters. The star commander stood in the middle of the room and surveyed what was the normal shambles for any quarters she had inhabited during all her warrior years. Since her failure to defeat Ravill Pryde, Joanna had shuffled or scattered or dropped even more of her possessions to different parts of the room and somehow created a more chaotic environment than any she had lived in before. If that was possible.

"Not packing at all. What is there to pack? Look at this junk. Would you bother to transport it to any other part of the universe?"

Diana stepped into the room and glanced around. "I see your point," she said. Horse, who had been waiting outside, now followed her in.

"You look uneasy, Horse," Joanna remarked. "Something like a warrior who has lost control of his 'Mech."

Horse stared at the floor. "I . . . I just wanted to say . . . that, well, it's not like me to . . ."

"Spit it out, Horse," Joanna said irritably.

"I was going to say . . . well, I'll probably miss your ugly face around here."

"I thought you did not even like me much."

"What's that got to do with it?"

"I do not know, Horse, I truly do not and don't know."

Diana smiled. "You two."

"We two what?" Joanna asked.

"You are so used to bantering and disputing about contractions that you do not even realize you have become friends."

"Friends with scum like Horse? You filthy freebirths are truly ignorant."

"Yes, Joanna," Diana said. "We *truly* are."

The three shared an uneasy silence. Years were contained in it.

"The DropShip has arrived," Horse said. "And guess what?"

"I do not guess." Joanna grouched.

"It brought an interesting passenger. The estimable Star Colonel Kael Pershaw."

"The walking dead man?" Joanna said.

"One and the same. They say he is on some kind of mission."

"Perhaps they are making Ravill Pryde a Khan," Diana said sarcastically. "I still do not know why he did not dismiss me. It makes me mad. I mean, after I spied and—"

"That is his punishment," Horse said.

"I do not understand."

"Keeping you with him. What better torture?"

"Maybe. It is more complicated than you think."

"Tell us."

"It has something to do with the way he is obsessed with Aidan Pryde, but I prefer not to talk about it."

Horse had never been particularly curious about other people's secrets, so he just shrugged and said, "As you wish, Diana."

Diana had a bizarre impulse to say, with affection and not lust, "I love you, Horse." She was glad to be able to suppress that impulse.

"Why is Kael Pershaw here?" Diana asked.

"For some devious reason, no doubt," Horse replied. "So devious that no one but him knows it—and maybe not even him."

"Yes."

Joanna took a last look around the room. "This is it. I

wish to see this room no more. I will wait outside for the DropShip to begin boarding."

Without a backward glance, she strode out of the room. Diana noted that Joanna's long, slim legs moved with a youthful vigor. Strange, she thought, I would be dragging my feet like they were in sludge. But no, not Joanna. A true Jade Falcon, despising her fate but going straight for its throat.

Haline called to Joanna as soon as she opened the door from her quarters. Apparently the younger warrior had been waiting for her to come out.

"What is it?" Joanna growled. "Unless your reason for stopping me is related to duty, I do not wish to speak with you on my last day here."

"Nor I you," Haline said in a sneering voice. All of the prydelings spoke to Joanna with just such contempt since her defeat. "But I am sent. Star Colonel Ravill Pryde will see you in his quarters. It is an order, Star Commander."

"I will be there soon."

Haline started to go, then turned back. "I would hurry if I were you. Star Colonel Kael Pershaw also awaits you there."

The information startled Joanna. When Haline was out of hearing range, Joanna looked at Horse and Diana over her shoulder through the still open door. "Why would that old molting falcon want to see me? Some long-delayed insult? A final humiliation?"

Neither Horse nor Diana could offer an explanation. Shutting the door, Joanna left them sitting there, and then headed off toward Ravill Pryde's quarters, muttering in consternation all the way.

16

Falcon Guard Headquarters
Pattersen, Sudeten
Jade Falcon Occupation Zone
1 August 3057

Joanna was not prepared for the latest collection of spare parts that was Kael Pershaw. The man had been taken apart and put back together so often that she could not tell anymore which part of him was prosthetic and which was still human. That single eye, glaring out from under a thick eyebrow—that had to be human. Half of his face, as ever, was masked, hiding behind whatever disfigurement was beneath. She thought the mouth was not reconstructed, or at least the half of it she could see coming out from behind the mask seemed real. One of the hands. Maybe an ear. But the reality of the rest of him certainly debatable.

The way he walked around the room had changed from the old Pershaw limp. One leg used to drag slightly after the other. Now he seemed to require great effort to move them both. He did not so much breathe as force his chest out and in. If either of his arms was good, she could not perceive since both swung with the same leaden motion. One of the arms was definitely fake, but she had forgotten which one.

Ravill Pryde's replacement parts, on the other hand, were entirely human—changes of expression, attitude, and even posture that Joanna took a special joy in. Around Kael

Pershaw he was nervous and deferential. Something was up, she could tell.

The only unaltered individual in the room was Galaxy Commander Marthe Pryde, a warrior as famous for her heroism as for the fact that she originated from the same sibko as the celebrated Aidan Pryde—one of the sibkos that Joanna had trained as a falconer on Ironhold. Joanna thought Marthe looked the same. Even though she was within shooting distance of undesirable warrior age, she still seemed young. Age was suggested only in her guarded eyes. For Joanna, Marthe's resemblance to Aidan was disconcerting.

"Star Commander Joanna," Pershaw said, his voice low and somewhat mechanical, as if electronically enhanced. "It is good to see you again. It has been a long while since Glory Station, *quiaff*?"

"*Aff*. Very long." Joanna did not like admitting that, since—in Pershaw's presence—it made her own advanced age so much more obvious.

"I, too, have not encountered Star Commander Joanna in some time," Marthe Pryde said.

Joanna stared at Marthe's outthrust hand as if she were being offered a dangerous reptile. But it was just a handshake, a firm and confident one.

What are they up to? Why are they buttering me up? Is this the way they treat a warrior on her way to becoming a nanny?

"Star Colonel Pryde," Pershaw said to Ravill. "You already know our mission. It is not necessary for you to remain here, *quiaff*?"

"But I—"

"It is not necessary for you to remain, *quiaff*?" Pershaw's voice had become harsh, a sound grating enough back in his command days at Glory Station, but uttered more like an edict from some god these days. Ravill Pryde bowed crisply to his superior and immediately strode out of the office. Joanna smiled, relishing the humbling of the man she hated so much.

Pershaw turned to her.

"I am here to revoke your reassignment, or at least postpone it for a while."

Joanna could barely contain either her elation or her surprise. "May I ask why, sir?"

"You would be wasted in such an assignment—"

"I believe that also."

"—and I have another task for you that would be eminently suitable. That is right, Galaxy Commander Pryde, *quiaff?*"

"Aff."

"Sit down, Star Commander Joanna."

"I sit only when I am tired. I am not tired now."

The perceivable half of Pershaw's mouth seemed to smile. Joanna did not know what gave her the impression, but she wondered if the hidden part of his face ever really duplicated the part that could be seen. Did the mask divide two independent halves of his face?

He raised his right arm, demonstrating that it at least was still a human part. The skin on the back of his hand was yellow and seemed paper-thin.

"As you wish." Pershaw paused and glanced for a moment at Marthe Pryde, who gave him a nod.

"When I dismissed Ravill Pryde," Pershaw began, "I told him he knew our mission. Strictly speaking, that is not true. Now that I serve the Jade Falcons as its chief intelligence officer, I find that I must often deceive others concerning my motives and my intentions. I regret that, but sometimes it is the only way to get the job done."

Pershaw's words seemed peculiar to Joanna. In all the time she had known and observed Kael Pershaw, she had always considered him at least a little bit devious, despite any Clansman's innate distaste for deception. What unsavory scheme was he cooking up now?

"The official story, Star Commander Joanna, is that the Jade Falcons have decided that you will be more useful to us here at the front, that you will be reassigned to a Falcon solahma unit. It is, after all, an assignment appropriate to, shall we say, your extensive service to the Clans."

At first Joanna could not speak, then the words came pouring out in a fierce torrent. "Solahma? You want to put me in one of those senility packs? Make me cannon fodder? And you see that as some kind of honor? I would rather tie myself to a short-range missile shot off in target practice. It is the same—"

To stop her flow of words, Pershaw help up a hand, or the facsimile of one. "I agree with you, Joanna. Solahma service is an honorable fate for most old warriors, but it would be a misuse of one so valuable as you. I feel fortunate that, at my age, solahma was not my destiny, and it should not be yours."

"What are you saying, then?"

"As I said, the official story will be that you have been assigned to a solahma unit, but what I have come here to tell you is that I have another mission for you, a secret mission that will bring you honor but not glory." He paused as if waiting for her response but Joanna was still too furious to speak.

"I have obtained evidence that enemy agents have infiltrated our ranks. As the head of the Jade Falcon branch of the Clan Watch, it is my duty, and my intention, to root them out. Thus far our intelligence is scanty, but we have reports of suspicious activity connected with one of our solahma units, peripherally at least, I need someone in place to—"

"A spy? You want me to be a *spy*?"

Pershaw again glanced toward Marthe Pryde, who seemed somewhat amused by Joanna's explosive reactions. He touched his half-mask with the back of his false hand, a gesture that seemed useless to Joanna. It was, after all, metal touching plastic.

Kael Pershaw studied Joanna for a moment, then his mouth twisted into something that must have been intended as a smile.

"That is one way of putting it," he said. "Let us say instead that I need you to assist me in gathering information crucial to the welfare and survival of Clan Jade Falcon."

Joanna did not know what to say. She just stared at Kael Pershaw, tried to gaze into his visible eye. One eye or two, he had always been hard to read.

"I have to give you credit. When I found out that I had no choice but to accept assignment as a canister nanny, I thought I could never be brought lower than that. Then you come here and tell me I am to join a solahma unit, and I think that must be the lowest I could sink. Now you tell me I am to become a *spy*. I have to inform on other warriors. Spy on aging warriors who have little more life to live. Pretend I am a loyal Jade Falcon and inform on my comrades? I was wrong before. Spying is as low as a Jade Falcon warrior can go. It is dishonorable for a warrior to stoop to deceit and intrigue. I cannot do it. Kill me now."

Pershaw shrugged. "You speak truly, Star Commander Joanna. As warriors, we Jade Falcons do not hold much store with secret warfare. We prefer the direct approach, the warrior's way of resolving conflicts. Yet the ways of war here in the Inner Sphere have taught us the value of intelligence, of gathering information and analyzing it for its strategic value in combat. We are not trained for the tactics of deception. Yet, I do not ask you to spy on your own kind. We are not concerned about loyal Jade Falcons. It is the Clan Wolf agents who are posing as Jade Falcons that we must root out. Strictly speaking, this is not a spy mission. It is an emergency measure to destroy a virus to save a healthy organism. You still look doubtful. But I can convince you, I assure you."

Joanna looked at Marthe Pryde, who nodded in agreement, then at Pershaw. "You did not mention Clan Wolf previously. I despise the Wolves."

"Then I have convinced you?"

"You are perhaps the only person who could have. Go on, tell me more if you will."

"You will do great service, Joanna."

"I only want to die well. That is my only goal now."

"And a noble one it is. But, for this mission, we need for you to survive."

Joanna looked away. "I was afraid of that," she said.

17

Solahma Number 34B Camp Site
Dogg Station, Dogg
Jade Falcon Occupation Zone
15 October 3057

Joanna had never seen a Jade Falcon warrior who looked as old as MechWarrior Bailly. Nor one as neglectful of his personal appearance. Nor one so bad-tempered that he made Joanna in mid-rage seem calm.

Bailly's face was permanently cemented into an expression of contempt. His mouth turned down at both corners, his cheeks were sunken, his brow heavily lined, and his eyes managed to look simultaneously angry and weary. His body was bent by age, something else Joanna had never seen before in a Jade Falcon warrior. Although he was obviously vigorous, his hands looked frail, with fingers slightly bent.

Almost from the hour of her arrival at Dogg Station, he seemed to have made it his new mission to torment Star commander Joanna.

"We don't get many star commanders here," he said. "ranking officers are *supposed* to die in battle and never become solahma. Only mere MechWarriors should live to become solahma. You must've been a real misfit to end up here, Star Commander Joanna."

Kael Pershaw had ordered Joanna to stay out of trouble, so she sucked in a deep breath, gritted her teeth, and vigorously suppressed the impulse to shove her fist into Bailly's face.

"You use contractions," was all she said to him.

His eyes widened, but he actually seemed pleased by the complaint. "We are solahma," he said with a shrug. "What need have we to stand on ancient rituals and ceremonies?" He turned to address the other members of the small unit that had gathered near the campfire. "We like contractions here, don't we?"

With nods of their heads and growled murmurs, the others agreed. Most of them looked old to her, but none so old as Bailly.

Ever since coming to Dogg, the Clan name for a small, uninhabited world that did not appear on any of the official maps, Joanna had been wondering how she could possibly carry out her mission. It was one thing for Kael Pershaw to command her to root out a Wolf agent, but why would any spy come to such a desolate place? Like Sudeten, the planet Dogg was a frigid and forbidding world, with winds that were, if anything, even fiercer. Why, she wondered, did the Jade Falcon commanders always seem to seek out such wretched stations for their troops? Perhaps it was to remind them of home, the nesting worlds hundreds of light years from the Inner Sphere. Forbidding places, those Clan homeworlds, yet Joanna knew that it was their very harshness that had made the Jade Falcons the fiercest of all the Clans.

"Speak as you wish," Joanna said to Bailly. "I despise contractions, but I would not stop others from using them."

"Oh?" Bailly said. "We hadn't expected you to be so agreeable. Your reputation suggested otherwise."

"You know of me?"

"Yes. For some of us you are celebrated. They think a Falcon Guard officer's an impressive addition to our little unit. Somebody to really despise. We understand, for instance, that you were one of the worthless Falcon Guards whose incompetence lost us the battle of Twycross."

"Incompetence! Let me tell you—"

"Tell me what?"

No, she thought, it would be wrong to respond to this imbecile. Anyway, he was right. Shame instead of glory had covered the Falcon Guards that day seven years ago. With the whole Cluster trapped in the Great Gash of Twycross, an Inner Sphere officer named Kai Allard had managed to explode charges hidden in the walls of the pass, setting off an avalanche that buried virtually every single Falcon Guard warrior under slag. Joanna had been one of the few who did not die, somehow digging her way out of her own BattleMech to survive.

"Nothing. I refuse to discuss Twycross."

"As so you should."

"What do you mean by that?"

"If I had been with the Guards on Twycross, I too would refuse to speak of it. I wouldn't even bother volunteering for solahma duty. I'd just take twenty steps into an ocean and ten steps back."

"Suicide is dishonorable."

"More honorable than bearing the shame of Twycross?"

"It was not—never mind. I see you are—"

"I'm what?"

"Forget it, Bailly." Some of the other warriors sitting nearby had been listening, but Joanna didn't care. It had been a month since she'd come to Dogg and already she was sick of them all. And even more sick of this place, where she didn't even have a cot or a foot locker for comfort. The warehouses near the spaceport were virtually the only real buildings at Dogg Station. Joanna and the rest of the members of the solahma unit slept out of doors.

She wrapped her rough patched blanket around her and settled down on the hard, rocky ground of Dogg to do the same thing she did every night—tried to make sense of this assignment. During her briefings with Kael Pershaw, she had learned that intercepted dispatches revealed that the Wolves had substituted at least one of their warriors for a true Jade Falcon in this unit. But why? Not only was the unit worthless solahma, but they were merely on garrison duty on a planet where DropShips came only once a month to refuel and to deliver nonessential materials for storage in a group of huge, semicircular warehouses that had originally been built by the Federated Commonwealth's logistics command.

Joanna had arrived on one of those DropShips, after a long and slow transit of almost four weeks. It had left her nerves on edge and her head full of questions. Dogg definitely seemed to be off the beaten path and the last place any spy would want to come. The only thing special about this world was its strategic placement along the supply routes so essential to Clan military success. Without the network of supply lines that brought in warriors and materiel from the far-distant Clan worlds, the entire Clan invasion and their current occupation worlds would have been impossible.

Joanna knew little about Clan DropShip and JumpShip operations within the occupation zone. Kael Pershaw had told her that they were so intricate that even some officers at the highest command levels had no idea how they worked. Most Clan warriors knew only that they had been transported here from the homeworlds, along with the necessary supplies, and that the means for accomplishing such troop movements were still secret from the enemy. It would make sense for the Inner Sphere to try to send a spy to a place like Dogg, trying to discover the route back to the Clan homeworlds. But the Wolves had no reason to spy on the Jade Falcons to learn that information. If they had placed an agent within the garrison troops on Dogg, they could only be up to no good.

Even the monthly DropShip did not remain long on Dogg. After delivering its cargo and reloading with other supplies, it quickly lifted off. Indeed, the whole operation was so routine that it was run by members of the technician caste. The only Jade Falcon warriors present were the members of this solahma unit whose duty was to defend the supply depot from attack. But it had not taken Joanna long to realize how absurd that was. If the supply depot had contained anything worth protecting, the Falcon commanders would never have assigned a collection of old, worn-out warriors as its protectors. That brought her back to her original question: Why would the Wolves want to place a spy here? After two months she was no closer to the answer to that question than the day she arrived.

For a moment she wondered if this whole mission was an elaborate lie designed to move her into a solahma unit without drawing her complaints. Perhaps Kael Pershaw, like Ravill Pryde, merely wanted Joanna out of the way.

No, she had already agreed to obey orders and return to the homeworlds for the nanny assignment. That would have gotten rid of her easily enough.

Anyway, Kael Pershaw was not that malicious. Or was he?

The puzzle was only giving her a headache. With a sigh, Joanna turned over to try to go to sleep, banging her head painfully on a rock as she did so.

18

Solahma Number 34B Camp Site
Dogg Station, Dogg
Jade Falcon Occupation Zone
1 November 3057

"Bailly's a real dogbrain," MechWarrior Karlac said one day, after observing a particularly caustic exchange between Joanna and the other warrior. The comment took Joanna by surprise because until now Karlac, with her downturned mouth and sad eyes, had been unfriendly. Age and frustration seemed etched into her face, permanent in her eyes. Her rough, weatherbeaten skin was darkened into what appeared to be a perpetual tan. She looked, in fact, like another Joanna.

Though it was rare for the real Joanna to socialize with other warriors, Joanna the spy had spent almost two months on Dogg trying to put on a friendly face. It was no easy feat, but what else did she have to do and how else might she glean information except through chance bits of information picked up here and there? Perhaps her efforts were finally bearing fruit.

"He gets on everybody's nerves at one time or another. Seems to know just what to say to rile you. He got to me with a remark about my chest."

"Your chest?"

"*Aff*. He said that I had rather a large chest for a Jade Falcon warrior, especially since our female warriors tend to be small-chested. He said that a warrior should be ashamed of having a big chest. Well, I did not know what he meant and I was foolish enough to ask him. His eyes had that nasty gleam, and he said they were so big they reminded him of the breasts of a mother. A freebirth mother, was the way he said it. I immediately went for his throat."

"As would I," Joanna said with a shudder. It was a deep insult to suggest to any trueborn that he or she was in any way appropriate to the role of freeborn parent. "That *stravag* has a talent for finding weak spots."

"He found yours, *quiaff*?"

"*Aff*. I am afraid so," Joanna said ruefully. "But I will get him for it."

"Let me know when you do, so I can be there to see it."

Karlac's remark made Joanna smile, a rare event in any situation. Just as suddenly a chilly gust of wind changed the smile to a frown and a shiver.

"A godforsaken place, Dogg, *quiaff*?" Karlac commented.

"Seems it is my destiny to be stationed in very cold places, except of course for those times when I have been assigned to worlds that were intensely hot. Either way, it makes riding in a 'Mech cockpit a memorable experience."

"Know what you mean. I do not know what is worse, feeling like you are trapped in a stove or a block of ice. But I would still give anything to be back in a cockpit again, anything but duty in this solahma group. I do not even feel old, do you, Joanna? If we only had 'Mechs or, failing that, good weapons. There are nights when I lie awake and hope somebody will attack us, so I can go out in a blaze of glory. I would like that, I think. A bit of combat at the end, then the eternal darkness."

This time Joanna's shudder was from the coldness of Karlac's words. Jade Falcon warriors generally accepted death as a blotting-out of existence, with the hopes that their genes would be accepted into the Clan genetics program or at least that their ashes might be deemed worthy for use in sibko-nursery nutrient solutions. In that, Joanna believed, would be a kind of immortality. She would be absorbed by many sibkin who would go on to high achievement in Clan warfare, and the ashes of some of the sibko's warriors might be fed to a new sibko, and so on. At any rate, she was not bothered by the concept of an eternity of darkness. She could not recall ever meeting any warrior who was—no trueborn warrior, anyway. It was the freeborn warriors who had been raised in the villages who tended to pick up such strange ideas.

"This place must have been a hellhole for the miners," Karlac commented.

"Miners?" Kael Pershaw had, of course, briefed Joanna fully on Dogg and its background, but she had a part to play. She was even getting good at it.

"Yes. Did you not know? Long before we came to Dogg, its only inhabitants were the crews of a trio of mining settlements. Supposedly, they excavated minerals which were used in jewelry."

Joanna made a face. "Jewelry? You mean that they dug up stones from this desolate world and shipped them across the stars for simple adornment? No wonder these Inner Sphere surats are so inferior. They do not understand the meaning of waste."

"Well, either the ores ran out or the popularity of the stones declined. I have heard that Dogg was virtually abandoned for nearly a century. When our forces came spoiling for a fight all we found was a weary garrison unit that surrendered without firing a shot. Even the supplies they were guarding turned out to be nonessential materials, except for a few weapons and, I am told, four or five 'Mechs in good condition, which we were able to convert and send into battle."

"So—just because some Inner Sphere merchant decided that this planet was a good place to store useless stuff, we have to follow his lead?"

Karlac looked at her suspiciously. Joanna wondered if she had gone too far in her efforts to draw out information that might be useful. She had told Kael Pershaw she was ill-suited for such a mission, but he had merely smiled in that insidious way of his. Intelligence-gathering required subtlety, and Joanna had never thought of herself as subtle.

"This place is quite valuable to the Clan," Karlac said. "There are not too many stepping stones back to the homeworlds that the enemy could not easily penetrate. But we can guard this roundabout route and, incidentally, perform some secret—"

Karlac stopped suddenly. She looked disturbed by her own words. And slightly embarrassed.

"Some secret what?" Joanna asked.

"I am sorry. I should not say. I forget you are new here. It is not up to me to spread company gossip, as it were. Forget I said anything."

Joanna tried to probe Karlac further, but the other warrior suddenly became taciturn, within moments slipping back into her earlier unfriendly manner.

19

Solahma Number 34B Camp Site
Dogg Station, Dogg
Jade Falcon Occupation Zone
2 November 3057

Joanna had enjoyed leisure times on a few rare occasions, but never before had she been forced to live day to day without any real duties, few scheduled activities, or any real purpose. The solahma unit on Dogg had been given a *stated* purpose—to be ready in case Dogg Station was attacked—but Joanna could see no sense to that at all. All she had seen while passing in and out of the warehouses that were virtually the only architecture on Dogg were packages and cartons of apparently trivial items. Why risk warriors, even mere solahma, over mess hall and bathroom supplies? The few weapons she had seen during a couple of forays into the buildings were outdated and powered down. They would be more trouble than they were worth to a genuine, combat-ready unit.

"We are all rusting here," she said to Karlac. "Why do we not at least guard the buildings?"

"What is the use of that? No one comes here to threaten the warehouses and they contain nothing of special value. Here on Dogg we solahma are just waiting for our chance to die."

"Maybe so, but do you not wonder about the way the

techs behave? They treat the place as their own little domain."

"It is true they seem very nervous when any of us is inside."

"Exactly," Joanna said. "They watch every step, as if we were thieves or intruders."

Karlac raised her eyebrows and shrugged, as if to say that what the techs did or did not do was all the same to her.

That night Joanna could not sleep. Though the air had turned unbelievably frigid, her restlessness drove her out of the comparative warmth of her rough blanket to go for a walk. Anything to keep from lying awake and staring helplessly at unknowable stars.

The solahma's sleeping ground was located on the other side of a hill, away from the warehouses. Heading now in their direction, Joanna noticed a curious aura of light hugging the hill's rim. Something must be going on at the warehouses, she decided, and picked up her pace.

Reaching the top of the hill, Joanna was astonished at the intense activity occurring around the big semicircular buildings. Sitting on the airstrip adjoining the warehouses was a DropShip, one that could only have arrived tonight because it had not been there earlier. The ship totally lacked insignia and was painted black as though to obliterate its identifying marks. Ramps thrust out from the bay doors leading from the cargo hold to the ground, where techs worked frantically—faster than Joanna had ever seen them move before—to load large, oblong metal structures onto carts with wide roadbeds. It took several techs to push and pull the carts away from the ship and through the wide open doors of the middle warehouse.

Standing on guard at the DropShip and all along the way were massive Elementals, the elite Clan infantry bred to be giants. Though not wearing their distinctive battle armor, they were nevertheless garbed for combat and scanning in every direction. Several kept touching their holstered sidearms as if they expected to use them any minute. They all wore Jade Falcon uniforms, but were too far away for Joanna to recognize their insignia. Since they had apparently come from the DropShip, perhaps they had been detached from their normal units for this apparently secret duty.

More Elementals stood outside the perimeter of activity.

They, too, continuously scanned the area around them. With their great height and slow, sinister way of moving, they resembled the fearsome apparitions that sometimes crept into the dreams of sibkin.

Seeing that it would be futile trying to get closer, Joanna decided to move sideways trying for a better view from another angle. Crouching low, her steps careful and quiet, she suddenly felt just like a spy—and worse, one spying on her own people.

While maneuvering in his skulking fashion, she nearly tripped over Karlac.

"Joanna!" Karlac hissed from her position on the ground. "What are you doing here?"

Joanna dropped down beside her and spoke close to her ear. "Just taking a walk. Could not sleep. I came upon this. What is going on?"

Karlac put a finger to her lips and nodded to her right. An Elemental, his powerful body and large head making his shadowy form seem like a moving tree, passed nearby. Karlac did not speak until he had gone.

"This happens about twice a month. The black DropShip arrives, and these tanks are unloaded and carted into the building."

"Tanks?"

"Storage tanks, looks like. They remind me of cryogenic tanks, but I really have no idea what they are used for. They are heavy, that much is for sure. These techs sweat more on these black DropShip nights than any other time."

"Where do the tanks end up?"

"That I have never been able to figure out. I have explored the buildings without ever finding a trace of the tanks inside. They simply disappear."

"Maybe we should investigate."

"We?"

"What else is there to do on Dogg? We can have some fun for a change."

"I am not sure—"

"What are you worried about? We are Jade Falcon, we have a right to learn what is being hidden from us. Otherwise it would be like admitting that we have earned solahma rather than being assigned to it, *quiaff*?"

"I am curious, yes—"

"That is the spirit, then. Tomorrow night we will go there."

"Night? Why not just go in during the day? They are not allowed to stop us."

"Ah, but they are watchful, *quiaff*? They will not expect a midnight visit."

"I suppose so. Agreed. Tomorrow night then."

Karlac soon left, but Joanna continued to watch the many deliveries being toted with such effort by the techs.

The operation eventually ended. The DropShip ramps were lifted and the bay doors shut with a clang. The bright lights abruptly switched off, and the Elementals disappeared into the black DropShip. Firing its thrusters the ship lifted off on orange flames, without—Joanna noted—having taken on any cargo for its now-depleted holds. It was unusual for a DropShip to go away empty. The way of the Clans did not condone waste, and this definitely was wasteful.

Joanna was about to return to the patch of cold, hard ground that was her bed, when she saw a man come out one of the side doors of the main warehouse. At first she thought it must be a tech because he was dressed in the standard coveralls and carrying a clipboard. He stood in the shadows and seemed to be looking about watchfully, then vanished inside the warehouse once more. Joanna waited a while longer to see if he would reappear, which he did, minus the clipboard. She was utterly surprised to see him head straight toward her, up the hill.

His pace was measured, but confident, with a youthful rhythm in the way he swung his arms. As he came closer, she saw that the man was now wearing warrior's fatigues. What little light Dogg's distant moon offered illuminated his profile as he passed. With his head held high and his back so straight, Joanna did not at first recognize him.

Then she saw that the man looked like Bailly, MechWarrior Bailly with a younger face and an unbent body. How could it be?

As Joanna twisted around to watch him continue up the hill, the movement created a faint rustle in the grass around her. The man turned and looked back.

His fierce gaze, so full of hate, left little doubt in Joanna's mind about his identity. It was definitely MechWarrior Bailly, not as young as she had first thought, but not as old as he pretended. Not seeing anything to further draw his suspicion, he resumed his journey toward the solahma camp.

Joanna followed cautiously, her escape and evasion training permitting her to escape detection. As Bailly reached the top of the hill, his back magically seemed to bend and his gait slow down to an agebound pace. In the last few steps before reaching camp, he looked like an old man whose age could have been measured in centuries rather than decades. Now she saw he had been playing a part.

Safely back in her sleeping area, Joanna lay awake for most of the rest of the night. Who was this Bailly? Was he the Wolf Clan agent Kael Pershaw had sent her here to discover? And what was his connection to the black DropShip and its mysterious cargo?

She would have to find the answers to these questions and also learn what the secret delivery was all about.

Well, she seemed to hear Kael Pershaw say, that is your job, *quiaff*?

20

Solahma Number 34B Camp Site
Dogg Station, Dogg
Jade Falcon Occupation Zone
3 November 3057

The next day Bailly was just as ancient in appearance and unpleasant in manner as ever. For the first time, however, Joanna noticed how exaggerated his responses seemed. The voice was too growly, the moves too dramatic, and he seemed to take too much relish in his more devastating comments.

Maybe Kael Pershaw would be happy now if she had finally discovered the spy after two months on Dogg. But she also realized that it did not matter so much who was spying, what Pershaw required was the why and the wherefore.

After witnessing the mysterious goings-on connected with the black DropShip last night, she was sure that whatever intrigue was involved, whatever spying was going on, it had to do with the deliveries of the black DropShip. And Bailly's presence meant he was also involved.

She considered the possibility that the black ship was a Wolf Clan vessel. That might account for the fact that it was painted over and all insignia obliterated. But if that were so, why was the cargo guarded by Elementals clearly decked out in Jade Falcon uniforms? Were the Wolves so deceptive that they would actually dress their own warriors in another Clan's colors? That was hard to say, she realized. Although

Clan warriors generally could not abide the idea of having the clothing of another Clan—or worse, that of another caste—next to their skin, it was possible that any Clan devious enough to use spies in the first place might stoop to the indignity of disguising their troops. Perhaps the wearers of the Jade Falcon uniforms were not true warriors at all. They could be bandit outcasts pressed into duty. Such people would not cringe at wearing the clothes of the warrior caste.

The whole issue of disguising identity confused Joanna. She was, after all, a Jade Falcon, and Jade Falcons hated deception, but who could say what the Wolves would do? As she had told Pershaw, the idea of pretending to be something other than what she was felt unnatural, even though she accepted the assignment. Hiding the truth about Ravill Pryde's unusual genetic legacy had been equally troublesome, although that at least made some sense.

This mission disoriented her. Joanna may have been an embittered warrior who tended to scoff at what others believed, but she was totally committed to the way of the Clan, the way of a Jade Falcon warrior, and that life had made sense even when she hated it. Now nothing made sense. Old men were young men, Clan Wolf sent spies, secret missions were taking place, black DropShips were materializing out of black skies. Joanna did not know what to make of it all. All she did know was that she needed to put some of this confusion into some kind of order—and, above all, get away from this ancient collection of useless warriors and back to—back to what? Back to Sudeten and Ravill Pryde and the next DropShip out to the nesting worlds to become a canister nanny?

The thought sent another one of her increasingly more frequent shudders through her. There was not a reasonable option in the lot. The only way to get one was to make it for herself. Perhaps she could hijack the black DropShip the next time it came, get at its controls, and fly it off to another galaxy, one where an over-the-hill warrior might still find acceptance. Of course she did not have the first idea of how to pilot a DropShip, but that seemed a minor obstacle in the face of her other dilemmas.

In the cold Dogg evenings, the solahma warriors performed a number of stunningly comatose activities. Some of them sat around the fire, murmuring tired tales of former days—of ancient battles and raids, of training as it was performed before the invasion of the Inner Sphere, of old BattleMechs that had probably gone to the scrap heap long ago. Others wrapped themselves up in ragged coverings or patchy fur and lay on the ground as if to retire early, but Joanna noticed that the eyes of many remained open but blank. A few did rudimentary exercises, but their diminished physical conditioning made their efforts painful to watch.

There was even one old warrior who sat staring into the flames, the light glinting off the metallic sheen of the neural implant tattooed over his face. He was one of those Jade Falcon warriors who had taken the short cut to glory, only to have his brain fried to a crisp within a matter of a few years. Joanna never heard the man speak a word, never saw him do anything except sit and stare, unseeing, perhaps unfeeling. The others laughed at him, joking that the only way anyone could get Pytor to move was to put a gun in his hand.

Even though it was a solahma unit, Joanna did not want to believe that this group was typical. Evenings in any Jade Falcon unit were usually quite lively. At the very least, warriors would prod or challenge each other in minor ways. Exchanges about warfare and strategy would go on until the early hours of morning. Arguments would break out and sometimes a tussle or two, all of it contributing to a noise level that was often deafening to anyone who did want to sleep. But it was always exciting. never had it been as enervating as the inactivity of this rickety bunch. They seemed to have lost all hope, all desire. There was not even any singing of the *Remembrance*.

Joanna could not stand the morose atmosphere right now, not with her mind racing madly with the previous night's mysteries. There were odd tensions in her arms that felt as if they would explode.

Karlac stood alone near the edge of the encampment, looking contemplative as she examined the charge level of her laser pistol. What in the name of Kerensky could she be looking at all this time? Perhaps she was merely faking while inwardly working out her own set of private mysteries.

Joanna strolled toward her, trying to look casual, just another decrepit solahma warrior seeking some relief from the constant boredom. She stopped as if to exchange a few words with Karlac—and, in fact, a few words were all she did say.

"It is time. Meet me where we met last night. About an hour from now when the rest of these walking corpses finally get to sleep."

"What is this all about?"

"Truth."

Karlac eyed her suspiciously, but nodded agreement. Joanna walked away. She noticed that her rate of breathing had increased and the tense feelings in her arms seemed changed—excited and not agitated, thrilled but not bothersome.

Before slipping out of camp, she made a careful survey of the pitiful scene around her. The only thing that seemed worthy of note was the fact that Bailly was nowhere to be seen.

21

Jade Falcon Warehouse 893
Dogg Station, Dogg
Jade Falcon Occupation Zone
3 November 3057

No techs were in sight when Joanna and Karlac approached the middle warehouse, but Karlac kept watch while Joanna tried the main door and found it locked. They had more luck with one of the windows near the rear of the building. Karlac wriggled in ahead of Joanna, who thought the aging warrior quite nimble for her age. How many others in this solahma unit could perform with more agility than they showed, she wondered.

Grabbing the ledge of the window, Joanna hoisted herself up and through the opening to the other side, which turned out to be a storeroom filled with small cartons. Labeling on the boxes indicated that they contained dehydrated food, the kind of rations that in their drab way satisfied hungry warriors long out in the field.

"That way," Joanna said, pointing to a door at the far end. It was locked, but Karlac managed to nudge it open easily.

"You show some skill at breaking into places," Joanna whispered to her as they stepped cautiously out into an empty corridor.

Karlac seemed taken aback by the remark. "In my sibko we often had to sneak around for supplies. Our falconer was trying to starve us, it seemed."

"Oh? I was a falconer once. The last thing we would do was deny trainees their rightful meals."

"Yes, well, I suppose different falconers use different methods."

"Ugly.'

"Yes, we thought so."

"You go first. You have been in this building more than I have."

"I never found anything before."

"You did not have me with you before."

"Are you always so confident?"

"Confident, and meaner than a cave bat. Let us go."

Passing through the storeroom's single exit, they came to a dark hallway with office doors on either side. Karlac tested several of the doors. All were locked. Too bad, Joanna thought, we might find out more from computer records than poking around in the dark.

Then they came to a double door, which opened into a vast area of storage cubicles that reminded Joanna of a battlefield cluttered with corpses and battered machinery. As they passed through the narrow aisle between the cubicles, Joanna noted that they were stuffed with tottering piles of moldy cartons marked with the Federated Commonwealth starburst, rusting metal parts apparently flung without logic into rusting bins, boxes bulging with computer printouts, decaying Inner Sphere weapons that—from the look of them—were also unserviceable, one strange cubicle piled high with cracking, lusterless ComStar infantry boots, another with nothing in it that Joanna could recognize. After a while, she did not bother to try to identify the contents of the individual cubicles. What she saw instead were abstract patterns, blobs and shapes with ragged borders.

Nothing in any cubicle offered any clue to the whereabouts of the storage tanks carted in with so much effort the previous night.

The general mess did make this warehouse, which Joanna had never entered until now, different from those whose interiors she had seen. The others were well-organized, arranged with the usual Jade Falcon sense of order. This area looked more like a terrifically extended version of Joanna's own normal quarters, that is, when she'd had quarters instead of a patch of hard ground.

But perhaps the mess was part of some larger purpose,

Joanna thought. Perhaps it was meant to persuade the typical Jade Falcon observer that nothing of value was there. Just the refuse and debris of defeated Inner Sphere armies.

A sudden noise came from a cubicle ahead of them. Both Joanna and Karlac reacted quickly, ducking into another cubicle whose contents were not identifiable but were certainly odorous. Nearly gagging on the smell, Joanna bumped against something so mushy that she didn't dare contemplate what it was.

The noise they'd heard had been a grinding sound. It was followed by some grunts of machinery, the sound of a door sliding open, then shut. This was followed by steps, at first muffled, then sharp as someone entered the aisle.

The two warriors huddled deeper into the cubicle's darkness. Joanna listened to the footsteps trying to tell how many people were coming. Only one, as it turned out, someone who hurried quickly past their hiding place. Joanna risked poking her head out beyond the partition to watch whoever it was go down the corridor.

"Bailly," she whispered as she ducked her head back in.

"What?" Karlac said. "Bailly what?"

"It was Bailly. I recognized him as he went past."

"You must be mistaken. Bailly could never walk that fast."

"You do not know Bailly then."

The moment she spoke, Joanna regretted it. Karlac wanted to know what she meant, which required telling her about last night's sighting of the less than aged version of MechWarrior Bailly.

"But why would he be faking his identity?"

"I do not know."

Joanna could not, of course, tell Karlac the full story. Nobody must know that she herself was here on a mission for the Watch.

"Maybe we should get out of here now," Karlac said.

"Go if you wish. I want to check out the cubicle he came from."

"Can you tell which one?"

"No, but how many possibilities are there?" The first cubicles they inspected yielded nothing noteworthy, then they came to one stacked with high piles of paper and boxes of used disks from outmoded computer systems.

"This is Inner Sphere garbage," Karlac said. "They must

have left it behind when our troops attacked. I cannot figure why we keep it around."

"Perhaps that is the point. Nobody can use this material anyway, so why would anyone bother to come poking around in here?"

"But—"

"No more talking. Let us have a good look around."

Joanna went over to a box full of printouts and pulled one out. As Karlac had suggested, they were indecipherable. Karlac held up some disks, arranging them in her hand like playing cards, and shook some dust off of them.

"These are no doubt coded, but by now the information would be useless to anyone."

"I know Jade Falcons are by nature against waste, but keeping such useless garbage around is—what are you smiling at, Karlac?"

"You. You have not given up. At heart you cannot be a solahma warrior. It means accepting your fate. But you question everything. I have noticed that ever since you came here."

Joanna was not sure how she felt about these words. On one hand it meant she was doing a good job of deceiving other people about how and why she had come to Dogg. On the other hand she was too much of the Clans not to be revolted by the idea.

"I am like that, too," Karlac continued. "I should be calmly looking forward to my death, the way the rest of them do. Not for me. Or for you. I see defiance in you, a refusal to accept our fate, to accept being consigned to the solahma heap. I am, I think, much like you."

"You do not know me."

Karlac looked startled, perhaps slightly wounded, by Joanna's abrupt response. Even Joanna was surprised at her sudden irritability.

Now silent, they worked on. Joanna wanting to investigate what was behind the boxes. When she tried to move one, however, it would not budge. She tried another. It, too, was immovable. It was obviously attached to the one below it. Then she tried to shift a middle one out. It was not merely wedged in between others, it was secured to them. Whether the bonding was some kind of glue or through mechanical means, she could not tell.

Putting her arms around a higher carton, Joanna pulled at

it with all her strength. Her grunting echoed through the massive storage area.

"Be careful, Joanna," Karlac whispered. "If that heap of cartons fell, it would make a noise that—"

"But that is the point. It cannot fall."

She explained to Karlac about the immovability of the cartons.

"But what is the point of joining all these boxes together?"

"Exactly. That is what we must find out."

"I think we should get out of here before anyone comes."

"I thought you said we were alike. Defiant, curious—wait, look at this."

Joanna pointed to a slight break between two piles of cartons. It was thin, not big enough even to insert a finger, but it could be discerned.

"However you get into this, you go through there," Joanna muttered.

"However you get into what?"

"I do not know what. But I am certain Bailly came out of here. Somewhere behind is something . . ."

She tested the surfaces of several boxes on each side. Nothing happened. She pushed at the boxes. Again nothing happened. She tried to pry them apart. Nothing.

"Maybe there is some kind of combination," Karlac suggested. "You know, touch the boxes in a certain order and—"

Joanna stared again at the boxes. "Well, your idea has potential. Let us see."

Touching one box after the other, first in one pattern, then another, Joanna was almost ready to give up when suddenly the touch of her hand produced first a deep rumbling sound, followed by the box-piles starting to separate from one another. There was a sliding sound at floor level as the opening widened to a few centimeters, then stopped.

Neither warrior could get through the opening. Joanna put her head up against it to look in with one eye.

"What do you see?" Karlac asked.

"Not much. It is pretty dim. But one thing it is not is more boxes. It is open in there. Some kind of passage probably."

"It could be just a hiding place, a place to hide in case of attack."

"That is for cowards. No warrior would hide during combat."

"I just meant that there might be—"

"Does not matter what you meant, unless we can get in there and see what it *really* is. And I do not think we—"

Out of frustration, Joanna kicked at one of the bottom boxes. The result of the kick was another rumbling sound from beneath the pile, followed by a soft beeping sound. The crack leading into the dark space slid all the way open with the same kind of grinding and grunting of machinery that Joanna had heard before.

Before them was a dimly lit elevator, its bottom raised just slightly above that of the warehouse floor. On one side a panel indicated three levels of destination. In the rear was a narrow bench.

"He came up here in this," Joanna said.

"What is down there, do you think?"

"That is what we will find out—"

"Joanna—"

"Come with me or not, Karlac. But I am going."

Karlac stepped into the elevator ahead of Joanna. "I would not let you go alone. I am cautious, yes, but I never back away from a good fight. And that is what I suspect may be down there. A good fight."

"Nothing would please me more," Joanna said, stepping into the car and pressing the bottommost button. The elevator started up with a muffled roar. As the car started to descend, they saw the portal of piled boxes closing up again.

Joanna and Karlac stepped into the next level down with weapons drawn, but it turned out none were needed. Extending away, lit only by the glow tubes of the elevator, was a long tunnel obviously in disuse. Joanna could just make out some rockpiles forming steep slopes down from the rock walls as well as a set of tracks going down the tunnel. In the dim light, she thought she saw the tunnel split into two more some twenty or thirty meters in the distance.

"Mining," she muttered.

"What?" Karlac asked.

"This tunnel, a mining tunnel. The elevator must have been used by the miners."

"Then it was concealed because the mines are not functioning anymore. We can go back up."

"No."

"But why not?"

"I am sure that Bailly came out of that elevator. There must be something down here on one of the levels. And I want to check every one. Are you game, Karlac?"

"If you say so, Joanna."

In the eerieness of the cavern, the dimness shadowing their faces, Karlac's voice echoed strangely. It had a hollow sound to it, as if she were not quite convinced.

"We will check level by level," Joanna said. "No point in going any further into this one, so—"

As Joanna turned to reenter the elevator there was a thunk so loud its echo seemed to go up and down the tunnel many times. The thunking was followed by a now-familiar grinding noise as the elevator doors began to close.

With a gasp of fright, Karlac leaped forward, just squeaking through the closing doors.

"Karlac, no, that is—"

Joanna's move toward the doors was too late and the two sides clanked shut, it seemed, in front of her nose. She banged a fist against it at the same time she heard another sound of machinery, the signal that the elevator itself was moving. From the sound, the car seemed to be going up.

Frustrated and angry, Joanna leaned her forehead against the cold metal door and felt the vibrations of the machinery against her skin.

22

Jade Falcon Warehouse 893
Dogg Station, Dogg
Jade Falcon Occupation Zone
3 November 3057

Joanna had been in some pretty dark places in her life, but none like this one. This darkness was absolute. For a moment she was afraid to remove her hand from the security of the cold metal door, where she could still feel a slight vibration, even with the elevator gone to another level. Keeping her body against the door for orientation, she holstered her pistol, but only with difficulty. She had to hold the side of the holster while slipping the weapon past her fingers.

Thinking that someone might come looking for her any moment, Joanna knew she had to locate as many points of reference as she could. Moving to the left side of the door, she ran her fingertips lightly up and down its rim. Nothing here. Careful to keep one hand on the door at all times, she moved to the other side. Nothing there either. Yet people on this level had to be able to summon the elevator. There should be a button, or palmprint scanner, or something. If it was not along the rim, where was it?

Making the same fingertip inspection outside the rim, Joanna came upon a thick cable attached to the wall. Following the route of the cable, she found what felt like a panel with shallow circular depressions. That had to be it, the control panel. She felt better—at least there would be a way out if nobody stopped on this level. She could wait a while, then summon the elevator.

But if anyone discovered Karlac in the elevator car, would that not make somebody suspicious enough to check all levels? Maybe not, if Karlac covered well. But Joanna could not be sure what she might do in any situation. Karlac was, after all, solahma.

Finding her way back to the security of the elevator door, she leaned against it and tried to collect her thoughts. Karlac's sudden vault into the elevator had caught Joanna by surprise. Karlac was a Jade Falcon warrior, not someone who should be struck by sudden panic. Joanna wondered if maybe fear of the darkness could make even a Jade Falconer behave uncharacteristically. But this pitch blackness did not send Joanna into a panic, so she found it hard to understand how it could frighten a hardened, battle-tested warrior like Karlac.

Unless Karlac was not hardened and battle-tested.

Unless Karlac was not a Jade Falcon warrior at all.

If not Jade Falcon, what? Was Karlac the spy from Clan Wolf? Even then, her behavior was puzzling. The Wolves were no more known for caution than the Jade Falcons. Wolf warriors might be devious, but their bravery was unquestioned. The worst thing about that Clan, in Joanna's view, was their tolerance of freebirths. Not only was one of their current Khans a freeborn, but he had originally been a bondsman from the Inner Sphere. Though that indicated a severe weakness undermining the entire Clan, it did not suggest cowardice. Stupidity, perhaps, but not cowardice.

If Karlac was not a spy, perhaps it was being consigned to the solahma scrap heap that had taken something out of her, dampened her spirit, deprived her of purpose and drained away the innate fierceness of a Jade Falcon warrior. Although Karlac's surliness mirrored Joanna's own, she lacked a certain . . . a certain toughness.

Is that what would happen to me? Joanna wondered. She thought of Karlac's cautionary reminders as they were investigating the warehouse. She thought of the listlessness of the other solahma warriors around the campfire at night, where not even the *Remembrance* was sung. Would I become so soft, so *deadened,* even after all my years as a warrior?

Joanna shook off those gloomy thoughts, which frightened her much more than any pitch darkness could. All she really knew was that Karlac, Jade Falcon warrior or not, could not be trusted.

Nobody could be trusted. Joanna was alone. The other warriors in the solahma garrison seemed to be misfits and failures, as beaten and defeated as whipped dogs. None of them could help her. The irksome Bailly was somehow involved in the secret operation involving the warehouse and the black DropShip. And Karlac was a confusion in a Jade Falcon uniform.

Getting to the bottom of the enigmas of this mission meant, she was sure, getting to the bottom of these mine levels to find the storage tanks—which had to be somewhere in this warren of tunnels—and to discover their purpose.

A rumbling noise, now familiar to Joanna as the sound of the elevator, started up, and the car began a new descent into the depths.

Not wanting to leave her perch by the door, Joanna realized that she had no choice. She had to move into the darkness, but only after drawing her laser pistol once more.

Four or five steps and she was thoroughly disoriented. First she walked sideways into a wall, the impact spinning her about until she was suddenly somewhere in the center of the tunnel. Joanna had no idea in what direction she faced. The elevator door could have been in front or in back of her. Then she became aware of the elevator's rumble to her right, and she turned her body toward the sound.

She held the pistol in front of her, pointing it where she thought the elevator door was. The rumble got louder and she thought she felt vibrations in the floor as the sound reached its peak—and passed. The elevator was descending to a lower level.

Joanna blinked her eyes several times even though the act seemed senseless. For a few moments she held perfectly still, trying to get her bearings from the distant rumble of the elevator. Then the sound abruptly stopped. The car had taken so long, it must have gone to the lowest level. The echo of its arrival seemed to travel up the shaft toward her.

The elevator had passed this level. Why? If captured, it was not in Karlac's interest to reveal Joanna's whereabouts, so the mission of the elevator's passengers must be elsewhere. This level, apparently long abandoned, seemed to have no importance to whatever operation was going on, which would explain the elevator passing by. She could die in here and her body would not be discovered until sometime in the next millennium. But she would get out. One press of the button on the panel, and the elevator would return to take her away. If the button worked. If it was even for the elevator and not some vestigial device from this level's mining days. For an instant Joanna felt something akin to panic and understood what might have so spooked Karlac.

No sound had come from the direction of the elevator shaft for some time. Whatever the car's last occupants were doing, they were doing it two levels below.

She could stay here and wait for something to happen.

Or she could summon the elevator and go find out for herself.

Joanna did not waste time considering the options. She knew what she had to do.

Walking carefully toward the point on the wall where she believed the panel to be, she felt along the wall until she found it. There were two buttons there. She pressed both.

For a moment she heard nothing. Then, from deep below, came a familiar rumble. And it came quickly toward her.

She had her pistol ready as the rumble stopped and the elevator doors opened with a rattling noise.

If there had been somebody in the car, Joanna would not have easily seen him. The interior light struck her eyes like a knife. At first she felt blinded. Her vision came gradually back as she heard the elevator doors begin to shut again.

Leaping with even more recklessness than Karlac had shown, she fell into the car and slid across the floor, knocking her head against the back wall. She did not lose consciousness, but many abstract shapes danced around her eyes as the elevator began to move downward.

When her vision cleared she looked toward the panel at the side of the car. A light was on next to the number for the third and lowest level.

But she had not pressed any of the buttons inside the car. Someone at the third level must have done it. Not blinking against the light, Joanna stood up and steadied her pistol with her none-too-steady hands. Her vision had mostly cleared, but there were still a few small dancing spots.

As she planted her feet in combat-ready stance, the elevator came to an abrupt stop and the doors in front of her began to open.

23

Jade Falcon Warehouse 893
Dogg Station, Dogg
Jade Falcon Occupation Zone
3 November 3057

There stood three techs, each one pointing a weapon at her. They obviously had the advantage. But they were only techs. So she opened fire.

Joanna hit the tech on the right in the mid-chest, her laser pistol powerful enough to slam the man backward a few meters before he fell, unconscious. His weapon skidded along a wall, sending out sparks in several directions.

She only saw the sparks peripherally because she was busy disposing of the tech in the middle, who got off a useless shot at the elevator floor after Joanna had temporarily deprived the tech of the use of her legs. Joanna dodged to her right to avoid the attempt on her from the third tech, whose laser beam seared by her shoulder without touching her. One more shot of Joanna's left this one sprawled on his face among some scree from the mine.

She stared down at the trio of fallen techs. They were all dead.

At the sound of footsteps behind her Joanna whirled, holding her pistol at the ready.

"Just me, Joanna," Karlac said, stepping forward into the meager light. She smiled oddly as she walked toward one of the fallen techs, then bent down to relieve him of the laser pistol still in his hand. She held it up, saying, "Mine. They took it from me."

This level was colder than the other one, its dampness seeming to seep in her bones. Joanna shivered.

"You let them capture you? Techs?"

"Let them? Is that not a bit cruel, Joanna? I am not as . . . as adept in my reactions as you. I did not expect to see techs with weapons! I had barely pulled this from my holster before the elevator door opened at the top level, and these three came charging at me. They disarmed me immediately, but I was still panicked and my mind was not working as a warrior's should."

Does it ever? Joanna wanted to say.

"You are so skillful, Joanna. Almost enough not to be . . ."

"Not to be what?"

"I was going to say solahma. Most of us are waiting for death, but when the time comes we hesitate, questioning the consequences of her actions. Not you."

"I do not know about that. I need to be in the fight, that is all I know."

"We should get moving. There may be others coming, these may revive—"

"Not soon, I would wager. They are dead."

"Perhaps we should get out of here before—"

"We have time," Joanna said, wondering at Karlac's foolishness. Did a solahma warrior lose all sense, along with everything else? Techs were carrying weapons! Something was going on and Joanna had to find out what. "I want to know what is going on down here. Did you discover anything?"

"Neg."

"Then we should explore."

Karlac did not look especially eager to do that. But it was obvious that she would not put up any more protests. Joanna would have her way.

Joanna checked out the nearest fallen tech. On his belt was a slim flashlight. Pointing it down the tunnel, she found it had a surprisingly powerful beam. She retrieved two more from the slumped bodies of the other two.

"One for you, one for me, and it is always useful to have a spare. Come, Karlac, help me get these freebirths out of sight."

The lifeless techs were dead weight that left Karlac and

Joanna sweaty and out of breath after dragging them out of sight of the elevator.

Joanna wiped the sweat from her face with the back of one hand. "I would guess that—whatever is going on here—this is the main level for the activity. I will go first. Stay close, *quiaff*?"

"*Aff.*"

The tunnel stretched far ahead of them, as far as the light beams would go.

"We have a long walk, I think, Karlac."

"Lead the way, Joanna."

There was a confidence and even camaraderie in Karlac's voice. Joanna did not mind the confidence, but the camaraderie was irritating.

She set a rapid pace, keeping her flashlight constantly in motion, examining the walls and even the ceiling for information. But this was just a mine tunnel. There were grooves in the tunnel floor where tracks had once been, but the tracks had apparently been removed long ago. There seemed to be a lot of footprints in the dirt and some ruts where vehicles must have passed.

Something was definitely going on at this level, but Joanna was suddenly not so sure she wanted to find out what. Now, wait a minute, she scolded herself. In all her life Joanna had never been cautious. This *stravag* Karlac must be rubbing off on her.

At first Karlac seemed to gasp a bit, as if struggling to keep up. But now, for once, she kept silent about her discomfort.

Then Joanna stopped and shut off the flashlight. The only light was from Karlac's, at the moment pointed directly at the tunnel door.

"Turn that off."

"But—"

"Turn it off."

Karlac obeyed and they were plunged into darkness, though not the same pitch black they had experienced at the other level. Ahead of them, the tunnel seemed to curve, and a dim illumination came from somewhere beyond that turn.

"What do we do now?" Karlac asked, her voice somewhat unsteady.

"If there is something waiting around that curve, I do not

want to go prancing in with these flashlights announcing our arrival."

"Good thinking, Joanna."

"You stay here."

"Right." Karlac seemed content with her orders.

Joanna edged forward toward the dim light, feeling her way along the wall. A slight dampness clung to the wall and the liquid that came off on her fingers had an oily feel.

She rounded the curve and saw that the light source came from far ahead. It was bright, illuminating the whole long passageway before her.

She returned to Karlac and told her what she had seen.

"We will go there, *quiaff*?" Karlac asked.

"Aff."

"Lead on, Joanna."

Moving in single file, the two warriors went around the turn toward the light. Gravel crunched beneath their boots and Karlac breathed heavily from their pace, which Joanna deliberately increased. Whatever else she was, Joanna thought, Karlac was definitely out of shape.

24

Jade Falcon Warehouse 893
Dogg Station, Dogg
Jade Falcon Occupation Zone
3 November 3057

Joanna and Karlac stayed close to the tunnel side as they came closer to the bright light. In the last few minutes Joanna had noticed a faint sound that was becoming a rhythmic rumble. At first she was not sure what the sound reminded her of, then she realized that it was almost identical to the steady turn in a canister nursery. Could it be that a genetic station was buried here deep beneath the surface of Dogg? No, that made no sense. Dogg was in the Inner Sphere, too far from the nesting worlds. The scientist caste would not even consider coming here. Scientists were meticulous about their own comfort. It had to be something else.

Joanna gestured for Karlac to stop as they came to an entrance. Standing with her back flat to the wall she let her head slide sideways to get a look inside.

What lay beyond the portal was an enormous cavern. It was more than a hundred meters high and its other end—what could be seen of it down long aisles—seemed a kilometer or two away. The aisles, seven of them, were lined with rows of metal structures whose purpose was not clear. The lighting, though it had seemed bright from the darkness of the tunnel, came from fixtures inserted at regular points along the aisles and some strips of light placed on the ends of the metal structures. Each of the structures reached nearly to the cavern ceiling. Strange four-wheeled vehicles with retractable cranes moved among the aisles.

A whirring noise made Joanna look to her right. In the second aisle a female tech had just climbed into one of the cranes and driven it to a place just beyond her sightline. The tech was soon back again, the flatbed behind her fully loaded. What she was hauling looked exactly like the storage tanks delivered and unloaded off the black DropShip the night before. Then the tech drove into the aisle and out of sight.

Joanna heard a scuffling noise to her left, then footsteps heading toward her. She retreated into the darkness, bumping into Karlac, who took a clumsy step backward. Two techs passed by without looking their way.

Joanna motioned Karlac a few more steps backward. "We have got to get in there, see what is going on," she whispered.

"But how?" Karlac sounded more dubious than ever. "In these warrior uniforms we would be noticed immediately, I think."

"We will appropriate a pair of uniforms. That is, if you do not—"

"Whatever you say, Joanna."

The two warriors went back to the portal and waited. Within moments the pair of techs made a return trip. Reacting quickly, Joanna and Karlac jumped the techs. Covering their mouths, they dragged the two men back into the tunnel. With a quick jerk Joanna snapped the neck of hers, and then helped Karlac dispatch the one she had hold of. Working swiftly but efficiently, she and Karlac then stripped the techs of their coveralls and put them on. Karlac's fit snugly, but the tall Joanna was conscious that her trouser legs and sleeves were a bit short. She would have to chance the possibility that no one would notice or find it particularly odd for a tech to wear an ill-fitting uniform.

"What now?" Karlac said, evening her sleeves.

"Take this." Joanna handed her a noteputer that one of the techs had been holding.

"What for?"

"Carry it like it means something to you. Techs like to walk around making frequent notations on these things."

"How do you know so much about techs?"

"I once had a tech named Nomad—dead now, I hope—who told me all about techs, little of which I wanted to know. A stupid, sarcastic freebirth, but he saved my life once. I guess I am grateful for that."

"If you had died, then—"

"Do not even say it, Karlac. Now, get rid of that warrior stiffness. Techs walk differently than we do. They stroll where we stride. They are in no hurry to get where they are going. Keep checking that noteputer and peer at everything as though it were important. If anybody speaks to you, use contractions. And speak with authority whether you know what you are saying or not, as though anyone with half a brain should understand you."

"I do not know if I can do any of that."

"Then keep your mouth shut, grunt a lot, and let me do the talking."

Joanna nudged Karlac ahead as they passed through the portal. Inside, the cavern seemed even more massive. The air felt cooler and clearer. Joanna saw a large air filtration and circulation unit located at one corner, which explained the difference in the atmosphere.

Joanna gestured Karlac toward a long table a few meters away. Joanna duplicated the tech manner well as they walked toward it, but Karlac's idea of carelessness made her gait too disjointed and loose. On the table's surface were several clipboards, each bulging with paper. Beside the table were two chairs. Joanna drew one up, while silently indicating that Karlac do the same. She whispered the word *casual* to Karlac as they sat down.

"What is this all about?" Karlac asked.

"Paper. Tech operations run on paper—computer printouts, graphs, invoices, blueprints, any paper on which data can be printed. If we find something now, it may help us know what to look for later."

Karlac glanced around suspiciously. She seemed more nervous than ever. "Well, all right. No one seems to be paying us any mind."

"Why should they? We are doing a job. Techs do jobs. Everything looks normal. Techs like to look busy, whether they are or not."

"You are so confident, Joanna. What if they find us out?"

Joanna was quickly losing her patience with Karlac's timidity, but this was not the time to make a scene. "So what?

We are warriors, are we not? Any trueborn warrior can outdo any freeborn tech in arrogance, *quiaff*? So they discover us, we just waltz out of here. What can they do to us, Karlac? What can anyone do? We are not just warriors, we are solahma warriors. We are meant to die soon in battle anyway. That gives us a certain advantage, *quiaff*?"

Karlac seemed unsure, but she said, "*Aff.*"

Joanna turned her attention to the papers on the desk, which at first seemed to contain merely a jumble of numbers and names. Reading the heads of columns, she was able to see that the numbers represented identification and location. But what were the names? She began to read through the list. Some of the names were bloodnames, many were not. Another code beside the names caught her attention. One said TWY10SEP3050-JFGUARDS-CHARLIEFIRE.

Joanna bit her lower lip to keep from reacting visibly. Someone else might not have decoded the notation so easily, but Joanna carried the same of Twycross and its date forever engraved in her memory. The notation was attached to a name, MechWarrior Fredasa.

The name meant nothing to her, but it was undoubtedly that of a warrior killed in the Great Gash on Twycross. She had not been personally acquainted with any of the Falcon Guard warriors who took the field on that day of *dezgra*, had, in fact, only been with the unit for a short time. A slower DropShip delivering replacement warriors and she would have missed the battle—and the disgrace—altogether. Joanna did not even remember the battle very well. She knew that she had killed at least one warrior from the Tenth Lyran Guards, and perhaps disabled another's 'Mech. But the confusion of the battle and her sudden burial under an avalanche of rocks had left the earlier part of the battle less vivid in her memory. Every suffocating detail of her escape from her 'Mech through an ocean of rocks was, however, too graphic.

She did not like thinking of Twycross. And she had thought of it every day since it had occurred. The Falcon Guards had been virtually wiped out on Twycross. The unit was only revived and Aidan Pryde given command because the Jade Falcons needed all the troops they could muster for the showdown with ComStar on Tukayyid.

Flipping officiously through the papers as though searching for some significant bit of information, Joanna noted that the entries were all of the same kind—a warrior's name, a place/date/unit code, and another number giving an aisle and place location. But all this was mere data. What did it mean?

Glancing around, she noticed a series of shelves built into the cavern wall, apparently with oversized screws set into deep anchors. The shelves were lined with tall, bright-colored volumes, many of which seemed to have page markers poking out from them. She decided to investigate.

"Keep up the act," she said to Karlac. "I will be right back."

Karlac looked frightened.

"I am just going over there," Joanna said, thinking that the fate of a solahma was a pitiful one. To become such a shrinking ball of fear . . . Taking a sheaf of papers from the table, she strolled in her best tech manner to the shelves. Selecting a volume at random, she opened it with studied casualness as if merely checking some data. The volume was a binder holding many pages of sheets similar to those on the desk and containing the same kind of data. Most of the names were checked off with a notation that said *dispatched*. More confusion, more strangeness.

Flipping through the pages, Joanna was about to shelve the volume when she noticed a whole page of names whose coded notation contained the letters TUK. Following the letters was the date of the battle on Tukayyid. Turning the page, she found four more sheets of names, all with the TUK designation in the code.

This time Joanna also noticed some names whose notation contained a JFGUARD. Looking closely down the list, she suddenly found one that was familiar, that of Star Commander Jula Huddock. Joanna had known her well.

Jula Huddock had been an older warrior on the verge of being relegated to a solahma unit, when she was suddenly reassigned to serve under Aidan Pryde and his newly organized Falcon Guards, a unit composed mainly of old warriors, troublemakers, and misfits, like Joanna, Horse, and Aidan himself. When Jula Huddock spoke, which was rarely, it had been in an astonishingly beautiful voice. Otherwise, she was someone who could be counted on to fight with silent eloquence in battle. Her combat skills had averted disaster at the fake city of Olalla, a collection of hastily constructed buildings intended to represent the genuine city.

She had fought well when the Com Guard ambushers had emerged from the counterfeit structures.

And Jula Huddock had been killed in action. Her *Executioner* had been destroyed by a missile from a ComStar 'Mech launched just before Jula Huddock's fatal fire exploded it.

Joanna sought another familiar name and found it. MechWarrior Obdoff of Trinary Charlie Talon, drowned during Aidan Pryde's daring maneuver at the Prezno River in which BattleMechs became stepping stones for other 'Mechs to cross the raging waters.

Checking for another name, then another, and still another, It did not take long for Joanna to see that all the TUK names belonged to warriors killed during the battle of Tukayyid.

The realization came as such a shock that she had to reach up and grab at the edge of the shelf for support. These, then were lists of dead Jade Falcon warriors.

Glancing around to see if anyone was watching, she slipped the pages listing Falcon Guard warriors killed on Tukayyid out of the binder and casually fastened them onto her clipboard.

Returning to the table, she quickly whispered her discovery to Karlac, who seemed more befuddled than ever by the information.

"Why would there be dead warrior names on these lists?"

"That is what we must find out. It has something to do with this storage area, and perhaps others like it. It also has something to do with the big tanks we saw being unloaded from the black DropShip. Remember when you said that they reminded you of cryogenic tanks?"

"Well, yes, but I did not mean literally—"

"You might have been on to something. What if they are storage tanks containing warriors or the giftakes of warriors?"

"Oh, Joanna, I do not think—"

"The techs, remember how they struggled to carry the tanks? That is consistent with my theory, *quiaff*?"

"Well, *aff*, I suppose. But there might be other theories that fit it too. The tanks might have contained combustible supplies or—"

"Do not even speculate. I understand that there are other

possibilities. The only way to find out the truth is if we investigate what *is* in the tanks."

"You mean, actually go look?"

"No, I mean, go up to a tech and ask what is going on in this secret underground place where just a few minutes ago we killed three people by an elevator and two more in the passageway outside. Of course, I mean go and look. What are we here for, anyway?" Even as a falconer charged with shaping warriors from silly little sibkin, Joanna did not think she had ever come across a Jade Falcon so unwarriorlike as Karlac.

"I wish I was sure of—"

"What is wrong with you, Karlac? You may be solahma now, but you were once a warrior—and even the least of our warriors is fearless. What happened to change you into a spiritless—"

"Do not be angry with me, Joanna. I will go with you. I just want to be sure we consider the conseq—"

"Yes, Karlac, yes, and the more we discuss, the more time there is for some tech to notice we do not belong in these filthy repellent uniforms of theirs. Let us go."

Dressed in their green coveralls, Joanna clutching her clipboard and Karlac her noteputer, the two walked casually to the nearest aisle, the third from the right. Joanna glanced over at Karlac, whose gaze was fixed steadily forward. Among all the strange things the other warrior had said or done, what bothered Joanna most was what she had *not* done. When she had called Karlac spiritless, Karlac had not so much as protested the insult. Any other Jade Falcon warrior would have taken a swing at Joanna, almost by reflex. A Jade Falcon was nothing if not fierce. Was this what the life of a solahma did to one?

Walking beside Karlac in this strange place, Joanna had never felt so alone.

25

Jade Falcon Warehouse 893
Dogg Station, Dogg
Jade Falcon Occupation Zone
3 November 3057

The last few steps before reaching the third aisle, they would have to pass a tech emerging from it. This tech's outfit was rumpled and he had obviously not shaved for some days. Although Joanna did not mind facial hair, stubble disgusted her. Dark and patchy, this man's growth of beard was particularly repulsive. She resolved, however, to show no reaction.

"Casual," she muttered to Karlac.

"I am, I am."

The tech glanced at them as they passed, giving them a brief nod, which Joanna quickly returned.

Two more steps and they were in the aisle. It was longer than she had thought, the structures on either side of it higher.

Farther down the aisle, techs worked busily. One drove a tall cart with a long crane on the end of it. He was using the crane to lift one of the big metal storage tanks to a position near the top of one side.

"We have to find out what is in these tanks," Joanna whispered to Karlac.

"If you say so, Joanna."

Though annoyed by Karlac's laconic response, Joanna

merely led her companion to the nearest storage tank, set nearly at floor level.

On a metal plate on the tank's side were numbers that resembled the ones on the sheets of paper she'd examined a few moments ago. They might be registration numbers, Joanna thought. At the top of the conical storage tank was a plexiglass circle that looked like a DropShip viewport.

Stretching her body, she looked down through the glass.

And grunted.

"What is it?" Karlac asked.

"There is a corpse inside, floating in some kind of clear solution. Nine-six-seven-three . . ."

Karlac did not catch on to Joanna's use of the numbers at first and looked momentarily puzzled, but she recovered and quickly faked entering the numbers into her noteputer as a pair of techs sauntered by, paying the two intruders no attention.

Joanna turned to Karlac. "All right," she said. "This is what I have so far. These storage tanks contain dead bodies of warriors who seem to be KIAs from our battles. They are being placed in preservative solutions in these storage tanks, shipped here in the black DropShip, labeled and numbered and stored on these shelves. But what is the purpose?"

"Are they being saved for genetic reasons, do you think?"

"Perhaps. I thought maybe it was to ship them back to the homeworlds so their ashes could be mixed with nutrient solutions. But since when did they preserve bodies for that? Last I knew, chosen bodies are cremated near the point of battle, after any necessary ceremonies, then the ashes are placed in an urn and shipped back. Whatever else is useful from the bodies—organs for possible transplant, bones for insertion in prosthetic devices, blood for reconstitution—is collected, and what remains of the remains is disposed of. Do you not think there is something wasteful as well as ghoulish about preserving an entire body, Karlac?"

"Of course. I would be afraid to be in such a tank. What if they are still conscious, even when dead?"

"What? What nonsense are you talking? When we are dead, we are dead. No consciousness at all. The only way we go into the future is through the gene pool or the nutrient solution. Why would you even imagine consciousness after death?"

"Well, I heard something about life after death once. Ever

since they sent me here my mind is filled with strange thoughts. Perhaps it is the idleness."

Joanna could barely believe her ears. "And so now, you, a Jade Falcon warrior fear death?"

"How could I? As a solahma warrior, the only honor that remains is to die so that younger warriors might live to see another day."

"I see fear in your eyes when you speak of such *stravag* waste as consciousness when you are dead."

"I am much changed since the day I came to Dogg Station," Karlac said sadly.

Joanna stared at Karlac for several seconds, then said, "Perhaps we should have this discussion for another day. We came here to investigate, *quiaff*?"

"*Aff,* Joanna."

"Follow me." Using a tech stroll and making frequent clipboard notations, Joanna began to study the numbers on the metal plates of the storage tanks she could see. Soon she realized that there was a pattern. Victims of a specific battle were kept together, and it looked like those from a specific skirmish within the battle were also grouped together. The numbers helped the techs to locate specific tanks.

Joanna glanced down at the list of Tukayyid numbers. Calculating mentally she figures they had to be in another aisle, probably two further down. After showily checking a lower-level storage tank, she and Karlac went back to the head of the aisle.

Just as they were about to pass into the open area, Joanna glanced toward the portal and stopped in her tracks at the sight of Bailly coming through it. He was again dressed as a tech and was not aping an aging warrior in his demeanor or movements. He glanced around, but did not notice Joanna and Karlac in their tech disguise.

Hurrying a little, Joanna guided Karlac past the next aisle and turned into the one she suspected was the storage section for the Tukayyid bodies. Glancing back, she saw Bailly walk by. He seemed headed to another part of the facility, and definitely seemed to know where he was going.

"That was Bailly," she told Karlac, who gave a start.

"How—"

"Later," Joanna said sharply. "We have work to do."

Karlac nodded but said nothing. She seemed distracted, even troubled. Well, no time to waste on her now, Joanna though. The important thing now was to find the storage tanks for the Tukayyid warriors.

They had gone almost two-thirds of the way down the aisle when they finally came to the Tukayyid section of this strange complex. Along the way they passed one or two techs at work. One adjusted a valve that no doubt controlled some aspect of the preservative solution. Another was engaged in wiping down some storage tanks. Other techs climbed like monkeys up and down the shelves using rungs welded onto girders as their ladders. Other pitonlike extrusions were set along the base of each shelf and they saw a tech moving hand over hand along the pitons to reach a different location.

"Some show," Joanna muttered.

"Show? What show?"

Joanna did not bother to reply. She had little use for Karlac now, and was only keeping her near to prevent her getting into trouble.

Examining the numbers on the sides of the tanks, Joanna saw that they were grouped according to unit. She glanced into one tank and saw there a MechWarrior whose face in death was still fierce—proper and fitting for a Jade Falcon warrior. But this particular section was devoted to a Cluster of Jaegers. "Where are the Falcon Guards?" she wondered aloud.

"Why them?" Karlac asked.

"Star Commander Jula Huddock," Joanna said. "I fought side by side with her."

By working out the number sequences, it was not long before Joanna located the Falcon Guard section. Unfortunately, all the tanks had been set in the upper reaches. Standing in the aisle, looking up, Joanna thought the shelves seemed higher than ever. "Well, if I have to climb, I have to climb."

"You are going up there?"

"Aff."

"Are you sure?"

"Why? Do you think I am too old to scale such heights?"

"No, I guess not. But heights make me dizzy."

"Why am I not surprised by that? Here, take my clipboard. I have Jula Huddock's identification number memorized. Wait here, and look busy. Remember you are a tech."

Without waiting for another dreary response from Karlac, Joanna grabbed the nearest rung and pulled herself up. A sharp pain immediately surged through her upper arm. I am getting too old for this kind of thing, she groaned inwardly, but stopped the thought immediately. No, it is just that I have been around this *stravag* Karlac too long.

Ignoring the pain, Joanna kept climbing, rung by rung, with a certain spry efficiency—the way she had seen the other techs do it. Stopping for a moment to check numbers, she noticed a tech at her level a few shelves away glance over at her curiously. She waved and went on.

Finally she came to the Falcon Guards section. Unable to resist a look into the first storage tank, she saw that it did not contain any Falcon Guard warrior she remembered. She was not even certain the man's face was familiar. Death had perhaps transfigured him.

Making a quick mental calculation, she figured that Jula Huddock's tank had to be three levels up and one over. Laboriously, now too tired to emulate the grace and skill of the typical clambering tech, Joanna managed to rise three levels; then, with a weary sigh, she swung hand over hand to the proper compartment. Thinking back to the day she had hung off the factory roof in the duel with the prydelings, she wondered how many more times she would have to perform such acrobatics.

Pulling herself up to the level of the storage tank, she checked the number on its side. It was the one she had memorized for Jula Huddock.

Swallowing once, she leaned over the top of the tank and peered in through the plexiglass. What she saw almost made her gasp aloud. To verify, she re-checked the number on the metal identification plate. It was correct. According to the manifest Joanna had examined, it was Jula Huddock's number. She looked back through the view glass.

The corpse in the storage tank was definitely labeled as Star Commander Jula Huddock, hero of the Olalla skirmish.

Only problem was, it was *not* Jula Huddock.

26

Jade Falcon Warehouse 893
Dogg Station, Dogg
Jade Falcon Occupation Zone
3 November 3057

After checking one more time, examining the almost characterless, smooth-skinned face of the body that had been substituted for Jula Huddock, Joanna prepared to descend once more. Peering down, she saw Karlac pretending to record data while inspecting some storage tanks.

Then she scrutinized the rest of the aisle, which was almost deserted now. A tech with a badge, apparently a supervisor, walked briskly down the aisle, then stopped to speak to another tech, who abandoned his task and left.

Joanna watched the badge tech come closer till he was only a few steps away from Karlac. What would he say to her? And would Karlac respond properly? Karlac was so intent on her pretense that she did not see him coming. Just as well. The fool might have tipped Joanna's presence with a quick tearful glance upward. Joanna waited tensely for something to happen, but the supervisor passed Karlac without a look, continuing on down the aisle and then disappearing around the corner.

Instead of continuing her descent, Joanna climbed higher until she was a shelf or two from the top. This vantage point afforded a view of the whole place. Joanna wanted to see whether any of the techs they'd killed had been discovered and the alarm spread.

But everything looked quiet and normal in the vast cavern of corpses, where the only sound she could hear was the rhythmic humming, which had become a gruesome sound to Joanna's ears. As before, various techs were carrying out their apparently routine duties among all these embalmed warriors. Scanning the huge area, Joanna noticed another section beyond the aisles filled with shelves and storage tanks. Seeing several closed doors, she guessed that these must be offices. A flash of movement caught her eye and she recognized Bailly moving down a far aisle, apparently headed in the direction of the offices.

Joanna climbed down the rungs, slower than she would have liked because her feet had to feel their way down. She was determined to find out what Bailly was doing in this place.

"Karlac," she hissed when she hit the floor. The other MechWarrior jumped, the clipboard almost flying from her hands. Joanna gestured for her to follow, though she was finding Karlac all but useless.

She went up to the end of the aisle and looked both ways to see if any techs were about. Seeing no one, she again indicated silently for Karlac to stay with her. Joanna did not want to lose Bailly, but they could not attract attention by moving with undue haste or excitement. They passed row after row of shelves, and the eerie sensation of being among all these dead warriors suddenly sent a shiver through Joanna. Cremation was the proper fate of a warrior's remains, not preservation like a pickle in bottle. It was more than undignified, it was offensive. Joanna was also finding the whole experience downright ominous. Again she wondered if perhaps Karlac's fears and fantasies were contagious.

She drew her pistol and nodded to Karlac to do the same. But it was not to defend herself against the spirits of Jade Falcon warriors that might be wandering this grisly place. It was to catch a spy, a Wolf clan intruder who was as unwelcome here as any stray dog. There, walking just ahead of them, was the filth who went by the name of Bailly.

Moving in the direction of the three offices, he had his back to them. Joanna motioned to Karlac as she ducked into the nearest aisle.

"It's Bailly," she said softly.

"But he is dressed like a tech."

"I know. I know. I told you I saw him here the other night after you left. He came in and out of the building, and he was dressed like a tech then too. He is involved in all this and we have to find out how. Can I count on you?"

Karlac stared at Joanna, her look one of complete bafflement. Then her face changed, as though she were remembering something. "*Aff,*" Karlac said and gave Joanna the warrior's salute.

There was no time to say more, no time to circle all the way around to the other end of the aisles to catch Bailly by surprise from the front. They would have to be quick and forceful and direct, which was just the way Joanna liked it. Bailly was almost to the offices now. Joanna hesitated only long enough to see what he would do next. He seemed to try the handle of the closest door and, apparently finding it unlocked, went in.

Here was their chance. Moving silently but swiftly, Joanna and Karlac made it to the door without incident. Joanna took the handle delicately, then twisted it ever so slowly to keep from making any noise. She opened the door a crack and then a little more and then a little more until it was wide enough for them to pass through without a sound.

Bailly sat in profile behind a large L-shaped desk, peering intently at a monitor screen whose glow was eerie in the dimness. Giving Karlac a shove toward the desk, Joanna swooped around behind Bailly. Startled, he looked up toward Karlac, eyes wide but without uttering a sound. Falcon swift, Joanna came from behind at the same instant and wrapped his neck in a stranglehold.

"Karlac! If he breaks the hold shoot him!" Joanna barked. She tightened her hold on Bailly's neck, then gave a sharp upward yank that took all the wind out of him.

"I am going to release my hold, but do not try anything," Joanna said. "I will break your neck if you even think of making any trouble."

Joanna let up slowly. Bailly's whole body slumped when she let go. He instantly grabbed his throat with one hand. He was breathing, but only with difficulty. Joanna drew her pistol and backed up a step, then grasped the back of the swivel chair and swung him around.

"Greetings, Bailly," she said.

He grunted, at first unable to speak. Then the words came out, haltingly and hoarse. "What are you doing here?" His voice was weak, almost defeated. But Joanna was taking no chances. This *stravag* was too tricky.

"That is exactly what I would like to know from you—what are *you* up to? What is this place?"

"You have seen the tanks by now, Joanna."

"*Aff,* and I know that they contain the bodies of warriors killed in combat. But for what purpose?"

Bailly shrugged.

"I do not have time for games, Bailly. I need to know what is going on here."

Bailly smiled. "Of course you need to know. You are a filthy spy, Star Commander Joanna. I suspected it from the beginning. You are too skillful a warrior to be solahma. Your reputation has traveled farther than you might imagine. No, the Clan would have a better fate arranged for you . . ."

Aff, a much better fate. Canister nanny.

"If I am a spy, what are you, Bailly?" Joanna demanded.

Bailly straightened up, almost to attention and said, "MechWarrior Alvar of Bravo Eye One, Second Falcon Jaegers Cluster, detached. Assigned to Dogg Station by the Jade Falcon Watch."

Joanna's eyes narrowed. *Kael Pershaw is famous for being devious, but would he assign two of us to this place? Not likely. Bailly obviously does not suspect that I am here at Pershaw's orders. Best to keep him talking.*

"Well, then, MechWarrior Alvar, with all our methods of storing genetic legacies while warriors are still alive, with our usual custom of collecting ashes for nutrients, why is it necessary to gather these bodies from the battlefield, preserve them in cryogenic containers, and transport them on black DropShips to this place?"

Bailly/Alvar shrugged again.

"I told you I do not have time for games, scum. I saw you here last night when the ship came and went. You will tell me what you know. Keep an eye on him, Karlac."

Joanna walked to the door, opened it carefully and looked out. All was quiet but for the internal humming of the tanks.

She turned toward Alvar. "Put your hands behind your head and get up." She prodded him at the waist with her pistol, nudging him around to the front of the desk. He would not try anything now.

"First I will tell you what I know," she said, coming up to close range and tapping the weapon against his chest. "And then you will tell me the rest."

27

Jade Falcon Warehouse 893
Dogg Station, Dogg
Jade Falcon Occupation Zone
3 November 3057

"We have been studying this place and examining the manifests that the techs have collected for each shipment, both those in and out," Joanna said.

"And?" Bailly asked.

Joanna never lost her stride. "They identify, by name and identification codes, Jade Falcon warriors fallen in combat during the invasion of the Inner Sphere. At first I thought that was who was preserved in the storage tanks, but some of those bodies are of warriors killed six or seven years ago, in battles like Twycross. And many were marked as already shipped out of the facility.

"Another puzzling thing was that their genetic usefulness would seem to have passed. The only use I could think of for preserving all these warriors was as a backup source for genetic materials in case something happened to the original legacies—perhaps an accident in a genetics storage center or if the scientists needed some DNA samples for other purposes. Yet, would obtaining such sources be worth the use of ships and manpower, plus the expense, necessary to provide DropShip transport and maintain such storage centers as this one?

"Then, after looking into one of the tanks up there, I recalled something I am not supposed to know, and it suggested something else, and I realized what this place is all about. How am I doing so far, Alvar?"

Alvar glanced at Karlac, then back at Joanna. "You watched the delivery last night, you found your way down here, you have investigated. Now we all know that this is a secret storage center. But tell me, Star Commander Joanna, why have you been doing all this snooping around?"

"The fact that you must ask reveals something about you."

"Your riddles are as ugly as your face. If you are not a Jade Falcon warrior, I must say that your act is a good one. You have the sound of a Jade Falcon, the swagger, the surliness . . ."

"I am Jade Falcon. I think you know that, Alvar—or whoever you are."

"It is true, Joanna," Karlac put in. "You are talking in puzzles and riddles. You are hiding something."

"What I am hiding is not at issue at the moment. It is what MechWarrior Bailly-Alvar-whoever is hiding—that is what we need to know. It is he who is giving the performance, the act, as he called it."

Bailly/Alvar looked momentarily flustered, then his face became meaner and more surly than ever. "What rot you speak! I could say the same of you. You could be the one who—"

"Enough of this *stravag* talk," Joanna barked. "Shoot him if he makes a wrong move, Karlac."

"Gladly."

"Now then, Alvar, if that is what you wish to be called, would you like to tell us your real name?"

"It is MechWarrior Alvar, as I said."

"No. I am sure there is no longer a MechWarrior Alvar—if there ever was one. Maybe he was killed in action in some battle. He could even be in one of these tanks. And who would ever have known if I had not been sent to root out filthy spies exactly like you?"

"Who sent you?"

"Kael Pershaw, one and the same. Saying you were assigned here by the Jade Falcon Watch was your major mistake, though not your only one. I am from the Watch, the *only* agent from the Watch."

"Pershaw told me that—"

"Do not even try. You are not a Jade Falcon agent. Whatever your name is. Clan Wolf sent you here to sabotage this facility."

"Sabotage . . ." Karlac said, a light coming into her eyes. "But I still do not understand the purpose of the facility."

Joanna was remembering Diana's discoveries in Ravill Pryde's personal file. "Our scientist caste is engaged in unauthorized genetic experiments. On Ironhold there is at least one genetics experimentation laboratory where they are mixing genetic strains for the purpose of creating even better warriors. They have been blending Falcon bloodlines with those of other Clans in order to breed certain skills and traits not usually prized in Jade Falcon warriors. I am told that, in the past at least, they arranged to obtain new legacies for their own private gene pool."

Karlac let out a gasp, but kept a grip on her pistol.

"The project began long before the Clan invasion, but I am certain it is continuing. That would explain why many of the new Jade Falcons seem so different from the true Falcon warrior. I believe they come from strains that the scientists have genetically altered and then placed in sibkos that also include a pure strain of Jade Falcon genes. Apparently even the scientist caste is not so deranged as to tamper with an entire sibko.

"It would not be hard for them to obtain genetic materials from Jade Falcon warriors. There are probably storage facilities for experimental sources of genetic materials in the homeworlds—and now this new one for collecting the bodies of Jade Falcon warriors."

"But why body storage instead of simply storing samples of genetic material?" Karlac asked.

"My guess is that gene samples are unstable and could be damaged in shipment unless special equipment is used. Remember how specialized is the machinery used during a giftake ceremony? If you could not, or did not, wish to use that machinery then it is easier to have the bodies always preserved and ready."

"I still do not understand why the Wolves would be involved."

"It is tricky. Apparently, many of our scientists admire Wolf warriors for various traits—a certain resourcefulness and knack for complicated strategy—traits not particularly valued by our warrior caste. The experimentation so far has centered on mixing Wolf genes with Jade Falcon genes. The results are striking. Repulsive, but striking."

"That is disgusting . . ." Karlac fell silent, her expression one of deep shock.

Joanna agreed wholeheartedly. The idea revolted her too, but she was glad to see that Karlac had not lost every trace of the pride bred into a Falcon warrior. "My guess about what happened next is that the Wolves, through infiltration or the interception of documents, discovered the secret project, were perhaps themselves shocked by it, then saw a way to use it. So typically devious. So typically Wolf Clan. Even as I think of it, it makes me sick, just like this bit of scum here."

Joanna leaned down to him. "What do you say? Am I right? You, a piece of Clan Wolf scum, and others like you, have infiltrated the secret genetic project for the purpose of sabotaging it?"

"You are scum yourself, Joanna."

Joanna suppressed the urge to counter Alvar's words with another blow. Instead, she went to the door, now slightly ajar, and checked the cavern outside.

"Everything all right out there?" Karlac asked.

"Fine, if you do not mind that a lot of techs are scurrying up and down the middle aisle as if looking for something valuable they have lost. Maybe they are just searching for a particular storage tank."

She turned back toward Alvar and resumed her speculations: "Having learned what our Jade Falcon scientists were doing, the Wolves decided to destroy the project through sabotage. They have been collecting their own dead and have found a way to get them placed in storage tanks like these, which originally held Jade Falcon warriors. The scientists, believing they are working with Jade Falcon genetic materials, would be unknowingly substituting Wolf genes into their precious mixes."

"Let me kill this filthy dog now," Karlac growled, barely able to contain her rage.

"Not yet, Karlac, but I applaud your newfound wrath. We need to explore this treachery more." Joanna returned her attention to Alvar. "As we were going through the aisles I did look into several of the storage tanks at the bodies preserved in them. Even before I climbed up to Jula Huddock's tank,

I was already dubious about what I had seen. Few of the bodies looked like warriors, especially not Jade Falcon warriors."

She leaned down toward Bailly/Alvar, whose face who puffed with rage.

"Why so angry, scum?"

He started to speak, then closed his mouth firmly, apparently using every ounce of will to hold his tongue.

"What is going on?" Karlac asked.

"This *stravag* is unhappy because I have insulted the Wolves by implying that Wolf warriors are inferior to Jade Falcon warriors, even though he knows the truth about these bodies."

Joanna paused, looking from Alvar to Karlac and back again. "But these are not Clan Wolf warriors either, are they, Wolf scum? No, I believe that the Wolves came up with the most malicious, revolting, *perfect* way to sabotage this project. The corruption caused by warrior genes would be mild. It would still result in effective, if lesser quality, warriors."

Alvar/Bailly started to drop his hands, but Karlac nudged him roughly with her pistol. "As you were, dog," she said.

Joanna thought of Ravill Pryde and the deviations from Jade Falcon characteristics he had shown, and knew she was right. She had also thought of a way to get the truth out of this Wolf trash.

"No, they have not scoured their battlefields for warriors," she said slowly, almost dramatically. "These tanks contain the bodies of freeborns—"

At that Alvar gave a kind of wounded howl and backhanded Karlac in the face, knocking her to the ground and the gun from her hand. With lightning speed, he scooped up the pistol.

"We are all three Clan warriors," he said quietly, obviously trying to master his rage. "The product of the most advanced breeding programs to produce the most superior specimens. Hear me out, Joanna."

Joanna had her pistol trained on him, but she signaled Karlac with a slight shake of the head that she was not ready to kill him.

"You have made some good guesses about what is going on here at Dogg Station, but I believe it is not the whole story. The truth may be even worse than you imagine."

"Oh, stuff it under a falcon wing," Karlac said. Again Joanna signaled her to wait and listen.

"The Jade Falcons and the Wolves have hated each other for a long time, and you believe that is enough to make Clan Wolf stoop to polluting the genetic legacy of another Clan. But no Wolf warrior would even *dream* of doing that. It is not the way of the Clans. It is not *our* way."

"You are right about me, Joanna. I am a Wolf, sent here by my Clan to find out why some of our merchant ships and tech assets have been making unauthorized runs to this uninhabited, apparently insignificant world in Jade Falcon territory. Can you honestly believe that the leaders of the Wolves would ever approve the sacrifice of our own precious legacies merely out of spite?"

He gestured out toward the storage tanks. "Some of these might be the giftakes of our own warriors killed on Tukayyid."

"Enough," Joanna said sharply. "How much longer must I listen to this speech about the honor of Wolf dogs?"

"Long enough for you to understand. I am telling you what the Wolves have already learned about all this. I was sent here on the same mission as you, Joanna—to find out what is going on at Dogg Station.

"Wolf intelligence first began to suspect something several years ago when we noticed peculiarities in our master log of ship movements, almost as though merchant and tech ships were being diverted from scheduled runs. We began to carefully track these movements until we were able to identify a pattern, and finally managed to piece together a route—a route that led in and out of Dogg Station from the battlefields of *both* our Clans—and to and from the homeworlds."

"You expect us to believe this birdlime?" Karlac scoffed. "It is just another one of your tricks to save your hide."

"You can believe me or not. A warrior has no need to lie."

"You are no warrior—you are a *spy,*" Joanna hissed. "Deceit and lying are you bloodname. Only deceit could have gotten you here in the first place—a Wolf warrior among a Jade Falcon solahma unit on a world deep within the Jade Falcon occupation zone? How did you get here, if not by deceit? And how have you gone undetected so far, except by lies?"

"True enough. I am here on a mission. Just like you, Joanna. Old or not—you are no solahma. You are nothing like the rest of the sorry specimens in the unit."

Joanna laughed harshly. "Am I supposed to thank you or slap you for saying that?"

"Slap him," Karlac muttered.

"Tell me more, scum. The black DropShip—Wolf or Jade Falcon?"

"Your insults do not harm me, Joanna. I know who I am. But to answer your question, sometimes it is one, sometimes the other. Can you imagine my reaction when I discovered *that*? I was sent here by the Wolves to find out what the Jade Falcons might be up to, only to learn that Wolf Clan ships are part of this whole filthy operation! Even worse, that Wolf warriors are being substituted for those of Jade Falcons for use in an experimental breeding program. An uncontrolled program, one for purposes defined by the scientists rather than the warrior caste."

Alvar handed the pistol to Karlac. "I believe this is yours," he said. Then he looked Joanna straight in the eyes, holding her gaze for several moments, something a Clan warrior seldom dared do to another. There was a sudden shout somewhere in the cavern outside, and Joanna used it as an escape from Alvar's disturbing gaze. She gestured toward the door.

"Karlac, have a look."

"Right, Joanna."

"See anything?"

"Something. Techs are scrambling around all the aisles now. Frantic, I would say."

"They have found out."

"Found out what?" Alvar asked.

"We left some debris behind us on our way here. *Human* debris."

Alvar grunted in disgust. "Cannot you Jade Falcons do anything right?"

Joanna strode toward him, for a moment intending to make him the next item of human debris. Then she realized his fate should not be her present priority. She holstered her weapon to remove the threat.

"We do not have much more time to talk," she said. "But tell me one more thing, Wolf spy. If the Wolves know all this, then why send a spy to Dogg Station?"

"Just as you assumed it had to be Wolf treachery, so we believed it could only be a Jade Falcon plot. After all, Dogg Station is one of your planets, *quiaff*?"

Alvar shook his head almost sadly. "Only the mind of a scientist could concoct a scheme like this one. But no scientist could have persuaded the High Council of any Clan to approve these genetic *experiments*." He spat out the word as if he could not stand the foul taste.

"The scientists of both our Clans, and who knows what others, have apparently placed themselves above the way of the Clans, have decided that only they know what is for the good of all. We warriors are bound by deep traditions and taboos, but the scientists are mere freeborns and they have no honor. We are supposed to be their masters, the warrior caste as the highest among the Clans, and yet these freebirths have been playing a monstrous game with the genetic legacies of both our Clans. It is shameless. It is *chalcas*."

It was a lot to take in, yet Joanna believed this Alvar/Bailly, this Wolf spy, this warrior of another Clan. Among themselves, warriors had no use for deceit. They did not need it.

"You are telling me it is not Wolves against Falcons, but an initiative from within the scientist caste," Joanna said slowly. "Scientists overreaching themselves, putting their own agenda above the way of the Clans. They are charged with creating the most superior warriors the universe has ever known, and they have become drunk with power. The end justifies the means—no matter how traitorous and disgusting."

Karlac was shaking her head in disbelief. "Filthy freebirths," she said.

The sound of the voices in the cavern grew even louder. Probably distorted by funneling within the narrow aisles, the sounds became eerie.

"Karlac?"

"They look fierce now. I am sure they have discovered the bodies of their comrades."

"We will be sitting ducks in this office," Alvar said, impressing Joanna with his calm.

"*Aff*," she said. "I do not think there is much more any of us can do here."

"Agreed. It is time to get this information back to our own Clans."

Joanna went to the door, roughly pushing Karlac aside. Obviously insulted, Karlac's eyes flashed with her newly revived anger. "I want you to do what I say," Joanna said to her in what she realized was her best falconer's voice. "It is important that—"

She did not finish the sentence. A tech with a pistol seemed to materialize out of thin air. Slamming against the side of the doorway first, he rushed into the room, his weapon aimed directly at Joanna. With her own pistol still holstered, he had the drop on her.

But not, as it turned out, on Karlac.

"Caught you," the tech snarled.

"Not yet," Karlac said and sent a beam through the tech's neck with the pistol Alvar had returned to her moments ago. "Where did this filth come from?" she said, stepping over the tech's fallen body.

He must have been crouching by the door."

"Listening? Good thing I killed him then."

"I am impressed by your ruthlessness," Joanna said. "Maybe I misjudged you, Karlac."

"You thought I was a spy, *quiaff*?"

"*Aff*."

"And when you stopped thinking that, you just wrote me off as a burned-out solahma warrior, *quiaff*?"

"Aff. You were too cautious, and you showed no revulsion at having to wear tech clothing and—"

"Enough. You are right. But sometimes I remember I was a warrior."

"And you still are."

"I hate to interrupt your mutual admiration," Alvar put in, "but I wonder how we are going to get out of here? There are armed techs like this one everywhere, and only one way out of the cavern. They will never let us leave alive."

"We will escape," Joanna said as she turned for the door. "Do not doubt it. We have one advantage the rest do not."

Joanna looked out and saw techs scurrying in and out of the main portal. The distance between here and the surface of Dogg seemed formidable. The way to the elevator would be as pitch dark as ever and the elevator the same monstrosity of a contraption. The odds were astronomically against her. Against them.

"What possible advantage could you mean?" Karlac asked.

"My advantage?" Joanna said, as she opened the door all the way and stepped through it.

"Yes."

"I am Jade Falcon."

28

Watch Command
Jade Falcon Command Center, Wotan
Jade Falcon Occupation Zone
15 November 3057

Kael Pershaw used his good arm to adjust the half-mask, which had slipped a centimeter or two to the side.

"I cannot speak freely, Joanna, but I will say this: what you have discovered may go far beyond some genetic machinations perpetrated by our Jade Falcon scientist caste. I have for some time suspected a network of conspiracy linking the scientist castes of many Clans—perhaps every Clan."

"But why? What are they up to?"

"I am not free to discuss that, especially with so much still based on speculation. But I have begun to suspect the scientist castes of somehow setting themselves apart, almost as if they had formed a separate Clan of their own. Frankly, it turns my blood cold to think of it."

Kael Pershaw's blood had always been ice, as far as Joanna was concerned. Turning any colder suggested temperatures that would make the icebound Sudeten Lake seem tropical.

"But your discoveries at least give some substance to my suspicions, Joanna. The information that you uncovered in your mission, which I have passed on to the Khan, has been divulged only to select Council members."

Steepling his fingers, he sat back in thought, making the expression on his ruined face more disturbing than ever. "We have, of course, eradicated the filthy freebirth techs on Dogg who unlawfully dared to take up arms."

Joanna's head still reeled at the implications of what she had turned up on her mission as Kael Pershaw's agent. She had no head for complicated plots, and the idea of a conspiracy involving the lower castes was almost beyond her comprehension. She was glad that her mission had been successful, but she was also glad it was over. It was time to return to normal, to the life of a Jade Falcon warrior, no matter where her fate would now lead. "What has been happening in the short time I have been away?" she asked.

"Much has been happening. At this very moment our Clan is fighting a Trial of Refusal against the Wolves. The Wolves' arrogance and their rejection of the way of the Clans have earned them many enemies, even within their own ranks. Ulric Kerensky's traitorous batchall, which led to our defeat at Tukayyid and the truce we must now live with, has finally caused all true Clan warriors to clamor for Wolf blood.

"Ulric was stripped of the office of ilKhan by the Grand Council. As is his right, he demanded a Trial of Refusal, and Clan Jade Falcon was elected to uphold the decision of the Council. Ulric has bid most of the Wolf forces and sent them swarming into our occupation zone. Some are offering honorable battle, while others are attempting to flee into the Inner Sphere. We are hunting down the Wolves throughout our space, wherever they are found. The battles will become great, and every warrior has a chance for honor or death."

"And I will be sent back to the nurseries."

"No, Joanna. This time fate appears to be on your side."

"You wish me to remain with the Watch, then?" Her voice dripped with scorn.

"No, Joanna, you will return to the Falcon Guards."

"I wish that, Star Colonel Pershaw."

"I thought you would. Be assured that your service on Dogg will be recorded in your codex. I will also brief Star Colonel Ravill Pryde, but not in too great detail, so that he may ease your reappearance among the Falcon Guards after assignment to the solahma unit. Otherwise, the success of your mission will remain secret for now. Others will not know of it."

"That is fine with me," Joanna said. "I am not proud of being a spy."

Pershaw's one visible eye seemed to widen.

"But you were good at it. If the Falcon Guards did not need you right now, I would have you permanently assigned to the Watch."

"The thought repels me. This is not warrior work, spying. I do not wish to die in the midst of a pretense."

"As a Jade Falcon warrior, I understand and pardon the offense you give me. I too would prefer to die in the field. As you can plainly see the only display of my combat abilities left to me now is the wreck my body has become. But I also must serve the Clan, and as leader of the Watch, as spymaster, if you will, I do so. Yet my hands long to be at the controls of a BattleMech. Sometimes this mask I wear to hide the burn scars on my face becomes like the deception I must practice to do my job. The spy mask hides the warrior face, and I hate it."

"I am amazed, Star Colonel, that you reveal these thoughts to me."

"Why, Joanna? We are very much alike, *quiaff*?"

"*Aff*. We are both mean as cave bats and twice as angry."

"I do not know if I would put it that way, but that does sum it up. Are you sure that you would not like to return here the next time you are up for reassignment?"

"*Aff*, I am sure. Are you trying to get me to show gratitude, Kael Pershaw?"

"Far from it. The universe would explode if you did."

"Do not tempt me. I might thank you then and welcome the explosion."

"Do not thank me just yet, or fate either. I have not told you the planet where the Falcon Guard participation in this Trial of Refusal will take place."

"What difference could that make? As long as there is a battle, I am happy. Where is the Falcon Guard battle going to be?"

Pershaw looked briefly away. It was strange to see him collect himself before speaking. He usually had no difficulty stating things bluntly.

"Twycross."

"Freebirth!" Joanna blurted.

Kael Pershaw nodded, but his twisted face was, as always, inscrutable. "Cursing does seem to be the logical reaction," he said.

29

Plain of Curtains, Twycross
Jade Falcon Occupation Zone
6 December 3057

Joanna could not have easily explained to anyone, not even Diana or Horse, what she felt being back on Twycross. Although she took no stock in the supernatural, she almost thought she saw ghosts in the strange shifting lights around her. Because the fierce wind, the awesome Diabolis, never ceased, the sands of Twycross were, it seemed, perpetually in motion. The redness of the sands and rocks made what little there was of available light also seem red. Shapes in the distance were indefinable. A rock could look like a BattleMech, BattleMechs standing together could look like a forest. The result was an obvious need for caution, a situation that automatically rattled any Jade Falcon warrior, for whom caution was cowardice.

For the moment the wind was too fierce and the swirling sand too dense for any engagements on the Plain of Curtains. Tomorrow the battle would be joined, but for now the Jade Falcons huddled in large geodesic tents and bemoaned their fate while trying to control their edginess at the inactivity. The Falcon Guards were particularly restless and more than a little irritable. Arriving on Twycross, they had discovered that they were the only front-line unit assigned to this Steel Viper-controlled planet for the Trial of Refusal. The other three units—the Fifth Talons, the Sixth Provisional

Garrison, and the Eighteenth Falcon Jaegers—were essentially garrison units, with much less combat experience than the Guards.

Ravill Pryde had been furious when he discovered how the Falcon Guards were being treated, forced to fight side by side with lesser units in what must surely be a minor part of the entire Trial of Refusal.

"Some of the taint that has stained the Falcon Guards since the original Twycross conflict is obviously still attached to us," he announced in an unusually emotional moment. "They will not waste other combat-ready units here, and saddle us with untested allies. Not only that, see who commands against us. The ancient Wolf Khan Natasha Kerensky. The Wolves insult us by sending an old woman to lead the fight against us. If she were a Jade Falcon, Natasha Kerensky would be dead by now or"—he glanced resentfully at Joanna when uttering his next words—"tending canisters."

Joanna chose to ignore the insult, but felt called upon to speak up for Natasha Kerensky. "Natasha Kerensky has displayed great skills as a warrior and a leader."

"Great skills?" Ravill Pryde said. "As a spy?" It was, of course, another calculated insult to Joanna, but she could not respond since no one else knew of her secret mission at Dogg Station. The other warriors thought she had been returned to duty in a time of need because of her vast combat experience. "She was in the Inner Sphere for years, posing as a Wolf's Dragoon. Like all Wolf Clan warriors, she is *skilled* in duplicity and deceit. I would not dirty my hands with her in honorable combat."

"Natasha Kerensky is a worthy opponent, Star Colonel. Wolf that she is, her accomplishments cannot be denied or belittled."

"Joanna you are old and cannot see this Wolf for the surat that she is."

After regarding her for a long moment, Ravill Pryde turned away while continuing to voice his complaints to the other warriors, who hung on his every word. Joanna had noticed differences in Ravill Pryde since her return. He was less cheerful, sharper to his subordinates, a bit melancholy around the eyes. Oh, he still pulled the smile and enthusiasm routine at times, but not so often and not so heartily. Was he nervous about the impending battle? Was he wondering whether he would test out in war as well as he had done in the Trials? Even he knew that warfare was more brutal and more complicated than qualifying tests and genetic legacy skirmishes. Joanna enjoyed her imaginings of a Ravill Pryde becoming tense and anxious.

Tired of the company of restive warriors, Joanna left the geodesic tent. She decided it would be better to suffer the brunt of the wind and the sting of the sand on her skin than be infected with even more impatience than she already felt. Diana joined her. They stood under an awning that was only partially effective against the ravages of the Twycross weather and stared into the patterns created by the whirling sands.

"See anything?" Diana's asked.

"Nothing."

"Does it look the same as last time?"

"Truth to tell, I have tried to forget this damnable place. What is worth remembering? All this red sand, these rocks, this wind, and a crushing defeat. No, I would rather view Twycross as a place where I have never been."

"How far do you figure we are from the Great Gash?" Diana asked.

"Not far."

It was known that the Wolves' Third Battle Cluster, 352nd Assault Cluster, and 341st Assault Cluster were camped between the Plain of Curtains and the Great Gash. The two sides had not made any agreement to take up these positions; it had just happened. Little was known of the exact Wolf Clan positions at present because the planet's atmospheric conditions made accurate detection impossible.

"Will we have to go through the Gash, do you think?"

"Maybe, but let us get into battle first, Diana, and see."

"I am itching for a fight. All this waiting irks me."

"Yes, I am eager also. Look at my hands. They are in permanent curl, as if already at the controls of my 'Mech."

"How do you like it? Your new *Summoner,* I mean."

"Well, so far I would say it is only a second-rate machine." Joanna hated the thought of going into battle in an unfamiliar BattleMech. She had been trying to become more familiar with the controls of the *Summoner,* but every time they refused to respond with the rapidity of her former 'Mech, she ended up so frustrated and angry that all she could so was pound at them with her fists. Joanna would have given her right arm to have her *Mad Dog* back. But the 'Mech had been assigned to Castilla while Joanna was away on Dogg, and Ravill Pryde would not reassign it to her.

"It would be waste," he had said. "We are glad that you have returned to fight with us in one more glorious battle, but MechWarrior Castilla has redesigned and reconfigured the 'Mech in the course of its repairs. Since it suits her skills excellently, it would be wasteful for you to reconfigure it to your requirements, then have Castilla redo it all over again after you leave for the homeworlds. There are three BattleMechs currently in reserve, survivors of the Tukayyid battle, although their pilots were not. Choose one of them, Joanna. No, do not even argue the point. It is my decision, *quiaff*?"

Joanna had reined in her anger and accepted the *Summoner* without further complaint.

"Aidan Pryde piloted a *Summoner* throughout most of his career, did he not?" Diana now asked.

"Yes, and he died in a *Timber Wolf* that he thought was bad luck. This *Summoner* is bad luck and a half."

"Stop it, Joanna. You are spooking me. You will not die. You will go on forever. Mean people do."

"Yes, I am mean and I hear that it is the miserable fate of mean people to die in bed."

"If you do not die in battle, you will die of apoplexy during one of your rages. I would not worry about bed."

Joanna chose not to tell Diana of her latest nightmares, where she lay in state on a bier and all the people she had ever known gathered around her body, with the ones she hated the most crowding to the front, apparently led by Ravill Pryde.

"I have requested of Ravill Pryde that our Star lead the way into battle. I want to be right in front."

"That should increase your chances of dying in battle."

"Do not be sarcastic, Diana. It is the way of the Jade Falcon warrior to desire the forefront of combat. If you want to transfer out to a different Star, then—"

"Not at all. I am happy to be here, and excited by the chance of being in the first assault wave. I was just making a small joke, very small. To tell you the truth, Joanna, I am so glad to be out of Ravill Pryde's office and away from the coregn job that I would wish for this battle to go on forever."

"You will have to resume your coregn duties afterward?"

"That is what Ravill Pryde says. I would try any ploy to be removed from the position, but if Ravill Pryde did not consider betrayal as cause enough for dismissal, what else would work?"

"Well, at least you see him for what he really is. Horse keeps defending him."

"Horse likes his spirit. And he says Ravill Pryde is one of the best leaders he has ever served under. Excepting Aidan Pryde, of course."

"Of course. Who could be better than Aidan Pryde?"

"Now *you* sound sarcastic."

"Sorry, did not mean to. Any talk of Ravill Pryde unnerves me, I guess. Aidan was a brave warrior, and a fine leader, but he had his flaws."

"I am happy to hear that."

"Oh? I forget that you have those ugly freebirth feelings toward a parent. Makes me ill."

"Glad to hear that too."

They paused, both lost in contemplation of the way the sands spiraled and, with their differing shades of red, created shifting, swirling patterns like the brilliant feathers of a proud bird.

"The bidding will take place tomorrow then?" Diana asked.

"Tomorrow. At dawn."

"How well do you remember this terrain?"

"Ravill Pryde also asked me that. I could not tell him much. It seems as if I was landed on the planet, immediately thrust into my cockpit, and pushed into battle. I was not on this side of the Great Gash for long, actually. A little combat on this plain and then we were suddenly in the Gash and just as suddenly buried under tons of rock and gravel. Most of my memory of Twycross is about suffocating and trying to dig myself out."

"And for that you had to bear the shame?"

"That is as it should be. We lost. We were stupid even. I hate the shame, but I accept it. I had little choice. I am Jade Falcon."

"That phrase covers everything, *quiaff*?"

"Aff."

"I hope to see the Gash. I wish we had more than just topological maps of it."

"You would like to see it? Maybe it would do me good to go back for a look too. Shall we?"

Diana was taken aback. "You mean, right now?"

"Yes. Now."

Joanna was already tightening her cloak around her, then pulling up the hood.

"Through enemy lines?"

"A fine challenge. Are you up to it?"

"Are you? It is a pretty long walk."

"For someone of my age. Diana, your sarcasm is—"

"Enough, enough. But what of standing orders? Would we not be violating—"

"Of course we would. What difference does that make?"

"Ravill Pryde will be furious."

"I sincerely hope so. But why worry about that? We are already punished for our acts. Me, by being sent away as soon as this battle is over. You, well, you are freeborn and—"

"Enough, enough. I see your point. Yes, I will go with you. But should we—"

Diana could not finish her sentence because Joanna had already stepped out from beneath the shelter of the awning and taken three steps into the sandstorm. The younger warrior adjusted her own cloak and hood and, feeling strangely thrilled by the act, quickened her steps to catch up with Joanna.

30

The Great Gash, Twycross
Jade Falcon Occupation Zone
6 December 3057

If Joanna had not been trapped in the pitch dark of the mines of Dogg Station, she might have considered the Great Gash at midnight to be the darkest place she had ever been. Shaking the sand out of her cloak and brushing it from her hood, she remembered the sensation of being buried alive here in her *Hellbringer*. But that time she'd at least had the dim glow of her cockpit instruments. Even that dimness had been brighter than any light reaching the floor of the Gash from the few stars visible in the murky Twycross skies. But the good thing was that the surrounding mountain walls were a barrier to the Diabolis and its maelstrom of sand.

"Eerie place," Diana commented. A deep gouge in the Windbreak Mountains, the Great Gash was aptly named.

"Did you expect otherwise?"

"Well, the good thing is that we are here, the bad thing is that we will have to return through that mess. That was one excruciating trek, Joanna. If I had not been following you, I would have gotten lost within seconds. What did you use for navigation?"

"Luck. Instinct, maybe. Old warriors still have a few tricks. I had to get here, so I got here."

"That gives me confidence."

"We are here, *quiaff*?"

"*Aff.* And my skin feels permanently pitted from the sand. Amazing that so much sand can get in through the small openings in our clothes. But one thing was very strange."

"What was that?"

"Where were the Wolves?"

"You saw the one tent, and we nearly tripped over a BattleMech foot."

"Yes. But we were never in any danger."

"We had our hoods up, our cloaks wrapped around us—hard to identify insignia or anything else. In a sandstorm, all warriors look alike under cloaks."

"If you say so. Now what?"

"You wanted to see the Gash. Well, this is it."

"It is so different than I expected. Not so high, not so wide as I had imagined it. Still it is high enough and wide enough to be very impressive."

"The spot where the battle took place should be close by. Are you game?"

"Game."

The place where the Inner Sphere warrior had set off an avalanche with explosive charges, burying most of the former Falcon Guards in this high mountain pass, was less than half a kilometer away. Joanna had not been sure she would be able to recognize the spot. All she had known was that she suddenly needed to revisit the site of her shame.

"I cannot see you anymore, Joanna."

"Take hold of my cloak."

"Why not use our beams?"

"Too dangerous. If there are any guards posted or Wolves camped in the Gash, we would become easy targets."

"Looks deserted. Maybe the Wolves find it as spooky as I do."

They headed further into the Gash. As the ground began to rise beneath them, Joanna was certain this must be the site of the Twycross disgrace. A few more steps, and then she stopped.

"Joanna?"

"Yes?"

"Just wanted to make sure where you were. I can see your outline now. A shadow on a shadow. Is this the place? Where it happened?"

"Yes. It makes me shudder."

"Joanna, such a human reaction. What is happening to you?"

"Who knows how many warriors and their 'Mechs are still buried here, beneath our feet? I do not believe we excavated all the dead."

"They could be ghosts inhabiting the Gash. Maybe they are watching us."

"Sometimes you talk like a fool, Diana. You and Ravill Pryde deserve each other."

"That is unkind."

"I hope so."

Though Joanna could detect from which direction Diana's voice was coming, she could not see even her outline. She looked up. Between the cliffs that formed the walls of the Gash, the strip of barely perceptible stars was wider at this point. The walls sloped backward rather than going straight up and down as in the other sections of the Gash. They were not as high either, although high enough. She reckoned the difference was due to the Inner Sphere secretly mining the walls with explosives and the subsequent avalanches. *Freebirths! And now we must fight another pack of them. Which is worse? Inner Sphere depravity or Clan Wolf treachery? The Inner Sphere, I suppose. The Wolves are a Clan, at least. And right now I would rather tear apart a Wolf warrior then one from the Inner Sphere. But either would do. Either would do.*

She was about to look away when she saw something.

"Did you see that?"

"What, Joanna?"

"A gleam of light. Brief, but I definitely saw it. A reflection of something, maybe. But where could the light have come from?"

"It was probably nothing. An optical illusion."

"We should return. Get back before daylight. There is nothing to see here. Nothing to—"

She stopped talking.

"Are you all right, Joanna?"

"Quiet."

The indefinable sound increased, and then suddenly she and Diana were pelted with a rain of gravel and stones. Some of them stung their heads. The stonefall lasted two or three seconds, then stopped.

Joanna brushed the dirt from her hair, realizing that most

of it went into the folds of her cloak. Diana came forward. "What was that? I mean, besides a lot of rocks and dirt falling on our heads."

"Somebody dislodged something up there."

Taking Diana's arms she led her to the other side of the Gash, where both stared upward. Another fall of stones came. Even in the dark, Joanna could see that what had caused the stonefall was some activity near the rim of the Gash's wall. A dim aura of light clung to the rim.

"What could it be, Joanna?"

"What does it look like?"

"Somebody is up there."

"My thought exactly. But who?"

"Maybe the ghosts have a club or—"

"No more joking, Diana. What do you really think?"

"The Wolves?"

"None other. They are up there doing something, and I doubt it is harmless. I think I will have a look. Are you up to it?"

"You mean, climb these walls?"

"What? Have you forgotten your training as a young hawk?"

"Well, no. But then we had some equipment, and it was not pitch dark. These walls are so steep."

"I think we can make it. It may be steep, but the ascent is better here than anywhere else in the Gash. The burial ground has elevated the level of the Gash's floor and the cliff walls are more gently sloped."

"That all seems logical, but I could be more convinced."

Joanna tied her cloak securely about her, then raced forward and leaped upward to grab a secure hold. Diana watched her for an instant, muttering a soft curse common among freeborn villagers. Then she tied her own cloak around her. Imitating Joanna, she leaped up to find a hold in the rock wall.

Nearing the top of the wall, the arms of both warriors ached. There had been surprisingly few slips or missteps during the ascent, but it had required greater effort than any survival-training climb either had ever made. Feeling around for handholds, scrabbling for footholds, looking for anything that could serve as a ledge—all of these delayed their progress. Still, Joanna knew they owed their success to their training as warriors. She, after all, had known the meticulous fierceness of the training from two perspectives, as a cadet and later warrior, and as a falconer.

Muffled sounds of machinery and a few faint voices drifted down toward them. Both machinery and voices became louder the higher they got, but never clear enough to define.

The rim was now just above them. Diana was alongside Joanna, less than a meter away. Joanna wondered if she felt the same deep exhaustion along with a contradictory urge to go on.

"What now?" Diana asked.

"Judging by the sounds, we are not far from the main activity."

"What do you think it is?"

"Some Wolf trickery, I suspect, but let us go see. Are you rested enough?"

"An odd question. I am about to collapse, with only the fear of a rather long drop keeping me going. Yes, I am rested enough. Let us go."

The rim had a slight outhang. Joanna pulled herself over it, then gave Diana a hand up. Diana whispered thanks, then the two surveyed the area. They were on a plateau all right, just as Joanna had suspected. Its terrain was relatively level, with trees interrupted only by some large rocks and clumps of trees.

Less than half a kilometer away they saw a hallucinatory scene—phantasmal shapes moving busily by the light of a few widely scattered fires. Hovering over it all like watchful giants were many BattleMechs. Also part of the scene was the constant going and coming of support vehicles making swift trips back and forth from the rim.

"We have to get closer," Joanna whispered.

"Aff."

"Separate a bit in case they have posted any guards."

"I doubt they have. They would never expect any of us to sneak through their lines, *then* struggle up the side of the Gash to have a look."

"Nevertheless, there is no sense in us being caught together. Go toward that big rock to the left. See it?"

"Hard to miss."

In a moment Joanna lost sight of Diana. She walked forward, taking slow, cautious steps. The ground beneath her feet was loose, but she doubted her crunching footsteps could be heard above the din of the Wolf operation.

As she got closer, she saw that many of the moving figures were techs. Some of them operated vehicles—forklifts and trucks with cranes. Others were driving carts. Some merely walked. All were carrying material toward the rim, where fighting positions were being constructed. Some positions were dug deep, with entrances that would allow 'Mechs a clear field of fire down into the Gash without exposing the 'Mech. Other positions were shallow. In them stood constructs of shattered armor plate and debris that were like grotesque parodies of 'Mechs.

Moving in closer Joanna saw that some of the objects were just scrap metal, others were complete 'Mech arms or heads. Techs ran power cables to these. With a flip of a switch a gigantic hand would close or an elbow would flex or the cockpit would light up. With a satisfied nod the tech would leave one shattered machine and go to another pile of electronics and armor plate and begin again.

The Wolves must have scavenged some Twycross salvage yard like the one on Sudeten where she had fought Cholas, Castilla, and the others.

Many Wolf warriors strode among all this activity, giving orders and sometimes carrying loads of explosives. They were like a colony of ants converging on the wrecks and adding packages of death to them. Other warriors were planting mines and explosives between the fighting positions.

She found Diana at the big rock, already waiting for her.

"I am waiting, Joanna. Explain all this for me."

"These *stravags* are hoping to spring an ambush. It is their way of trying to repeat the original Twycross humiliation. Natasha Kerensky hopes to suck us into the Gash, then unleash all this on us."

"I do not get it. An ambush? With scrap and bits and pieces of 'Mechs?"

"I suspect that those piles are just part of her plan. If I observed correctly, they are placing explosive devices in those piles and laying mines throughout the positions. First real 'Mechs fire from hidden positions along the Gash rim. Our forces reply by jumping up to the rim to attack the sham 'Mechs that we can actually see. Once the Wolves see us charging these positions, the real 'Mechs pull back under cover. Our forces land among these piles of junk, and are trapped in the middle of a minefield, with exploding 'Mechs all around them. The real 'Mechs then counterattack and finish off the survivors."

Diana shook her head, trying to clear her thoughts. "They assume that we will assault the Gash. They assume that we will close with the forces on the rim. They assume that we will be stunned into inactivity by the minefields. They are gambling on many assumptions about how we will react."

"Yes but do you not see that that is exactly how Ravill Pryde will react? It is as if Natasha Kerensky were sibkin with our commander. She is taking a gamble, but one worth taking."

"This also explains how we slipped through the Wolf lines so easily. They have diverted so much personnel and materiel up here."

"It must have been part of her plan all along. She has put all of her effort into luring us into the Gash and spoiling our passage through it."

"Spoil is a mild word for it."

"I am a mild person."

"That has always been your problem."

"You are getting more sarcastic every day. Be careful. You might wind up as sour as me."

"My ambition exactly."

Diana would probably have been amazed if she had known how much her words disturbed Joanna, even though humorously intended. The older warrior had a momentary vision of Diana in the future, feeling the same resentments Joanna had felt. She did not want that, but—even worse—she could not figure out why she should be concerned about it. The fate of Diana, who would probably die in the midst of some daring exploit, was of little consequence to Joanna.

"What do we do now?" Diana asked. "I am afraid you will say go down the way we came."

"That is so. But first I want to see more. Let us circle around, see what is in the rear of all this."

"Your curiosity stuns me."

"Has nothing to do with curiosity."

"What, then?"

"War."

Keeping well away from the main activity, the two made their way to the other edge of the encampment, beyond the rows of support vehicles. There they discovered more BattleMechs being prepared by techs for combat.

"Joanna, would not the sheer size of so many BattleMechs make some of them visible to our forces when daylight comes?"

"That mountain on the other side there would effectively mask this contingent from us until the battle begins. They are counting on our reconnaissance units not thinking to look up here. Another gamble, but safe enough, I think."

An impressive campfire lit a wide area. Working nearby, Wolf officers were busy with the logistics of the operation. An officer would make an expansive arm gesture, and immediately a chain of events leading out of the encampment would take place, with warriors running, vehicles being driven in and out, all accompanied by the strange, subdued babble of many people speaking in low voices.

"We must get closer," Joanna said.

"Very daring of you."

"Are you being cautious?"

"Not at all. I am eager to see more."

"Good. Extreme caution brings out the worst in me."

They moved forward. Joanna gestured toward some trees to their left, and the two strode toward them without any attempt to stay out of the flickering light of the campfire. Joanna had counted on the officers being too busy to notice them as anything more than a couple of workers on a detail.

From within the small cluster of trees, they could observe the Wolf endeavors in relative safety. Something was happening near the campfire, where several warriors were gathered in a loose circle.

"What are they doing?" Diana whispered.

"Listening to someone, it seems."

"I wish we could hear, then this would—wait! Who is that?"

A warrior dressed in a field uniform bearing the insignia of a spider with a red hourglass on its back stepped from the circle. A woman of regal bearing, the first thing one noticed about her was her red hair, which was like a fire around her pale face. The second thing noticeable was that she was much older than the average warrior. She could, Joanna thought, be anywhere from sixty to one hundred, an age range that few Jade Falcons reached as warriors. The other warriors clearly deferred to her.

"I knew it," Joanna muttered. "I knew she would be behind all this."

"That, then, is Khan Natasha Kerensky?"

"Of course. Red hair and haughty and old, it could be no one else."

"She must be ancient, more ancient than—"

"Older than even I am? She is and, even with her advanced age, she is one of the best warriors in the Wolf Clan."

"Even in the village where I grew up we heard about Natasha Kerensky. But I know little about her."

"I have to admit, even looking at her now, with all the years marked on her face, that Natasha Kerensky impresses me, too. I do not know the full story, but I know she spent many years with Wolf's Dragoons in the Inner Sphere and became known as the Black Widow. Maybe it was there she learned deceitful techniques, or maybe they come naturally to members of the Wolf Clan, maybe it is something mixed into their nutrient solutions. The most sickening thing I know about the Wolves is that they even elevate traitors to high position. Their other Khan is a freebirth from the Inner Sphere."

Diana was agape. "I have heard of this before but I still cannot believe it. A freebirth as Khan? How can it be? We Falcons do not even allow freeborns to—"

"Perhaps we will talk of this another time," Joanna said. "Right now we must find out what Natasha Kerensky is doing here."

"If we are to climb back down the Gash and be back to base before daylight, we should go now."

"Daylight on Twycross? You are optimistic."

"At any rate we should not get trapped behind enemy lines."

"We got through them easily before, we can do it again. I need to find out more."

"Need? You have changed, Joanna."

"Quiet, Diana. Tell me what you see when you look at Natasha Kerensky."

Diana shrugged and spoke quickly, in the style of a report. "For a person her age, her physical condition is clearly laudable. She walks youthfully and with a strong stride."

"Do no confuse haughtiness with youth. She would not dare walk like an old woman, anymore than I would."

"She must have been beautiful once."

At that moment Kerensky turned, and the firelight lit her face weirdly. The age was even more evident, but so was the beauty. Eyes that threatened devastation seemed to look directly at Joanna and Diana, and they both shrank back a bit, even though they knew she could not possibly see them.

"Joanna, we have to get back to camp or—"

"Wait. Be patient. Let us see what we can find out."

What they discovered, however, was not what they expected, and it so disgusted Joanna that she nearly broke cover and ran straight into the Wolf encampment.

While they watched, an officer came to Natasha Kerensky and whispered something into her ear. She nodded and walked toward the fire. From around the other side came two figures.

"Joanna! They are wearing Jade Falcon uniforms!"

"Maybe they are spies. The Wolves might be trying to infiltrate our outfits. It would not be un—"

Diana recognized the pair a second later than Joanna, and she gasped at the sight.

"Castilla! Cholas! What are they doing here?"

Joanna could not speak for a moment. She pushed her hands against the trunks of a pair of trees and held tight, so tight that a thin stream of blood ran down the tree bark from each of her hands.

"Joanna! What is it?"

Joanna struggled to control herself. When she spoke, it was in a tense but steady voice. "They are the spies, infiltrators."

Kerensky conferred with Cholas and Castilla, nodding frequently at their words. Then she put a hand on their shoulders, giving each a squeeze, as if in acknowledgment of a job well done.

"Why did I not see it?" Joanna muttered.

"How could you possibly—"

"Kael Pershaw told me that the Wolves were substituting their own for new Jade Falcon warriors."

"Substituting? But how?"

"They kidnap new warriors before they arrive at their units. They change the codexes to match the physical description with that of the replacement."

"What do they do with the ones they kidnap?"

"What do you think? Kill them."

Diana suddenly retreated into the trees. The sounds of her retching followed. When she returned, her face was grim.

"Freebirth bastards!"

"Strange words for you to use, but I agree. I should have known. Right away I knew there was something off about those two. They were too close, almost intimate, they even talked of coupling together in a strange way, like what they call romantic. And they spoke of love as if such an emotion were not both ridiculous and repugnant among warriors."

"I know, I know. But I thought they were just deviant Jade Falcons and would straighten out when they became real warriors. But even Wolf warriors from the same sibko do not act like that, do they?"

"Not if they *are* from a sibko. Perhaps they are freeborns or even bondsmen from the Inner Sphere corralled into doing dirty work for the Wolves. It does not matter who they are."

"But it does! This . . . this is sickening."

"Put those thoughts out of your mind. We must remain calm, objective. The question is not who they are. That we already know. The question is, what are they up to? And, in one way, that seems clear. They are bringing information about the Falcon Guards to Natasha Kerensky. It could be nothing else."

"I will kill them!"

Joanna stared at Diana, seeing the rage in her eyes, seeing herself in Diana.

"Perhaps you will. But not now. If we kill them, say, as soon as they leave this camp, their bodies might be found."

"We can hide bodies."

"Even so, if they are not in their 'Mechs when the battle begins, Natasha Kerensky might get suspicious. No, we let them live. For now."

Diana shuddered. Joanna's calm tone frightened her.

"Something has happened to you, Joanna, since you left us. You have returned from wherever you were with a much craftier outlook. You were not assigned to another unit, as Ravill Pryde said. You were a spy yourself, Joanna, *quiaff*? No, do not even speak. It must have been an appalling experience. I will do whatever you say, and be a spy, too. Your spy."

"Good. Now then, since Cholas and Castilla are leaving, we can follow them to learn their route back to our camp. I have no wish to return the way we came. But do not follow too close. I would hate to see them dead too soon."

Cholas and Castilla glanced at each other as they passed near the trees. It was obvious that the glances, even to unsentimental observers like Joanna and Diana, was one of deep affection.

"Yes," Diana muttered. "I must kill them."

"You could. You could kill them. And their death would be shameful. But think how much better to humiliate them."

Diana stared into Joanna's almost amused eyes. "You have changed, Joanna. You seem less Jade Falcon, more—"

Joanna was instantly angry. "I am Jade Falcon. Have no doubt about that, Diana. I am Jade Falcon to the core. Like you, I want to tear those two apart. But I want them to feel the pain. Let us go, we can debate this later. We must not let those traitors disappear on us. Come."

Diana's feeling were confused as she and Joanna left their hiding place. Even though she had previously despised Cholas and Castilla, the idea of their being spies was almost too much for her to absorb. It was too evil, and evil was a concept that had always bothered Diana. She could accept bad behavior, cruelty, rudeness, even the insults about her being freeborn—all of these were despicable, but they were not evil. They were part of being Jade Falcon. Evil was much more abstract. And what if Cholas and Castilla, being of another Clan, did not even consider their actions evil?

Diana shook her head, trying to rid her mind of these thoughts. They were not even worthy of a Jade Falcon warrior. She had spent too much of her life as a freeborn and all her attempts to place herself completely into the mold of a Jade Falcon warrior were eroded by ideas from outside the Jade Falcon tradition, the warrior's way of life. She wanted to be able to say firmly, as Joanna did, "I am Jade Falcon," without the accompanying qualifications. *I am freeborn, but within me are the genes of Aidan Pryde and I deserve to be accepted fully by trueborn warriors, as is my right.* Shaking her head did not shake away such thoughts.

Briefly, she looked back at the Wolf encampment. It was an eerie scene—the flickering firelight and deep shadows, the intense activity, and the huge BattleMechs hovering over it all like the powerful behemoths that they were.

31

The Plain of Curtains, Twycross
Jade Falcon Occupation Zone
7 December 3057

No real dawn on Twycross. Just a slight change in the darker reds of the sand and rocks. Eventually, a sensory shift that felt like daylight even though it did not look much like it. It tasted more like day than night. Sky intermittently visible. Patterns of sand, sharper-edged. Sand like fire.

Joanna did not give Ravill Pryde much chance to reprimand her and Diana. Though he had started out saying they had no right to conduct unauthorized night reconnaissance, she quickly interrupted and told him what they had discovered, leaving out the part about Cholas and Castilla. Luckily, he did not ask how they had returned from the plateau, so she did not have to lie about following the two spies down a gradual path leading to the Plain of Curtains. Nor was she forced to mention how Cholas and Castilla were guided back to the Jade Falcon camp under Wolf Clan guard.

"Obviously the Wolves knew we would check inside the Gash for explosive charges," Ravill Pryde responded bitterly. "So those freebirths are planning to humiliate the Falcon Guards again at the very place our dead are buried. I knew they were devious, but I did not think another Clan would stoop so low as to borrow strategy from the Inner Sphere. Why not fight us honorably, according to the way of the Clans?"

"I think Natasha Kerensky is desperate," Joanna said.

"Why should that be? The Wolves are fierce fighters, their 'Mechs—the ones we have seen—are in good condition, their supplies are—"

"I think they do not have sufficient forces on Twycross. Even taking into account that we traveled at night and the visibility was miserable, the Wolf camp seemed spread out and their manpower thin. Natasha Kerensky would not stoop to such tactics as ambush unless she—"

"What else can you expect from that disgusting old woman?"

His comments about Kerensky always seemed forced. The thought crossed her mind that Ravill Pryde might be a spy, too; that he, too, might have been inserted into the Falcon Guards to undermine them; that he—but no, that was impossible. Too many people had known Ravill Pryde since his marvelous Trial victory and his early win of a bloodname. Kael Pershaw had mentioned meeting Ravill Pryde several times before he had come to Sudeten. Pershaw had even commented that the Jade Falcon leadership believed Ravill Pryde would eventually rise to become Khan, no doubt one of the youngest Khans in Clan history.

No, Ravill Pryde had to be a true Jade Falcon warrior. No substitution was possible. The only infiltration Ravill Pryde represented was a bizarre genetic contrivance which, though effective in breeding a new kind of warrior, was repellant to anyone, like Joanna, who believed only in Jade Falcon ways and in the greatness of the Jade Falcon warrior. Until more was known abut the genetic experimentation, it seemed reasonable for her to assume that Ravill Pryde's effectiveness as a Jade Falcon officer could be affected by his Wolf genes. To her his behavior would always be suspect.

"I respect Natasha Kerensky," Joanna insisted.

"She is you, I expect."

The remark surprised and angered Joanna, but she held back the emotions, merely asking, "Why do you say that?"

"She is an effective aged warrior and you have also shown us that a warrior can be strong in spite of your years. In defiance of your years, I might add."

"Will you revoke my transfer to the homeworlds then?"

"I did not say I had changed any of my beliefs about aging warriors. Most are a liability to combat units, but there are a rare few who have moments of effectiveness. As I am sure you will in the battle to come."

"Spare me your kick in the behind compliments. Instead, tell me where will we engage the Wolves."

"A few kilometers from here, on the Plain of Curtains."

"I wish to lead the assault."

"You will be more valuable in reserve. The garrison Clusters will strike at the Wolf flanks while the Guards go straight through their line. Star Captain Evlan will head the main force with Echo Nova, sending her Elementals ahead, both to scout and to interfere with Wolf progress. Command Cluster will enter the fray on her near right flank while I take Delta and the rest of Echo in a massive flanking movement on the left. We should engage fully at this point here."

He pointed out the location on the command terrain map.

"That is too close to the Gash. She wants to lure us there."

"I can see that. But I believe we can inflict enough damage before she is able to start withdrawing any troops through the Gash, as I expect she will. Besides, we should not tip our hand that we know her ambush strategy yet."

"What are you going to do about it?"

"That will depend on Natasha Kerensky. I want her to proceed with confidence, so that we can prepare our own ambush."

"Our own ambush?"

"*Aff*. A psychological ambush, if necessary."

"Psychological ambush? What is that?"

"You will see."

"I do not know that I wish to. I prefer prowess to psychology."

"As do I."

"Then why even contemplate it?"

"Because it might work. You will have to adjust, Joanna. We Clans have learned much from this invasion of the Inner Sphere. If we are to succeed we must apply some of this knowledge to our own ways, especially since it looks as though Natasha Kerensky intends to use Inner Sphere tactics."

"I do not agree. The way of the Clans must be sufficient."

"Then perhaps you deserve to be reassigned."

"Ravill Pryde—"

"No, not now. We can settle all this later. And in the field do not forget to address me properly, with my rank."

"Star Colonel Ravill Pryde, I request permission to ready my *Summoner* for the coming battle."

"Granted, Star Commander Joanna."

A sense that sand is thick in the cockpit's air, although there are no signs of it on any surface, and the air was filtered. A sense that, when it moves forward, toward a battle already engaged, the Summoner *has problems with footing. A sense that something is affecting balance and that the dizziness that lurks in the cave of its pilot's eyes will soon emerge.*

Joanna switched off her commline so that she could hear, muffled by the *Summoner*'s thick skin and the subtle creaks inside her neurohelmet, the first sounds of combat. Hitting the button to reopen the channel, she heard the warrior yelps and screams, boasts and challenges, groans and moans of pain of pilots in their cockpits. But there were more sounds of victory than distress. The battle was obviously going well for the Jade Falcons. Ravill Pryde directed the fighting in a crisp cool voice. Even for Joanna, who still detested the man, the sound of his voice was encouraging, the import of his words inspiring. They made her want to get to the fight sooner.

She should have felt insulted at being held in reserve, yet she did realize that, to Ravill Pryde, it must make sense. She was an old warrior and, from his point of view, not worthy frontline material. She also had too much experience to be wasted as front-line cannon fodder. As for Joanna, all she wanted was the chance to dispose of as many of the despised Wolf warriors as she could.

She had a good chance for glory in this battle. Fate was on her side and, though Jade Falcon warriors did not feel bound by the workings of fate, they did consider its influence. Joanna had survived Twycross before, she had survived Tukayyid and Glory Station; indeed, she had survived countless battles in her life. She could survive again. But would she achieve the one kind of survival so essential to her? To pull herself out of the rubble of her fate and continue on as a warrior? Sometimes she thought she could endure even greater shame than Twycross if so doing would win her the privilege of finishing off her life as a Jade Falcon warrior.

For a moment the turbulent atmosphere of the Plain of Curtains jumbled her commline signal. First came some static, and then she heard, muffled but discernible, a strange new voice. "Hall, get the Three Hundred and Forty-first to the rear. Have the Thirteenth form on this side of the Gash. Alert the Eleventh to be ready."

Then another, softer voice said, "Roger, Nat . . ." And then the new voice faded and was gone. After some more static, the regular Jade Falcon chatter came back on line.

Joanna strained to hear more, but only the familiar sounds remained. Nevertheless, she knew what she had heard. It was only the first syllable of the name, and of course it could be some other name, or even some other word, but Joanna was certain that it was Natasha Kerensky's voice she had heard. Firm, strong, and sounding younger than her years.

It excited her to hear Kerensky's voice. She had seen the woman, she had heard her, she had known about her for a lifetime, it seemed. Now, if only she could fight her . . . Then she realized she would. Joanna did not know how she knew it, but she did.

The battle itself, a bizarre sight. BattleMech torsos above the swirling sands. Disembodied beings floating precariously.

A *Stormcrow* came charging at Joanna's *Summoner,* its right-arm medium lasers sending a chain of beams at her. But the *Stormcrow* pilot must have been disoriented by the weather conditions, for its shots went wide. Joanna let the Wolf pilot fire again before responding with her LB-X autocannon, sending a burst of cluster munitions at the light machine. The submunitions dispersed from their canister more slowly, another apparent result of the strange atmospheric conditions, but enough hit to score some critical hits on the body armor of the *Stormcrow*. This 'Mech seemed poorly named, for it did not thrive in the storm, and in fact stumbled backward with little grace. Joanna started to move in on it, but another 'Mech, an *Executioner* bearing the insignia of the Falcon Guard Trinary Delta, began firing at the *Stormcrow* from the other side. Before she could challenge this thief of her opponent, the *Stormcrow* exploded. Seething with fury Joanna looked for another target.

The battle was well engaged now. 'Mechs faced each other, green lances of laser light, gouts of fire from missile launchers, and the sharp crack of autocannon all mixing together. Armor pieces flew with the sand, sometimes carried high above the fray, then dropping onto other BattleMechs. Sometimes these armor fragments chipped off other armor, their destruction becoming part of the enemy assault. Choosing a *Warhawk* as her target, Joanna was about to trigger a missile salvo when Ravill Pryde's voice came over her commline.

"Star Commander Joanna!"

"Roger, Star Colonel."

"I do not choose to have you in the battle yet. Retreat."

"Retreat? I do not retreat."

"You do now, *quiaff*?"

Instead of responding, she flung another question at him. "You dare to insult me in the midst of battle? Shame me again? That is too much even for you. I will—"

"Joanna, your insubordination, *in the midst of battle,* is foolish. Follow orders. I have strategy as well as command in my favor."

"But I—"

"No more protest. I wish to hold you in reserve."

"What of my Star?"

"Only you. Deploy them into the fight, then move to the rear, or I will personally destroy your 'Mech!"

Her rage made her feel like a 'Mech whose heat levels were rising too fast. Had that *stravag* Wolfspawn sucked her into this situation just so he could augment her shame, make it easier for him to transfer her back to the homeworlds? Or perhaps there was no motive; he merely hated her so much that shaming her was second nature to him. Yet she had brought him essential information. That alone should have earned her the privilege of being in the heat of the battle.

Was the man a traitor, after all, the spy, as she had originally thought? Was his scheme to make the ambush happen? Maybe Kael Pershaw had been wrong. Had Ravill Pryde been inserted into the Jade Falcons via some deep concealment even before his Trial, had his victory been arranged and his bloodname bought, had he been assigned to the Falcon Guards—all to ensure the Wolves one victory in a Trial of Refusal that no one could have foreseen?

The rational side of her mind noted that, even for Clan Wolf, such a plan would be too far-fetched and far-sighted. No Clan leadership, not even the Clan scientist caste, could depend on one thing following another so precisely. Ravill Pryde had to be a Jade Falcon warrior. She had observed a firmness in his voice suggesting that he did, in fact, have a plan, and that she was part of it. For the moment she had to believe that. She *would* believe it. It was the only theory that made sense of his actions.

Feeling like some kind of coward, she barked orders for her Star, then began to back her *Summoner* away from the battle.

Diana's voice immediately came over the commline. "Joanna! What are you doing?"

"Malfunction. I will be right back."

"Everything looks fine."

"Do not be insubordinate." Joanna knew that besides echoing Ravill Pryde's tone, she was again being deceptive. Her experience as a spy had perhaps ruined her forever. "In the meantime, MechWarrior Diana, fight well and do not forget to keep an eye on the twin gauges, *quiaff*?"

"Aff," Diana responded sullenly. "Twin gauges" was a code term they had agreed to use whenever referring to Cholas and Castilla over the open channel. It might sound strange to other warriors, but was unlikely to tip off the two Wolf agents.

The battle disappeared from her viewport, its bursts of fire replaced by blowing veils of shifting, swirling red sands, and the work of the BattleMechs became an unsteady shifting field of blips on her scanner screens.

The heat of the plain made the interior of a cockpit feel as if the whole 'Mech were in jeopardy from internal heat rises. But its heat monitor showed the normal settings. Strange, softly grating sounds, the sand itself hitting and sliding across the 'Mech surface. Occasionally, warring 'Mechs, seen through the sands in the distance, looked like battle scenes out of some nightmare, with too many reds and confusing shadows. Damaged 'Mechs stumbled past her, to safe places where techs could manage makeshift battlefield repairs.

More frustrating than the views of the battle were the

sounds coming over the commline. Cool voices of 'Mech pilots reacted to attacks, reported damage, encouraged each other with warnings and praise. Ravill Pryde, clearly in control, snarled out orders and reported his own successes while noting the achievements of others. Such reports only made Joanna more agitated, more wrathful. What could she say when the battle was over? That she had demonstrated her skill at being in deep reserve? Ravill Pryde had not even given her the rearguard duties of guiding repair operations or alerting reserve forces. Though Joanna did not want to believe that Ravill Pryde had in some way double-crossed her, the idea kept recurring.

With nothing else to do, she monitored the progress of the battle. It seemed to her that the Jade Falcons had gained the upper hand early and were maintaining it. Few losses had been recorded so far for either side, but considerable damage was being done.

Then she heard Star Captain Evlan report to Ravill Pryde, "The Wolves appear to be retreating, Star Colonel. Several have already slipped into the Gash. And, sir? According to our count, the Wolves have not sent their full bid of BattleMechs up against us."

"I realize that, Star Captain."

"Request permission to pursue."

"No, Evlan. Do not, repeat, do not follow the Wolves into the Gash at this time."

"Sir—"

"All units. Do not enter the Gash. Destroy any stragglers on this side, but do not advance further. Permit the Wolves to enter the Gash if they head that way."

There was a great deal of confusion over the open line as Jade Falcon warriors protested Ravill Pryde's command. The main theme of their protests was that the order violated Jade Falcon custom.

"I am happy to see our warriors protest so vigorously," Ravill Pryde said. "Our fighting spirit lives on!"

"Then why hold us back?" asked an officer whose voice Joanna did not recognize.

"Remember the shame of Twycross. We must not duplicate that. Those Falcon Guards rushed into the Gash too quickly. But we are the new Guards, the heroes of Tukayyid. We will not allow those lowborn Wolves to underestimate us. We will not repeat the error of Twycross, warriors!"

If a crowd cheer could be transmitted over a commline, it would sound like the reaction that followed, a concatenation of fighting spirit and approval of Ravill Pryde's inspiring words. But that was followed by a long period of relative silence which seemed to make Joanna's cockpit feel hollow. Then, over an open frequency came the voice she had heard before. It seemed to thunder about her.

"I am Khan Natasha Kerensky of Clan Wolf. I have sent my troops away. I wait in the Great Gash of Twycross to meet and slay any Jade Falcon who thinks more of himself than he should, and prefers courage to wisdom. Come now. Your time is at hand."

Then Ravill Pryde's voice followed on the secure channel.

"We have received a challenge from Natasha Kerensky of the Wolves for possession of the Gash. What say you, warriors?"

"Reject it," said one voice. "Natasha Kerensky is an old woman unworthy of a single contest against a Jade Falcon. Further, she is a traitor to the Clans who has associated with Inner Sphere scum. The shame of fighting her would outweigh any glory gained in the battle. She merely wants to degrade us with the bid. We can accept a proper bid of her own best warrior, but not her."

Other warriors echoed those sentiments. Ravill Pryde then called on several officers, all of whom refused to dirty their hands in a duel against an impossibly ancient Wolf warrior, in spite of her fame and notoriety.

"Star Colonel Ravill Pryde," Joanna screamed into her own microphone, twisting its flexible cable with her hand as she brought it closer to her mouth. "I wish to speak to you over a private channel."

"Granted, Star Commander Joanna." There seemed to be a strange pleasure in his voice. "Speak, Joanna. Time is short. The Wolves may be preparing even more traps."

"I should be the warrior to fight Natasha Kerensky."

"And why is that?"

"You must know why. I am the oldest warrior under your command. It is not shameful for me to engage her in battle. Also, I am the only survivor of the first Battle of Twycross. My deep shame will, in turn, shame her."

"So be it. You have convinced me, Star Commander." There was a strange sound in his voice that Joanna could not quite define. It seemed to her that he was not sufficiently surprised, nor did he offer the protest that she might have expected. Then it hit her. He *wanted* her to be Natasha Kerensky's opponent. The freebirth scum has planned this the moment he heard Natasha's challenge. That was why he had protested so little at the reluctance of the other warriors. He had almost *encouraged* their reluctance. This was what Wolf genes did to a Jade Falcon warrior. At least, in Ravill Pryde's case, they created deceitfulness. The Clan should send him to Kael Pershaw for the Watch instead of keeping him in a command position.

Ravill Pryde allowed Joanna to listen in on his transmissions to Natasha Kerensky. The notorious Wolf warrior was obviously angered at Joanna's selection. She asked if Pryde was too frightened to take her on himself. He said no, that Star Commander Joanna had a *long* and distinguished career. She was sufficiently skilled to dispose of an aging Wolf relic. If seething could be communicated over commlines, then that was the source of the angry static that followed Ravill Pryde's comment. Finally, Natasha Kerensky announced, with well-concealed rage, that she accepted the Falcon champion.

"Oh, and one more thing, Khan Natasha," Ravill Pryde said, his voice imperious and sneering. "That little ambush you have planned up on the plateau? Withdraw all your forces from there. I will not allow Star Commander Joanna into the Gash until the withdrawal is complete. Your troops there are useless to you anyway, since I am not as stupid as Adler Malthus and would not commit any forces into the Gash until I know it is safe. If this is to be a contest between two skilled warriors, then it should remain so, without any help from above. An individual contest, fairly designed and fought, that is the way of the Clans, *quiaff*?"

Joanna was not certain, but the squawking sound on the commline might have been a reflection of Natasha Kerensky's surprise and irritation that the ambush had been discovered or it might simply have been static caused by Twycross's erratic atmospheric conditions. However, Natasha Kerensky agreed to Ravill Pryde's demand and vowed to remove all Wolf forces from the plateau.

"We are on a private channel now, Joanna," Ravill Pryde announced. "As you know, I and our comrades depend on you to bring honor to the Falcon Guards this day."

"Spare me your florid speeches, Ravill Pryde. We hate each other and have from the beginning, *quiaff?*"

There was a long pause before Ravill Pryde responded. "I do not know the specifics of your mission with Kael Pershaw but, whatever it was, it has generated a definite change in you, Joanna. You are suspicious, you see complexity where before you would have seen simplicity."

Since Diana had voiced the same thought to her, Joanna wondered how true it was. Inside, she felt the disgusting need to examine matters even she would have preferred to remain in ignorance of varied possibilities. Well, she would get rid of this tendency toward inquiry soon enough. She simply did not like it.

"While we are discussing complexity," Joanna said, "why did you need to resolve this challenge in this way? You could have accepted the challenge yourself, Ravill Pryde, *quiaff?*"

"*Aff.* You are quite . . . perceptive. You have a talent for analysis I would never have suspected. I will explain, and you can argue my decision later. I welcome that, in fact. I could not fight her. I am young, she is old—whoever won, I would earn no honor. Defeating an ancient warrior brings no glory. Losing to her, though unlikely, would be even worse. So you are, you see, the logical choice. If you win, you bring glory to yourself. If you lose, well, you have been shamed before."

"And, if I do lose, perhaps you can win the glory after all by avenging me."

"Perhaps."

"You should become a Wolf, Ravill Pryde. Your shades of meaning do not suit the mouth of a Jade Falcon. You are a new breed, Ravill Pryde, and it is no wonder I hate you so deeply."

"Most people believe you hate everyone."

"Which gives you a special place of honor, Ravill Pryde, for I hate you more than any other."

"So be it. I will cherish your words, Star Commander Joanna. Now, ready yourself for the battle. Proceed into the Gash."

"What about the ambush?"

"Natasha Kerensky has just sent word that the evacuation of the plateau has begun and will be completed momentarily."

"Can you trust her?"

"She is Natasha Kerensky—according to you, a great warrior in spite of her origins."

"And her origins are the problem. The Wolves are not above springing more traps. We should prevent them."

"What do you suggest?"

"Send warriors to make sure. Have them go on foot, so that the Wolves will know we are not appropriating their ambush."

"Warriors? Abandoning their 'Mechs in the middle of the battle?"

"The battle is now between myself and Natasha Kerensky. You can pour cement in all these 'Mech and turn them into statues for all the use they are now. I will not be in position for twenty minutes. We have plenty of time for some warriors to get to the top of the plateau on foot."

"All right, I will assign some warriors to this duty. And I must say I am much impressed with your newfound sense of caution, Star Commander. Since you suggested the mission, I will let you plan it. It will give you something to do while you await your contest with Natasha Kerensky."

"Fine. Since MechWarrior Diana accompanied me on our unauthorized mission last night, she may guide them along the path. I choose MechWarriors Cholas and Castilla to accompany her."

"You have some reason to choose those two?"

Joanna hoped her slight hesitation was not noticed by Ravill Pryde. "Why would I have a reason? Do you question their abilities for the assignment?"

"Not at all. They show fine potential as Jade Falcon warriors. But you did fight them once, and Diana had her own fracas with them."

"Now it is you who are being suspicious. Send others then."

"No. As I told you, I will allow you to make the choices. I will detach MechWarriors Diana, Cholas, and Castilla for the assignment."

Joanna regretted being so devious, but the ability to deceive was becoming part of her character, too, with all the other changes Ravill Pryde and Diana had observed. She would have to rid herself of them someday. But today was not that day.

"One more thing, Ravill Pryde, *quiaff*?"

"*Aff*. I realize this is a private channel, but please get used to addressing me by rank as I ordered you."

"I will take that into consideration, Ravill Pryde. You ordered me to the rear *before* Natasha Kerensky's challenge, yet you seem to have been planning to conserve me for this battle all along, *quiaff*?"

"*Aff*. I knew a proper use for you would emerge somehow."

"No, not *somehow*. You knew all along. I think that you engineered this confrontation yourself, in some private conversation with Natasha Kerensky."

"You can think that, but she did issue the challenge herself."

"But you engineered it, *quiaff*?"

"Well, an angry Natasha Kerensky may not have perceived a tactic or two but, as I said, she issued the challenge."

"You are not going to tell me more?"

"Is there more to tell?"

"I am sure of it."

"As I told you, Joanna, you have become most suspicious since your return."

"And perceptive, you said that, too."

"I did."

"You are loathsome, Ravill Pryde. Star Colonel Ravill Pryde."

She switched off that line and, after a moment of subduing her anger, spoke to Diana on their private frequency. "I will be glad to be alone with those two," Diana said, upon hearing her orders.

"Diana, this is not an opportunity for assassination. Unless, of course, the traitors reveal themselves."

"You expect them to, do you not?"

"I did not say that." She paused for a moment because it struck her that Ravill Pryde had used the same kind of evasive tactic on her only moments ago. Why had it seemed necessary? she wondered. "If I am to fight this battle, I just want those two under observation, *quiaff*?"

"*Aff*."

As she signed off and started her *Summoner* toward the Gash, Joanna thought back on her lies. Most of them were not lies really, just evasions—answering a question with a question, making the protest that avoided the reply. As before, she regretted them. Yet, reconsidering her achievements at Dogg Station and reviewing her improvised deceit here on Twycross, she also wondered why she was deriving so much pleasure from such lies and evasions.

32

The Great Gash, Twycross
Jade Falcon Occupation Zone
7 December 3057

It was as if Joanna were seeing the Great Gash through her 'Mech's eyes. It seemed smaller to her, narrower. From her seat high in the confined cockpit of her *Summoner,* its walls did not seem so high. However, the difference could have been technical rather than geological. After all, some felt that certain distortions were useful, allowing the 'Mech pilot better mobility, a better sense of location, a concentration on the matter at hand without interference from peripheral phenomena. In a sense, technology could reduce the perception of the Gash.

However, there were other, stranger differences. Sound, after the roar of the Plain of Curtains, abruptly diminished. Except for the distant and hollow murmur of the Diabolis winds, there was nothing to hear inside the Gash. In war, silence was more ominous than noise. Then came a series of resonant thumps, which Joanna's scanner showed to be Natasha Kerensky, in her *Dire Wolf,* one of the heaviest of all OmniMechs. She was entering the other end of the Gash, as arranged. Each step Joanna's *Summoner* took would register in Natasha Kerensky's ears as a similar, but somewhat lighter, thump.

Joanna, estimating from the increasing louder sounds of the other 'Mech, slowed her own pace. She wanted the match to be initiated at the place where the avalanche had occurred, about a third of the way in from the Jade Falcon end of the Gash. That part of the Gash was somewhat wider and its uneven terrain would give Joanna's often unorthodox fighting tactics more room. Furthermore, she thought there was something appropriate about avenging her own shame in the exact place where it had originally occurred. Making it even more appropriate was the knowledge that Diana was up there on the plateau with the wretched Castilla and Cholas.

Checking the time, she realized it was nearly dusk, although dusk on Twycross might be something of a contradiction in terms. The clash between the Jade Falcons and Wolves had begun a couple of hours after dawn, yet the day was almost over. Although Twycross had a short daylight period, it seemed to her that the time should be nowhere near dusk. Should the contest between her and Natasha Kerensky be a long one, it could last well into the night. But that did not matter. Nightfighting or dayfighting, on level or rocky terrain, with odds against her or in her favor—none of it had much significance to Joanna. She merely needed the combat. She needed to put a BattleMech through its paces and turn another 'Mech into a fireball of molten armor and expanding plasma. It was only right and proper. She was, after all, Jade Falcon.

The sounds of the approaching *Dire Wolf* grew steadily louder. Joanna had nearly reached the burial ground of the old Falcon Guards and their BattleMechs.

The path up to the plateau seemed, to Diana, longer than it had the night before. Of course, then it had been downhill, and her and Joanna's concentration had been firmly on tracking the pair of spies. Yet, it was not the exertion of going up that seemed to prolong the time. With the way her adrenaline was racing, she could have run up the relatively steep path. It was the necessity of maintaining a pace casual enough to prevent Cholas and Castilla from becoming suspicious that seemed to make the time drag.

It was also the anticipation of reaching the plateau. Diana wanted to finally get there and see what Cholas and Castilla would do. It seemed to her that the order Joanna had given her of guiding the strange pair up was an implicit command to dispose of them. Nevertheless, Joanna had provided a number of explicit instructions. Executing the two outright would not really satisfy Joanna's dictates.

She glanced back at Castilla and Cholas, who remained about four steps behind her. The path was wide, so there was plenty of room for them to walk closer to Diana. She was sure they were holding back on purpose.

As she reflected on her experiences with these two, it suddenly became evident to her that Cholas and Castilla could *only* be together. Even in a group of the prydelings, they seemed to set themselves apart. In the honor duel with Joanna, they had actually seemed to function better in tandem than individually.

If Diana had not known they were spies, their intimacy might have bothered her. She still would have despised them, but their behavior would have seemed merely odd rather than completely abhorrent. Jade Falcons, after all, did often form comradeship, but there was only a mild familiarity in them. Most often, such relationships resembled the loose alliance that had formed between her, Joanna, and Horse, characterized by some casual banter, a sense of cooperation in duties and tasks and—most important—an ability to fight side by side skillfully and successfully. Many times one of the trio had saved one or even both of the others.

But, deep down, there were too many barriers to being close, all of them related in some way to the Falcon Guards. Joanna could not quite overcome her distaste for freeborns sufficiently to embrace, or even touch, Diana or Horse. Horse, who had been closer than any other warrior to Aidan Pryde, genuinely went his own way and was too independent to be anything more than someone you could count on in a scrape. For Jade Falcons, and especially the Falcon Guards, that was perhaps the best definition of friendship. Diana felt so much in awe of the other two that she felt almost subservient to them, an ally, the hanger-on lucky enough to *be* a hanger-on for the two Jade Falcon warriors she most respected.

But Cholas and Castilla—that relationship went beyond such casual friendships. There was something tangible between them that Diana could not define. It reminded her of the old books Horse had pressed upon her, especially those parts which she could not really comprehend—the stories where one male and one female apparently sensed some kind of destiny together and they described their feelings for each other in excessively emotional words whose meanings and nuances usually eluded Diana. They experienced extraordinary events or went on obstacle-littered quests because of their profound, and sometimes chaotic, feelings for each other. The stories often involved such difficult-to-grasp concepts as love, romance, passion, personal devotion—all ideas that Diana could translate into simple Jade Falcon terms, but could not understand in the intricate terms suggested by the stories.

Well, the fates of such lovers were often tragic, and Diana hoped this romance between Cholas and Castilla, if that was what it was, would follow that tradition. Even if they had not been spies, Diana felt they were an unhealthy influence on the Falcon Guards. From the beginning, Cholas and Castilla had been anomalies, and anomalies were detrimental to a good fighting unit. How long could any Jade Falcon warriors endure two of their kind? Sooner or later, someone would have killed one or the other out of pique.

Underlying her confusion about the pair, Diana also felt an important sense of relief. Cholas and Castilla were *not,* after all, Jade Falcon warriors, so their actions did not reflect upon the Clan. Their lives were pretense, deceit, and so did not place the way of the Clan in question, as it would have if they had been genuine.

As Joanna had once said to her, "Diana, sometimes I think there is more Jade Falcon warrior in you than in most trueborns. Perhaps it is the uniqueness of your spawning . . . I do not know. But you believe more strongly in the beliefs, obey the codes more obediently, fight with more determination. For any who would look, you embody the virtues that all warriors ascribe to."

Remembering that, Diana also recalled Joanna's words from the night before, about the freeborn bondsman from the Inner Sphere who had, in Clan Wolf, earned a bloodname and become a Khan. For a moment, she imagined herself earning the Pryde bloodname, but that was a dream beyond dreaming, a fantasy that was more than fantasy. Or was it?

They were nearing the end of the path. Diana told herself she must put all these disturbing thoughts out of her head. Cholas and Castilla could easily gain the advantage if her mind was clouded with fantasy. She looked back. They were still there, still physically close. Castilla, it seemed to Diana, leaned a bit *too* close to Cholas, as if she meant to defy Diana with her love.

There was a slight curve in the Gash, and so Joanna did not see Natasha's *Dire Wolf* until it was very close, even though her scanners, accurate inside the Gash, allowed her to track the enemy 'Mech all the way. First the left arm of the 'Mech, swinging slightly, appeared, and Joanna noted that her opponent had reconfigured it with a Gauss rifle instead of the usual large laser. As the torso became visible Joanna observed its short-range missile setup and took note of its antimissile system. She was glad she had also replaced her own long-range missiles with SRMs, much more useful in the confined Gash location.

The enormous machine, heaviest of Clan BattleMechs, lumbered around the curve and then came to a stop facing Joanna's *Summoner*. The *Dire Wolf* had never been to Joanna's taste. It was too big, too thick. Its legs, with their large, rounded knee joints, were too wide and gave the impression of being fat. The rest of its body seemed perched on those legs like a visitor, a hawklike bird about to fly off the legs and away—although, Joanna noted now, the overall effect was less of a bird than an insect, an insect of prey, the kind that bit off the heads of other insects after conflict or sex. That description might just fit Natasha Kerensky, Joanna thought. She was, after all, called the Black Widow.

Joanna did not believe in giving imagined life to a BattleMech, for it made one forget the threat of the pilot inside. However, she had to admit to herself that, at this moment, the *Dire Wolf* gave off a humanlike energy, a readiness for battle, a sturdiness of stance that duplicated a warrior's resolute bearing before battle.

Briefly, Joanna felt something rare for her. An abrupt pang of fear. Not fear for her life, or even that she would fail in battle, but fear that she would not do well. This *Dire Wolf* seemed such a massive challenge, especially when guided by such a legendary warrior. Fortunately, she quickly recovered her equilibrium, knowing she was up to the challenge, up to *any* challenge.

The *Summoner* was, after all, a quicker 'Mech, though speed would not be much advantage in the Gash, except to run away. It was also a more efficient 'Mech in spite of its relative lightness, giving away thirty tons to the 100-ton

Dire Wolf. Freebirth, Joanna thought, my *Summoner* is even a taller 'Mech. From my position, I can look down on the great Natasha Kerensky. What could be the problem?

At dusk, the abandoned encampment on the plateau looked even more ghostlike. From the still-smoking embers of the campfires, thin, wraithlike ghosts emerged and floated upward. Recalling her previous night's jokes about ghosts, a cold shiver went up and down Diana's spine. Vehicles had been left abandoned and there were gouges in the dirt where mighty BattleMechs had walked. Some of the gravel was blackened from the fire of jump jets as the 'Mechs had jumped away, and the faint, oily fuel smell was a gift left by the machines as they had lifted into the sky.

"Those freebirths!" Cholas exclaimed as if he had not seen the encampment before. "Did they think they could *cheat* the Jade Falcons of victory? Scum!"

"What do you expect from the Wolves?" Castilla said. "They fear us as the day fears the night."

"What?" Diana blurted out inadvertently. "As the day fears the night?"

Castilla raised her eyebrows in what might have been disdain of Diana's ignorance. "That was just something one of our falconers used to say. She used to say, you will fear me like the days fear the nights, and I will be the night for you, my foolish hawks."

For a moment, Diana almost believed Castilla, who finished off her explanation with a faint shaping of her distorted mouth that almost resembled a smile. Castilla's explanation was credible, for Diana knew from her own training days that a falconer could get quite bombastic when addressing cadets. But all it really proved was that Castilla and Cholas, whose reaction to the abandoned camp Diana found a bit overdramatic, had experienced some kind of military training. It did not, and would never, make them Jade Falcon warriors, new breed or otherwise.

The three walked through the camp toward the plateau's rim, their weapons drawn in case the Wolves had left behind some ambushers. But the camp was definitely abandoned. No surprise. Natasha Kerensky, despite her guileful ways, was a warrior of her word. If she claimed she had ordered her forces to leave the site, then they had left.

The piles of mined debris remained, higher and thicker. In

the waning light of day they looked to Diana like a series of haystacks, an image that would hardly have occurred to most Jade Falcons who, unlike Diana, had not experienced freeborn village life.

Cholas and Castilla, now walking ahead of Diana, picked up their pace as they neared the rim. He whispered something to her, and she nodded. Diana tensed and slowed, determined to keep her distance while keeping them in sight. At the same time she located spots that would offer her good cover if she needed it.

During their walk, all three could hear the footsteps of the two BattleMechs down on the floor of the Gash. Echoes gave the sounds abnormal resonance. Diana kept special attention on the sound of the *Summoner* and recognized immediately that Joanna had halted her machine where the avalanche had occurred. Reduced to the sound of one advancing BattleMech, the noises coming up from the Gash became hollower and even eerie. Before the three reached the rim, Natasha stopped her *Dire Wolf* and the air became ominously silent.

Then someone fired and there was a blast of light visible along the rim, silhouetting the mounds for a moment before fading. Afterward, the plateau seemed darker, as if night had descended suddenly, announced by the firing of one 'Mech on another. But nights did fall quickly on Twycross, Diana knew. Nights so dark they distorted the senses. The darkness made her especially alert.

A good thing, too, for just then Cholas and Castilla whirled around and began firing at her.

The *Dire Wolf* did not move, Natasha waiting for Joanna to bring the fight to her. *Well, we could stand like this and try to stare each other down, I suppose. She wants me to make a move, I'll make a move.*

Keeping her pace slow, Joanna advanced in her *Summoner*. After five steps, she fired her PPC and its crackling bolts of energy struck the other 'Mech on its right torso. Some armor flew and bounced off the Gash's walls. The *Dire Wolf* took a step backward, a move that caught Joanna off-guard. She had hoped to damage its anti-missile system by concentrating some fire on that side, and she might have scored a lucky shot on it. Withholding her fire, she stayed where she was, daring Natasha Kerensky to make the next move.

But the Wolf warrior's next move was a surprise. Instead of fighting, she spoke to Joanna on the commline.

"Star Commander Joanna, I am giving you the chance to retreat. This Gash is a confined area. Most of our weapons cannot be used to full effect. Fragments from our armor will bounce off these walls and become weapons in themselves. We will be at each other's throats waiting for that single lucky hit to take out the other. There is no skill in this, no opportunity for a warrior to prove her mettle."

Joanna was too puzzled to respond easily.

"Star Colonel Ravill Pryde has already discussed this challenge with you," Joanna replied. "If you give up, the Gash belongs to Clan Jade Falcon, and the entire battle is ours."

"You misunderstand me, Joanna. I'm not giving up. I'm giving you a chance, a chance to avoid repeating your old shame. I'm giving you a chance to avoid ignominy in your Clan annals."

Joanna was not used to such ideas, but she knew she would disagree even if she understood the motives behind them.

"You talk of shame, Natasha. What of the shame in the retreat you suggest? That would not look good in the annals, I think."

"If it was recorded at all. Or if your name was even used. You're a minor warrior, Joanna, the kind whose name doesn't often get recorded. I'm willing to propose an alternate challenge to Ravill Pryde, one that will make this little encounter so insignificant that it will probably never be reported."

"Your cowardice is as blatant as your reckless use of contractions, Natasha Kerensky. I am not afraid of you."

"I didn't for a moment think you were. I just wish to stop this inglorious skirmish in favor of a—"

"I will kill you, Natasha Kerensky."

Natasha's laughter was so loud it seemed deafening even over the commline. "I'd probably like you if I knew you, Star Commander Joanna. I'm sorry our battle must take place. I'm sure you are here due to the treachery of your commander. I know all about him. He's a rodent who—"

"Oh, shut up, Natasha. I know about your spies. I know they were reporting to you even last night. I know—"

She stopped, realizing that she might have said too much. The transmission between her and Natasha was not going through a private channel. Ravill Pryde was undoubtedly monitoring them. He would want to know about the spies, and Joanna would have to tell him. But that did not seem to matter while she was caught up in this strange palaver with Natasha Kerensky.

"I'm not sure how you know what you know," Natasha said softly, "but it impresses me that you're sharper than I had thought. I'll suggest this. We can have a fairer battle out on the Plain of Curtains. Same challenge, but a more warriorlike combat than us bouncing off the walls of the Gash."

"And what will you do if I agree?" Joanna said. "Attack me from the rear as we go out? We can hardly go out side by side, as you can see."

"I'll wait here until you're on the Plain. I won't follow you till then."

"You are a warrior of Clan Wolf. You plotted an ambush on that plateau up there hoping to lure the Falcon Guards into the Gash and repeat the humiliation of the past. Now you do not want to fight here because, without the ambush, it is inconvenient. With all that, I should trust you?"

"I am Natasha Kerensky. My word is—"

"Truth to tell, Natasha Kerensky, your word may indeed be trustworthy. I suspect it is. But the essential piece of news I have for you is that nobody dictates the rules to me. I do not do what my enemy says is right. I do what I say is right."

"You're independent then?"

"I am Jade Falcon!"

Joanna did not wait for further words from Natasha. Instead, she triggered an SRM salvo at a rock formation on the Gash wall above the *Dire Wolf*. She had not aimed it directly at the *Dire Wolf* because she was not yet sure whether she had impaired or even destroyed Natasha's antimissile system in her earlier attack, and Joanna was not prepared to waste a shot just yet. The missile exploded the rocks and sent a small avalanche down toward the 'Mech. The alert Natasha Kerensky countered by taking a step toward the *Summoner* so that the bulk of the rockfall missed the *Dire Wolf* altogether, although the fringe of it knocked off some shoulder and back armor.

She came at the *Summoner,* her Gauss rifle and lasers blasting away. Joanna felt her 'Mech tip backward dangerously as it absorbed several ruinous hits. She countered with a steady firing of her PPC, hitting the *Dire Wolf* again and again. Many shots ricocheted off the Gash's walls. Rocks and armor fragments seemed to fall together in a density resembling a storm.

Joanna, in the taller 'Mech, lowered her LB 10-X autocannon and aimed it outward at the *Dire Wolf*'s SRM missile rack, realizing that the shot could be suicidal as well as murderous. She was almost right, as the explosion of the fully armed missile rack rocked the Gash, and shrapnel slammed against the *Summoner*. Joanna had to guide its steps backward, down the slight hill to the point where the burial ground of the original Falcon Guards began. As the smoke cleared and the debris fell, she found the height advantage reversed. At the top of the rise, the *Dire Wolf,* its left shoulder missile rack a tangle of metal and wiring, looked down at her. Natasha Kerensky continued to press on, using her remaining weaponry recklessly but efficiently as Joanna's 'Mech took hit after hit.

For a long while Diana crouched behind a large rock and tried to discover the whereabouts of Castilla and Cholas. It had not been pretty, her retreat from them, but it had made sense. Rather than staring down two weapons fixed on her, she had fallen to the ground, where she got off a couple of ineffective shots, then rolled away, jumped up, and took off at a run. She did not want to trade shots with them when she could do better by seizing her own advantage later.

Now, behind the rock, she wondered why they had not pursued her. They had obviously stayed behind for something. When they had talked together before turning and firing, had they worked out some kind of plan, one bigger than merely doing away with Diana, one that might even affect the battle below? It had to be something like that, else why attempt to murder Diana?

The Great Gash duel, after the first shot and burst of light, had become silent. That was unusual for any combat, especially one involving a Jade Falcon warrior. What could be happening? she wondered.

At first dark seemed near-total, but Diana's eyes adjusted somewhat, and she thought she saw movement near the rim, on the other side of one of the Wolf transports. Her perception was verified by the sound of the vehicle's engine starting up. Diana needed no more motivation than that to leave the protection of the rock and run forward, toward the vehicle. She was not sure what Cholas and Castilla were planning, but she knew she had to stop it.

As she started to run, the fighting in the Gash began again, the flashes of light coming like lightning from below. The sounds of devastation and damage were loud and reverberating.

Joanna felt battered as shot after successful shot sent her *Summoner* reeling. With her 'Mech's back against the Gash wall, and its front facing up toward Natasha's BattleMech, Joanna found that she had difficult gauging her return fire in these narrow confines. A couple of her SRMs sailed over the head of the *Dire Wolf* and did more damage to distant rock than to the intended target. Her PPC and autocannon fire also went awry as Natasha Kerensky worked on hitting the upper limbs of the *Summoner* with an intense precision. The old woman seemed able to maintain a varied pattern of fire. What concentration she must have, Joanna thought. I must duplicate it.

A flashing light indicating damage came on at the side of Joanna's control panel. The outline of the *Summoner* on the main screen showed a red aura around the end of the 'Mech's right arm. Several shots from Natasha, all concentrated on the same area of the right arm, had hit the extended range PPC. There was a moment of hesitation, then an explosion and the lower arm seemed to come apart. The impact of the explosion sent the *Summoner* sideways along the Gash wall. Regaining control, Joanna saw that the arm was partially severed at a point where a wrist would be on a human being. What remained of the PPC hung down uselessly, a construction of wires and red-hot metal. She tried to move the arm, which would elevate only halfway with no side to side movement. As part of her arsenal, it was gone, as good as amputated.

Screaming with rage, Joanna focused on the *Dire Wolf*'s torso. Now was the time to see whether or not Natasha's antimissile system was still operative. Although she found that the overall imbalance caused by the damaged arm threw her aim off slightly, a missile did graze the side of the *Dire Wolf*'s torso, chipping off a slab of thick armor as it flew by. Something had to be wrong with the *Dire Wolf*'s antimissile system, a piece of information that encouraged Joanna greatly.

Swinging the good 'Mech arm around as she also swung the *Summoner* itself away from the wall to face the *Dire Wolf,* she used the advantage of her lower position to fire a burst of cluster munitions from the autocannon against the other 'Mech's legs. She did not bother to gloat over her direct hit as she simultaneously aimed several missiles at the already damaged missile rack on the *Dire Wolf*'s left shoulder. She had perceived many live missiles in the rack's tangles and she hoped to explode some of them.

She did, exploding almost all of them.

The *Dire Wolf* careened sideways from the explosion and its recovery of balance was hampered by the Gash wall it rammed against. Joanna smiled, knowing that the collision with the wall would, at the very least, send a massive neurological pulse through the neurohelmet and into the aging head of Natasha Kerensky.

But the *Dire Wolf* came away from the wall firmly on its feet and, with the best speed a lumbering OmniMech could manage, charged at the *Summoner,* its Gauss rifle spitting fire. The undamaged arm of Joanna's 'Mech took a dangerous hit, and the lower part of the arm started to bob up and down. It was out of her control, she realized, as she frantically pushed her joystick and felt no response from the arm.

The *Dire Wolf* was closing in on her. Hoping to slow it down, Joanna triggered an SRM blast toward its torso. At the same time, she realized that a strategic retreat might be in order. She would have to jump her 'Mech backward.

Engaging in her jump jets, she felt a sharp jolt as the *Summoner* abruptly began its rise toward the top of the Gash walls. Another jolt told her that Natasha, firing from below, had scored another hit on the *Summoner*'s left leg.

As Diana sprinted forward, she saw that Cholas had stepped out from behind one of the piles. But he did not see her yet. He was waving the vehicle on as it headed toward the pile, its tires launching gravel and stones into high arcs. Diana saw immediately what they were up to. Cholas was waving at Castilla, who was driving the vehicle, to push one of the dummy 'Mechs down into the Gash, where he had probably pinpointed the *Summoner*'s present location. If Cholas timed the fall well, the pile of junk with its explosives inside could do a lot of damage to Joanna's 'Mech.

Cholas was moving too fast for Diana to manage an accurate shot on him. Anyway, Castilla had enough warrior instinct to continue on, whatever happened to her compatriot. Diana had to disable the vehicle first.

Stopping and taking careful aim, she ruined the right front tire and left rear tire with two quick shots. It was enough to make the vehicle swerve from its path and come to a screeching stop. Diana heard Castilla jump out of the vehicle's far side. She was momentarily visible behind the vehicle, but dodged back as Diana got off a shot at her.

With Castilla pinned down, Cholas was already running in a zigzag pattern toward the vehicle, firing intermittently at Diana, who went into a crouch and looked for cover. She found it in back of a mound of 'Mech parts that had not been included in the ambush. For a moment it occurred to her that her current position must resemble what Joanna had experienced during the honor duel against these same two warriors. The predicament might have drawn a smile, but she had to attend to returning the fire of the desultory shots that came from the disabled vehicle, followed by the footsteps of Castilla and Cholas running in the other direction. Diana sprang up to follow.

At the disabled vehicle, she peered around it and saw the pair of dark shadows several meters away, running with impressive speed and threatening to disappear into the blackness. Diana felt her best move would be to ignore caution and merely pursue them.

The sounds from the Gash shifted. It seemed as if the fight was moving toward the Plain of Curtains. Did that mean that Joanna was being defeated? Could she be retreating?

The two Wolves came to a jeep, leaped into it, and quickly got it running. Instead of aiming toward a pile at the Gash rim, they drove directly at Diana. Seeing that the jeep's windshield was flattened against the hood, Diana stood her ground and fired into the vehicle. Her shots were so steady that they forced Castilla, at the wheel, to veer away from the shots and forget about crushing Diana beneath the wheels.

The two leapt from the jeep, one on each side, as it careened onward. Diana also jumped aside as it sped past her, hit one of the large rocks that were all over this plateau, and flipped over.

Diana did not watch the fate of the vehicle. Her attention was on Castilla and Cholas, who had apparently abandoned the search for any more Wolf vehicles to use, and were running toward the rim. Diana raced after them, expending some useless fire at their adeptly maneuvering bodies.

All three were stopped in their tracks for a moment as the missile rack and part of the upper torso of Joanna's *Summoner* briefly appeared above the rim, then dropped back downward. Cholas took a futile shot at it, and its beam arced over the Gash like a single colored rainbow.

As the *Summoner* descended toward a targeted point several meters to the rear, Joanna found that she could only move the lower part of the 'Mech's left arm in a small upward arc. Natasha's last hit had damaged it as well as the leg, but it was movable.

Natasha Kerensky had apparently calculated the *Summoner*'s landing point, for her *Dire Wolf* lumbered steadily toward it. Gauging her progress and steadying the left arm's arc until it was lined up with a point just ahead of the *Dire Wolf*'s path, Joanna fired her autocannon. Her aim was slightly off. A few of the submunitions gouged the *Dire Wolf*'s shoulder, but most struck in front of the 'Mech. Joanna thought she had done little damage until she observed, as she landed, that the *Dire Wolf* swayed to the right. But Joanna had to attend to her own landing before she could assess the extent of the *Dire Wolf*'s damage.

The landing itself was rough. The *Summoner* swayed, the havoc Natasha had wrought on its left leg throwing it off balance. Joanna suspected the landing was made uneven because one of the 'Mech's arms was completely useless and the other was partially disabled. As she located the *Dire Wolf,* she did another test of the left arm. It barely moved. The weapon was all but useless.

For the moment the *Dire Wolf* seemed propped up by the Gash wall. Joanna could see the large hole she had blown out of the 'Mech's right leg. It started at the knee and went downward in long pointed gashes almost to the enormous

'Mech foot. Inside the hole, wires dangled and some myomer bundles appeared to have been pushed inward.

"Best you can do is limp," Joanna said aloud softly. "Unfortunately, the only effective weaponry I have is a rack of SRMs with only a few salvos left. Unless you lay down on the Gash floor where I might be able to tickle your toes with my autocannon. Well, no fight was ever won by muttering."

Slowly advancing toward the *Dire Wolf,* she triggered a series of missiles, alternating targets from side to side. One missile caught the *Dire Wolf* as it tried to straighten up and get back to the center of the Gash. It hit the right arm at shoulder level and, in a clean slice, separated the arm from the torso. Joanna was so surprised by the effectiveness of the shot that she almost forgot to maintain her attack. But she could not resist thinking. *Well, that equalizes us—almost, anyway.*

Something had to be wrong with the *Dire Wolf*'s internal systems. The missile should have passed right by the 'Mech and landed ineffectually further down the Gash. A pilot would never have walked her 'Mech into a shot like that. If it was not the 'Mech systems, then it had to be the pilot herself. The earlier jolt when the *Dire Wolf* crashed against the Gash wall may have thrown off Natasha Kerensky's equilibrium. Maybe she was dazed or unconscious.

Well, not unconscious, Joanna thought, as the *Dire Wolf*'s Gauss rifle initiated a fierce attack on the *Summoner*. The rifle fired low, blasting her left leg in several places. *Freebirth! She wants the* Summoner *as disabled as her 'Mech.* Joanna concentrated her missile fire on the *Dire Wolf*'s left arm, hoping to disable it or its weapon before Natasha could finish her. At the same time she tried to maneuver the *Summoner* out of the Gauss rifle's line of fire. But the Gash was too narrow at this point. Any adjustment she made, the rifle easily tracked.

Suddenly the Gauss rifle made a vital hit on the *Summoner's* right hip joint, and this time it was the turn of Joanna's 'Mech to bounce off one of the Gash walls. With no use of her upper limbs, Joanna could not regain balance. The *Summoner,* veering off the wall, twisted grotesquely and collapsed.

Suddenly Joanna and the *Summoner* were on their backs. Ferociously Joanna slammed the controls one way and then another. Only the left leg moved at all. Her missile rack tracking system was offline, damaged by the fall. She could manually fire the remaining salvo, but it would just go straight up and fall back on the Summoner. A unique kind of suicide, Joanna thought, but not her style.

Uneven sounds of 'Mech footsteps told her that the *Dire Wolf* was limping forward slowly. To deal the final blow, no doubt. Joanna looked out through her viewport. All she could see was the high wall of the Gash and some of the sky. Suddenly, there was a speck coming out from the top of the wall. Whatever it was, was coming straight down, right toward the *Summoner,* it seemed. Joanna soon realized it was a body. The person's arms flailed, accompanying a scream that reverberated through the Gash, with several fading echoes that went on long after the body had landed somewhere at the *Summoner*'s feet.

When Diana recovered from the surprise of the *Summoner*'s brief appearance over the Gash rim, she saw only Cholas ahead of her, still gazing toward the rim. As she moved toward him, her pistol raised and sighted on him, he suddenly turned to fire at her. But Diana shot first. She hit him in the arm, forcing him to drop his pistol. Cholas quickly knelt to pick up the weapon with his other hand. But Diana was already racing toward him. She grabbed him around the neck and forced him sideways, at the same time kicking away the pistol, which skidded across the gravel. She stunned Cholas with a blow against the side of his head with her own pistol barrel.

Scrabbling around the ground to make sure the now-limp Cholas was between her and Castilla, who she was sure was between them and the Gash's rim, she shouted, "Castilla!" Her answer was a futile burst of fire that went far over Diana's head. It seemed to come from near the rim.

"Do not shoot, Castilla! I have your—Cholas here, and I can kill him easily."

"So what is that to me? Kill him."

But Castilla's voice was shaky, unconvincing. She was still acting the part of a Jade Falcon warrior.

Diana peered toward the rim intently, but she could not see Castilla. The Twycross atmosphere, even this high up, tended to compress distances, as well as distort shapes. A voice could also sound as if it came from one place at one time, another a moment later, without the person moving a centimeter.

"I do not believe you really wish his death. Or there is something strange about your love."

"Love? Diana, do not be absurd."

"I have seen your vile looks at each other. And I know you are not Jade Falcons. You are spies sent by the Wolves."

"Diana—"

"Do not even try to deny it. I saw you two here last night, as did Joanna. If not spies, why did you turn on me here?"

"It was Cholas. He said *you* were a spy, and you were to execute us."

"That is feeble, Castilla. Let us stop this talk. Surrender your weapon, and you will save Cholas' life. His life means nothing to me. I can take it easily."

"Kill him then." Castilla's voice seemed closer. Diana surveyed the area for movement but still saw no moving shape, no suggestive shadows.

"One more chance to save him, Castilla."

Castilla did not respond.

"All right then."

Diana did not intend to kill Cholas—not yet. She pushed his body to a sitting position, aimed a shot past his head, and then quickly shoved his body down to sound as if it had struck the ground.

Castilla's scream was like no sound Diana had ever heard. It had pain in it, along with a ferocious anger. And it did not stop. It came at Diana from behind like a truck bearing down on her. With no time to even figure how Castilla had gotten behind her, Diana whirled around, but not fast enough. Castilla leaped out of the darkness onto her.

She seized Diana's neck in her hands and began to squeeze, apparently oblivious to the pistol in Diana's hand. Struggling to breath, Diana tried to angle the pistol for a shot, when suddenly she felt her wrist being grabbed and slammed onto the ground, the pistol flying from her grip. She could not see, but knew that Cholas must have come awake, seen the two warriors struggling, and instinctively grabbed Diana's arm.

"You—you murderer!" Castilla screamed. Her pressure on Diana's neck increased and Diana's vision began to cloud. But her hearing was still clear. She heard Cholas call out, "Castilla! I am all right."

"Cholas?"

For a moment Castilla let up on her pressure. It was a moment that Diana knew how to take advantage of. Twisting her body, she was able to bring her free arm around and, pushing at Castilla's face, fling her back. Castilla's hands came away from Diana's neck.

Diana wriggled away, feeling with her hands all around her for her pistol, for any weapon to use against this pair. At the same time she heard the repugnant conversation between the two spies.

"I thought she had killed you."

"One of her lies. I will never leave you."

"Nor I either."

Diana forgot about her search for the weapon. With a scream as frightening as Castilla's had been, she leaped to her feet and rushed the two lovers. At that moment she had never hated anyone more than she hated them. What right had they to display such feelings, even if they felt them? What right had they to feel love?

With her considerable warrior strength, she knocked both of them to the ground. She rolled over onto Castilla and began hitting her in the face. Her blows were fierce as she focused on the evil, twisted mouth. When Cholas tried to break them up, Diana merely shoved him off.

Castilla was unconscious before Diana stopped raining blows. Still enraged, she whirled to locate Cholas. He had found her pistol and was raising it to fire at her. Diana did not care about the weapon. She did not fear it. She was Jade Falcon.

Diving for his legs, she tackled him and brought him down. A momentary flash of reason told her to go for the pistol, which she did. Over and over she slammed the arm holding the pistol against the ground with both her arms. Blood flowed out of the cuts on Cholas' hands, but he held on. Diana dug two of her fingers into a cut. Cholas screamed and released the pistol. Diana picked it up.

Suddenly the rage went out of her. She had the advantage anyway. She need not kill Cholas. She need not kill either of them.

She stood up slowly and gestured with the pistol for Cholas to get up, too.

"Help Castilla," Diana ordered. "You will carry her back to our camp."

"So you can accuse us, have us executed? Why should I?"

"I think a coward like you values his own life so much you will seize any chance to prolong it."

"I am no coward. But I see I have little choice. We will let Star Colonel Ravill Pryde resolve matters."

He knelt down and braced Castilla against his knee before standing up with her in his arms. They looked to Diana like something out of one of the books Horse liked so much. The hero carrying his loved one in his arms for some kind of purpose that they termed romantic. Cholas took a step toward Diana, his body apparently relaxed. Then he stiffened and flung the body of Castilla forward. Caught by surprise, Diana fell backward, the dead weight of Castilla on top of her.

When she had extricated herself, she saw Cholas running toward the rim. He was soon enveloped in darkness. She chased after him, but could not find him right away. Then there was a flash of fire from down in the Gash and she saw Cholas outlined against it. He had climbed onto one of the piles and was trying to loosen something. Something he could use as a weapon perhaps. Cool and steady, Diana, took aim and fired. Cholas shrieked, stood, and fell backward, off the pile and over the rim of the Gash. She heard his scream echo through the Gash as he fell.

Diana almost regretted the accuracy of her shot. Why had he not clung to the pile or landed on this side of the rim? She had wanted to take him back, to relish his and Castilla's humiliation at the hands of the Jade Falcons. But that pleasure was to be denied.

There was more fire down below, and she suddenly recalled the battle taking place there. Standing at the rim, she looked down and muttered angrily as she saw the deep trouble Joanna was in.

"Call Star Colonel Pryde and announce that you have yielded. I would have you live, Star Commander Joanna."

Although she heard Natasha's voice and had heard the *Dire Wolf* approach, Joanna was not sure of her position. Her sensors indicated a position just beyond the *Summoner*'s feet.

"Somebody fell, Natasha. From the plateau up there. Who was it?"

"I could not tell. It wears a Jade Falcon uniform. What

was a Jade Falcon doing up there in the first place? Some kind of Jade Falcon treachery?"

Could the body be Diana's?

"Is it a female warrior?"

"The body isn't recognizable in any way. Why do you even care?"

Natasha is right. Why do I care? If it is Diana, then it is Diana. Yet I feel something strange. A concern, perhaps. It is as I felt when Aidan Pryde was killed. It is—but I may be dead myself soon, so no matter.

"I give you the chance again, Joanna. Your weapons are now useless to you. You cannot even move your arms and legs."

One leg. The left leg. I know I can raise it. Natasha Kerensky must move to where I can see her.

"If I walk away, your humiliation is complete, Joanna. Twycross doesn't seem a lucky place for you."

No! Do not walk away. Come closer, where I can see you. Only one way I can get a chance at her and that is to make her try to kill me.

"That is the point, Natasha. Finish me off. I do not wish to endure the shame here a second time."

There was a long pause. "Yes," Natasha said slowly. "It is true. You deserve a good death."

The *Dire Wolf* stepped forward and now Joanna could see it. She did not waste time, for it would only take a moment for Natasha to fire her Gauss rifle. Already, the *Dire Wolf*'s left arm was lowering as Natasha bent her torso slightly forward, clearly intending a shot into Joanna's cockpit.

This is it, then. The leg has to be clear. Yes, I can move it. Does she even notice it raising up?

"You are a worthy opponent, Jo—"

The sentence remained unfinished. Joanna had raised her left leg to a point left of Natasha's cockpit. Then she moved it in a rapid shift to the right, while lightly touching the control that ignited the jump jet attached to the leg. The flame shot out in a violent orange burst and enveloped the *Dire Wolf*'s cockpit like a hungry, fiery mouth.

Joanna kept the jet firing long after the cockpit of the *Dire Wolf* had melted into slag. The pilot inside was incinerated. Natasha Kerensky, legendary warrior and a Khan of the Wolves, victor of more battles than there were stars in the night sky, was dead.

Joanna released her finger from the control, and relaxed her body.

"And you were also a worthy opponent," she said wearily and passed out. Above her, although she saw none of it, the *Dire Wolf* swayed for a short time and then fell. It nearly landed on Joanna's cockpit, but something—perhaps a burst of Diabolis rushing through the Gash, or perhaps just the imbalance from its damaged leg—made the 'Mech veer sideways and land right next to the *Summoner,* face down.

Up above Diana had watched the contest in alternating anger and cheer. When it looked like the *Dire Wolf* would destroy Joanna, Diana wanted desperately to somehow jump to the Gash floor to help Joanna. Then, when she saw Joanna manipulate the 'Mech leg and destroy Natasha Kerensky, for a moment she was not able to comprehend what had happened. When the *Dire Wolf* settled next to the *Summoner,* she knew the battle was over.

Joanna's all right. She has to be. Joanna cannot die, ever.

When Diana returned to where Castilla had lain, she was gone. Castilla was not seen again on Twycross, and the Jade Falcons assumed she had managed to get off the plateau and join the rest of the Wolves in their escape from Twycross.

Epilogue

Jade Falcon Garrison
Pattersen, Sudeten
Jade Falcon Occupation Zone
31 December 3057

The Falcon Guards had returned to Sudeten.

"One question has been on my mind for a long time, Star Colonel. You said something about a psychological ambush of Natasha Kerensky. What did you mean?"

Joanna was determined to study Ravill Pryde closely as he gave his response. If he lied, she wanted to search his face and watch his body movements for any clue to it.

"Is that not what we did, Joanna? I could have fought her myself, and I was willing to accept the risk, and even shame, of facing Natasha Kerensky. Still, as you have said so often, I was not battle-tested, not a veteran warrior, and it seemed to me as commander that the match required someone who could be as wily, and as ruthless, as Natasha Kerensky. So I declined the challenge and, given the strong opinions I expressed about combat with Natasha Kerensky prior to the battle, I knew that none of my officers wished to dishonor themselves by taking up her challenge. They were lies, of course. Already the psychological ambush was in process."

"Let me ask this: You knew that their refusal would rattle the old warrior?"

"Very perceptive, Joanna. You continue to surprise me."

The man's smile was ugly. For that matter, Joanna decided, Ravill Pryde was ugly, and deceitful, and too small. But he was crafty, she had to give him that, and he was a brave leader, as his command of strategy and fighting prowess had shown during the entire Battle of Twycross. In the last stages of the battle, while the Wolves were escaping in DropShips, he had charged among them without waiting for his troops to catch up. But what new kind of leader contemplated psychological ambushes?

"The rest of the psychological ambush should be clear, Joanna. Natasha Kerensky had issued a worthy challenge and, from her point of view, we had responded in an unworthy fashion. You, Joanna, were the final facet of my psychological ambush—the key to it, really."

"Because I am old, too. Not as old as—"

"Your age was the key factor. And therefore the psychology. But I knew you would win. And therefore the ambush. The fight merely had to be set up correctly, and I did that, *quiaff*?"

It pained her to admit, "*Aff,*" especially since Ravill Pryde obviously thought so highly of himself for his strategy. Ravill Pryde, for all the glory he had brought onto her name, was as repellent to Joanna as ever.

Now she and Ravill Pryde stood near Sudeten Lake. It was a rare day on Sudeten. An impossible day. The breeze was balmy, the day extremely pleasant.

"What about my assignment to Ironhold?" Joanna asked.

"Revoked. But do not credit me. Martha Pryde gave the order. I still believe you are too old and would be more useful elsewhere. Kael Pershaw asked for your return to the Watch. Will you go?"

"No. I do not wish to be a spy. I have had enough of them."

"Martha Pryde advises you to accept your role. The Clan needs you as an inspiration as we heal our wounds and wait the next call to action."

"You are getting florid again, Ravill Pryde. If ordered by Martha Pryde, I will go anywhere. I respect her. But, if she gives me the choice, I do not choose to be an inspiration. I am Joanna, Star Commander Joanna, if you wish, and I am a Jade Falcon warrior, and that is all I wish to be."

"So be it. I do respect you, Joanna. I do not like you, but I can use you in the Falcon Guards."

"It is my place."

He nodded and abruptly started to walk away. "Star Colonel!" she called after him.

He turned. "Yes, Star Commander?"

"You beat me unfairly in our last fight. I wish to fight you again, to even the score."

"In BattleMechs?"

"In any kind of fight. Barehanded in a Circle of Equals, if you wish."

"Perhaps it will happen. Sometime. But you must provoke me, Joanna."

"Oh, I will do that."

"You might."

"Might?"

He shrugged and resumed his walk.

"How about one of your sporting contests?" she called after him. "How about a swim across the lake here?"

His shoulders went up and down slightly as if he had laughed, but Ravill Pryde walked on.

"I can swim circles around you," he shouted back, however.

"Show me."

He stopped walking and looked back over his shoulder. "No, Star Commander. I have given up contests, games. They are useful for new warriors to display skills. But for us, we who have seen real combat, well, we have already displayed our skills, *quiaff*?"

He looked so strange, standing there, short and thin to the point of fragility. Like a child in adult clothing. But he also stood like a Jade Falcon warrior, confident and defiant.

"*Aff*, Ravill Pryde."

He threw her a smile and then continued on.

Joanna walked to the shore of the lake. She was angry now, angry at Ravill Pryde for treating her challenges so lightly. He must understand that his victory over her was the one remaining humiliation she must avenge. And it seemed she had proven herself adept at avenging humiliations. In spite of the calm of the day, the lake water was, as usual, turbulent and cold. Small floes of ice still bobbed on its surface.

"Freebirth!" she muttered and kicked off her boots and removed her jacket.

Plunging into the water, she was astonished by its intense

frigidity. It made her body cold immediately, in spite of the insulation of her jumpsuit. She had an impulse to turn back and give up the swim, but—once she started a task—she had to finish it. Perhaps that was the secret to her survival.

She heard a splash behind her. Had that scum, Ravill Pryde decided to compete with her after all?

The presence in the water of a competitor urged her on. She did not force her strokes, but executed them in the steady rhythm she had been taught nearly three decades ago as a sibko cadet. It was painful to maintain a fierce kick in the icy waters, especially when an ice floe threw the kick off, but she swam on. It was also hard to concentrate when your head felt like it was turning to ice itself.

The water increasingly resisted her hands as she tried to slice them in smoothly, then pull them back toward her hips in an even stroke. Joanna did not know how she did it, but her stroke got stronger, her legs kicked harder.

But she could not shake off the competition from the other swimmer, who kept up with her, but just behind. She dared not turn to sneer at Ravill Pryde, nor did she want to waste vital energy with an insult or a boast about beating him.

Ahead was a large piece of ice. Reacting quickly, she slipped underwater and swam under the floe. She did not have time to watch the scene below her for long, but she had a glimpse of an impossible beauty of flowers and aquatic life. She emerged on the other side of the ice floe and took in a deep breath. The warm air created strange sensations in her cold lungs.

Now she could see the other side of the lake, the cliff rising from the water. Her strokes became fiercer, splashing water high. She heard similar splashing just behind her.

For the last few meters, Joanna kicked as hard as she could, moved her arms with all the strength she could muster. She could feel herself accelerate—and sense her pursuer speed up accordingly.

There were only six meters left as she felt a challenge from her competitor. From somewhere within her Joanna found the extra energy, the additional power to surge ahead and reach the cliff wall first.

Feeling extraordinary, she pulled herself onto the wide, deep ledge where most swimmers who crossed the lake rested before the return swim, unless they chose to climb the sheer face of the cliff. Settling herself onto the ledge, trying to feel the warm air, she looked down and saw her competitor lifting himself out of the water. "But it is only you, Horse."

In one smooth movement, graceful for a man of his bulk, Horse pulled himself to a sitting position on the ledge.

"Only me? Are you disappointed? Who did you think it was?"

"Ravill Pryde."

Horse laughed. "In that case, he would have been sitting here, awaiting your arrival."

Joanna could not even get angry at Horse's baiting.

"I can beat him, Horse. I can beat him."

"You seem different, Joanna."

"Will everybody stop telling me I am different? I am the same. Well, with a little glory attached perhaps."

Joanna could not have explained it to anyone, but with Horse she felt comfortable. He was freeborn, yes. Stubborn, sarcastic scum, yes. But comfortable. She was not even sure she hated him anymore. Him and Diana. Stupid freebirths.

"The really strange thing, Joanna, is that you look happy. Different or not, that's a change, and a frightful one, to boot."

She smiled. He was right. Swimming across the lake had made her feel happy. It would not last. She liked being angry too much. But, for the moment, it was all right to feel happy. They sat silently on the ledge for a long while. Then Joanna spoke:

"I have never earned a bloodname, Horse, but look what has happened. I have proven myself. I even have a fragment of history, a line in *The Remembrance*— '. . . for on Twycross on the day that the Wolves lost a Khan, it was the aged Joanna that flew and slew.' Not bad. Do you think my ashes will be mixed with the nutrients for a sibko, Horse?"

"Maybe. But first you have to die. I am sure there are a few Wolf whelps who would like to do you that honor."

"Good. I too would like a chance to rid the universe of a few more Wolf freebirths."

"Why don't you just travel to one of their camps, walk in, and challenge them?"

"A fine idea, Horse. I will consider it. Who is that out there, just this side of the big ice floe?"

Another swimmer was heading toward the ledge. It was Diana. She climbed onto the ledge, caught her breath, and said, "I did it. You should have seen his face. He brought his hand down so hard on that desk he values so much that he got all the papers on it mixed up. Some even fell on the floor without him picking them up immediately for a change."

"Slow down, Diana," Horse said. "What are you talking about?"

"Did you find a way to resign as coregn?" Joanna asked.

Diana took a moment to compose herself, then spoke. "Nothing as trivial as the coregn job. Remember, Joanna, the night in the camp when you told me about the freeborn Khan in Clan Wolf?"

"Yes."

"Well, I have thought about it a great deal. *And* I recalled what Ravill Pryde told me about how, since both my parents were trueborn, my genetic makeup was almost trueborn."

"But not," Joanna said. "You can never be trueborn when birthed naturally."

"I suppose it is true. Technically. But a case can be made, and I intend to make it."

"A case?"

Diana nodded and could not resist an accompanying smile. "I confronted Ravill Pryde in his office. I told him that freeborns become bloodnamed warriors in Clan Wolf, and that I am as close to trueborn as I am to freeborn so that I am neither, as he said himself, and that both my parents were in a sibko from the Pryde line.

"He asked me why I was bringing up all this information. And I told him. 'Star Colonel Ravill Pryde,' I said, 'for all these reasons, I demand to compete for a bloodname when the next Trial of Bloodright for a Pryde name occurs, and further, I demand that, as one of the current bloodnamed warriors of the Pryde line, you sponsor me.' "

Joanna and Horse looked at each other, amazed. "Diana," Joanna said, "you surprise me. But that is not possible, is it, your competing for a bloodname?"

"Possibly not. I went on to remind him about how I exposed the Clan Wolf spies, and that on Twycross he had told me I was due a reward for my bravery on the plateau. He said that, as a reward for that, a bloodname was somewhat extreme."

"I admire your tenacity, Diana," Joanna said, and Horse nodded agreement. "But I doubt that even Ravill Pryde, for all his vaunted skills, can pull that one off."

Diana's face clouded slightly, but she smiled. "I do not know, Joanna. Things are changing. In the Jade Falcons, we have new breeds of warriors, even genetic experimentations of bizarre proportions. We do not know what will happen to the invasion of the Inner Sphere once this truce is up, or even if the truce might not be broken beforehand. You, Joanna, have not only redeemed the Falcon Guard shame of Twycross but have become part of history. In a universe like this, with so many alterations in my own short lifetime, who can say what will happen to any of us? Horse, you could become a high command officer."

"Not likely."

"Joanna, you could decide that your destiny is with a canister nursery"—Joanna's grunt was scornful—"or you could be killed by a Clan Wolf whelping looking for his own line in the *Remembrance.*

"And I could compete for a bloodname. Things change."

Horse gave one of his low rumbling laughs. "Or, on the other hand, we could all drown trying to swim back across Sudeten Lake."

"Which I think we had better do," Joanna said. "The air is turning cold again."

Without looking at each other once, the three dove off the ledge, almost in unison, and began the long swim back.

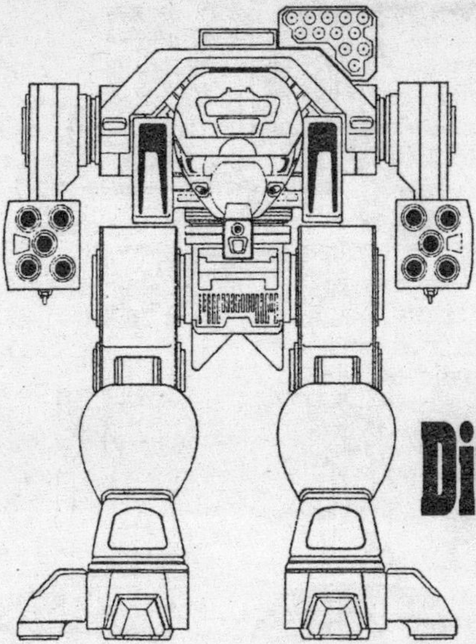

Dire Wolf

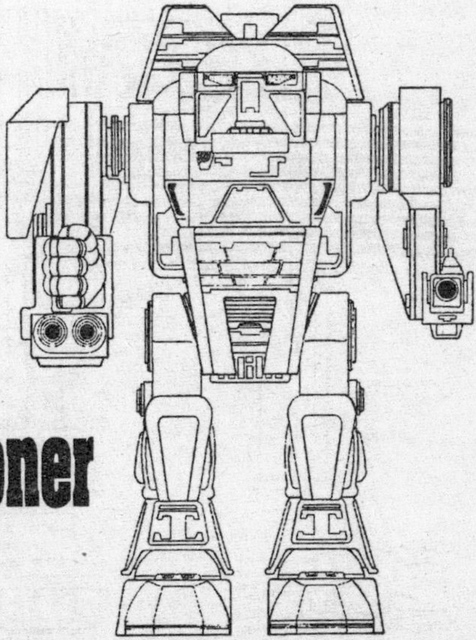

Executioner

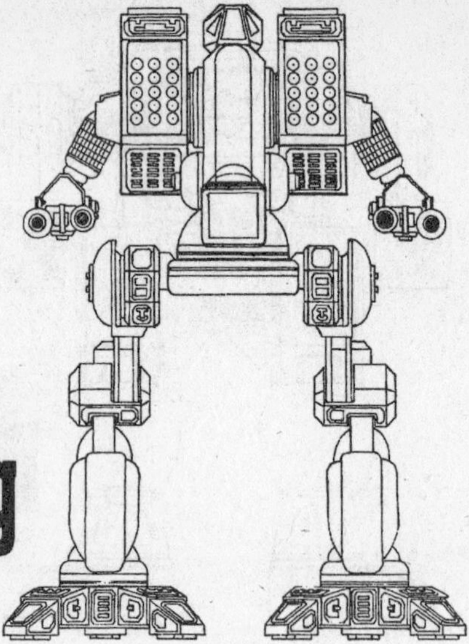

Mad Dog

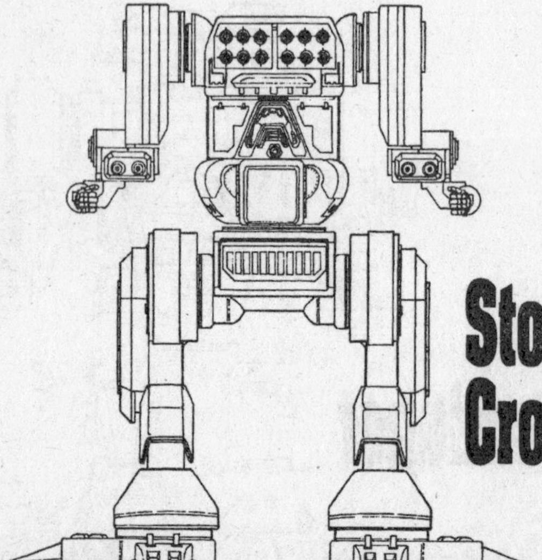

Storm Crow

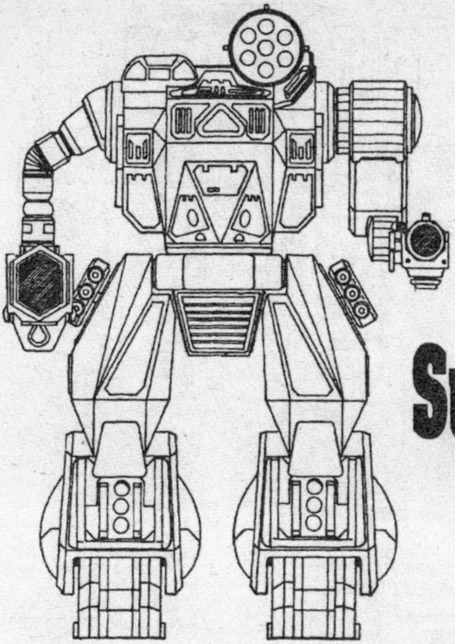

Summoner

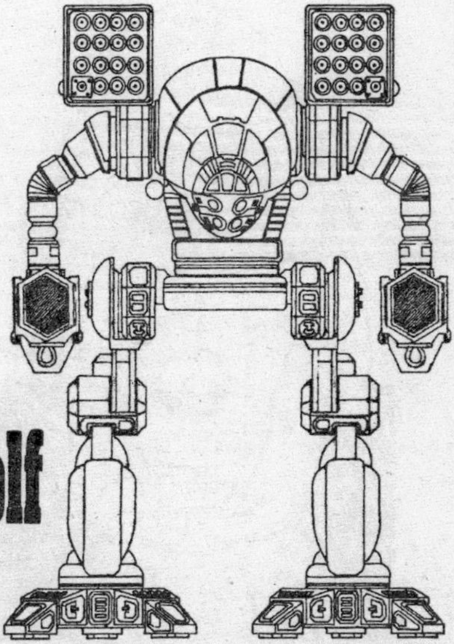

Timber Wolf

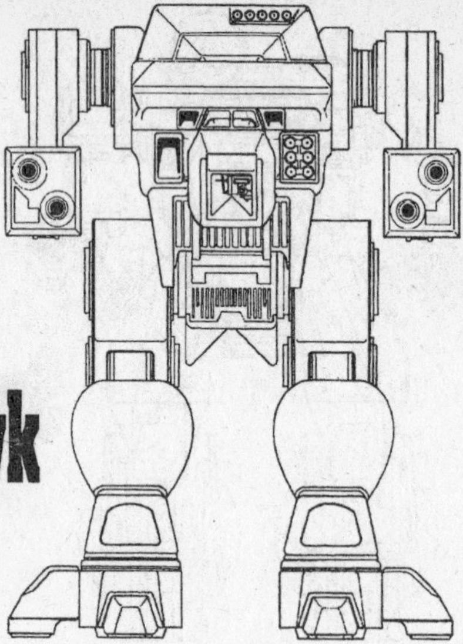

Warhawk

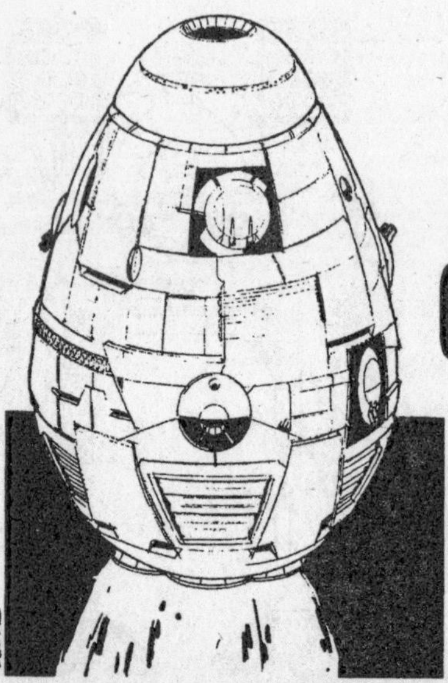

Overlord

Read on for more exciting action in the Battletech universe. . . .

Battletech 1: WAY OF THE CLANS, Legend of Jade Phoenix

By Robert Thurston

In the 31st century, the BattleMech is the ultimate war machine. Thirty meters tall, and vaguely, menacingly man-shaped, it is an unstoppable engine of destruction.

In the 31st century, the Clans are the ultimate warriors. The result of generations of controlled breeding, Clan Warriors pilot their BattleMechs like no others.

In the 31st century, Aidan aspires to be a Warrior of Clan Jade Falcon. To win the right to join his Clan in battle, he must succeed in trials that will forge him into one of the best warriors in the galaxy, or break him completely.

In the 31st century, Aidan discovers that the toughest battle is not in the field, but in his head—where failure will cost him the ultimate price: his humanity.

Battletech 2: BLOODNAME, Legend of the Jade Phoenix 2

By Robert Thurston

TRUEBIRTH—Born in the laboratory, these genetically engineered soldiers train to be the ultimate warriors. They are the elite pilots of the Clan's fearsome BattleMech war machines.

FREEBIRTH—Born of the natural union of parents, these too are soldiers, but pale imitations of their truebirth superiors. Despised for their imperfections, they fight where and when their Clan commands.

Aidan has failed his Trial of Position, the ranking test all truebirth warriors of the Clan Jade Falcon must pass. He is cast out. Disgraced. His rightful Bloodname denied him.

But with a Bloodname, all past failures are forgiven. With a Bloodname comes respect. With a Bloodname comes honor.

Aidan will do anything to gain that name. Even masquerade as the thing he has been taught to despise.

A freebirth.

Battletech 3: FALCON GUARD, Legend of the Jade Phoenix 3
by Robert Thurston

A CLASH OF EMPIRES
In 2786, the elite Star League Army fled the Inner Sphere, abandoning the senseless bloodshed ordered by the Successor Lords. Now, almost three hundred years later, the Clans, heirs of the Star League Army, turn their eyes back upon their former home. Nothing will stop them from raising the Star League banner over Earth once again.

A CLASH OF ARMIES
For two years, the Clans' BattleMech war machines have overwhelmed the armies of the corrupt Successor Lords. Now, at the gates of Earth the Clans must fight one final battle, a battle that will decide the fate of humanity for all time.

A CLASH OF CULTURES
For Star Colonel Aidan Pryde of Clan Jade Falcon the battle is more than a question of military conquest. It is an affirmation of the superiority of the Clan way, a way of life he has sworn to uphold despite his fear that the noble crusade has fallen prey to the lust and ambition of its commanders.

Battletech 4: WOLFPACK
by Robert N. Charrette

THE THIRD AND FOURTH SUCCESSION WARS
THE MARIK CIVIL WAR
THE WAR OF '39
THE CLAN INVASION

WOLF'S DRAGOON WON THEM ALL

Now, in 3005, the Dragoons have arrived in the Inner Sphere. No one knows where they came from—no one dares ask. They are five regiments of battle-toughened, hardened MechWarriors and their services are on offer to the highest bidder.

Whoever that might be. . . .

Battletech 5: NATURAL SELECTION

by Michael A. Stackpole

THE CLAN WAR HAS ENDED IN AN UNEASY PEACE. . . .

Sporadic Clan incursion into Inner Sphere territory supply mercenaries like the Kell Hounds with more work than they can handle. . . . border raids sharply divide the Federated Commonwealth's political factions, bringing further instability to the realm standing between Clans' goals and anarchy.

And while secret ambitions drive plans to rip the Commonwealth apart, Khan Phelan Ward and Prince Victor Davion—cousins, rulers, and enemies—must decide if maintaining the peace justifies the actions they will take to preserve it. . . .

Battletech 6: DECISION AT THUNDER RIFT, The Saga of The Gray Death Legion
by William H. Keith, Jr.

WINNER TAKE EVERYTHING

Thirty years before the Clan invasion, the crumbling empires of the Inner Sphere were locked in the horror of the Third Succession War. The great Houses, whose territories spanned the stars, used BattleMechs to smash each other into rubble.

Grayson Death Carlyle had been training to be a MechWarrior since he was ten years old, but his graduation came sooner than expected. With his friends and family dead and his father's regiment destroyed, young Grayson finds himself stranded on a world turned hostile. And now he must learn the hardest lesson of all: It takes more than a BattleMech to make a MechWarrior.

To claim the title of MechWarrior all he had to do is capture one of those giant killing machines by himself.

If it doesn't kill him first.

Battletech 7: MERCENARY'S STAR, The Saga of The Gray Death Legion
by William H. Keith, Jr.

AN OPEN BATTLE OF MAN AGAINST MACHINE

The Gray Death Legion. Mercenary warriors born out of treachery and deceit. Now the time has come for their first assignment serving as the training cadre for farmer rebels on the once peaceful agricultural world of Verthandi. And although MechWarrior Grayson Carlyle has the knack for battle strategy and tactics, getting the scattered bands of freedom fighters to unite against their oppressors is not always easy. But the Legion must succeed in their efforts or die—for the only way off the planet is via the capital city, now controlled by the minions of Carlyle's nemesis, who wait for them with murderous schemes. . . .

Battletech 8: THE PRICE OF GLORY, The Saga of The Gray Death Legion

by William H. Keith, Jr.

THEY RETURNED AS ENEMIES WHEN THEY SHOULD HAVE BEEN HEROES

After a year-long campaign in the service of House Marik, Colonel Grayson Carlyle and the warriors of the Gray Death Legion are ready for a rest. But there is no welcome for them at home base. The soldiers return to find the town in ruins, their families scattered, and their reputations destroyed. Rumors fueled by lies and false evidence have branded them as outlaws, accused of heinous crimes they did not commit. With a Star League treasure at stake, Carlyle's need for vengeance against unknown enemies thrusts him into a suspenseful race against time. But even if he wins, the 'Mech warrior must ally himself with old enemies in a savage battle where both sides will learn.

Battletech 9: IDEAL WAR
by Christopher Kubasik

FIGHTING DIRTY

Captain Paul Masters, knight of the House Marik, is well versed in the art of BattleMech combat. A veteran of countless battles, he personifies the virtues of the Inner Sphere MechWarrior. But when he is sent to evaluate a counterinsurgency operation on a backwater planet, he doesn't find the ideal war he expects. Instead of valiant patriots fighting villainous rebels, he discovers a guerilla war—both sides have abandoned decency for expediency, ideals for body counts, and honor for victory. It's a dirty, dirty war. . . .

Battletech 10: MAIN EVENT

by James D. Long

BATTLES FOR A BATTLEMECH

Dispossessed in the battle of Tukayyid, former Com Guard soldier Jeremiah Rose wants nothing more than to strike back at the Clans who destroyed his 'Mech and his career. Dreams of swift vengeance turn to nightmares when every effort he makes to rejoin the fight to protect the citizens of the Inner Sphere is rejected.

Forced to win a new BattleMech by fighting on the game world of Solaris VII, Rose recruits other soldiers from the arenas to create a new mercenary unit and take his grudge back to the invaders.

Unfortunately, Rose is long on battle experience and desperately short on business skills. Turning a band of mismatched MechWarriors into an elite fighting unit becomes harder than he imagined when Rose is forced to fight his fellow MechWarriors in order to fight the Clans.

Battletech 11: BLOOD OF HEROES
by Andrew Keith

HEROES FOR A DAY

Melissa Steiner's assassination ignited fires of civil war, and now secessionist factions clamor for rebellion against the Federated Commonwealth. The rebels plan on gaining control of the Skye March, and thus controlling the crucial Terran Corridor. Throughout the March, civil and military leaders plot to take up arms against Prince Victor Steiner-Davion.

The final piece of the plan requires the secessionist forces to gain access to the planet Glengarry and the mercenary group that calls it home: the Gray Death Legion.

When Prince Davion summons Grayson Death Carlyle and his wife, Lori, to the Federated Commonwealth capital, the rebel forces seize their chance to establish a garrison on Glengarry.

The rebels didn't expect the legion newest members to take matters into their own hands. . . .

Battletech 12: ASSUMPTION OF RISK

by Michael A. Stackpole

THE FUTURE OF THE REALM

Solaris VII, the Game World, is the Inner Sphere in microcosm, and Kai Allard-Liao is its Champion. Veteran of the war against the Clans, he daily engages in free-form battles against challengers who wish his crown for their own.

There is no place he would rather be.

Then the political realities of the Federated Commonwealth intrude on Solaris. Ryan Steiner, a man sworn to dethrone Victor Steiner-Davion, comes to Solaris to orchestrate his rebellion. Tormano Liao, Kai's uncle, redoubles efforts to destroy the Capellan Confederation, and Victor Steiner-Davion plots to revenge his mother's assassination.

In one short month, Kai's past, present, and future collapse, forcing him to do things he had come to Solaris to avoid. If he succeeds, no one will ever know; but if he fails, he'll have the blood of billions on his hands.

Battletech 13: FAR COUNTRY

by Peter Rice

THE DRACONIS COMBINE

claimed the loyalty of regular soldiers and mercenaries alike. But while the soldiers fought for honor, the mercenaries, the MechWarriors, fought for profit, selling their loyalty to the highest bidder. When a freak hyperspace accident stranded both Takudo's crack DEST troopers and Vost's mercenary MechWarriors on a planet for which they had no name, survival seemed the first priority. But that was before they captured one of the birdlike natives of the planet and learned of the other humans who had crashlanded on this world five centuries before. Then suddenly the stakes changed. For Takuda was sworn to offer salvation to the war-torn enclaves of human civilization, while Vost was only too ready to destroy them all—if the price was right!

Battletech 14: D.R.T.

by James D. Long

DEAD RIGHT THERE

Jeremiah Rose and the Black Thorns, flush with success against the Jade Falcons on Borghese, head to Harlech to draw a new assignment. Their only requirement: Their new job must let them face off against the Clans.

They find more than they bargained for. Their assignment: Garrison duty on Wolcott—a Kurita planet deep in the heart of the Clan Smoke Jaguar occupation zone. Wolcott is besieged, but protected from further Clan aggression by the Clan code of honor.

Wolcott makes a useful staging area for Kurita raids on Smoke-Jaguar-occupied territory.

The pay is good. The advance unbelievable.

But they have to live to spend it.

Battletech 15: CLOSE QUARTERS

by Victor Milán

SHE WAS THE PERFECT SCOUT

Resourceful, ruthless, beautiful, apparently without fear, Scout Lieutenant Cassie Suthorn of Camacho's Caballeros is as consummately lethal as the giant BattleMechs she lives to hunt. Only one other person in the freewheeling mercenary regiment has a hint of the demons which drive her. When the Caballeros sign on to guard Coordinator Theodore Kurita's corporate mogul cousin in the heart of the Draconis Combine, they think they've got the perfect gig: low-risk, and high pay. Cassie alone suspects that danger waits among the looming bronze towers of Hachiman—and when the yakuza and the dread ISF form a devil's alliance to bring down Chandrasekhar Kurita, only Cassie's unique skills can save her regiment.

All she has to do is confront her darkest nightmares.

Battletech 16: BRED FOR WAR

by Michael A. Stackpole

A PERILOUS LEGACY

Along with the throne of the Federated Commonwealth, Prince Victor Steiner-Davion inherited a number of problems. Foremost among them is the Clans' threat to the peace of the Inner Sphere—and a treacherous sister who wants to supplant him. The expected demise of Joshua Marik, heir to the Free Worlds League, whose very presence maintained peace, also endangers harmony. Victor's idea is to use a double for Joshua, a deception that will prevent war.

But secret duplicity is hard to maintain, and war erupts anyway, splitting the Inner Sphere and leaving the Federated Commonwealth defenseless. And when Victor thinks things can get no worse, word comes that the Clans, once again have brought war to the Inner Sphere.

THEY'RE HERE
NOW GET OUTTA THEIR WAY
BLAST YOUR WAY THROUGH THE GALAXY with collectable BattleTech 'Mechs from Tyco. Major Adam Steiner in his Axman leads his First Somerset Strikers to take back the Inner Sphere from the evil fury of the Jade Falcon Claw!
Each 'Mech comes with its own MechWarrior® and a full arsenal of heavy firepower!
Plus a special Battle Damage feature—one well-placed shot can turn a 'Mech into a WRECK before you can say "particle projector cannon"!
BRING THE BATTLE TO *YOUR* HOMEWORLD!
Look for the full BattleTech line!
Nicolai Malthus piloting Toad
Pytor in Hunchback
Zack Hawkins in Mauler
BATTLETECH®
NO GUTS, NO GALAXY™
TYCO®